Anything Goes

Center Point
Large Print

Also by Richard S. Wheeler and available from
Center Point Large Print:

The Two Medicine River
Richard Lamb
The Fate

Anything Goes

RICHARD S. WHEELER

CENTER POINT LARGE PRINT
THORNDIKE, MAINE

This Center Point Large Print edition
is published in the year 2016 by arrangement with
St. Martin's Press.

The text of this Large Print edition is unabridged.
In other aspects, this book may vary
from the original edition.
Printed in the United States of America
on permanent paper.
Set in 16-point Times New Roman type.

ISBN: 978-1-62899-941-9

Library of Congress Cataloging-in-Publication Data

Names: Wheeler, Richard S., author.
Title: Anything goes / Richard S. Wheeler.
Description: Center Point Large Print edition. | Thorndike, Maine :
Center Point Large Print, 2016. | ©2015
Identifiers: LCCN 2015051492 | ISBN 9781628999419
    (hardcover : alk. paper)
Subjects: LCSH: Large type books. | GSAFD: Western stories.
Classification: LCC PS3573.H4345 A83 2016 | DDC 813/.54—dc23
LC record available at http://lccn.loc.gov/2015051492

To my wife, the one, the only Sue Hart

Anything Goes

1

The silence was deadly. The show might as well be playing to an audience of cigar store Indians. Half the seats were empty. August Beausoleil hoped that Helena would be one of those cities where people habitually arrived late. But he wasn't seeing any new arrivals pushing their way along the rows. The opera house seemed a giant cavern. Opera houses were like that. They seemed largest when they were empty, more intimate when they were jammed.

From his perch at the edge of the proscenium arch, he studied the vast gloom beyond the hissing footlights. Ming's Opera House, in Helena, in the young state of Montana, was a noble theater just up the flank of Last Chance Gulch, where millions in gold had been washed out of the earth just a few feverish years earlier.

And now, opening night, those who had braved the chill mountain winds were sitting on their hands. Who were they, out there? Did they understand English? Were they born without a funny bone? Why had a sour silence descended? A miasma of boredom or ill humor, or maybe disdain, had settled like fog over the crowd, what there was of it.

The show had opened with the Wildroot Sisters, Cookie, Marge, and LaVerne, strutting their stuff, singing ensemble; Sousa marches melded into a big hello, we're starting the show. And all it got was frostbit fingers tapping on calloused hands. Beausoleil could almost feel the dyspepsia leaking across the arch onto the wide stage.

The show was his. Or most of it. Charles Pomerantz, the advance man, owned the rest of it. He had done his usual good job, plastering Lewis and Clark County with gaudy red playbills and posters touting the event, booking hotels, hiring locals, stirring up the press, handing out free passes to crooked politicians, soothing the anxieties of clergymen with bobbing Adam's apples, and planting a few claques in the audience. Who weren't doing much claquing at the moment.

Beausoleil doubled as master of ceremonies, and that gave him a chance to stir the pot a bit, sometimes with a little jab, or a quip, or even a hearty appreciation of wherever they were.

He grabbed his cane and silk top hat and strutted into the limelight, Big City man in gray tuxedo, in the middle of arctic tundra.

"Ladies and gents," he said. "That was the Wildroot Sisters, the Sweethearts of Hoboken, New Jersey. Let's give them a big hand."

No one did.

"LaVerne, Cookie, and Marge," he said. "Singing just for you."

Dyspepsia was in the air. Time for some quick humor.

"Citizens of this fair city—where am I? Keokuk? Grand Rapids? Ah, Helena, the most beautiful and famous metropolis in North America—yes, there you are, welcoming the Beausoleil Brothers Follies."

Well, anyway, waiting for whatever came next. No one laughed.

"We've got a great show for you. Seven big acts. Please welcome the one, the only Harry the Juggler, who will do things never before seen by the human eye."

Harry trotted out, bowed, and was soon tossing six cups and saucers, breaking none. And when it was time to shut down, he pulled one after another out of the air and set the crockery down, unharmed. He bowed again, but the audience barely applauded.

"And now, the famed Marbury Trio, Delilah, Sam, and Bingo, from Memphis, in the great state of Tennessee, doing a rare and exotic dance, a lost art, for your edification."

It was, actually, a tap dance, and they did it brightly, the dolled-up threesome syncopating feet and legs and canes into rhythmic clatter that usually set a crowd to nodding and smiling. But the applause was scattered, at best. This crowd didn't know a snare drum from a bass drum.

"Next on our bill is the monologuist and sage,

11

the one, the celebrated, the famous Wayne Windsor. Welcome Mr. Windsor as you would a long-lost brother fresh out of the state pen."

They didn't.

Wayne Windsor trotted out in a soft tweed coat, a string cravat, and a bowler, which he lifted and settled on his balding head. He would do his act in front of the silvery olio drop downstage.

Another bomb, Beausoleil thought, retreating into side-stage shadows. Windsor was also known as The Profile, because he thought he had a handsome visage from either side, with a good jut jaw and noble brow and long sculpted nose. He had contrived to take advantage of this asset, speaking first to the left side of the audience, giving those on the right a good look, and then when that portion of the audience had absorbed his famed profile, he shifted to the other side, treating the viewers on the left to his noble nose and jaw.

The act was a good one. The Great Monologuist always began with an invitation.

"Now tonight," he said, "I'm going to talk about robber barons, and I want anyone who is a genuine, accredited robber baron, or any other barons, to please step forward so we can have some fun at your expense."

That was good. Robber barons were in the news. Helena had a few. The Profile had a knack. Beausoleil thought it might crack the ice this sorry evening, but it didn't even dent the silence. The

12

Profile fired off a few cracks about politicians, added a sentiment or two, and finally settled into one of his accounts of bad service on a Pullman coach, while the Helena audience sat in stony silence. It was getting unnerving.

Was something wrong? A mine disaster? An election loss? A bribery indictment? Nothing of the sort had shown up in the two-cent press before the show. The trouble was, the week hung in balance. A bad review, three bad reviews in the three daily rags, and the Beausoleil Brothers Follies would be in trouble. A touring show bled cash.

He eyed the shadowy audience sourly, and came to a decision. He talked quietly to two stage-hands, who told him there were few tomatoes this time of year in Helena, but plenty of rotten apples, which would do almost as well.

"Do it," he said.

They vanished, and would soon be sitting out there in the arctic dark, surrounded by surly spectators and bystanders little comprehending the subversives in their midst.

"I knew it," said Mrs. McGivers. "I saw it coming. You should pay me extra. It grieves my soul."

"I didn't know you had one," he said.

Mrs. McGivers and her Monkey Band would follow, after The Profile had ceased to bore his customers. Like most vaudeville shows, this one had an animal act, and the Monkey Band was it.

Mrs. McGivers, a stout contralto, would soon take the stage with her two obnoxious capuchin monkeys, Cain and Abel, in red-and-gold uniforms, and an accordionist named Joseph. Cain would pick up the miniature cymbals, one for each paw, while Abel would command two drumsticks and perch with a little drum in front of him, looking all too eager.

And then the music would begin, with Cain clanging and Abel banging, and Joseph and Mrs. McGivers setting the pace and melody, more or less. It was usually good for some laughs. And sometimes the beasts would add a flourish, as if they were caffeinated, which maybe they were. The result was anarchy.

August Beausoleil loathed the monkeys, who usually spent their spare time up in the flies, careening about and alarming the performers. The Profile had complained mightily when something had splatted on his pompadoured hair. Beausoleil sometimes ached to fire the act, but good animal acts were tough to find and hard to travel with, and Mrs. McGivers usually gave better than she got. It was better than any dog or pony act he'd seen.

But he had one surefire way to turn a show around, and this was it. When at last The Profile had ceased to bore and offend, the master of ceremonies announced the one, the only, the sensational Mrs. McGivers and her Monkey Band.

Quick enough the olio drop sailed into the flies, revealing Mrs. McGivers, the monkeys seated beside her, one with cymbals, the other with drumsticks. And Joseph, the accordionist, at one side. The audience stared, lost in silence. Would nothing crack this dreary opening night?

Mrs. McGivers had come from the tropics somewhere, and the rumor was that she had killed a couple of husbands, but no one could prove it. She used a jungle theme for the act, and usually appeared with a red bandanna capturing her brown hair and a scooped white blouse encasing her massive chest, below which was a voluminous skirt of shimmery blue fabric that glittered in the limelight. She looked somewhat native, but wasn't. She wore sandals, which permitted her smelly feet to exude odors that offended performers and audiences alike.

Her repertoire ran to calypso from Trinidad and Tobago, mostly stuff never heard by northern ears, which usually annoyed the audience, which would have preferred Bible songs and spirituals as a way of countering the dangerous idea that man had descended from apes. There, indeed, were two small primates, wiry little rascals dressed in red-and-gold uniforms, making dangerous movements with drumsticks and cymbals in hand.

She turned to Beausoleil.

"You're a rat," she said.

Joseph, the accordionist, took that as his cue,

and soon the instrument was croaking out an odd, rhythmic tune, and she began to warble in a nasal, sandpapery whine stuff about banana boats and things that no one had ever heard of.

Mrs. McGivers crooned, repeating chords, giving them spice as she and her monkeys whaled away. The capuchins gradually awakened to their task, led by the accordion, and soon Cain was whanging the cymbals and Abel was thundering the bass drum, with little attention to rhythm, which was actually intricate in Trinidadian music. The whole performance veered toward anarchy, which is what Mrs. McGivers intended, her goal being to send the audience into paroxysms of delight.

Only not this evening in Helena, in the midst of stern mountains and bitter winters.

Were these ladies and gentlemen born without humor?

Abel rose up on his stool and began a virtuoso performance on the bass drum, both arms flailing away, a thunderous eruption from the stage. And still those politicos out there stared across the footlights in silence.

Very well, then. Beausoleil quietly waved a hand from the edge of the arch, a hand unseen by the armored audience.

"Boo!" yelled a certain stagehand, now sitting front-left.

"Go away," yelled another stalwart of the show, this gent sitting front-right, four rows back.

The capuchins clanged and banged. Mrs. McGivers warbled. Joseph wheezed life out of the old accordion.

The two reporters, front on the aisle, took no notes.

"Boo," yelled a spectator. "Refund my money."

The gent, well known to Beausoleil, had a bag in hand, and now he plunged a paw into it and extracted a browning, mushy apple, and heaved this missile at Mrs. McGivers. It splatted nearby, which was all Cain needed. He abandoned his cymbals, leapt for the mushy apple, and fired it back. Any target would do. It splatted upon the bosom of a politician's alleged wife.

This was followed by a fusillade of rotten items, mostly tomatoes, but also ancient apples and peaches and moldering potatoes, drawn miraculously from sacks out in the theater, and these barrages were returned by Cain and Abel, who were born pitchers with arms that would be the envy of any local baseball team.

Mrs. McGivers was miraculously unscathed, the war having been waged by her two capuchins. Joseph, too, was unscathed, and continued to render calypso music, even imitating a steel guitar with his miraculous wheezebox.

It was a fine uproar. Suddenly, this dour audience was no longer sitting on its cold hands, but was clapping and howling and squealing. Especially when Abel fired a soggy missile that splatted upon the noble forehead of the attorney general. The Helena regulars enjoyed that far more than they should.

After a little more whooping, Beausoleil, in bib and tux, strode purposefully out onto the boards, dodged some foul fruit, and held up a hand.

"Helena has spoken, Mrs. McGivers," he said. He jerked a thumb in the direction of the wings.

She rose from her stool, awarded him with an uncomplimentary gesture barely seen on the other side of the footlights, and stalked off, followed by the capuchins, and Joseph, and finally some hands who removed the stools and instruments.

"Monkey business! Give them a round of applause," Beausoleil said, and immediately the audience broke into thunderous appreciation.

The two bored reporters were suddenly taking notes.

All was well.

The rest of opening night was well nigh perfect. Indeed, Mary Mabel Markey, the Queen of Contraltos, got a standing ovation and repeated demands for an encore, which she supplied so abundantly that Beausoleil almost got out the hook to drag her offstage. Mary Mabel was getting along, was fleshy, and used too much powder to hide her corrugated forehead. She was sinking fast, and Beausoleil had hired her mostly out of pity, since she could no longer find work in the great opera houses of the East and Midwest. But she was also becoming impossible.

There were more acts after the intermission and, finally, the patriotic closing in which all the acts combined with a great huzzah for the waving flag.

The rotten vegetables had rescued the show, once again. It annoyed August Beausoleil. It meant his acts weren't working. It meant financial peril. It hurt the reputation of the Beausoleil Brothers Follies. There were neither brothers nor follies in it, but that was show business. The audience had gone home happy.

2

August Beausoleil stared at the greenbacks and coins in the battered lockbox. The evening's take was a hundred forty-seven dollars and fifty cents. Forty-five were gallery seats, sold at fifty cents. The rest were dollar seats. There were also some free passes, given to local bigwigs and press and bloodsuckers.

That was not even his gross. He owed Ball's Drug Store, seller of advance reserved seats, two percent. And he owed Ming's Opera House seventy-five. And he owed the Union Hotel for the rooms. And he owed the printer who did the playbills, and his partner Charles Pomerantz, who ran up expenses as the advance man, his costs. There were other costs, too. Chemicals for the limelight, chemicals for the footlights. The publicity spending he had to do, drinks for guests.

Running a variety show through western towns was a tough proposition, and it required near-sellout bookings. He usually had seven acts, too many for small-town vaudeville, but he hoped that the size and depth of the show would start tongues wagging and purses opening. It was folly, but it was also a bet, and August Beausoleil didn't shy from a good bet.

Ming's had emptied, and the lights were mostly doused. But the evening was far from over. He had been in the business all his life, ever since he was a hungry boy edging his way through the theaters of Manhattan, making a nickel here, a dime there. His instincts told him that this night was going to bring trouble.

Indeed, a gent in handsome attire worked through the shadows to the arch, climbed to the stage, and found the proprietor of the Beausoleil Brothers show in the wing.

"Your show, is it?"

"Hope you enjoyed it, sir."

"We did until a rotten apple landed on my wife's dress, ruining it. She wishes to be reimbursed, and tells me the cost is fourteen."

"I see," said the proprietor. "And you have some

evidence, do you, that the dress is beyond repair, can't be restored, and of course you have a bill of sale, and all that?"

"Now see here. The dress is ruined and one of those infernal monkeys did it. The show was so bad that it got all the spoiled fruit in Helena tossed at it."

"I agree, sir, that monkey act is really beneath our standards."

"Beneath your standards! You hired it on. Now you can pay the piper."

"Ah, but the monkeys were entertainment. There wasn't a smile all evening until the monkeys took offense. And after that, sir, the show was a great success."

"Well, fork over. I don't have all night. My wife waits in the hansom cab."

"Who did you say you are?"

"I didn't. I'm the attorney general, Carruthers, and that's all I need to say."

Beausoleil digested that. "Here, sir, are two tickets to tomorrow's performance, absolutely free. Give them to your friends."

"Two dollars."

"Well, then, four reserved front-center orchestra seats, something only a well-connected person can hope to acquire without paying a premium."

The gent stared. "It's late. I'm tired. My wife is angry. Otherwise I'd be digging into that cash-box."

"Here. My compliments. On the house. Enjoy the show tomorrow."

The dandy vanished into the gloom, clutching some prize tickets, and in the distance a door opened and closed.

Beausoleil thought that the monkeys had saved the show. When the barrage of spoiled fruit sailed in, no one out there expected Mrs. McGiver's capuchin primates to return the fire. Yes, it was worth it. The whole audience erupted with glee. The show would have a good run in Helena. A few free tickets wouldn't hurt anyone. Give them anything but cash.

He contemplated the hotel, the awaiting bed, but he knew the night was not over. She would show up. She always did on a night like this. So he waited, and in a couple of minutes there she was, storming across the dark boards, the ultimate, the memorable, the sublime stage mother. He would listen, she would storm, and he would wind up his day.

"Fire that act," Ethel Wildroot said. "I don't want to be in a show with Mrs. McGivers. It's a blot on my name."

"I think you're right," he said. "Of course the monkeys saved us."

"Saved us! They drove everyone out of the theater. The show's dead in Helena."

"They broke the ice, Ethel. They returned the compliments. After that, it went perfectly."

"I'm putting you on notice; we'll leave the show unless you unload that immoral woman and her tropical parasites."

He yawned. "That it?"

"I'm just getting started."

"Pull up a stool."

"No, I'll stand, and you will sit, and you . . . will . . . listen."

August had succeeded in the business by being agreeable, but now he knew she was going to discover his limits.

"LaVerne's ready to move up. She's been rehearsing. She's got the songs, and she's ready for the big time. The East Coast circuits big time, not here. I thought you might want to show her off. Get rid of the deadwood around here, like the monkey act, and that fat old Mary Mabel Markey. She makes me want to screech. I won't even be in a theater when she opens that cavern of hers and bats fly out."

Ethel was alluding to the star of the show. A little shopworn, but still capable of packing them in.

"I hadn't thought of her songs as bats," he said. "They're said to carry rabies."

"She's got a thousand bats nesting in her gums. But LaVerne, she's young, shapely, and she can wow the crowds. She has her own teeth."

"And you want to pull her out of the Wildroot act?"

"Certainly not. She holds it together. The girls are stupid, she's not."

This all was odd. LaVerne was actually a niece, and the other girls, Cookie and Marge, were Ethel's daughters. Ethel was a stage mother in reverse.

"She's got the songs. 'Sweet Rosalie.' 'Empty Stockings,' and 'You're a Daisy.' You've got to listen. Better yet, throw her in as an olio act. She'll show you a thing or three."

"Nice to have your counsel, Ethel."

"I'm not done yet. You think you're getting off easy? Not this opening night in this dumb town. It's worse than Peoria. And Peoria's the end of the line. Now that hotel room, it's impossible. There's four of us and two beds. LaVerne needs her own room, and since I'm her manager I'll join her."

"One room, one act," he said. "That's how it is."

"What a cheapskate."

"And I'm getting rich by mistreating you," he said.

She laughed. There was that about her. "Make LaVerne a separate act, and then she gets a room."

"You've got three salaries in your act. Buy a room for her."

"If we don't walk out on you first. This show, it's an embarrassment."

He didn't say they were welcome to.

She whirled into the gloom, and he heard the theater door snap shut.

Everybody wanted something. He felt the lonely, dark theater around him. In rare moments it was bright-lit, packed with cheerful people, a certain mysterious joy rising from the crowd. But mostly it was like this, a hollow place waiting for those few minutes.

He wanted things, too. A show on solid footing. A hit act or two.

He'd been at it since age nine, when he hung around theaters, wanting the pennies or the occasional dime he'd collect to run an errand, get a sandwich for a showgirl, take tickets to someone, carry a stagedoor Johnny's bouquet to his dream girl. He never knew his old man. His ma started raising him fiercely enough, in a basement cubbyhole, but then she would go away for days, and then show up and feed him, and then go away for weeks, and he had only his wits and a little knowledge that at stage doors people wanted something or other, and he could run it down and get a tip—sometimes. Sometimes not. Sometimes he spent a hungry night atop a steam vent in the big city, the dank warmth the only thing between himself and bitter cold. But there was always the next show coming in, and actors who wanted stuff, and he got good at getting it, and got good at understanding how it worked. And there came a time when people on the streets would ask him if a show was good, somehow trusting in a boy's verdict, and there came a time when he had actual jobs, sometimes taking tickets, sometimes doing the books, sometimes working as a stagehand. By the time he was eighteen he was a veteran of show business, and by the time he was twenty-three he was doing his own variety shows—not big time, but on the roads of rural America. He'd never done Broadway; he'd made his way in smaller venues. And now the new thing, vaudeville, cranked out by Tony Pastor, clean stuff, good for ma and pa and the brats. His shows were a little more gamy. He was playing to miners and cowboys and their silky ladies. But it was vaudeville, the new thing, and it drew crowds.

He turned down the lamp and watched it blue out. The theater was black and yet he knew his way. He'd been in so many that they were no mystery to him. Some of these opera houses had towering flies, where curtains whirled up out of sight. Some had draw curtains, flooding across the stage. Those were the cheaper deals, and they slowed the show.

He felt the rush of cold air, and eyed the empty street for footpads. The hotel was four blocks distant, but the editorial sanctum of the *Independent* was two blocks straight down the gulch, and next to it was the *Herald*. He'd go see. Sometimes he could get a good idea of how the show would go in a town by reading a review.

The *Independent* was well lit. Light flooded the street. He saw within a couple of compositors, someone in a sleeve garter who was reading proof and a walrus-mustache man who looked to be the one putting the morning edition to bed. He entered. The place was hot.

He headed for the one who was poring over some handwritten pages.

"I'm Beausoleil, from the show. Have you a review I might look at?"

"Suit yourself," the gent said, not moving.

August Beausoleil had been in plenty of printing plants, and knew something about ink. It leapt out at you. While you were protecting your front, it nabbed you in the rear, and sometimes ruined a coat or a shirt. He edged gingerly toward the compositors, who were garbed in grimy smocks, which did little to protect their hands, which looked like they'd never wash clean, and in fact they didn't wash clean.

"Got a review for the show?" he asked one.

The man nodded. The review was sitting in a half-filled form consisting mostly of pre-cast advertisements. Beausoleil couldn't read the backward type, but he knew what to do. On a spike next to the form were the galley proofs, so he gingerly tugged his way through until he found what he wanted. It was lacking a headline. The compositors would add that later. He yanked the galley proof free and smeared a thumb with sticky ink. He laid it on an empty stone and read.

"So-so show at the Ming," was the opener. It

started with an all-out condemnation of the monkey act, but then had a kind word about The Profile, Wayne Windsor, whose humor was "piquant." It announced that Mary Mabel Markey was so-so, and looking a little shopworn. But it had a good word for the opening act, the Wildroot Sisters, who were "fresh and maidenly and a delight to the eye."

It praised the other acts readily enough, and even encouraged readers to lay out a little for tickets and an evening of good fun.

Well, no disaster there.

The *Herald* was less active, but there was one duffer setting type.

"Got a review?" Beausoleil asked.

"Review? Nah, he went to bed. Try about nine. We hit the alleys about eleven."

Beausoleil stepped into deep dark, not having the slightest feel how the Beausoleil Brothers Follies would fare in the cold capital of Montana. There would be three more shows: Friday, Saturday matinee, and Saturday evening. And a lot of bills to pay.

Wherever Mary Mabel Markey went, she hunted for a confessional. She always had a lot of confessing to do. She was guilty of the sin of vanity, which was a version of the sin of pride, which was one of the Seven Deadly Sins.

The Vicariate of Montana did not have large congregations, except in Butte, which was Irish and Italian. But there was a nondescript redbrick church in Helena, off the gulch, which she soon discovered. She needed to confess for the good of her soul. Being a big draw in vaudeville was something that needed forgiveness.

Late that morning, the top-billed performer with the Beausoleil Brothers Follies found her way to the Church of Saint Helena, and discovered an empty confessional and a waiting priest on the other side of the screen.

She plunged in and settled herself.

"Forgive me, Father, for I have sinned," she said.

This was the familiar ritual. She was an Irish girl. Her name wasn't really Markey; that was a theater name. It was O'Malley. Her birth name was Mona O'Malley.

"I have committed vanity," she said.

"Well, the Lord requires humility," the priest said. "But I don't quite grasp what it is that gives offense."

"I am too proud. I'm in show business. I'm in vaudeville. I'm at the top, and proud of it. I fought my way up, and now there's no one better."

"Ah . . . I wonder a little about this, my daughter."

"Pride is the worst sin. It excludes God from my life," she said. "I confess it whenever I reach a new town."

"Ah . . . I'm sure the Lord is most merciful, but perhaps you could say a little more about this."

"Father, show business is wicked. And I've climbed the ladder. The higher I've gone, the more wicked things I do, so I need to confess them all and be forgiven."

"I wonder if you could tell me a little more," the priest said, sounding a little confused.

"I insist that the posters and playbills put my name first."

"Well, that's wicked, all right, if you don't deserve it."

"But I do deserve it. The company wouldn't be profitable without me."

The priest paused. "I think it might be wicked to think it if it's not true, or if you attach more importance to your presence than is merited, my daughter. But I find no sin in assuming your rightful place."

"Well, that's just for starters. I make a point of abusing my rivals. I'll never say a good word about anyone else in the company."

"Yes, that's a venial offense," the priest said. "You would do better treating others as you wish to be treated. Yes, there's something that needs repentance. But I don't quite see it as one of the Seven Deadly Sins."

"Well, I do. Take my word for it. I could spend twenty minutes giving you a list, but there must be others waiting. I've done it all. I'll do whatever you say. Just give me my absolution and penance and I'll be gone."

A pained silence exuded from the other side of the screen.

"Daughter, penance for what?"

"For all of it. For being in vaudeville."

"How is being in vaudeville sinful?"

"I put myself on display and sing."

"Do you sing things that offend our Lord?"

"No, but maybe He thinks I do."

"Do you behave in a manner that evokes lust or evil thoughts?"

"No, but who can say?"

"Are you dressed modestly?"

"Mostly. But the corset's so tight I have no breath."

"You've examined your heart and believe there is wickedness in the very business? Vaudeville? It compels you to sin?"

"Yes, Father, that's just it."

"Then it would seem you should leave vaudeville. But you can always be forgiven, even in vaudeville. Temptation is one thing, sin is another."

"I knew you'd say that. Thank you, Father. I'll say a few extra prayers."

More odd silence, a sigh, and then the mumbled absolution in Latin, the words strange and puzzling, strangulated as they passed through the screen. It felt just right.

She enjoyed that. He would never forget it. His first encounter with a vaudeville star. Tonight, he would be mulling it in his mind, confused and unhappy. Hers was not the usual act of contrition. That was how she affected people. She departed, knowing she would feel just fine until the company reached Butte, the next venue. Then she'd have to find another confessional and unload. Meanwhile, she thought, she was free to be whatever she felt like being. Whoop-de-do!

She had grown up in the jammed tenements of Gotham, the daughter of desperate Irish parents who had fled the Famine, traveling steerage to the New World and hope. The cold tenements were worse killers than the famine. One in five died each year of consumption, and indeed, the lung disease soon took her mother. But little Mona O'Malley, as she then was known, survived, and so did her father, who first swept streets and then delivered bags of coal for the parlor stoves of the comfortable classes.

There was one bright thing about Mona's mother, Eileen. She could sing. She brought from Ireland a whole repertoire of ballads, lullabies, and sometimes strident songs full of pride and fight. And these she sang, and these did Mona absorb, somehow delighting in each song. Her mother sang until her last hours, sang even after consumption had ravaged her throat and her voice was a hoarse and crackling rumble and there was blood on her lips. And when she died, Mona's father said it had to be; everything had to be. He was a fatalist, and whatever happened had to happen, and Mona kept wondering why her mother's death had to be, and why her father didn't grieve.

Mona was very thin, and sometimes weak from not getting anything to fill her, and she took to wandering the bustling city, a pale child of ten, looking for anything to snatch for her stomach. Even the seed some people fed to birds. One day she saw a street entertainment: a man with an accordion and a monkey with a cup, looking for pennies and dimes. And she saw people listen to the man, who had great mustachios, and put coins into the monkey's cup. Mona hastened back to the tenement, a room she and her father shared with five other people she barely knew, and there she found a cup that no one had stolen. She took it.

She hastened uptown to a place where there

was a little park and people strolling, and they looked clean and pink compared to everyone in the tenement, who was waxy and gray. She set her cup on the grass, back from the paving stones, and sang. She didn't mind it if people stared. She had utterly no self-consciousness. She knew her mother's songs, so she sang them, and soon people listened, and some smiled and drifted on, but sometimes someone put a coin in her cup. Later some boys stole the coins, but her career was launched in that hour, and she sang the ballads, and when mothers with perambulators came by, she sang lullabies, all six her mother had sung, and the women listened and studied Mona and sometimes added a coin. She learned to empty the cup frequently, and slide the coins into a pocket, and after that she kept what had been given.

Then she bought things her body cried for. She bought pastries at a bakery. She bought an apple. She bought some potatoes to take to her father. She presented them to him proudly when he returned at dusk after a day working for the coal and ice merchant. He eyed the potatoes, and her, and flew into a rage.

"Stealing are you, shaming me are you?" He smacked her.

She didn't reply.

"You get what you deserve," he added. "That's the way of things."

She had an old sweater and a couple of pinafores, and these she gathered, tied into a bundle, and walked away. It wasn't cold, not yet. She never saw her father again, though once she saw a wagon like his, with a man like him, driving across a street ahead. She had no wish even to find out whether it was John O'Malley, the fatalist who thought everything was meant to be except that his daughter had earned an honest living.

She was not yet eleven.

Now she patrolled the crooked streets of Helena, blotting it up. It was a city in flux, barely a state capital, without a capitol building but with a good commercial district that hemmed the winding gulch that had turned a few miners into rich men and spawned a busy city. She saw bureaucrats in suits, and far more men in dungarees. She saw few women, and wondered why. Up a hill was a modest governor's residence, only slightly larger than a comfortable private home. She wondered where the legislature met, and where state offices were housed. Maybe it scarcely mattered. Montana was a work in progress.

She liked to get a feel of a place, but Helena was eluding her. She thought she would do better in the saloons, and that was where she was headed anyway. It was a bright fall afternoon, and the saloons would be empty, but that didn't matter.

Most of them lined Last Chance Gulch, and some bore the usual names she had encountered in the West—The Mint, Stockman, Pastime—but some carried evocative names: O'Leary's, The Shamrock, Harrigan's.

She chose O'Leary's, pushed into a wall of sour odor, and let her eyes open to the gloom. A wide barkeep with a soiled apron eyed her.

"Sorry, lady," he said.

It was not customary for a single woman to pierce these male sanctuaries.

She saw only half a dozen patrons, all with mugs of ale before them. Not a whiskey glass was in sight.

"I will sing," she said.

"Lady, I said, there's the door."

"I'm Mary Mabel Markey and I will sing."

"Who's that?"

"You can buy tickets. Seven at the Ming."

"Mark, let her sing," a gent said.

She placed her portfolio on the bar and withdrew some sheet music. There were several titles, which she fanned out.

"Fifty cents, signed by Mary Mabel Markey," she said.

She stood back a bit, selecting a spot where all six of the guzzlers could study her, and then she paused, drew a breath, and sang. This one was a lively jig, one of her mother's, rhythmic and rollicking. Her voice carried outward. The barkeep scowled. She knew he was thinking it'd soon be over and she'd be gone.

But now, as always, she caught them nodding, feet tapping, shoulders swaying. It always was like that. She finished the jig.

"There now," she said. "I'm Irish, and I'll sing a medley, every one of them learned from my ma. She died of the lung disease long ago, and left one thing behind. The songs of the old country."

She sang once again, needing no backup, no instrument, just a cappella to half a dozen working men—hod carriers, dustmen, who knows? Her voice was untrained and hadn't changed in all the years she had sung on street corners. She sang without elegance, no vibrato, no finesse, no punctuation to catch a breath. That voice had never been shaped by a maestro in a music academy, but it was sweet, and better still, it was earnest; more than sincere, it was honest and true. She sang the way her mother did, daughter emulating mother, and she saw that they liked that, and even Mark, the saloonkeeper, liked it and allowed a small smile to lift the corners of his mustache.

When she had finished she let silence settle.

"It's my pleasure," she said, not defining just what pleased her. "The sheet music sells for fifty cents, and I will sign each one."

First one old bloke ambled over and laid out two quarters. She lacked a pen, but she had a good pencil, and she signed the name that the customers knew. Little did they know that she was Mona and that she was an O'Malley, and some of them, if they listened closely, could name the county where she was born. Then the next one bought, and another, and she sold five in all, with one sour holdout.

"I'll give you a kiss instead," she said, and planted a kiss on the old duffer's dandruff-caked brow.

She hadn't changed at all. She was the ten-year-old girl with the cup.

At noon, August Beausoleil pounced on the *Independent*, only to find that the paper had pounced on him. He found no review, but on the front page was a lengthy article, or rather, an outburst. A deacon in a local congregation had not liked the show, and had voiced his complaints to a friendly reporter, who had written them up and added the weight of the paper's concurring opinion to them.

The show, it said, was an affront to decency. And morals. Most especially, a certain act featuring monkeys.

> The act featured certain musical material
> from the tropics, with morally objection-
> able rhythms and offensive appeal to the

baser instincts of the sort not on display in more northerly climes. That it had a corrupting influence on the audience is beyond cavil. What started as stern rectitude in the silent viewers soon turned into lax and ludicrous amusement as the ugly little beasts, devoid of human dignity and spirit, began to maul melody and inject anarchy into the proceedings.

That for starters. But the deacon and the paper were not content to trash Mrs. McGivers.

The songs rendered by the opening act, known as the Wildroot Sisters, were not of the sort to elevate moral and ethical sensibility, but to debase both singer and listener. The catchy rhythms were quite the opposite of what might be rendered by a trained and spiritual church choir, offering melodic praise to the Almighty.

Neither did the operators of the show escape.

The very name of this abomination, at the Ming Opera House, The Beausoleil Brothers Follies, tells the entire tale. It is an effort to Frenchify and Latinize good American tastes, and as such it subverts all the efforts of the Founding Fathers, guided by their respective congregations, to create a nation that would truly be The City on the Hill.

Wayne Windsor didn't escape, either.

There was a monologue, rendered by a vain eccentric who would turn from one side to the other, which lacked both humor and grace, and poked ridicule at the better classes of people, the empire builders who are subduing this continent and turning it into something close to paradise. The callow, shallow fellow doesn't hold a candle to the builders of the Republic.

And one of the early acts, The Marbury Trio, who performed with metal taps on their shoes as they did complex routines while dressed in tuxedos and silk top hats, came in for some of the worst of the assault.

To put a woman in men's clothing, with two men beside her, and have her do pirouettes and rattle the boards with the metal on her feet, debased not only the woman who was subject to such public gaze, but also the audience, unused to seeing such coarse violations of whatever is sweet and retiring and fair in American womanhood.

The piece recommended that the show fold and depart the precincts at once, or failing that, that no one should purchase a ticket, and in any case the chief of police should be on hand at all performances to step in and cover wanton dancers and issue summons for all infractions.

Beausoleil sighed. The show was a long way from Manhattan. For decades, variety shows had been somewhat racy, or deliberately offensive, often mocking anything that might be considered traditional. But in the early eighties, a New Yorker, Tony Pastor, had cleaned it up. He was the godfather of vaudeville, and every show he put together was considered suitable for any viewer. That careful approach had been picked up by Keith and Albee as they built their vaudeville circuits. They enforced the rules relentlessly. An act that violated certain standards got pitched out.

This wasn't a Keith circuit show, and Beausoleil had no contractual arrangements with the kings of vaudeville, so he and Pomerantz were free to assemble whatever acts appealed to them and to their audiences. Maybe someday the vaudeville magnates would swallow all the small shows like his, but not yet. There was plenty of room in vaudeville.

He read the material once again, and liked it. He'd sell out tonight, and for the rest of the run. He couldn't have written a better review.

"Boy," he said to the kid hawking the papers.

"Here's two bucks. Put a paper in every saloon and barbershop in the gulch, and keep a dime."

"Holy cats," the kid said, staring at the two greenbacks.

"I'll take another," Beausoleil said, and hurried toward the hotel, hoping to catch most of the acts.

He was lucky. There in the lobby stood Delilah Marbury.

"Get a load of this. Do your worst," he said.

"Skirts or pants?"

"Show some leg," he said.

"You worship the golden calf," she said.

"Mainly yours. And whatever else is attached."

"So does my husband."

"Which one?"

She laughed. The act was new, and tap dancing was new, and some people thought it should be done in blackface. In all of variety there were only a few tap acts, and he had wanted to try one out. He soon discovered that these people were dancers, day and night, cold and hot, and a stage was nothing but an excuse to tap and click and drag a foot and rattle the boards. He hadn't made up his mind about them. He usually ran them third, between two stronger acts. This was their first tour. The three were from Memphis, where they had picked up the motions and the rhythms on the waterfront. They made a good olio act, and that was proving handy whenever he was having a tough time with sick performers, or boozy or hungover ones. But the jury was out on the Marburys.

"August, we've got a new routine, and tonight's the right time to try it. I'll be in a skirt."

"Wear a tutu," he said.

"If you post bail, I will."

"Delilah, don't let them slow you down. Don't let me slow you down. If you've got something to give to those people out there, they'll know it and they'll buy it, and they'll clap, and I'll back you. I like talent. I like whatever it is that catches people in their seats and brings them to life, and brings them to cheering for you. That's why I'm here. That's what I'm looking for. It's not just the show, it's the magic. It's what makes some acts grand, and some acts flop. If you've got it, you've got me every step of the way."

She gazed at him, almost like a frightened doe. "I guess we'll find out," she said. "We're going to tap a love story."

Tap dance a love story. What would it be? A triangle, the three of them tapping away?

"The hall might be empty tonight."

"We'll see about Helena," she said. "Maybe there's a lesson or two in an empty hall."

He liked that.

He returned to sunlight and headed up the slope on Broadway, looking for city hall and the coppers. He didn't know the name of the chief, but he would learn it. He found the place, most of a square block set aside for local government but not yet built up.

The top constable was named Will Riley, and he was in, chewing on some junior constable for something or other. August never caught what.

But in a moment he was free.

August pierced the cigar smoke–coated room, and offered a hand to a man who had been feasting too much and too long and now had trouble holding his trousers up.

"August Beausoleil, sir. I own the show."

The top cop grunted, licked his lips, and waited.

"I thought you and the missus might enjoy the show, so I brought you some tickets. Front-center, third row, best in the house, perfect for variety. You get to look up every nostril."

He laid a pair of green tickets on the battered desk.

Riley eyed the tickets and grunted. He studied Beausoleil a little, and smiled.

"We'll be there. Behave yourself."

That was all there was to it.

"If you want two more, for tomorrow, matinee or evening, let me know," Beausoleil said. "Courtesy of the whole troupe."

"I bet," Riley said.

Beausoleil headed for fresh air, but then realized he was next door to the Lewis and Clark County Attorney. So he entered.

The gent was as skinny as a weasel, but mostly bald.

"Beausoleil, here, sir. I run the show at the opera house. A quick question. Is there some ordinance or local law I should know about?"

"Ask me after you've broken it."

"We want to give people a show they'll all enjoy. Especially women."

The skinny man yawned. "Good afternoon," he said.

"Would you like a couple of tickets?"

"I knew it. Soon as you walked in. You're here to grease the skids."

"Thought you might enjoy the show. We're proud of it. There's something for everyone in it."

"Time is precious, sir, and I don't squander it on entertainment."

"You have a list of the pertinent ordinances?"

"In the ledger." He jerked a thumb toward a gray ledger book. It was thick. The city fathers had been busy.

It wasn't hard to see where this was headed.

Beausoleil lifted his hat and headed for the pebbled glass door. The man stared, measuring the impresario for a black-and-white–striped costume. Walking through that door into the hall was like stepping out of a bat cave.

You never knew what you'd find when you and your company hit a town. The chill weather brought bold blue skies and a pine perfume off the mountains. There was an early dusting of snow up high, making the world virgin. He liked Helena as a place to visit but he'd never live there.

He'd done what he could. It was up to the acts now. The newspaper assault had made the rounds by now, and everyone in the company knew that there might be trouble. Some places didn't like to be entertained. Or they thought anyone in show business rose straight out of some devil's lair. But sometimes it was the reverse: show people sensed a holier-than-thou town and resented it. And their resentment showed up in the acts, no matter how professional they were. Some things couldn't be hidden. Beausoleil had occasionally gotten rid of an act because there was something about it that caused trouble. Sometimes nothing more than an attitude. Something that was a little like spitting on an audience. Take this, you rummies. Like it or leave.

But that was rare. More common was simply that each venue was different. Some acts played well in some towns and not others. Some acts bombed in a town that enjoyed variety and welcomed any company that rolled in. What prompted these shifting welcomes was a great mystery, and August Beausoleil had tried out every theory he could come up with, without getting anywhere. Running a road company was largely guesswork and instinct. But there was one thing he could always do: stay alert and try to head off trouble.

He stopped at Ball's Drug Store to see how advance sales were going, and wasn't surprised to learn that ninety reserved seats for the night's show had been sold, and more for the matinee and finale. Maybe his instinct was right: that newspaper piece had stirred things up.

As the day faded and the lamps of evening were lit, Beausoleil found himself in an anxious mood, which was unusual. He was a veteran showman, a veteran with road shows, and he usually took trouble with aplomb. But not this evening. There was nothing but a hostile, even nasty, newspaper piece between him and an ordinary show night, but somehow this article, with its brooding menace, threatened him, threatened the show, threatened trouble of a legal and political sort, trouble that could mean jail and fines and ruin.

He ate lightly, a bowl of soup, and could stomach no more. At the opera house he found the acts were tense and silent. So the newspaper assault had affected his people the same way. As showtime approached, it became plain that the evening would be a sellout. Crowds waited their turn at the ticket window, plunking down dollars, picking up green tickets, entering the quiet opera house a block above Last Chance Gulch.

He stirred through his people, who were dressed

47

and waiting, ready for the curtain to sail into the flies and the Follies to begin.

"We're going to be just fine, just fine," he said. "A grand crowd. Enjoy yourselves."

A few grinned. Others didn't.

"We'll bail you out," he said.

Only Mary Mabel Markey smiled. She looked like a woman who had just been shrived.

Showtime. As always, seven minutes after the appointed hour. The limelight was lit, casting brilliant white illumination across the center of the stage, creating an anticipation of good things to come.

August Beausoleil, in his tux and stiff white bib, appeared suddenly, waited for the packed house to quiet, and welcomed these Helena people to the Follies.

"We are delighted to be in this handsome city, among such fine people," he said. "And now, to open our show, please greet the Wildroot Sisters."

The curtain flew up, and the limelight caught the girls in bright pastels, crouched together, and then they exploded out and into their first number, a lively heads-up song about big things coming.

August studied this crowd from his perch at the

wing, and thought it looked good. Every seat had been sold, and now the crowd was settling in for the evening. In the third row was the police chief, and next to him what appeared to be a twenty-year-old wife, or a mistress or daughter. That was good news. The gals strutted, the accordion wheezed, and the girls won a quiet round of applause from an audience that seemed content enough.

Next was Harry the Juggler, who soon was tossing bowling pins, then tea cups and saucers, then baseballs, and then a mix of them all. Harry's act was short. People could take only so much tossing, even when the items were likely to break, which is what the audience waited for. He got polite applause. He'd do a second stint in the second act, juggling two knives and two scimitars. He was missing a finger, and August always wondered if that had been a juggling disaster. Harry was a loner, spoke Latvian or something, and sent his pay somewhere.

Next came the Marburys, one of the acts that was criticized in the press for violating womanhood.

"It's my delight to present, for the first time in the great state of Montana, the tap-dancing Marburys, who will show the world what's new."

They tapped out from the wing, Delilah in a calf-length frothy skirt, short by most standards but definitely female attire, and they soon were in an arm-in-arm pirouette, or buck-and-wing. August never knew the terminology, but the trio's obsession with bright dancing and intricate tapping was captivating the audience. And no one was complaining.

But August Beausoleil had a feel for things, and he knew that this crowd was waiting, and he knew what they were waiting for, and he hoped there wouldn't be another rotten fruit fight.

She was next. He sprang out into the limelight, feeling the heat of the device, bowed, and waited dramatically until there was deep quiet.

"And now, ladies and gents, one of the great attractions, brought to you from far across the Caribbean seas, in the tropics, in a world that few of us have ever known. The one, the only Mrs. McGivers and her Monkey Band."

The olio rose on the old gal, with the capuchin monkeys Abel and Cain on cymbals and drum, and her sagging accordionist wheezing his bellows to life. This was what they were waiting for out there, something scandalous. She let them absorb the rhythms, study the cheery little monkeys, and then she began singing, her corpulent body rising and sagging, her melodies hoarse and alien. The cymbals clanged, and the drum got banged, at first in an orderly manner, but the anarchistic monkeys were soon improvising, and leaping up on their seats, their arms gonging and hammering, even as the music became dissonant and at war. It was not a good sale for calypso.

Helena's theatergoers hardly knew what to make of it. But there was no flying fruit. And he heard an occasional chuckle. They were getting it: this began as languid tropical music, and was turning into anarchy, and that was the fun of it. She was the conductor of the Chaos Symphony. And some of those people were grinning.

Mrs. McGivers stood and swayed, formidable, like a tropical banana queen. The audience began to enjoy it. It didn't matter what she sang; no one could understand a word of it anyway, and the monkeys were more entertaining than the singer.

And no fruit. No rotten tomatoes.

Then the accordionist switched to a new tune, one Beausoliel hadn't heard before, a little like an organ grinder's street corner music, and sure enough, the monkeys pulled out tin cups and leapt into the two aisles, shaking the cups, which had a couple of pennies in them, soliciting coin from the audience. And the gents out there indulged the monkeys and pleased their wives by dropping nickels and dimes and even quarters into the cups, while everywhere people stood or craned necks to watch the rascally little monkeys extract boodle from pockets. And then, as fast as the accordionist had started this monkey business, he switched to another song, new marching orders, and the monkeys bounded for the stage and presented the loaded cups to Mrs. McGivers. She stood, bowed handsomely, accepted the coins like a priestess accepting a sacrament, and made her queenly way offstage.

There were some chuckles out there. This audience had gotten its money's worth. Beausoleil watched Mrs. McGivers, just offstage, empty the cups, slide the coins into a pocket, and go back for an encore, which was strictly calypso, restoring the tropics to Helena's Ming Opera House once again.

"Wasn't that fun! That was the famous Mrs. McGivers and her Monkey Band. Let's tell the world about her talented act." He waited for the final ripple of applause. "And now, my friends, the woman you've been waiting for, the one, the only, the celebrated Mary Mabel Markey."

She swept in, her posture erect, her shoulders thrown back to make her look a little more svelte. She had started to sag, but now, in the limelight, she exuded a brassy command of the whole world.

The audience clapped, glad to see the star of the show, the legend, the top-billed singer, with her accompanist, who played a flute. And then an odd thing struck Beausoleil. His star seemed distraught. Maybe that wasn't the word. He had no word for it, but she was taut and uncomfortable, this woman who was totally at ease singing in any place, for any group. It passed, but when she launched her first song, to the counterpoint of the flute, it wasn't as serene as usual. He couldn't say what was ailing, only that even though she seemed the same as ever, she wasn't. And listening carefully, he decided her voice was troubled. He suspected that two decades of singing on a stage, or maybe a street corner, had coarsened her vocal cords. He didn't know. But something wasn't right.

She sang a ballad about mothers, and another about sweethearts, and a final one about courage, and when she was finished, she bowed, and the audience clapped politely, and that was the heart of it. Polite clapping.

It troubled him more than he cared to admit. He was suddenly worried about her; she was the most stable person in the company. She was the one he could count on in any emergency. If half the acts took sick, she could fill the bill. But there she was, a shadow over her as she slipped into the wing. He caught her hand, and she pulled it away. There was no encore.

It was just a passing moment. She'd be fine. But it would not vanish from his mind, even as he strode out to introduce the final act before intermission, which was Wayne Windsor, The Profile.

"Ladies and gentlemen, welcome the king of comedy, the legendary Wayne Windsor," he said, hastening the show along to cover the odd mood left by Mary Mabel Markey.

The Profile trotted out, bowed to the right audience and the left audience to give everyone a fine view of his noble brow and jut jaw, and then addressed the multitude:

"Now, I have it from the local paper, the excellent *Herald*, that there's some people of the better class in town. That's good news. I should like to meet you. Are there any people of the better class out there? Please wave a hand, and maybe we can all gather right here, in front of the footlights."

Beausoleil did not spot any waving hands out there. It was going to be a good evening. The Profile would say kind things about the better class. Some smiles were already building up.

"Surely," he said, "there are some better-class people in Helena. I'd be disappointed if there is not one person in this beautiful city who is not of the better class."

There sure was a lot of silence out there.

"Actually, the paper got it right. There is one person of the better class in Helena. Can you guess who?" He paused. "I'll give you a hint." He pointed a finger at himself.

The crowd laughed. Windsor smiled, and posed for a Napoleonic moment.

"Now I reached this status by inventing a form of accounting, a method widely used to keep the ledgers of both government and commerce. This accounting has a new feature, which directs one percent of all revenue into a certain charity, with offices in Kentucky, Argentina, and Australia, as well as the Principality of Monaco. . . ."

The audience had settled down to some good times, and was listening sharply for heresies and scandals. The Profile was doling out scandals slowly, making sure to shift his feet, giving the lucky listeners another view of his visage.

Beausoleil hurried to the Green Room looking for Mary Mabel, and found her alone, staring sternly at the wall. He knew better than to ask if she was ill.

"I'll sub LaVerne Wildroot for the last," he said.

"You will not."

"She won't hold a candle to you; it's just that you need a break."

"I don't need a break, and if you sub her, you can put me on the next train to New York."

"You're a little out of breath."

"What do you expect? Helena's not sea level."

"Yes, and Butte's much higher. You might have a bad time of it. You'll be up a mile, I understand."

"I will be out front, singing, every day, every performance."

"Mabel, you'll have top billing on this show. You don't need to worry. I'm giving you a break. You're worn-out. There's some young talent that can fill in."

"I am who I am. I am no one else. I have been the same all my life. I sang on street corners, and

I'll sing until I can't. And when I can't you can put a yellow rose on my coffin."

He knew he had to ask the hard question. "All right, Mabel, but what if you can't sing well? Bad tonsils. Nothing comes out."

"Not sing well? That will be the day I die."

She sat there glaring, as granitic and unmoving as Gibraltar. He reached across, plucked up her icy hand, and squeezed it. She didn't respond.

He hurried up to the wings, wondering how the monologue was progressing. One thing about Wayne Windsor: every night was different, and sometimes there were a few jokers in his deck. He peered out from the edge of the arch, and saw exactly what he hoped. This crowd was devouring every word, sometimes anticipating Windsor ahead of his punch lines. The various acts hung around in the wings, just to scoop up whatever he was dishing out. He offered fresh talk in a show loaded with routine.

And there was Ethel Wildroot, over in the opposite wing watching The Profile. August Beausoleil sometimes wondered if the old gal had set her cap for the man. She rarely missed an act. August made his way behind a rear curtain, found her listening raptly, and summoned her back into the darkness.

"I may need the new act," he said. "Is LaVerne ready?"

"But you've given me no notice!"

"It may not happen. Mary Mabel's sick. Or at least she's off her form. I want to be ready."

"I'll go tell LaVerne and the accordion."

"Ethel. I'm not saying it'll happen. It's to be ready. Clear?"

"You could make it happen. You're the boss."

"I respect my talent, Ethel. Try to, anyway. All these years, I've respected my talent."

She glared. "Well, make up your mind. If I tell the girl she should be ready, then she's going on, whether or not Mary Mabel quits on you."

He took a chance. "Then don't tell LaVerne anything, Ethel. Mary Mabel's an old trouper, and she can put the sun into a new orbit."

"She can't stop old age," Ethel said.

"Well," said Wayne Windsor, winding it up. "I will go forth and tell the world that there's no one of the better class in Helena, Montana."

People chuckled, and then clapped. Windsor awarded them with both profiles.

6

Mrs. McGivers sat comfortably in the wing, watching the second act. Unlike most of the performers, who retreated to the Green Room or out the side door for some air, she preferred to watch the performers. Sometimes it was instructive. More often, she caught mistakes and blunders and had something to enjoy.

Her act would be on soon, and she and Joseph would do things a little differently. He would use a guitar, and the Monkey Band would be racier than the first act. She was very good at undulating to Caribbean rhythms. And the end of the act would be anarchy when the monkeys took over.

Just now, though, the Marbury Trio was leading off, a sudden switch by August Beausoleil. He sometimes did that, when he was not entirely confident the variety show was doing well. One indicator was empty seats. If people returned after the break, that was a good sign. If some had abandoned the theater, that wasn't so good. But Mrs. McGivers' own peeks upon the sea of faces had led her to believe they had a happy crowd that cold Helena evening.

But now the audience was quiet. The tap dancers were tapping, a fiddle was making music, and the routine was going well. This time, though, Delilah was in a tuxedo and pants, like her two dancing partners, and all three had a gold-knobbed walking stick they used as a baton, and sometimes to punctuate a musical verse with a rap on the boards.

Mrs. McGivers thought it was just fine. Three great dancers doing great footwork, the taps clicking and rattling out into the dark, beyond the limelight. But not even the perfection of the act, the astonishing footwork, toe and heel tapping, the rattle of taps on boards, was loosening up the crowd for the second act.

Cain and Abel sat beside her, leashed, watching the tapping, which was new to them. They were imitating what they saw onstage, making their monkey feet go, swaying the way Delilah swayed.

Messing with other people's acts was taboo, but Mrs. McGivers didn't care. There had never been a rule that contained her for long. She turned the capuchin monkeys loose.

"Go wiggle your butts," she said.

The little devils could hardly believe their good fortune. They eyed her, eyed the trio in the spotlight, and sprang out. The dancers, to their credit, didn't falter. The monkeys leaped right in and imitated the trio, while a ripple of delight rolled back through rows of seats. It took a moment for those at the back of the opera house to catch on In the bright light were five, two monkeys and three tap dancers, all rat-tat-tatting along. Delilah, never one to miss a chance, handed her black walking stick to Cain, who went into paroxysms of joy, hammering the boards in perfect rhythm as the fiddler speeded up the game.

Now the crowd was undulant, whispering, tapping feet, and pointing. Cain and Abel were so integrated into the line of dancers that they seemed a part of the act, as if it had been rehearsed that way from the start. But it hadn't.

"What's this?" asked Beausoleil.

"A little pepper," Mrs. McGivers said.

"They got loose, eh?"

"Smart little devils," she said, which won an arched eyebrow from him.

He watched the tap dancers bow and exit, tapping their way off the stage, led by a pair of delinquent primates. Then, as the clapping subsided, he hastened out to introduce the next act, which was Wayne Windsor, doing another monologue.

Delilah Marbury stormed straight at Mrs. McGivers, who sat quietly.

"You ruined it. You wrecked the act."

"Probably needed wrecking, girl."

"We're dancers. Not some Punch-and-Judy show. Don't ever do that again."

"You have a good act, sweetheart. Just needs a little spice."

"Spice! We're dancing, and that's all we do. And we're good at it. I'm going to have it out with August."

"Guess you will, sweetheart. And don't be surprised by what he says."

Out front, the boss was introducing the next act. "And now, for your delectation, the finest comic in the country, the one, the only Wayne Windsor!"

The finest comic in the country hastened out for his second appearance, caught the light, allowed it to shine upon his left profile, and then his right, and smiled.

"I certainly enjoy Helena, Montana," he began. "It has great newspapers. I'm especially taken with the *Herald*. I was talking to one of its reporters a while ago, and I said, 'Sir, what are your qualifications? What makes you a good reporter?' And he eyed me sternly and he said, 'A quart a day.' Now I immediately knew I was in elevated company . . ."

Beausoleil returned, unbuttoned his tuxedo, and stood, listening.

You never knew about Windsor. Once in a while he caused a ruckus. Mrs. McGivers had seen moments when the audience was ready to lynch him. The man was a phenomenon. He did have a standard routine, but most of the time he improvised, somehow coming up with good quips and funny anecdotes that had a local flavor. He was superb at his craft, which was tickling the funny bone of audiences wherever the show performed.

When there was music out front, people in the wings could talk a little, but not when there was a monologuist or a silent animal act. So she sat and watched and listened, as interested in Beausoleil's responses as in the performance. And in truth, the boss was listening carefully, because Windsor was on perilous ground. Reporters got the last word.

"I asked this fellow what a reporter's job is, and he said a really good reporter hunts around for the truth and then hides it. I said, 'How do you hide it,' and he said, 'By printing it on the front page, where no one believes it.' "

That seemed to evoke a chuckle. Windsor decided that his other side needed exposure to the limelight, so he shifted and let the white glare fall upon the left-side view, with the high brow, fine long nose without a wart, and jut jaw tapering into a handsome neck.

The limelight flickered a bit. It was achieved by training a hot flame upon a block of quicklime, which threw out the eerie light that performers loved. In Windsor's case, he somehow became incandescent himself, throwing brightness out upon his rapt listeners. It was some trick, and sure wasn't anything she had picked up in the tropics. Some performers had all the luck, and he was one of them. Audiences enjoyed him even if they didn't love him. His comments were usually barbed, and while that evoked a few laughs, it sometimes evoked some rotten tomatoes. Either was just fine.

She saw the juggler waiting his turn. If juggling baseballs and cups and saucers was entertaining, the next stint with sharp blades would be riveting. How he managed to keep those knives and scimitars in the air at once, without cutting his hand off, was something of a mystery, though once he said that the knives were heavily leaded to the exact weight of the big scimitars, so he didn't have to vary the throw. One of these days, a scimitar would crash down on his neck like a guillotine, and that would be the end of the act. The audiences always hoped to see it, but he disappointed them. She scarcely knew him. He ghosted about, not really part of the company, and barely making friends.

Meanwhile, The Profile was having a fine time. "So I asked this reporter from the *Herald*, I say, 'Who edits your stuff? Who decides what goes on the page? Who corrects it?' And he says, 'The advertisers do.' He says, 'Peruna Tonic wields the blue pencil.' He says that the editor whom every reporter dreads is Mrs. Stewart's Bluing. She wants to get the yellow out of every story, and make it perfect blue-white, with no yellow tint anywhere. 'I tell you,' says he, 'there's no editor in the business like Mrs. Stewart's Bluing.'"

She heard an appreciative chuckle. The Profile was steadily scoring, pushing back against the local paper. Even as Delilah Marbury had gotten back into her tuxedo and pants just to affront the paper, so was The Profile nibbling away at the paper. And it wouldn't stop there. The whole vaudeville company would, in its own way, even the score.

The boss was enjoying it. A show that fights back is a show that gets itself an audience, and if Wayne Windsor wanted to even things up with the *Herald*, that was just fine.

When Windsor was done tickling their funny bones, he awarded them with left and right profiles, and trotted off. A fine round of applause lured him back for a bow, a quick right and left, and then he was done.

"Now how about that, ladies and gents? The incomparable Wayne Windsor," said Beausoleil. "And now, the one you've been waiting for: the world's finest juggler, straight from Vienna, Harry Drogomeister. Please welcome the one, the only man who will put himself in harm's way to show you his unparalleled skills."

Harry trotted out, armed with a lot of blades, including steel knives with heavy handles, and scimitars, curved swords with slasher edges on the interior curve, useful for beheadings. He didn't speak much English, so he simply bowed, this way, that way, accepting the ovation, and then he picked up the knives, two lethal weapons, and casually flipped one upward, and another, and another, deftly catching each as it descended, his hand clasping the handles, never touching the blades, faster and faster, until the limelight glittered off of flying steel. Then he caught them, set them down, and picked up a scimitar, ugly, sinister, menacing. He slashed air with it a few times, ran a finger along its wicked edge, and finally pitched it upward, where it rotated slowly before descending blade-first, and the juggler caught the handle and sent it looping up again.

The audience was rapt. What reckless thing were they seeing?

He added a second, each one requiring that it be caught by the handle and deftly tossed upward. People studied his hands, looking for missing digits and scars, but they saw none, or at least none was visible across the footlights. He whirled his swords faster and faster, making the loop smaller, a prodigy of deft maneuvering, and then collected the scimitars and bowed.

But he was not done. His next feat was almost beyond imagining. He started with the knives, adding them one by one, and slowly added the scimitars until he was juggling six deadly instruments, each one treacherous, each one requiring the most delicate propulsion. How he did it no one knew, but it always impressed Mrs. McGivers as something that required voodoo. It was simply beyond human sensibility.

But there he was, out there, in front of hundreds of people, some of whom hoped to see a disaster, while others feverishly prayed that the juggler would not shed gouting red blood all over the stage.

Which he did not. Somehow he plucked the scimitars out, set each one down, and then the knives, and never let any of them clatter to the boards.

He had worked up a sheen. He bowed, and listened to polite applause. Mrs. McGivers had never heard wild applause or huzzahs or bravos following this act. It was the applause of respect and relief, and maybe thanksgiving. For that is what she always felt when the juggler was done. There he was, whole, not dripping blood or writhing on the boards, killed by accident.

It was not just the audience. The whole company breathed relief when the juggler walked safely into the wings, while a stagehand picked up all his sinister hardware in the limelight. The audience had turned somber, and she spotted a few customers abandoning their seats. It was not, she thought, an act for children.

Mary Mabel Markey would be next. But Mrs. McGivers didn't see her. She was usually stationed in the wing, ahead of her act, ready to bloom onstage, somehow flowering sweetly as she paced into the brightness.

August Beausoleil was looking for her, too. He was ready, but where was the star of the Follies?

Where indeed? The best quick sub would be the Wildroot girls, but they were lounging in the Green Room. Beausoleil nodded to Mrs. McGivers, the unspoken gesture meaning to go look for the leading lady. So she abandoned her comfortable seat and lumbered toward the stairs, and only then did she encounter Madame Markey, panting, heaving her way forward, her face white and distraught.

She pushed right past Mrs. McGivers, and

nodded to the master of ceremonies, who studied her briefly, nodded, and stepped into the light to welcome the top-billed singer and star of the Follies, who looked strangely chalky and afraid.

Mary Mabel Markey hurried to escape, feeling out of sorts. She slipped on a plain street dress, found her shawl, and headed through the Green Room hoping no one would waylay her.

But there was August, and she was trapped.

"Want to take a walk, Mary Mabel?"

"No, I'm tired, I'm going to bed."

"I think we'd better talk."

"Tomorrow," she said, heading for the stage door and the velvet cold of Helena at about eleven at night.

"I'll come with you," he said. "I like to escort a lady to safety."

"I'm not going to talk about it, so forget the gallantry."

She was alluding to the evening's performance, which she had struggled through, barely completing three songs, out of breath, off key, her stage presence lost, and that ineffable quality that had made her the queen of the vaudeville palaces utterly gone. The audience had welcomed her, then grown restless, then silent, and when it was over, the applause was tepid. She had smiled, stormed offstage, and neglected the final bow.

But as she stormed into the night, momentarily disoriented, not sure where the hotel was, he stuck with her. The last of the theatergoers were drifting away. Some of the cast had switched to street clothes and were heading for the nearest saloon. There were several lining Last Chance Gulch.

August Beausoleil would not be put off, and he caught her elbow and navigated down the steep grade.

"The air is thin here, and a singer can't get enough of it," he said.

"I told you I wouldn't talk about it."

"I was thinking some rest might help. We all wear ourselves to shreds on tour."

"I will not leave the show, and the show needs me, and you'd fall flat on your face if it wasn't for me."

"You are quite right, Mary Mabel. Absolutely. You're the draw."

He helped her down a long stair that took them into the gulch, where there was a little light spilling from windows. The quiet air bit at her cheeks and ears. Helena was cold and hard.

"But," he added, "I'm thinking you need a few days' rest, and we'll manage. Some time with your head on a warm pillow should give you more air."

"I don't need air. And I have no intention of letting LaVerne Wildroot substitute for me. She'd drive the crowd right out the door. You'd be paying refunds."

"I haven't heard her. She has some songs worked up, Ethel says."

"Ethel has a tin ear."

"The mothers of entertainers tend to have tin ears, yes. Mary Mabel, your slot is yours. I'm simply hoping that a little bed rest will put you back where you belong."

"You won't get rid of me that easily, August Beausoleil."

"It's my object to keep you."

"Then we won't talk about this again."

"We may have to if your act continues to weaken your hold upon your admirers."

She relented a little. "I won't be toyed with," she said.

He nodded. They both knew he wasn't toying with her. He was a discreet and sensitive impresario, with a knack for placating unhappy talent. She would give him that. He said no more, but she knew it was far from over. She felt out of breath; the mountain air didn't seem to satisfy the craving of her body for more oxygen. Her pulse raced, and she ached. She wondered sometimes why she was a performer. No one in the business lived quietly, safe and rested in a nest somewhere.

If Helena did this to her, how would she survive

Butte, which was much higher? She felt dizzy again, and felt his firm grip on her elbow, steadying her. They headed up the Gulch, found the dim-lit door to the hotel, and entered. It wasn't much warmer inside the tiny lobby, but somehow it was welcoming.

"I will see you to your room."

He never did that. It alarmed her. She ran through the reasons, and concluded that he was escorting her to her door for the worst of them: he feared she would collapse before she got to her room. He had read her well. She was wobbly on her pins, rasping for air, and she hurt. Her vocal cords hurt. They often hurt a bit, but not like this. Her voice had thickened. During her act, the sweetness that had won ardent admirers had vanished, and what emerged this night was thick and nasal and without the maidenly quality that had made her a celebrated singer with a silvery high range.

He paused at the door, while she dug for a key.

"You've given your all to the Follies, Mary Mabel. I know you'll continue."

"If that's a warning, lay off."

"I need to do some accounting," he said. "We had a full house."

He tipped his hat and vanished. She was angry with him for no good reason. She'd had a miserable night, sometimes so faint onstage that she wondered if she should sit down and sing from a chair. All those Mary Mabel Markey admirers had been disappointed. It wasn't blatant. She had pushed air through her throat, forced her lungs, delivered every ounce she could, even as she grew horrified and desperate at her own performance up there in the limelight.

She'd had a few bad nights, sick nights, nights when the stage was so cold, or so hot, it made her dizzy to sing. But nothing like this night, which is what terrified her. She slipped the skeleton key into the door, and swung it open. It wasn't the fanciest place in Helena—show people didn't live like that—but it had a soft bed, a taut red blanket drawn over it, and a good white pillow in a slip that wasn't yellowed. Tonight any bed would be paradise.

She slipped down the hall to the water closet that served six rooms, found it empty, and prepared herself for the night to come. She washed her face in cold water, studying it. She was still young, or at least not seamed and gray. She had a dozen more years at the top of the heap if she wanted that. But she didn't like this dizziness, or the aching arms and chest and neck, so she hastened to her room, slipped into her white flannel bedclothes, and tumbled into the bed.

But the weariness wouldn't release. Her racing pulse wouldn't slow. She lay angrily, not wanting to know what was troubling her, and not wanting to learn about it from stupid doctors who didn't know, either.

In the morning she sought out Marcus Aurelius Flannigan, MD, who practiced in the front parlor of his home on the other side of Last Chance Gulch. It had to be a morning appointment; she had a matinee that afternoon, and an evening performance. There were two doctors in Helena, so she chose the one with the most imposing name, on the theory that he knew more.

He welcomed her and led her to his parlor, fitted up as an examination room, with square bottles lining the walls and instruments of torture lying about.

He wore a gray swallowtail coat, and had a closely cropped beard, and hair in his nostrils.

"I am Mary Mabel Markey," she said, but that elicited no response. "If you are overly familiar with me, and talk about it, I will consider it an offense against me."

"I practice medicine," he said, and nothing more.

"I may have the vapors. Find it out at once, and give me some powders. I have a matinee this afternoon."

He pursed his lips, registering that. "What powders do you have in mind?" he asked.

"You're the doctor. Take twenty years off me."

"Well, if you'll take twenty off me, I'll take twenty off you," he said. "Sit right there and tell me what's ailing you."

She seated herself on an examination table, eyeing him suspiciously. She was fussy about who did what with Mary Mabel Markey.

"I'm waiting," he said.

"I am dizzy. My strength vanishes. My neck and arms hurt. My left arm. My chest hurts. I have no air. I can't get enough. It's the altitude. I'm cold at night. My throat bothers me, especially when I sing 'Sweet Lover Be Mine.' My throat's a little better when I sing 'Wayward Girl, Whither Goest Thou?' But I have trouble with the high notes, and the lowest ranges seem a little coarse. Not like me at all. And I almost fainted, twice. And they were all waiting in the wings for me to keel over, but I foiled them."

"I am going to see about your circulation," he said.

"I don't circulate."

He had one of those listening tubes in hand, and pressed it on her chest, suspiciously close to her bosom, but she let it pass. He listened carefully, moving the instrument about, being all too familiar, but what could you expect of a man named after a Roman emperor?

"Breathe in and out," he said. He was listening at her side, her back.

He took her pulse, his hand firm on her wrist, his eye on a pocket watch with a second hand. He poked around in her mouth, the fountain of her fame, with a tongue depressor, using a carbide lamp for illumination. Tongue, gums, nostrils. Neck glands. He also peered into her eyes, one by one, with some sort of lens, which annoyed her. That was all the apertures she intended for him to examine. Knee tap. He checked her ankles for swelling, his hand lingering there, probing.

He asked the usual questions. How long have you felt this? You get faint standing up? How about sitting down? What powders are you using? Have you had any other examination?

She was inclined not to answer him because he was becoming personal, and she was Mary Mabel Markey, and doctors who wore swallowtail coats were obviously suspect. Clothing could cloak incompetence. Where did he go to medical college, and what was he doing in a raw, tawdry town like Helena, full of politicians and miners and crooks?

No one in his right mind would live in Montana except to get rich quick and get out.

"Your pulse is high, ninety-five, and erratic. Your heartbeat's erratic and not regular. Your left ventricle's misfiring, is the way I could best put it. You have heart trouble."

"I do not. It's the altitude."

He sighed. "That'll be three dollars."

"What do you mean? Are you done with me?"

"You just announced that my diagnosis is wrong, and it's altitude. Three dollars, and you may head for your matinee."

"Of course it's wrong. So why should I pay?"

He stared out the window for a moment. "You're in great peril of an attack. You've had some small ones. There's not much to do for it but lose weight. You would profit from losing ten or fifteen pounds."

"I am Mary Mabel Markey and I won't listen to malicious talk."

"You would also do better at lower altitudes. You'll breathe better at sea level. And certainly live in less peril."

"I knew it. My rivals have paid you off. I'll want some powders now."

He contemplated that. "I saw no major problems with your throat. But it would take special lighting equipment, incandescent light beamed in, to tell you more. Until Helena's got electricity, I'm limited. But I would suggest temporarily retiring from your company, and spending a few months at a seashore."

"I want powders."

"Any powders I might prescribe would have no effect on your heart, nor would they improve your breathing, and they'd probably weaken your voice."

"But they'd stop pain."

"Dover's Powder, opium, would stop pain, and so would any of the cough syrups with opium in them. They would all damage your voice. And the longer you use them, the higher the dose you'd need to subdue your demons."

"I want powders."

He eyed her gravely. "I'm sure you do. And they would be your ruin. When you sing 'Sweet Lover Be Mine,' you may not receive the ovation, the response, you expected."

She saw that he was not going to budge, so she pulled out two dollars and slapped them on the examination table.

He eyed the two dollars, eyed her, and nodded. An odd amusement filled his face. But he didn't argue.

She left in a tantrum, headed for the nearest apothecary shop, purchased a bottle of Dover's Powder in tablet form, and some Williams' New England Cough Syrup, opium in an alcohol solution, and headed for the matinee.

8

The house was filling up. August Beausoleil eyed the rough crowd, wondering what brought them to the matinee on a bright autumn afternoon. They were miners. The matinee price was seventy-five cents and two bits for gallery seats. They would enjoy the show, have money to spare for a few drinks before heading for the outlying gold mines. Or so he was told. They were not gentlemen in cravats, and there were few women out there.

That was unusual. In most places, matinees were for women and children, who could see the show and reach their homes safely before dark. But not this crowd. He saw bearded men wearing bib overalls, pale men who worked far from sunlight. Men with big, rough hands. And one or two with a flask in hand. Many of them lived in remote barracks and hadn't seen a woman in a week.

A quiet descended as curtain time neared. These were men starved for company, starved for entertainment, ready to lap up whatever was put on their plate. It would likely be the best sort of audience, generous and happy and forgiving, if one or another performer failed.

All right, then. The audience had settled. He nodded, and the curtain rolled skyward, revealing himself, center stage, in the bright white light of the lime. This would be a dandy afternoon. A faint foreboding skittered past him, and he ignored it.

"Ladies, gents, welcome to the Beausoleil Brothers Follies," he said. "We're here in beautiful Helena, the proudest town in Montana. Now, to welcome you, meet the Wildroot Sisters, Cookie, Marge, and LaVerne. Let's give them all a big hand."

Indeed, applause rose upward as the three young ladies danced out, in the order by which they had been introduced. And quickly, they broke into song, "Yankee Doodle Dandy," always a good opener that swelled up a little national fervor.

Beausoleil discreetly abandoned the stage, and waited in the wings.

The girls wore shimmery taffeta, rose and turquoise, which rippled with light and movement and added to the luster of the opening. It was all fine, fine, another opening, another matinee.

Several acts appeared, juggling, tap dancing, and the audience delighted in them, and waited for the one that had brought them. Beausoleil knew they were waiting, didn't quite know why, but knew he'd soon find out.

Mary Mabel sat quietly, almost remote, dressed in her show costume, her corset giving her a wasp waist and pushing her bosom high. She was oddly serene. Usually, as her turn loomed, she was blooming with energy, some inner fires heating up for the performance. But now she watched, distant, all too quiet.

"You're fine, Mary Mabel?" he asked.

She replied with a little wave of her hand. It was a white hand she rubbed with sheep lanolin daily to hide the wrinkles. Now it was soft and languid. She peered up at him with enormous eyes, and smiled. Her quietness disturbed him almost as much as the agitation that had given a ragged tone to her act the day before.

"The show is a king," he said. "It commands us."

She nodded, still strangely quiet, the shadowed light hiding her from him.

"All right, here we go," he said.

She stood, languidly.

He adjusted his tuxedo, made sure the attached white bib was reasonably clean, and plunged out just as the applause was fading. He was always conscious of pace, and hated dead moments. So now he strode into the shocking light even as the clapping echoed through the hall, and waited for all those miners to settle into the next act, the big act, the one he knew had brought them, the one for which they had laid out seventy-five cents and slipped into a theater seat.

The light momentarily blinded him, as usual, but soon enough he could make out those rows of males before him. And he could smell them. This was not a perfumed crowd, not for this Saturday matinee.

"And now, the lady you've been waiting for, the one, the only Miss Mary Mabel Markey! Welcome our sweetheart!"

Some of those miners cheered; most clapped amiably, and settled into their seats. She moved languidly past the arch, into the light, and somehow instantly quieted the crowd. Some performers could do that. Her mere presence was all it took.

She smiled right and left, almost a Wayne Windsor performance, letting all those lusty men have a gander at that hourglass form.

This would be good, he thought. He guessed she'd sing three. Usually it was two, but a little adoration sometimes stirred her juices.

She would sing a capella. She usually did. That was one of the qualities that had made her a legend. She smiled, took a breath, and began. But she produced only a squawk. She smiled, nodded, touched her throat, and plunged in again, and that yielded another throaty rumble. She seemed puzzled. The whole house was watching, transfixed.

She smiled, captured a breath, and tried again, this time landing heavily on a note, until it died. She seemed utterly bewildered. How could this be? She peered right and left, and offstage, and there was no help. She smiled helplessly, cleared her throat, and tackled her opening of "Blue Eyes" once again, only to have it strangle in her mouth. She seemed utterly befuddled.

Beausoleil was just as befuddled, but he was a veteran at rescuing beached acts, and hastened out, blinded by light.

"A bit of laryngitis, is it?"

She nodded.

"We'll see if things clear up. Ladies and gents, our beloved Miss Markey is out of voice, at least for the moment. This is most regrettable, but can't be helped. We hope our favorite singer will be fine for the next act."

But she was shaking her head.

"We'll count on it," he said.

That crowd slowly absorbed it. They wouldn't be hearing their favorite, Miss Mary Mabel Markey. Not this afternoon. The miners stirred, restless, uncertain about something. Mary Mabel bowed, meandered offstage, in no hurry, and with no particular concern about all of this. He glanced her way, puzzled, wondering who to run next. Probably the tap dancers. The show needed some-thing lively just then, something to wipe away this odd interlude.

And then some fellow out in the house was talking. He stood up.

"You mind if I come up there? We have a little something for the lady," he said.

"After the show, sir. Time to roll out the next act."

"It's a gift for Miss Markey, sir. We came here to present her with something. It's gotta be now, or we'll lose our chance."

August Beausoleil was flexible. You had to be flexible, sometimes bending backward, to run a variety show. He'd always argued that every town had a surprise waiting for him. And so he waved the man forward, with a flourish, and then hastened backstage to find Mary Mabel, who was standing numbly in the wings. There was something plenty strange about her.

"Come," he said.

She strode out obediently, ahead of him, and

won a lively round of applause, even as the miner, a black-bearded fellow, clambered up a stair to the boards.

He was carrying a little white box, and seemed perfectly at home on the bright side of the lights.

Beausoleil steadied Mary Mabel Markey, who seemed as slippery as soft butter, and steered her around so she was facing the gent.

He grinned, nodded to some of his friends out there, and plunged in:

"Ma'am, me and my crew, we got to thinking that you're the girl we'd like have serenade us. We saw your picture in *The Police Gazette*, and one of us heard you in St. Louis, and said you're a nightingale, and you can sing for us any time. Anyway, we've decided you're The Montana Nugget, meaning no offense of course, and we got together to give you a nugget, one of the biggest ever hauled out of the ground around here. This one's over an ounce, and it's all for you."

He handed her the box. His crew cheered. The rest clapped. She slowly undid a blue ribbon, pulled open the pasteboard, and spotted an irregular blob of native gold.

She smiled, lifted up the shining gold for all to see, and then planted a big smack of a kiss squarely on his hairy lips. And she added another and a big squeeze for good measure. And one more to make the point.

"You're my boy," she said, in a voice bordering on basso.

Beausoleil shook the man's hand. "And your name, sir?"

"Aw, just call me Fandango."

"All right, Fandango, you've brought blessings to Miss Markey, and pleasure to the Follies. We all thank you. What a fine audience! Montana takes the cake."

Fandango retreated to to his seat, Beausoleil welcomed Wayne Windsor, and hastened to the wing, looking for Mary Mabel. He found her meandering back toward the Green Room, and steered her in. They were alone, with just one lamp lit.

She plunked herself in a chair.

"What's the story?" he asked.

"Oh, I'll get past it," she muttered, still basso.

"Your throat?"

"The cough syrup. And the pill."

"Show me."

She found a handbag and handed it to him. He opened it, found the brown bottle of Williams' New England Cough Syrup, and the pasteboard box of tablets. The labels didn't say much, but he didn't need to learn what he already knew.

"We'll sub for the evening show, and your second act," he said.

Then she was crying. He knelt beside her, pulled her close, gently wiped her flushed face, ran a hand through her uncombed hair, and kissed her softly on her forehead.

"You're my star, and you always will be," he said.

"I was born that way."

"Come out for the curtain call," he said.

"I'm so dizzy."

She seemed almost inert as he held her, and he wondered if she would ever grace his stage again. He could feel it, something ebbing within her. He wondered how ill she was, and how deeply the pain ran through her body.

"Wayne's winding up," he said. "You rest."

He trotted upstairs, and found Windsor showing his right and left profiles to all those miners. He had managed to win them over, and now they were chuckling regularly. He was still mining the *Herald* story.

Ethel Wildroot aimed straight at him, and it was too late for him to escape.

"She was drunk!" Ethel yelled.

Beausoleil thrust a finger to his lips. Talk in the wings was forbidden during the silent acts; you could whisper something during the musical ones. Yelling was a felony.

"Drunk as a skunk," she added, deliberately loud enough to reach the first few rows.

Beausoleil shook his head, and grabbed her elbow, and steered her away, finally reaching a rear corner of the commodious backstage.

"No, she wasn't. She's sick."

"Sick, my eye. Why are you covering up?"

She still was loud enough to disturb Windsor's act, so he just pressed a finger to his lips, and to hers.

That turned her into a hissing teakettle.

"The woman's an old drunk," she whispered, loud enough to rattle windows. "I don't know why you put up with it. Treating you that way. Her voice's gone to seed, and the way she abuses it, it's done. She's a has-been. Yet you stick with her, mollycoddle her. What's the matter with you? There's talent, there's good voices, there's people like LaVerne, ready to step up, to fill the stage and shine, but you stick with that derelict."

"Later," he said softly. "Not now. You're out of line."

"You don't even give LaVerne a chance. She could turn this around. She could knock all those miners out of their heads."

"That isn't what we have in mind, Ethel," he said, softly enough so maybe she would get the message. He could hear Windsor winding up. It was odd how rhythm played a role in his monologues, and the faster the laughs lapped each other, the closer he was to finishing.

"Gotta go," he said, abandoning her. But she boiled right along beside him.

"That whole business. She doesn't have laryngitis. She has whiskey-itis. And it's wrecked her voice. And you pay her three times more than she's worth. She's thirty-nine!"

"Ethel—stop."

She smiled suddenly and patted his arm. "You know what you're doing," she said.

Ethel Wildroot was elated. LaVerne would do a solo at last. Ethel discovered LaVerne in the Green Room, playing solitaire.

"Get ready. You'll sub for Mary Mabel second act."

"Who says?"

"He's got no choice. You get yourself gingered up and be ready."

"What did he say?"

"He said Mary Mabel's sick, and if she's better, she'll go on. Actually, she's drunk."

"I haven't done the songs in days."

Ethel glared at her. "Now's your chance."

"I should be happy?"

That was the trouble with LaVerne. She didn't come from theater family. Not like Ethel's daughters. Marge and Cookie looked too much like their father, the comedian Wally Wildroot, which was why Ethel brought her niece LaVerne into the act. LaVerne actually looked like Ethel herself, halfway pretty. Marge and Cookie had inherited all the wrong features, and they weren't going anywhere in vaudeville. Rotten Wally Wildroot had sired two jut-jawed girls with bad voices that were beyond redemption, even though Ethel had paid for lessons. They were doomed to be blues singers in Memphis, but Ethel wasn't ready to tell them that. Not yet. They had bad teeth, too. LaVerne could sing when she felt like it, but she didn't care if the audience was ten people or two hundred. It sure was hard to create a good act.

"What'll you sing?"

"Whatever you want."

"You'll sing 'Waltz Me Tonight,' and 'Ta-Ra-Ra Boom-Dee-Ay.' And for an encore, 'Warm My Hand.'"

"All right," LaVerne said, and returned to her cards.

"LaVerne, I've brought you into the act, and given you top billing. You owe me a performance that they won't forget. This afternoon. Now. Get ready."

"Sure, Ethel."

"I'll get you more money. You'll reach the top. All I'll want is an agency fee."

"Sure, Ethel."

"The second act's coming right up. Shouldn't you be talking to the music?"

"Just tell him."

The music was any of several people in the show. The Wildroots borrowed an accordionist or a fiddler, or sometimes a clarinetist, and gave him a couple of dollars.

"I'll get Willie," Ethel said. Willie made music for the tap dancers.

LaVerne was no Mary Mabel Markey. She needed backup. Ethel hastened to the stage door, where Willie usually smoked cheroots and watched the pedestrians during matinees, and there he was, fingers stained brown, sucking a fat nickel cigar.

"LaVerne's subbing for Mary Mabel, so be ready," she said.

"It's LaVerne's big chance," Willie said.

"It's only a matinee, Willie."

Willie smiled. "Have her show some ankle."

"You would say that, wouldn't you?"

"Bunch of miners out there."

It wasn't a bad idea. She'd advise LaVerne to appeal to the male animal.

"Vaudeville's elevated and spiritual," she said.

Willie grinned maliciously.

The second act rolled along, the Helena afternoon bright and chill. Harry the Juggler put on a good show, but nothing compared to a sword swallower. There were only a handful of those, and they all played the big circuits back east. Imagine slowly lowering a double-edged sword, right to the hilt, down your gullet. People always waited for the sword swallower to eviscerate himself. But so did they wait for Harry to behead himself with those flying scimitars, and that was almost as good.

She had seen Harry lose a scimitar only once, when a gust of air hit a playhouse back in St. Louis, pushed open a double door, sending a gale straight across the stage. It also blew out some footlights. Harry had picked up the scimitar, smiled, and did the deal all over. Except for the missing finger, Harry was unbloodied even after a dozen years in variety shows. But he was so quiet that some people thought a stray knife had cut out his tongue.

The miners clapped politely, and Beausoleil introduced the tap dancers again, and the trio did that strange loose-jointed clatter that Ethel couldn't call a dance, and couldn't call gymnastics, and probably came out of some plantation somewhere down south. Oh, well. Vaudeville was always trying out new acts, and sometimes one clicked. Not this one, though. Ethel knew it was doomed. Tap dancing was a passing novelty, and there wasn't enough to it to catch an audience.

LaVerne stood quietly in the wings. She had on a short green skirt and scooped blouse, mostly because Ethel had told her to wear that outfit. Willie's accordion sagged across his belly.

Beausoleil trotted into the bright light.

"And now, ladies and gents, something special. Mary Mabel Markey, once again."

It was as if an anarchist had thrown a bomb under the duke's carriage.

"Mary Mabel Markey, the world's sweetheart, is going to hum her songs tonight, gents and ladies. You know the words. She knows the words, but they're locked up in her throat this rare afternoon. So may I present, the world's sweetheart, Mary Mabel Markey."

Mary Mabel swirled out of nowhere, head to toe in pale blue velvet, with only a strand of pearls to relieve the sky blue gown.

She would hum, sore-throated, a capella.

And she did. She started softly, so softly the audience strained to hear her, but slowly Mary Mabel Markey triumphed over lyrics, and let melody steal her act, melody rising from her throat, low and soft as velvet, sweet as whispered love.

The effect was unearthly. Ethel was enthralled, in spite of a wish to tear the opera house to pieces. Mary Mabel swayed softly, small and vulnerable, yet powerful and sweet. Not a word was spoken. Her lips never formed them, but only formed a soft aperture. When she finished, and the opera house was caught in quiet, she bowed. And her audience leapt up and cheered.

LaVerne, across the stage in the opposite wing, stared. The accordionist yawned.

Mary Mabel started another, soft as a lullaby, her throaty voice rising from some new place in her body, almost down in her stomach. It never broke. It had innocence in it, somehow trans-forming Mary Mabel Markey into a woman waiting for her lover. Beausoleil watched from the wing. The other acts, drawn to this phenomenon, were watching too, the Green Room abandoned. And then when it was done, Mary Mabel took her sky-blue bow, and bowed again, and vanished.

It was not a tumultuous applause, but one suited to the mood, warm and polite and affectionate. Somehow, Mary Mabel Markey had triumphed over her sore throat. She disappeared, not pausing to stand offstage, gone for the rest of the matinee.

August Beausoleil looked pensive. He was thinking about all this. They all were. But finally, after an unduly long pause, he headed into the white light, nodded at the miners, and very quietly introduced Wayne Windsor, The Profile.

"I'm the two-spot following the Queen of Hearts," Windsor said.

Ethel listened a bit, curious about the miners out there, wondering whether they would simply shut out Windsor, but he soon was digging up chuckles. Windsor had his own gifts.

"Be ready," Beausoleil said.

"LaVerne?"

"You've been asking."

He was shuffling the acts again. She hastened to

the Green Room, found LaVerne at her solitaire, bullied her to the stage, and collected Willie from the alley behind the opera house.

"Ladies and gents, something special now, direct from Brooklyn, New York, the Miners' Heartthrob, LaVerne LaTour. Welcome Miss LaTour."

"The what?" Ethel asked, pushing her niece into the limelight. She heard scattered applause as LaVerne stumbled out, smiled, waited for Willie to crank up his squeeze box; then she bowed, did a little pirouette, and plunged into "Waltz Me Tonight."

She wasn't half bad. She kicked up a little, displayed that slim ankle, worked at seducing the crowd, and sailed through without winning any hearts. She knew it, and worked harder at "Ta-Ra-Ra Boom-Dee-Ay," which somehow didn't work on this crowd, either.

Ethel watched, revelation opening her mind, aware that this niece of hers lacked talent, would never have talent, and no amount of rehearsal and revamping the act would give her talent. She was adequate as one of the Wildroot Sisters, buried in three-part harmony, but not solo.

Ethel glanced at Beausoleil, who stared impassively. The impresario had seen plenty of nondescript acts come and go, and this one just went and wouldn't return.

He smiled at Ethel, and that smile spoke a million words.

There was no encore. LaVerne could read applause as well as anyone. She and Willie retreated to the wings, and Beausoleil trotted out.

"Give that lady a big hand," he said. "LaVerne LaTour. The Brooklyn siren."

The crowd didn't.

It was odd how careers ended in vaudeville. One day you're on, in the white light, the next day you're barely someone's recollection.

LaVerne looked relieved.

Mrs. McGivers and her Monkey Band were out there, and the crowd was already buzzing with delight at the sight of the capuchin monkeys in gold-and-red uniforms. Suddenly the whole stage was tropical. That was the thing about Mrs. McGivers. The audience just knew it was about to have some fun.

Ethel caught up with LaVerne, who was returning to her card game.

"He shouldn't have put you so close to Mary Mabel," Ethel said.

"I can figure it out as well as anyone," LaVerne said. "So quit knocking me."

That's how the new act vanished. Not a word of rebuke, not a word of regret. In truth, LaVerne didn't really care. But Ethel cared. The Wildroot Sisters act didn't earn much; it had to feed three singers and their manager. And pay a musician. LaVerne wasn't a bit disappointed, but Ethel was.

She rebuked herself for luring her niece into

the business. The girl would have been happier living in prosaic wedlock and motherhood somewhere, rather than on the circuit. And this tour had barely started.

Ethel heard the raucous sounds of the Monkey Band, the erratic cymbals, the crazy drumming, the rowdy Mrs. McGivers. That was a good act; vaguely scandalous, though it was hard to say why. It was Mrs. McGivers herself who oozed impropriety of some sort, looking loose and wicked.

Ethel remembered when she and Wally Wildroot were an act. He was a mean comedian, the sort who jabbed and sneered and stabbed. And she was his foil. She in her blond wig. He would ask a question, she would reply, and he would have fun at her expense. She played the dumb blond lady, and he played the superior sophisticate. That was okay, but what wasn't so much fun was the offstage relationship, which was no different from what went on in front of those heckling audiences. After two baby girls and years of abuse and comedy that wore thinner and thinner, she had quit the act cold. She walked out. And it turned out his act was no good alone, without some female to ridicule, and he hated her for it. They never bothered with a divorce, just drifted this way and that, and he disappeared. Last she knew, he was in New Orleans in some steamy dive, making a two-bit living. And she had put together the Wildroot Sisters, which barely survived, even in two-bit shows like this one.

She needed a new act. She knew the entire art of making a joke. She wondered whether she could make it as a comedienne, making fun of some male oaf. Turn the tables. Would these miners enjoy the switcheroo? Could she pull it off? She sure didn't know, but she needed an act, and she knew how to do an act, and it would work if she could find the right foil, a male who'd be her punching bag. There had to be somebody in the outfit, but she couldn't think of anyone. Could she make wiseacre comments as Harry juggled? Could she and Mrs. McGivers trade insults? Could she work out a comedy routine with August? She sure didn't think so. August was practically a saint. She'd never heard him give offense to anyone. Too bad. That was one reason it was a third-rate show touring weary little burgs out in the West, far from the big time. Really big-time operators always wounded everyone around them.

10

Ginger. She would never be anyone else. She would have no surname. She would be known only as Ginger. She was not sure she liked the name, but it was as far removed from her real name as she could make it. Her real name would be buried this day, all three parts of it, and never again spoken. That part of her had ceased to exist.

Some of it was to conceal herself from her family and its minions, who would be watching hawk-eyed for the young woman with the birth names she had abandoned. By choosing to be Ginger, she was escaping a velvet prison. She was taking great care not to be discovered and forcibly restored to her mother and father. She was an only child, and that had been part of the trouble.

Weeks earlier, she had bought coach tickets that would take her to Butte, Montana, on a roundabout route. She hoped to meet Destiny there in the mining town, but there was no assurance of it. She only knew she had to do this, was desperate to do it, and would have no regrets, no matter what the outcome.

Her father was the supervisor of the Union Pacific division that probed from Utah up into the mountainous reaches of Idaho, and served the mining towns scattered across the state. She had lived most of her life in a generous home in Pocatello Junction, a haven of space and sunlight and comfort, even as the rude town bloomed into a civilized city serving ranches and reservations nearby.

There, in sunny circumstances, her parents had doted on her, and turned her into a musical prodigy, through constant employment of the best tutors. She could sing sweetly, and with all the nuance of an educated voice. She could play the family's Steinway as masterfully as she could sing ballads, opera, light opera, and hymns. She was a prodigy, a marvel for her eighteen years, a peer of anyone ever taught in the salons of New York.

She had practiced dutifully, performed for her parents and their affluent friends, won the attention of choir directors and orchestra conductors. Her mother doted on her, found vicarious delight in her, boasted of her, demanded that she continue her musical career, and insisted that she surrender everything else in her life. All of which was seconded by her father, who offered to spend whatever it took, bring in whatever tutor was required, to turn her into the most accomplished daughter in all of Idaho, if not the West.

All of which had grated more and more upon her as she realized how totally she was her parents' puppet, the rag doll who was permitted no ambition of her own but was simply the hope chest of every dream her mother harbored. That she was an only child only made matters worse. That she lived in a small town, just setting aside its rude frontier beginnings, only threw a light on her, and made her much more visible than if she had been a prodigy in, say, San Francisco, or Chicago.

But this nightingale in the gilded cage had discovered that the attention lavished upon her was a prison, that no one had ever asked her what she would like to do with her life, that no one had noticed the deepening melancholia as she watched the world through barred windows. She had few gentleman friends; her parents would not allow her to cultivate any.

She had struggled to carve some liberty out of her schedule, but all these efforts, timid at first, and then more urgent, had been sloughed aside, dismissed with a maternal smile, a small joke, a wave of a ring-encrusted hand. Somehow, in the preceding months, she had realized that she had to escape or die. Yes, she believed, die. If she stayed longer, her mother would own this daughter, possessing everything.

Ginger, a chosen name, was as far removed from her nature as she could imagine. Ginger was sharp and bright. Ginger was spunky. And there never had been a Ginger in her father's family or her mother's.

She had to escape. Vanish and never be found. She hadn't the faintest idea of what to do, and didn't even know how to make a plan and execute it. But as adulthood approached, so did desperation. One day, while reading the Pocatello paper, she discovered a tiny story about a vaudeville company traveling through the Northwest. The Beausoleil Brothers Follies would play in Helena that November, then Butte, then Philipsburg, then Missoula, and then head for the coast. She barely knew these places. She barely knew what sort of acts appeared in a vaudeville show. But they employed singers, and she could also play the piano with virtuoso skill, or so they said. And she had secretly mastered a few ballads, not just arias or hymns, but songs real people sang. Ballads about love.

She wished to audition in Butte. In vaudeville! The Union Pacific would take her to Ogden. The Utah & Northern would take her to Butte. She knew something about railroads; her father ran them. She was not lacking in cash. She had always been free to indulge herself in dresses and suits and skirts and shoes and parasols and gloves. Cash was there for the asking.

She knew a little about vaudeville, or at least variety theater. Small shows had come to Pocatello, gotten a crowd, and left. Her parents had disapproved of them. Barbaric entertainments, not suited for people of substance. She didn't know whether she approved of them, but now she saw the Beausoleil show as a vehicle, a carriage to a new life, whatever that life might be.

Of course she could say nothing, not even express a wish. She would horrify her singing coach, her piano teacher, her other tutors, and her parents. Vaudeville? That would be like throwing away her life.

One day she bought a coach ticket to Ogden, and another from there to Butte. She would need to intercept the vaudeville company and audition for it. Her heart was not aflutter. She would plan and execute this escape, and if it failed she would find something else. She would be unescorted, and she knew that could pose dangers, but there was no point in worrying about anything. She was not anxious. The day she decided she would no longer be a prodigy, she ceased worrying. She accumu-lated greenbacks, eventually acquiring a hundred dollars, which she concealed in various pockets.

She wondered whether she might feel a pang upon slipping away. These were her parents, after all, Will and Mazeppa Jones, and they had nurtured her, given generously to her, developed her skills. She knew she would miss her father; he always distanced himself from her mother's obsessions. Her mother she would not miss. She bore no love for her daughter, who was little more than a shell to carry a bag of ambitions.

When the cold day arrived, she marveled at how calm she felt. Anything at all would be better than the oblivion she faced at home. She dressed discreetly, not wishing to call attention to herself. She shipped one bag ahead, via express, and would collect it in Butte. The other bag she nonchalantly carried with her. An inner voice whispered that all this was harebrained, but what did it matter? It beat being a prodigy. She had given little thought to what she would say when she contacted the vaudeville company. Nor had she created an act, a performance. All that would come.

She was, at eighteen, handsome. Thin but not slight. A warm-eyed oval face framed with brown hair. She lacked the curves gentlemen liked, but it didn't matter. She could sing, and she would get paid for it, and that mattered. What she would do with herself if she got on board the show, she didn't know. That was part of the pleasure of it. She hadn't the faintest idea how she would live, who she would befriend, and what her future might be. She supposed she was all innocence, given her cloistered life as a prodigy, but she knew she wasn't. Her parents were urbane people who lived in a wide world, and she had a good idea of what lay ahead.

She boarded the train unobserved, settled into the green horsehair seat, and felt the engine yank the couplings and roll the wheels of the coach under her. The conductor, stern in blue serge, took her ticket and smiled.

"We're on time. You'll connect," he said.

She murmured her thanks. She realized, too late, that she knew many of the conductors in that division; they knew her father. But she was lucky this time. In Ogden, she boarded the Utah & Northern, a plainer coach with wicker seats. And again, no one knew her, the red-nosed conductor was no one she had ever seen, and soon she was rolling north, to the mysterious copper mining town of Butte, and Destiny.

She watched the untouched wilderness tick by, caught whiffs of smoke from the engine ahead, heard its mournful whistle, and waited to begin a new life.

Butte finally rose up ahead, a haze of gray smoke, a sloping city, the largest in Montana, surrounded by breathtaking alpine vistas. It bristled with life and grit. When the train finally squealed to a halt, and its engine shot steam from its valves, she clambered to the gravel station platform, bag in hand, wondering what came next.

She corralled an open hack, driven by a skinny gent in a stovepipe hat, and in turn received a once-over from the man. She realized she was an unescorted woman.

"I wish to be taken to a proper hotel," she said. "Near the opera house."

"That would be the Butte—if you can stand the tariff," he said, still puzzling her out.

She nodded. He slapped lines over the croup of his dray, and the bony horse clapped its way up a gentle grade, which grew steeper as the roadway headed toward the forest of headframes ahead, where shafts plunged into the hillside, taking men into the darkness below and bringing rich copper ore up by the carload.

So this is where she'd meet Destiny, she thought.

"You in show business?" he asked, impertinently.

"I'm not in any business."

"Butte Hotel, it might not want show people."

He annoyed her. He was fishing. She kept her silence and let him wonder about her.

He turned, at last, and halted at a smoke-grayed structure.

"This is East Broadway. The playhouse's west, West Broadway, almost in sight," he said.

The hotel seemed nondescript, but so did all of Butte. She paid the man his thirty-five cents and added a dime, and headed into the hotel, where a clerk looked her over with pursed lips. It puzzled her. Butte was famously uninhibited.

But a dollar and a half in advance put her in a generous room with a water closet down the hall. Butte was electrified, and she enjoyed the novelty of incandescent light when she pushed the switch.

It was deep in the afternoon. She didn't know what to do next, but saw no virtue in mooning about, so she descended two flights of creaky stairs, reached the cold street, and headed west on Broadway, looking for Maguire's Grand Opera House.

It was not hard to find, its pretentious front shouting its importance. It was dark. A playbill on its side advertised the Beausoleil Brothers Follies, beginning the next evening. Mary Mabel Markey was the top-billed act, and half a dozen more were listed, none of them familiar to her, but she knew they soon would be. There was an empty box office with a small sign that said reserved seats were available at several places it listed.

She spotted a side door, found it open, and started up a gloomy stair. Far above, she saw warm light. Well, nothing like asking. She headed upward, reached a second-floor foyer, and found a small reception area, and beyond it an office, where two men were conversing beyond an opened door.

She knocked boldly, and they eyed her. One of them was the nattiest dresser she had ever seen. He wore a purple broadcloth suit coat, fawn trousers, a starched white high-collar shirt with an ascot tie, a black pearl stickpin, and spectacles.

The other gent was plainly dressed in a dark suit, but he had a sharp, hawkish gaze.

"Yes?"

"I'm seeking to audition for the variety show tomorrow, and I wish to know how."

"Audition? You mean, as an act?" the natty man asked. "I'm afraid this isn't the time or place. You'd need to do that when a show's assembled."

"I'm Ginger," she said. "And I sing. I'm trained."

"Well, young lady, I'm John Maguire. This is my theater. Ginger, is it?"

"That's it, first and last and middle name. I sing, and I wish to be given an audition. At least tell me who to contact when the show arrives."

The other one, the hawkish one in the dark suit, answered her. "I'm the man," he said. "Charles Pomerantz. It's my show."

"You're early?"

"I'm the advance man. Ahead of the show. Making sure it's promoted, boarded, fed, ticketed, and all that. You are, you say, a singer? What's the act?"

"When I sing for you, you'll see. I'm a pianist, too."

There was a long assessing gaze. "Ginger, my dear, I was just thinking about a libation and dinner. May I invite you to dine?"

11

Pomerantz steered her to the Chequamegon Café, a fancy joint. The locals called it The Chew Quick and Be Gone, but it was often patronized by the copper kings. And the food was tasty.

"So, Miss One Name, what'll you have to drink?"

Ginger hesitated. "I'll let you order for me," she said.

He got the message. She didn't know one drink from another. For that matter, she probably had never been in a saloon or an eatery like this one.

"You old enough?" he asked.

"I wouldn't know," she said.

That was honest enough. He ordered a bourbon and water for both of them. His gaze told him a lot about her. Her clothing was well made and tasteful. Her manners were cautious. Her clear-eyed gaze suggested that she was not afraid.

"So, you want to leap in, join the show," he said. Now he caught a flash of agitation. "I would like to try."

"You ever seen a variety show? With acts? You got an act?"

She stared, registering that. "I'll let you decide," she said.

"I don't do the deciding. August Beausoleil does."

"He's one of the brothers?"

"There's only one. The name, Beausoleil Brothers, that's for appearances. The more brothers, the bigger the show."

"I guess I've learned something," she said.

"In vaudeville, everything is for appearances. Why are you here, looking to get into vaudeville?"

She stared, dreamily. "I thought I might enjoy it."

"You running away from home? There likely to be cops and warrants and detectives chasing you—and making life hard for me?"

"I'm Ginger now. That is enough. I won't say any more."

The waiter served the drinks.

"Cheers," Pomerantz said. He sipped.

She sipped, grimaced, hid it, and sipped again, coughing slightly.

First one.

"You tell me," he said. "What kind of trouble are you running from?"

"None. And I'm Ginger, and that's all you'll know."

"You come from people with some money. You're wearing it."

"I am Ginger," she said, sipping again. But she smiled. There was something feisty in her.

He ordered lamb chops for both of them, with a Waldorf salad and mashed potato.

"Okay, now it's my turn," she said. "What's the top act in your show?"

"Mary Mabel Markey."

"She sings. I sing."

"And she wouldn't want a rival around, Ginger."

"I wouldn't sing what she sings. I . . . would learn other songs."

"Such as?"

"Sentimental favorites, things like that." She straightened up in her seat. "I'm trained for opera. But I wouldn't sing it. That's what they wanted, but not what I want. I'll use what I've learned—but I'll choose the songs. I'd sing ballads. I know lots of ballads. When I gargle, I gargle ballads."

He smiled. That was funny. But none of that was

107

a bit promising. He was slowly getting the picture now: a girl on the brink of adulthood, in a gilded cage, the canary chirping for her parents. She had fled. This is where she hoped to begin anew, and far away from her cage. He sighed. It wouldn't happen. He'd occasionally dealt with people who wished to audition for the show, and it all came to nothing. A girl would dream, and the dream would crack apart. But he wasn't prepared to shatter any dreams. Not yet, anyway.

She ate quietly, employing her tableware with daintiness and discipline. She had gotten manners somewhere. She sipped the bourbon carefully, in tiny measures, determined to master it. And she probably would. Anyone who could sip an unfamiliar and fierce drink like that must have an iron will. She seemed oddly innocent and yet formidable at the same time, which intrigued him.

"I'm simply the advance man," he said. "I'm usually far ahead of the show, but Butte's the big one. The opera house has a thousand seats, and we mean to fill them. If we make money here, we'll be in better shape for the rest. And we're scheduled to extend our stay if it's worth doing."

She was listening, eating slowly, and carefully observing everyone else in the place. He could only imagine what she was studying. She was the best-dressed woman in the café, and she probably knew it. He wondered if she had ever been out after eight o'clock.

"I'll be staying for the opening, ready to plug holes," he said. "Then I'm off to Philipsburg and Missoula. I have a simple task: making sure that it all goes right. Philipsburg has no electricity but a nice new opera house. Not well equipped. So I make sure we've got lamps, footlights, and all that gear, and the oils we need. You never know. Our hotel may be far from the theater, and we need means to get our people back and forth. A sleigh, a buggy, a wagon. I have to find bed and board for twenty-some people. Sometimes I can get a bulk rate. Sometimes I have to pay in advance. Sometimes something goes haywire, and there are no rooms, or an eatery closes, or the owner decides to charge more for a breakfast because show people are supposed to have lots of money. Or a printer didn't print our tickets, and we need some, and fast. Or they didn't paste up the play-bills and no one knows we're coming. That's what I do. I make it all work, and there's no room for error."

"You don't decide what's in the show," she said.

"That's my partner's job, and he's got the judgment for it."

"And everything's going to be all right in Butte?"

He hesitated. "On my end, yes. But not on the other end."

"Trouble with the show?"

He smiled. "Nothing for you to worry your head about. And nothing to start you dreaming.

Show people all have that fantasy. You hope you'll fill in, be discovered, do better than the act you're subbing, and then you're on your way, audiences worshiping you, stage-door Johnnies waiting to escort you, all that. It's the dream."

"All I dream about is making my own life," she said.

He'd heard that, too. From runaways like this girl, escaping something unbearable, risking everything just to flee their homes. Usually with good reason, if not good sense. More often boys, escaping fathers. He watched her sip and eat, always dainty, always trusting. She trusted him, foolish girl. She brimmed with quiet strength, and the more he sat across from her, the prettier she became. And it wasn't the bourbon speaking. She was uncommonly lovely.

There was an impenetrable wall about her. Whatever he had garnered through a dinner had been gotten from intuition. She was Dresden china.

"There's nothing I can do for you," he said.

She smiled. The Chequamegon was noisy. Butte was noisy. Every shift change amounted to a racket, with shouts, chuffing steam engines, bells, whistles. The city never slept.

"What comes next?" she said.

He wasn't quite sure what she meant. She was gazing, unblinking, at him.

He arched a brow, and stared at the mustachioed barman.

"This part I know nothing about. Except what I've read in trashy novels," she said.

"How old did you say?"

"Old enough."

"You are reckless, and it will get you nowhere."

"I am unaware of it. No one has instructed me."

"And you want to be taught."

"When I left my home I left everything behind."

"And you suppose you can discover a way to become an entertainer. No, my little canary, you cannot do it. You must have an act."

She laughed suddenly. "I don't even have stage fright," she said.

He thought for a moment about the delight of being her instructor, opening the curtains, awakening her to a new world, the limelight where it had never shone. She was waiting, and he had only to pay the tab, collect her on his arm, and escort her a short distance, and close the door behind them. For her, there would be mysteries upon mysteries, revelations and maybe moments of fear, but no regrets. Not just then, anyway.

He could not fathom what was inhibiting him. Not scruple. He had none. But then he knew. She was too innocent. She was too sheltered and utterly unaware of traps, of cliffs, of slippery slides into hopelessness. She might fall crazily in love with a man who could not return it. More likely, she would pack up in the morning and head back to wherever she came from. And for once in his life, he would harbor regrets.

"Sing for me," he said.

"Here?"

He saw the flash of fear upon her. "Where else? An audience you must capture. They're eating. They're with friends. They're drinking."

The restaurant hummed. People conversed. Dishes clattered.

It amused him. She stood, gathering courage, and faced him. "It is called 'Cielito Lindo,' " she said.

"De la Sierra Morena,
cielito lindo, vienen bajando,
Un par de ojitos negros,
cielito lindo, de contrabando."

She sang it sweetly, but with voice enough to catch the restaurant. Heads turned.

"Ay, ay, ay, ay,
canta y no llores,
porque cantando se alegran,
cielito lindo, los corazones."

A strange quiet settled now. What was all this? Charles Pomerantz confessed to being surprised, which was, for him, a major concession. His vocation was to prevent surprises. Her French horn voice caught his ear. It was not the sweet and virginal voice he had expected.

"Ese lunar que tienes,
cielito lindo, junto a la boca,
No se lo des a nadie,
cielito lindo, que a mí me toca . . ."

A dark youth busing dishes quietly joined the chorus. "Ay, ay, ay, ay . . ."

So did several patrons. They were swaying in their seats. Was this one of those songs that drew people into it?

And they clapped when she was done. She smiled serenely at them and rejoined Pomerantz. Patrons turned away. The evening's amusement had passed.

"There are many verses," she said. "And people create their own. It's much enjoyed by mariachi bands."

He hadn't the faintest idea what such a band was, and wasn't about to confess it, but he would find out sooner or later. She was somehow annoying him. She was exuding superiority. She was better bred and letting him know it.

"If you have an act, you'll need your own music. Not someone else's. Not a folk song," he said, gently.

She looked bleak. "I have none of my own. I know almost every ballad that's been caught on paper. I know Stephen Foster. Lullabies that came across the sea. Songs my grandmother sang, and songs I learned from music teachers. Songs they got from their home countries across the sea. The songs have come together, and we learn Irish lullabies and English sea shanties. I have all those, but nothing that would suit your show."

"Put them into an act, and try out somewhere," he said.

She stared, smiled, and nodded. The crowd was thinning.

"I'll walk you to your hotel, wherever that is."

"The Butte. And I can manage."

He ignored her, paid the tab, helped her throw a shawl over her shoulders, and walked beside her, filled with odd thoughts. He wished she would pack up and go home, stop being Ginger and start using all her real names. She was too sheltered to be out in the hurly-burly world, especially show business. People didn't just get hurt; they nosedived, they sank, they made bad choices. They tried powders and pills. They trusted the wrong people. She had no idea. She'd been raised in a garden, high walls around her, kept that way by protective parents who didn't want their little girl to grow up. And they no doubt congratulated themselves.

"So, Ginger, I enjoyed the dinner. And I wish you success," he said as they paused at the door.

Inside the door, and up two flights, was her room, rented for one night.

She was hoping for more, but he made no commitment. He would introduce her to no one. She should get the hell out of Butte, and out of her dreaming.

"Thank you. I've never done that before," she said. "Singing for my supper."

"No, I was just curious. Not for your supper. Just curious."

She eyed him, sudden mischief in her eyes. "Odd how evenings end," she said.

He thought maybe she was a lot more experienced than he had supposed.

She entered, digging for her room key, and that was the last he saw of her.

The show would arrive in Butte around eleven, barely in time for an advertised matinee, and the telegram from Beausoleil indicated there was trouble.

12

Mary Mabel Markey was enthralled. Butte lay before her, stretching up a long grade, its stacks churning smoke into blue skies, the busy city glittering and shimmering. She loved the thought of all those people, people who might show up soon at the opera house. Butte was Irish. Her own.

She had spent hours traveling through wilderness. There was hardly human habitation between Helena and Butte, and the view from the coach window was monotonous forest and anonymous emptiness. Give her a bright city anytime, especially a brawling, sprawling one like the copper mining city with all its miners and millionaires.

Butte was high, hugging the continental divide, and an island of purpose in a lifeless land with nothing but mountains and forest. At the crest of the city were scores of headframes, the mines that tore copper and silver and a little gold out of the earth. The place deserved an opera house and deserved a great variety show like the Beausoleil Brothers.

The train screeched to a halt, huffing steam and pouring ash upon the platform, as brakemen opened doors and set steel stools on the gravel. They all must hurry: it was eleven thirty and they had a matinee at two. She spotted Charles Pomerantz waiting with several open carriages and two wagons, ready to speed the company to the opera house. He was a fine advance man, knew what was needed and got it there at the right time. The acts and props would go straight to Maguire's Opera House. The bags and trunks would go straight to the hotel, where performers would find them in their rooms, later.

She spotted August Beausoleil, first off the car,

in earnest conversation with his colleague, no doubt about her. She was the problem, and enjoyed it. August had persuaded her to abandon the narcotics, especially the cough syrup with opiates, and that had restored her voice—a little. Enough to permit her to do the opening act of the final show in Helena. But she was dizzy, reeling, her heart flip-flopping, her chest hurting, her left arm aching, and she barely reeled off the stage after one song. The audience clapped only politely and thought she'd imbibed. Little did they know she could barely stand up, much less dish out a lively song.

Let the two of them worry out there in the smoke. She was the top-billed act, and she'd sing or they'd carry her out. They were frowning, earnest in their exchange, occasionally glancing back at the enameled green coach that was, even then, discharging a steady stream of the show people.

Beausoleil had settled quietly beside her on the trip to Butte.

"I think it's time for you to get some bed rest," he said. "Skip Butte. There's a hot springs near here, chance for you to soak and get better. Fairmont, it's called. Hot water, right out of the ground. Just sit in hot water and get strong."

"Over my dead body," she said, and meant it.

"That's nearly the way it worked last eve," he said. He had helped her off the stage when it appeared she would keel over at the end of her first song. She had suddenly lost breath and balance, and he caught her just before she tumbled.

"I'm singing. Every performance. I wouldn't miss Butte for anything. This is my city. These are my people. Right here, buster."

"Mary Mabel, Butte's higher than Denver. Up against the continental divide. You'll not get enough air in your lungs to sing. I'd prefer to see you strong and with bellows pumping down the road. Sing for us on the coast, at sea level."

"I'm top billed. They buy tickets to see me."

He had hit a wall of granite.

That had ended the exchange, but it wasn't over. The two owners were talking earnestly in the cold wind on the platform, while carriages were wheeling the acts up the hill.

She stepped down to the platform, the brakeman offering a hand to steady her, and headed straight toward the owners.

Charles Pomerantz lifted his derby and nodded.

"Miss Markey, how good to see you," he said. "Your admirers are awaiting you, and in Butte, they're legion." He smiled. "And I'm at the top of the list."

"Someone around here wants to cheat them out of the price of a ticket," she said. "And it won't be me. I'll be on that stage. The first performance is what gets reviewed in the dailies, and they're going to review me."

"You're an admirable lady," Pomerantz said. "And you're ready, of course, and fit to sing?"

She eyed him. "I'll be on that stage, singing." She was going to add, even if it kills me, but decided that would not be politic.

"Air's smokey here," he said. He glanced at August. "We're prepared to give you paid leave, Miss Markey. We want you full of zip when we reach the West Coast."

"If you reach the coast without me."

She had played her ace. They couldn't survive without her. This second-rate company would fold, the acts wouldn't get paid, and there'd be a lot of talent trying to hitch a ride back to civilization. And they knew it.

They didn't like it. But she had them. There was no way they could push their top-billed act out of town and let some little songbird pretend to put on a performance.

August smiled suddenly. "Take the carriage," he said. "You'll be dropped at the opera house. Rest before the show."

She eyed the carriage, ebony and open to the November chill. The hack driver was eyeing her as if she were a piece of hanging beef. She entered and settled, drawing a robe over her, and the hack driver slapped his nag into motion.

Her heart was tumbling again, and she didn't like it, but she wouldn't give in to it. It had all come down to stark options now: do or die. A few minutes later the hack turned onto Broadway and pulled up before a fancy-fronted opera house, all noble pretense, except that it would seat a thousand, and was as big as any, anywhere.

She wondered about paying the man, but he shook his head, helped her out, and pointed toward a side door. She found herself in a huge, dark auditorium, but there were incandescent lights on the stage, and people moving about. She grabbed a seat-back to steady herself. Her pulse was racketing around again.

She made her way to the bleak stage, where hands were putting the props in order. And there, watching, was a man whose reputation preceded him, John Maguire, dressed just as she had known he would, in a purple swallowtail.

"I believe I have the great honor of meeting one of the finest names in variety theater," he said. "Miss Markey, Butte welcomes you."

He not only clasped her cold hand, but reached down to plant a kiss on her cheek. She already liked Butte, and now she was filled with sublime delight. The most admired theater man in the West, kissing her cheek. Her heart skipped.

She peered out upon row after row of seats, a wide stage, majestic wings and flies, everything on a grand scale. It suited her. This was the great city of the Northwest, and these were her people, and here she was known and celebrated. She would sing to them, lullaby them, awaken them to love, stir ancient memories of a greener land, poke them with humor, smile and feel them smiling back. She had waited long for this, a Celtic celebration, a communion with all those lonely men, imported from across the sea by the copper king, Marcus Daly, and put to work in those terrible pits thousands of feet below the sunlight.

It made her heady, dizzy, and she retreated to the Green Room, passing people who were putting their act together. Mrs. McGivers had loosed her capuchin monkeys, and they were swinging about, looking for trouble. Harry the Juggler was unloading scimitars, and the Wildroot girls were opening a trunk, digging at costumes. There wasn't much time. The matinee crowd would flood in soon.

Mary Mabel Markey careened to a dressing room, found it solitary, lit by a single incandescent light hanging on its cord. It was as quiet as a confessional, and she wished there would be time to find a real confessional, in this city teeming with Irish, and confess to the sin of pride, the sin of having an act, of being in variety theater, so she might assuage her pride. But there was no priest here, and no church anywhere near this opera house, and her yearnings would have to wait for a while. Maybe between the matinee and the evening show.

She tried her voice, just a bar or two, and didn't like it much. But it would have to do, and what she lost in hoarseness she would make up in sweetness. She knew how to sweeten music, make it sugary and honeyed. Today she would slather honey on all those off-shift miners. She would give the most memorable performance of her life, there in Butte, there before the men from County Clare, or County Kilkenny and County Cork.

It was cold. The great barn of a theater carried a chill wrought by icy air flowing out of the mountains. It might warm with a packed house; it might not bother other acts, but it bothered her. She chose her sky-blue velvet dress because it was warm, and because she looked smashing in it, and she would woo her miners in it, and she would feel their longing, as they sat out in the dark, peering up at her, lit by incandescent spot-lights.

She spotted John Maguire in the wing, and approached him.

"Miss Markey, what an honor. Rarely has this house seen the likes of a singer of your reputation," he said, plucking up her cold hand again.

"It's the Irish in me. I'm singing for an audience that'll pick it up," she said.

"They'll let you know it," he said. "But not loudly. You'll bathe in it, my dear."

"I've never bathed in anything but water," she said. "This will be a novelty."

August Beausoleil approached, looking stern.

"I've talked to the fiddlers, and they'll cover for you, see you through if your voice cracks."

"My voice is fine, and I'll chase them off the stage."

"Alone, then?"

"This is my town, and this is my hour, and this is my act."

He didn't like it. He was preparing for the worst, and fiddlers were good backup, carrying a song if a voice vanished. That was a veteran showman for you, anticipating trouble and dealing with it ahead of time.

But he annoyed her. She felt a great thump in her chest, and she met his steely gaze with one of her own. Maguire watched intently, missing nothing.

"We'll have a sellout," Maguire said. "Nine hundred advance, and the rest being picked up right now." He led her to the arch and drew the curtain aside. The house was starting to fill up. Miners, but more. Wives and children, old men, and plenty who didn't look Irish at all, because Butte was Cornish and Italian and Slavic and Norwegian and Russian and Spanish and Greek.

"Good crowd, since it's snowing."

"Snowing?"

"All the time, all winter, in Butte."

"We were lucky to get in, then."

"It was close."

Then, somehow, it was curtain time, and the house lights dimmed, and the footlights cranked up, and the spotlights threw their beams, and there was August Beausoleil, all gotten up in his tux and bib, striding out there, welcoming the crowd, urging them to enjoy the show, and enjoy the famous Wildroot Sisters, and their medley.

The curtain flew upward, and the gals plunged in, bright and saucy, with plenty of flounce.

The Butte crowd enjoyed them, and enjoyed the acts, and laughed at The Profile, and clicked right into the tap dancing, and howled at Mrs. McGivers and her Monkey Band, when the unruly little devils went into their anarchist mode. It was a grand show, and Butte was a grand city, and they were in the grandest opera house in the region.

"And now, the one you've been waiting for, the lady who gets a hundred proposals a day, the one, the only Mary Mabel Markey," August was saying.

Her heart tripped. That was a new one, a hundred proposals a day. She glided out, feeling the spotlights, feeling a thousand gazes watching her, the blue velvet, the smiling Irish eyes. All that warmth made her dizzy.

She welcomed them, and told them she would sing for the best audience ever, and then, in the hush, sang "Your Big Blue Eyes." She was in fine voice, and her honey spilled over the footlights, and when she was done, there was a pause, and an affectionate swell of happiness, just as John Maguire had predicted. She waited for that outpouring to ebb, and then sang "The Cradle

Song," and again her people sitting in row after row loved it, and she was dizzy with love, and she volunteered a third song this opening in Butte, "The Ribbon on My Finger." Oh, yes, they loved that, too, and everything was perfect, and the world whirled.

She bowed, and the world turned white, brighter than limelight, brighter than sunlight, and she felt herself floating, carried up through the flies, out into the snowy heaven, into the blinding white until she could see no more.

13

The headlines said it all that afternoon: "Markey's Finale"; "Singer Dies"; "First Act, Last Act." The newsboys hawking their two-cent tabloids on the corners put it in their own vernacular: "Croaks on Stage," one was yelling. "Read all about it."

For August Beausoleil, it was a moment of anguish, one he foresaw, and one he was helpless to stop. Mary Mabel Markey had simply dropped dead. One moment she was concluding an oddly tremulous act, the next, she toppled, slowly, flailing, to the boards, convulsed twice, and lay still. He knew in a paralyzed moment that she was gone, that her heart had quit.

Strangely, his first thought was to forgive her.

125

Those in the wings watched, galvanized by the moment, unsure of what to do. He knew.

"Drop the olio," he said. The olio was a canvas backdrop that lowered downstage, permitting olio acts to perform in front of it while scenes were changed upstage. After a long moment, the tan curtain descended, even as a first stirring of the audience caught and spread.

His performers rushed to the fallen singer, turned her onto her back, sought life, and stared helplessly. She was gone. The clock was ticking. Harry the Juggler was patting her, pumping her, but life had fled.

There was a terrible instinct in August to continue the show, keep it rolling. Just a seizure, folks, and here's the Marbury Trio. But he could not. These people had just witnessed death. His people were huddled over Mary Mabel Markey, staring at him, waiting for something, and that something was up to him. Even John Maguire, restless in the wing, waited for him. And so did his colleague, Charles Pomerantz. All waiting for him.

In his gray tuxedo, stiff bib at the neck, he stepped into the bright glare of the footlights, and walked to the center of the stage.

"We grieve Miss Markey," he said. "This show is over. We will honor your ticket stubs at a special matinee tomorrow. We will cancel tonight's show in honor of our beloved Mary Mabel Markey, and will honor tickets at a future show. Thank you, good people, for coming this afternoon."

The audience sat, restless, unable to begin its exit.

John Maguire stepped into the light.

"My friends, I will be at the box office to refund the price of your tickets," he said.

The two of them hastened offstage, even as the shocked audience stirred. August knew he had done the right thing. If he had tried to keep the show going, his performers would have faltered, and the audience would have ached.

"There will be very few refunds," Maguire said.

But August was already absorbed with the things he must do. First, to arrange her burial, to deal with any officials, to find her relatives, if any. Death brought sudden tasks. It all fell upon him. And he still had to keep the show going, keep his company afloat, fill those seats or perish.

There, backstage, the Wildroot Sisters stared, frightened. Mrs. McGivers sat beside Mary Mabel Markey, holding the dead woman's hand. Ethel Wildroot, on her knees, stared, looking for signs of life. Wayne Windsor sat beside the singer, patting her occasionally, as if to wish her back to life. Others—musicians, stage hands, performers—all watched desolately, deep in their own thoughts. Mary Mabel Markey's white face, distorted when she fell, now had slipped into serenity. Her wrinkles somehow vanished. August thought that she had run her course, had succeeded, and was content even as her spirit drifted away.

A whiskery doctor with a Gladstone bag appeared, knelt beside the fallen, and listened with a stethoscope, and shook his head.

"Mr. Maguire got me," he said. "There's nothing I can do. She was gone even before she fell down. I'm so sorry. I don't think it could have been prevented."

He stood.

Two burly men in dark suits appeared. "Brogan Mortuary," one said.

Maguire had been busy. Beausoleil was grateful. It was Maguire's city, and he knew what to do. They all watched silently as the mortuary men lifted Mary Mabel Markey into an ebony hand-cart and wheeled her away. The stage, lit only with one overhead lamp, was gray.

Then it was all back to August.

"No show tonight," he said. "Matinee tomorrow, and the evening show. We may make other changes in the schedule. I want to honor our great lady. But I don't yet know how, or about a funeral, or any of that. You're free this evening."

"August," Mrs. McGivers said, "God bless you."

That was it. Somehow her benediction completed the moment. The knots of people gradually abandoned the boards, and vanished into the late afternoon.

Charles Pomerantz corralled him. "We should talk to the papers," he said.

"And say what?"

"That Mary Mabel Markey could hardly wait to play Butte," he said.

"You know what, Charles? That's exactly right. Play Butte, almost a home to her. Her town. Play Butte, no matter how she hurt."

August had the sense that there were things undone, decisions looming, but for the moment he couldn't think of any. He found John Maguire sitting quietly in the box office, and paused to thank him for the arrangements.

"No one wanted a refund, August. Not one," Maguire said.

"We're doing a matinee tomorrow, and the rest, I don't know. What would you say?"

"Extend here. I'm dark for three days after you've booked me." He smiled wryly. "You have a publicity bonanza."

"I hadn't quite thought of it that way," he said. "But Mary Mabel would like it. She loved Butte. Charles and I are off to talk to the papers."

"There's the *Daily Post*, the *Evening News*, the *Inter-Mountain*, the *Miner*, the *Montana Standard*, and the *Reveille*, which is an obnoxious rag. Each copper king has one or two."

"Any to start with?"

Maguire smiled. "Get their slant, and use it." He added that they were clustered a couple of blocks south, gaudy rivals, keeping a sharp eye on one another.

The two principals of the company headed into a wintry evening with overcast skies and icy knives of snow in the wind

"You can handle this, August? I'm off to Philipsburg tomorrow, but I can hold off a day."

"We've both been around the block," Beausoleil said. "There's a hole in the show, and you'll need to patch the playbills."

"Just some white paper. Unless you've got something up your sleeve."

"White paper," Beausoleil said. "A show without a top act. We're a week from a replacement. Someone from Chicago if we're lucky, New York, more likely."

"There's local talent."

"Mary Mabel was the draw. They knew her. They lined up to see her."

Pomerantz conceded it with a nod.

They turned into the first paper they came upon, *The Standard*. Beausoleil was glad to meet a wall of heat after two grim blocks with alpine cold jamming into his flesh.

He spotted four compositors plucking up type and filling a stick. And two reporters, scribbling on sheets of newsprint. Compositors were wonders. They created lines of type, one letter at a time, working upside down and backwards, then slid the completed line into a form that would print the page. Even more wondrously, reporters and compositors were often one and the same. A man would get the story and then compose it as he plucked up the type.

But now a redheaded young man in a thick waistcoat rose and headed toward the visitors.

"We're from the show," Beausoleil said. "Would you like something on Mary Mabel Markey?"

"We're pushing deadline, but a bit, sure," the newsman said. "Jake James here."

He escorted them to his battered oak desk. "Now then?" he asked.

Beausoleil made the introductions and then plunged in. "Mary Mabel Markey was our top-billed act, you know. We thought she was marvelous. That voice, that presence. She drew crowds wherever we went, because she was sweet. And tender, like a mother singing a lullaby. And she was Irish, and that's why she was so eager to play Butte. This was homecoming for Mary Mabel. This was the most important engagement of her life." He paused. "And at least for one act, she enjoyed the thing she dreamed of, the thing she pined for. Singing in Butte."

Pomerantz continued. "We're in shock, let me tell you. After that olio drop rolled down, the rest of us crowded around her, wishing life into her, holding her hand, but she was gone. There were tears, sir. There was the deepest silence and respect I've ever witnessed. We just want you to know, officially, that the principals and the acts here all grieve the greatest lady in American vaudeville."

The young man scribbled away for a bit, and then eyed them.

"Any plans?"

"We're working on them," Beausoleil said. "We're going to have a funeral. She's going to be buried right here, in the city she loved. And we'll put up a stone, knowing all her admirers will be looking for the grave, and we'll have a funeral in a big place, a place where people can come, which we'll announce."

"What about the show?" James asked.

"We're dark tonight, of course. And tomorrow, we've scheduled a matinee for those who didn't get to see an entire show this afternoon. And beyond that, we're working things out. We'll extend our stay in Butte for two performances, to be announced."

"You think you'll draw without Mary Mabel Markey?"

"We think people will flock to the show, just to honor her," Beausoleil said.

Jake James grinned suddenly, as if this were some sort of private joke, but he dutifully got it down. "This is a good town to make a buck," he said.

"You know what I'd like?" Pomerantz asked. "I'd like people to bring bouquets to put on her grave. Mary Mabel's spirit would rejoice."

Jake James let his pencil hover, and set it down. There might not be a story.

"Mr. James," Beausoleil said. "Let me tell you a bit about show business. Those of us who survive in the game don't know from month to month whether we've got a job. We ache to see those seats filled, because if they aren't, we're done. We ache to entertain, to make people laugh, or smile, or chuckle, because if we don't, we're done. If there's a lot of empty seats, we're done. Or maybe we just worry ourselves down to nothing. We have bills to pay: hotels, meals, railroads, and rental of halls. And if we don't pay them, we're done.

"So, sir, we do what we can to stir up interest. Mary Mabel Markey really did like Butte, and really did dream of playing here, because Butte's Irish. We really do want to honor her, because she topped our show, and because we were her friends, and we cared about her. She was always doing things for us. And there were real tears shed among us, when she lay there, on the boards, gone from our lives. And as for a funeral, we want a big one, because we really think she would have wanted a big one, one that people will remember. And the two of us, we own the show, we want her to be celebrated, and we think Butte's the perfect resting place for her. This is what she would have asked for.

"So, sir, you're right to think we want to fill our theater seats, and right to think we're making what we can of this, but that's not the whole deal. The whole story is that this vaudeville company grieves Mary Mabel Markey. Every one of us has memories, thoughts of Mary Mabel's many kindnesses and, yes, quirks, the things that make us mortal, stumbling along in a world we don't always understand. And it's going to be hard for our players to perform. And Mr. James, you can print up all of this if you want to. I'm talking straight, and you're welcome to put quotation marks around every word."

Jake James stared out the window into the dark November dusk, and nodded.

"It's a good story, Mr. Beausoleil, and if I don't write good stories, I might lose my thirty dollars a week, and if all those people who buy the paper don't read what I wrote, then I won't last as the top-billed reporter around here. You'll see the story in the morning."

14

Ginger pounced. She had been waiting in the opera house. When she spotted August Beausoleil, a somber man who seemed to be carrying a heavy load, she addressed him.

"Mr. Beausoleil," she said, stepping up. "I would like to audition."

He studied her a moment, saw a handsome young woman, and shook his head.

"I'm Ginger," she said. "I've a trained voice and a good repertoire."

He smiled. "Not now," he said. "I couldn't be busier. I'm burning up the wires, trying to get some box office."

"I sing," she said.

"I know you do. My partner told me about it. But Ginger, my dear, even if you sing like a nightingale I wouldn't hire you. I need more than a singer; I need a draw. I need a name. I need a top-billed show-stopper."

"When you're less busy, sir, may I sing for you?"

"Oh, I don't know. It's all a waste of time. I need seasoned people."

She felt the tide ebb from her. At least he wasn't simply brushing her off.

"I—I have one question. May I sing at Miss Markey's funeral?"

That startled him. He smiled. "Look, you go talk to Brogan Mortuary. They're doing all that. Tell them I said you could sing your song. I don't know a Catholic funeral from a Hindu one, so I don't know what they want. But tell them I said it's okay. Can't do any harm."

He tipped his hat, and hurried off. She stood in the darkness of a wing, a single bulb throwing a little light across a mysterious darkness.

She paused, studying the great expanse of stage, the curtains that sailed up and down, the props in the wings, ready to roll out in an instant, the upstage, the downstage, the footlights, the spotlights, the row upon row of stern seats, canted upward to give everyone a view. There was not a soul in any of them.

She had been nurturing a fantasy: She would sing into the dark theater, unaware that there was an auditor watching from some distant row, and the auditor would stand after she was done, and tell her that she was hired. That it was utterly beautiful.

But it was only a fantasy. She studied the empty barn of an auditorium, seeing no life at all. But she stood downstage center, and tried an American ballad she loved. She liked being on a grand stage, all those seats, row upon row, fading away into darkness.

"Oh Shenandoah,
I long to see you,
away you rolling river.
Oh Shenandoah,
I long to see you,
away, I'm bound away,
'cross the wide Missouri."

She liked the silence. Her voice felt silky. She tried another.

"Oh Shenandoah,
I love your daughter,
away, you rolling river—
Oh Shenandoah,
I love your daughter,
away, we're bound away,
'cross the wide Missouri."

There was no one to hear her, and that was fine.
The opera house itself seemed to welcome her,
and tuck her song into its walls, and that was fine.
She sang two more verses, and it all was good,
and no one heard a word. Then she wrapped her
shawl about her, and headed into the blustery
November day, and soon found the Brogan
Mortuary, where Miss Mary Mabel Markey lay,
waiting for the last act.

The place was quiet, and dark, and smelled of
incense. She found a small silvery bell, and rang
it. And out of the gloom a bearded man rose up,
black as the River Styx.

"Madam?"

"Are you Mr. Brogan?"

"I am. Are you in need?"

"Mr. Beausoleil suggested that I come. I would
like to do a song, 'Ave Maria,' at Miss Markey's
rites."

"I see," he said. "You are?"

"Ginger."

"Ah . . ."

"First and last, Ginger."

"A stage name, then. Well, come along, and let's talk."

He led her to a small office, lit the overhead lamp, and motioned toward a chair.

"Mr. Beausoleil suggested that we do what we could, by way of a service. We've asked Monsignor Murphy to officiate, and there immediately arose some questions. Is the deceased a Catholic, and in good standing? A theater person, you know. That's how it is. We've been unable to find out, so Monsignor has reluctantly concluded that the proper course is for him to assist in a simple prayer service. He'll open, Mr. Beausoleil will eulogize the late departed, and the monsignor will offer a prayer for her salvation. And of course, yes, your song would be fitting and sacred. We'll fit it in. You're talking about Franz Schubert, of course?"

"Yes."

"Yes, fitting. How kind of him to send you along. Now, we've scheduled it for tomorrow at eleven. It must not interfere with the matinee. They're scheduling matinees each day, in the hope of recovering what they lost yesterday. One today, of course. But you must know that. How shall I list you in the program?"

"Ginger."

He smiled suddenly. "Ginger it is, then. Please be here ahead of eleven, so we can seat you in the first row. Now, will you need accompaniment? We will have a pianist."

"I will sing a capella."

"I take my hat off to you theater people. I would want to hide behind a pipe organ."

"Where will Miss Markey be buried?"

"Mountain View. Immediately following the ceremony."

"How will I get there?"

"It's a long way. The cast won't be there; they have a matinee. But I believe Mr. Pomerantz will represent the troupe. Maybe he'll take you."

She worried it all the way back to her hotel, where she had engaged the room for another night. Couldn't they respect Mary Mabel Markey enough to set aside the matinee? Was that show business, or just the Beausoleil Brothers Follies at work? Bury their top act on the run? Well, she knew what she would do. She would sing the beloved Mary-song in a way that honored the woman they had come to bury; sing it in a way that it had never been sung.

Was it the right song? Would a song honoring the Virgin be the thing for a vaudeville singer? Maybe she should choose something else, something more suited to Mary Mabel Markey. She had mastered it in Pocatello but had never sung it at a recital. It wouldn't have been suitable there.

Much to her surprise, the service was at the

Maguire Opera House. Long before eleven the next morning, every seat had been taken. The cast, Miss Markey's only relatives, filled the first rows. And Ginger, dressed in white, was among them, at an aisle seat. The crowd waited expectantly, in deep silence, not so much as a cough disturbing the quiet. An upright piano stood at one side, downstage. The curtains were open. At eleven, the stage lights came up, shining down on Miss Markey's simple coffin, which rested on a pedestal draped with gilded cloth.

The monsignor appeared, wearing a black suit with red piping, and addressed the silent throng. "We are here to celebrate the life of our beloved Mary Mabel Markey, and to hasten her ascent to an eternal life with the angels," he said. "Now let us pray."

Next was August Beausoleil, this time in an immaculate black suit, entirely at home on that stage, before that quiet crowd.

"I will talk a bit about our dear departed. Every member of our company is grieving this hour for a remarkable woman who was the backbone of our show.

"She was intensely private, but once in a while shared bits of her past. Mary Mabel was not her name; I don't know what it once was. I know that she was Irish, that she grew up in New York, and from earliest childhood found a way to survive by singing the songs her mother had taught her.

Songs she remembered after her mother had died. Singing as a girl on street corners for a bit of loose change. Singing for passersby. Singing for her supper, for those songs would give her the only food she had, and the corners of the city offered her the only shelter she had.

"But out of it came a miracle. Her very life depended on pleasing people, and that was her salvation and her secret road to success. When someone liked her song and gave her a generous tip, that was a clue. When someone listened to a song, walked away, and never looked back, that was a clue. So she was in the hardest school of all, and failure was not a grade, but death or starvation. But gradually, being a woman of courage and intelligence, as well as a woman who learned without help how to employ her voice, gradually she turned herself into an instrument of beauty and joy for countless admirers. Mary Mabel Markey wrought the raw material into the most successful female singer of our times, and not one step along the way was easy."

Beausoleil talked of the way Miss Markey had become the single thing she wished to be, a singer, and how that had shaped all her life, to her last hour, when she sang because she had to, sang against the wishes of the show's managers, sang because she was there, in Butte, among her people.

"Mary Mabel Markey gave the world songs that

141

linger in our hearts. Tomorrow, a year from now, and when you are old and gray, you will be hearing her songs in the concert hall of your memory," he concluded.

It was amazing how that crowd devoured August Beausoleil's eulogy. They were starved for Miss Markey; they wanted every intimate detail, and he gave them whatever he knew of a woman who was largely private and distant from them all.

After he sat down, the monsignor invited Ginger forward.

"And now, a sacred song in honor of all womanhood," he said, judiciously.

Ginger had never faced a crowd like this. She made her way to the stage and peered out upon the sea of quietness, brushed her white dress, folded her hands together, and began.

> "Ave Maria,
> gratia plena,
> Maria, gratia plena,
> Maria, gratia plena,
> Ave, Ave, Dominus . . ."

Ave Maria, full of thanksgiving, Maria, full of thanksgiving, Maria, full of thanksgiving, Ave, Ave, God . . .

And so began her solo. There alone on the stage, she let her voice soar far out into the great opera house, soar to every corner, soar to every heart.

Then a strange thing happened. Joseph, Mrs. McGivers' accordionist, quietly stepped away from his seat in the first row, made his way to the stage, and settled at the piano, and soon was adding its notes to her voice. She was momentarily flustered, but he was perfect, and the piano only amplified the moment, and the words, and sent them sailing on the wings of white keys and black.

"Benedicta tu in mulieribus,
et benedictus, et benedictus,
et benedictus fructus ventris . . ."

And then it was done, and the last sound from the last key faded into the hall, and there was only the deepest silence. She waited for a moment, and then retreated to her seat, and the pianist quietly returned to his. There were gazes upon her. She settled in the safety of her seat, and waited.

"Let us pray for the departed," said the monsignor.

And they did. And then the priest blessed the crowd and sent them on their way.

She watched, suddenly alone, not part of the company, unknown to them all. The Butte crowd collected quietly outside, where an ebony hearse, drawn by four jet horses with black plumes, stood waiting. By prearrangement six of the troupe gathered about the coffin and carried it outside to the hearse and slid it inside the glass-paneled chamber. And then, with a stately clop of hooves, its driver, in a black silk stovepipe hat, steered the ebony hearse toward the cemetery, far away.

She watched. Her part was done. She felt oddly lost.

Then Charles Pomerantz approached her.

"I will give you a ride, if you wish," he said.

An enclosed hack, armor against the Butte wind, awaited, its bundled-up driver eager to move.

The crowd was watching him and her. The company gathered on the street was watching. They would not be going. They would be snatching a bite if they cared to before the show, and preparing for the matinee that was looming just ahead. Charles Pomerantz and the girl in white, the girl unknown to them, would represent the company at the graveside service.

He held her hand, to help her up, and soon she was seated, with a buffalo carriage robe about her, while he settled beside her. The carriage rocked gently down a rough road.

"Ginger, that was magnificent."

"Well, thank you, but most sacred songs are like that."

"Your voice. Never have I heard such a voice, and such an offering, in any opera house. Or any concert hall. Or anywhere else."

She glanced at him, suddenly shy. He was gazing intently.

15

A biting wind hastened the monsignor through the burial rite. Two employees of the funeral home were on hand, no one else from Butte. Ginger shivered in her summery white dress, with only a shawl to turn the cold. Charles Pomerantz stood patiently, the representative of the touring company.

He was the only person present who knew Miss Markey. Ginger had not met her. The priest wasn't sure Mary Mabel was in good standing, but he was offering her the benefit of the doubt, and gently laboring through the burial, though he was blue with cold. He was doing as best as he could, because death was the greatest mystery.

It was an odd end for a nationally known and acclaimed performer, Charles thought. Burial in utter obscurity, no friends gathered at the grave. The company would pay for all this, and a head-stone, too, and it would carve a hole deep into the working funds that supported the tour. He lacked even a flower to lay upon her plain pine coffin. She would be buried as anonymously as she had started, a girl struggling to survive on the streets of the city, not unlike August Beausoleil. She deserved more.

Then it was over. "Ginger, go wait in the hack," he said. "I'll thank the priest."

The monsignor was climbing into a black topcoat.

"Those of us who were Miss Markey's only family thank you, Father. She is lost to us, and found above."

"We may all trust in it," the priest said, and hastened toward the mortuary hack, which would hurry him back to his rectory.

Ginger fled to the thin protection of the hack, where the driver huddled against the cold, and moments later Charles climbed in and pulled the lap robe over both of them. A great quiet settled upon them as the driver steered the reluctant dray straight into the wind. Pomerantz had a sense that things were unfinished, that Mary Mabel was waiting for more. Maybe what was needed was a wire to someone back east, announcing her death. But who? She had lacked a family, and found one in her admirers. Maybe that was the thing: let the press know, and the world would know.

The hack rolled up the gentle slope toward the opera house. The chastening cold had vanquished traffic, and Butte seemed almost deserted. There were more dogs than people on the sidewalks. Smoke scraped the streets.

"Where to, Ginger?"

"It doesn't matter," she said.

"You're at the Butte Hotel. I'll drop you there."

She peered out of the breath-silvered isinglass window. She was no longer shivering, the carriage robe warming her.

"I want to thank you for singing. I've never heard a finer voice. And not just a voice, either. I've never heard a more accomplished voice, a voice that was tutored by someone, wherever you came from."

"Thank you."

"You're at the end of your tether. You don't know what to do."

"I will make my way."

"You came to join the show."

"Yes."

"I never saw anything so compelling. You, dressed in white, with your wavy hair, mahogany colored, like my mother's, all alone, without so much as a pianist, standing there poised, your hands folded together at first, wholly absorbed in the gift you would give us."

She eyed him, her brown eyes wide.

"Franz Schubert, was it not? Is your repertoire mostly classical—opera?"

"It's everything. It was the wish of my . . . mentors . . . to be able to entertain them for any occasion."

The hack driver pulled up at the hotel. She pulled the carriage robe off, thanked him, opened the flimsy door, and stepped down.

She started toward the hotel.

He threw open his door.

"Ginger!" he said.

She paused, orphaned, in the cold.

"Please join me."

The driver looked impatient. He wanted to escape that crushing air.

She turned back, shivering again, the blue shawl a poor defense against the bitter wind. But she clambered in.

"The Chequamegon," he said, and the weary horse once again lugged the hack along hard-frozen streets.

"Ginger, will you marry me?" he asked.

It shocked her. It shocked him even more. He had no idea why he had asked. The thing had simply erupted.

She could make no sense of it. She stared at him, stared at the cold city, stared ahead, even as he tucked the carriage robe around her.

She smiled. "I'm not your ward," she said. "And I don't know anything about you. But it was sweet of you. It was the nicest compliment."

He was beginning to think he didn't know anything about himself, either. The question hung between them, like a light throwing illumination in all directions. What was it about her? Her looks, something like his mother. Her bravery. She volunteered to sing at a funeral all alone, with no help, for people she had never seen before. Or something else. Only now, as the hack climbed another grade, did he realize that she had knocked him over. Theater men were immune to all that. Especially womanizing ones like himself. He could not fathom what had made him so reckless. Now, if she began to smile, he'd have to retreat from that precipice.

They reached the restaurant. It was midday. He hurried her in, paid the driver, and led her toward warmth. They settled into a booth in deep silence, the moment oddly choreographed with nods and smiles and courtesy. She still was cold. He settled his topcoat over her lap. The impulsive question was forbidden turf now. And yet it governed everything they said and did. He supposed it had been a lapse, a folly, something that had escaped harness.

He ordered tea for her, a whiskey for himself, and still she sat in silence.

"You asked. I will tell you about me," he said. "I'm Polish. My parents brought me here at age two from Warsaw. I'm Jewish. There were troubles in the old country and promise in the new. I'm thirty-three. I'm from Brooklyn. I've been in this business since eighteen, when I sold tickets. I did accounting. I managed acts. I speak Polish, Yiddish, English, and some others. As you probably guessed."

He was referring to the slight accent that rolled up some letters and words.

She nodded, her warm gaze registering everything about him: The combed-back hair, starting high on the crown of his head. The sallow flesh, the dark eyes, peering out from bags.

The plainness of his features. He could never pass for dashing or handsome.

"No one has ever proposed before. Especially not an older man."

He was almost twice her age. "And who is Ginger?"

"She is what you see before you, and all else has passed and will never be seen again."

"So I have proposed to a new woman."

"I am eighteen. That is the age of consent, I believe."

"And, you have had male friends, boys?"

She shook her head. That was the past. He could see the curtain sliding down.

"How do you live? Where is home?" she asked.

"Home is my suitcase. I live in hotel rooms ahead of the show, or sometimes with the show, and at the end of the tour, I rent a room until the next tour."

"And what would you do with me?"

"The same."

"I would have to like the business," she said. "That's why I left . . . where I grew up. Why have you proposed to me?"

"I don't know. I have no idea."

She colored a little. "I can imagine. You've had many women."

"Yes. A few. Ah, more than a few."

"And you're an accountant!" She had turned merry.

"A thousand women, and none of them got into the show."

"Would this marriage last one night, one week, or one month?"

He shrugged. "I don't know why I asked, and I cannot see into the future. I apologize. It was an impulse. I shouldn't make light of it."

"Yes," she said. "Neither can I see ahead. But never say never."

"I don't audition acts," he replied.

"It's the best offer on the table," she said. "And now and then there'll be a piano. I need a piano in my life. A piano's more important than singing. So you're stuck with it."

He sat, nursing his drink, oddly cheerful, confused, wary, curious, regretful, and even afraid, all at once, which was too complex to sort out.

"Cheers," he said, lifting his glass.

They toasted it.

"I think I like you," she said. "But we'll see."

He knew he would remember this moment as the jackpot play of his life. But what would he take off the table?

"Where and when?" she asked. "I'm ready right now."

He hadn't thought about that. Down the road, maybe. This would take some getting used to. He could live with her for a while, see how it might go.

"Shall we find a justice of the peace?" she asked.

"In for a dime, in for a dollar," he said, not quite believing any of this.

"Over the cliff," she said, a quirky smile building.

"The matinee's playing? You want to wait for the company?"

"You're already weaseling out," she said.

"I am not! I just thought we might invite the acts. Witness the follies."

"You've got thirty seconds. Now or never."

He lifted her hand, squeezed it, and kissed it gently.

"My white dress is fine, but I'd like my coat," she said. "And you can buy me a bouquet."

It took an hour or so. Ginger checked out, they caught a hack to the courthouse, they completed a license, she as Ginger Jones, and they scouted up a justice of the peace who said he'd do the deed in half an hour after he was done with an assault and battery case. It was odd: instead of doubts, Charles had only delight coursing through him. There were no but, but, buts. He could not explain why a normally cautious man was stepping over a cliff believing he would land safely. He could not imagine what he would tell August, his confidant, when the deed was done. And he was curious about what Ginger thought, whether she was having a flood of doubt. How little he knew her.

"Do you have doubts?" he asked.

"No. The time when I had doubts was when I left my home, took a new name, and headed here. I don't have a single doubt. There's no turning back."

"Do you love me?"

She ignored him. "Should I call you Charles or Mr. Pomerantz?"

"Suit yourself. Shall I call you Ginger or Mrs. Pomerantz?"

The judge invited them in, eyed them skeptically, and studied the bride. "Where'd you run away from?" he asked.

She paled for the smallest moment. "Make me a proper woman," she said. "And be quick about it."

The judge laughed. So did two smirky clerks serving as witnesses. He extracted a hidebound text and rattled it off, enjoying the embarrassment when Ginger and Charles could produce no ring, and continued on, amusement in his bearded face. An older man, a younger woman of great radiance, and some adventures ahead. They cheerfully repeated the vows. Stuck with each other for life, until one or another croaked. The judge pronounced them man and wifey, his little joke, and they shook hands with him, and Charles handed him a fiver.

"I don't suppose you'll have a reception or

banquet," the judge said. "If you do, I'll come and toast the happy couple."

"You're not invited," Ginger snapped. She hadn't liked the ceremony, and Charles didn't blame her. Marriage wasn't frivolous, even if the judge treated their union as a joke.

The judge nodded, grinned, and saw them out.

They headed into the late afternoon, both of them in a funk. The matinee was over. Miss Markey was buried. The Butte wind whipped. And now they were strangers in paradise, scarcely knowing how to cope with their union. He took her hand, squeezed, and was rewarded with a smile, and then a flash of delight in her eyes.

"You ready to tell the world, Mrs. Pomerantz?"

"Call me Ginger," she said. "I have no other name."

16

The act was a disaster. August Beausoleil was auditioning local performers, hoping to plug the hole in his show. But Cohan and McCarthy, from the Comique, in the nearby smelter town of Anaconda, were about to get the boot.

This was an Irish act; the vogue in vaudeville was acts that made fun of the various peoples flooding to America. Most of these were performed by the very people who were being ridiculed. Blacks were doing blackface acts. Irish were doing drunken Irish acts. Like this one.

Cohan did a somewhat drunken Irish clog dance, and McCarthy showed up to insult him, and soon enough there was a brawl, with the pair whaling away at each other, both of them in well-padded suits to take the whacking of canes.

Some people apparently found this hilarious, especially the Irish audiences in Butte and Anaconda. Actually, there were some amusing moments, but the proprietor of Beausoleil Brothers Follies hoped to find something better.

With the help of John Maguire, who owned the opera house, he was looking at local talent. He'd wired agents on both coasts and Chicago, and had not come up with anything to fill out his show bill, especially an act that would draw crowds. And Butte was a long way from anywhere.

"Thanks," he said. "We'll let you know shortly."

"We're filling the Comique every night," Cohan said.

"Comedy, that's the trick," said McCarthy.

August nodded. They paused, expectantly, and then quit the stage.

"Any more?" Beausoleil asked.

"You could try skits," Maguire said. "One-act comedies, ten or twelve minutes. There's a show at Ming's we might get down here."

Beausoleil had seen the ads in the Helena

papers: Mr. Roland Reed, in *Lend Me Your Wife*. On other nights the actor starred in *The Woman Hater*: "Reed as the Misogynist; Reed as the Bigamist; Reed as the Lunatic," read the ad in the *Helena Independent*.

Good fun, at least around Helena.

The stage was empty, lit by a clear glass bulb. The matinee was over, the evening show a way off. He had put LaVerne Wildroot into the matinee against his better judgment, and the crowd was neither inattentive nor delighted. That had been plain to Ethel, and she was no longer promoting her niece. She hinted that she was putting some-thing else together, but he discounted it. That was show business talk. Everyone was working on a new act.

The afternoon crowd had been good enough. Not a sellout, but not bad. The aura of Mary Mabel Markey still hung over the show, and over Butte. There were seats available for the evening show, but the next shows were not selling advance seats. And without her, unlikely to sell, even in a great theater town.

"Well, maybe I'll go out and do a two-step," Maguire said.

"Knock 'em dead," August said.

He stared into the cavernous theater, deep in shadow, a place that could crush dreams as well as make them come true. "Any dog show around here?"

Dogs were always welcome. Dogs jumped through hoops, caught anything thrown, did their own ballet, howled in unison, and bowed to audiences. Dogs, ponies, tigers. An animal act was a good deal.

The stage door popped open, boiling cold air through the darkened house, and Charles Pomerantz appeared, with that mahogany-haired girl at his side, still in white, but bundled up in a blue scarf and wooly hat and gray mittens. They made their way across the bleak stage, and down to the orchestra, where August was nursing his melancholia.

"Tell me you just hired a great act," Charles said.

August sighed.

"You've met Ginger. She sang. She is now Ginger Pomerantz."

Ginger looked pretty solemn.

"Congratulations, Charles. It's number thirty-three, right?"

"No, this is real. This is serious. A justice of the peace, an hour ago. You're the first to know."

"Oh, number seventeen!" August said.

"You want me to show some paper?"

This had to be some sort of joke, so August grinned. "Well, miss, you want to audition now?"

"No, I won't sing for you," she said. "Anyway, you've heard me." She turned to Charles. "But this is my husband." She caught his hand and held it.

It was dawning on August that this was real, or at least an improvement on most of the theater jokes he was familiar with. Maybe the punch line would show up in a few days. Maybe this was one of those endless gags.

"Ginger, is it? Forgive me. I've been rude. If this is your wedding day, permit me to wish you all the best."

Charles was enjoying it, even if Ginger was not.

"We'll want to celebrate," August said. "Maybe after the show this eve?"

"Yes," said Maguire. "Please allow me to host a gathering. And my congratulations. This is all a surprise. But show business is nothing but surprises, right? And we'll want to toast the happy couple. Will you be putting an act together?"

There it was again. Not even an emergency marriage could trump the business.

August stared at this unlikely couple, noting that they were smitten with each other, serious, and somewhat mysterious.

"Tell me the story," he said.

"She propositioned and I proposed," Charles said.

She reddened, but said nothing.

"It was a lost cause. Her hair's the color of my mother's. That lowered all my resistance, and after that, she was driving and I was along for the ride."

She eyed him nervously, and eyed August and

John nervously. But she caught the crinkle of flesh around their eyes, and smiled herself.

"And what are your plans?" John Maguire asked, closing in on the question that August had been too polite to ask.

"She'll travel with me, and with the show, and we'll see," Charles said.

"And will there be a home somewhere, like Brooklyn?"

"Wherever he is, that's my home," she said. "I'm not a performer, but I'd love to be in the company. And I'd love to be with Charles, wherever he goes."

Something sweet in her caught August.

"A trouper! Well, Ginger, welcome to the Follies," he said, and clasped her hands in his own. The glacier had melted. But he was still waiting for a punch line.

"I don't know who's more surprised," Charles said. "You, me, or her. None of this was by design, and all of it is pure good luck."

"I believe in omens," Maguire said. "Who can explain these things?"

"We're off to Philipsburg," Charles said. "When we can. The local train leaves at dawn, alas."

A flash of a smile, and a surrendering gaze from the bride, and they vanished into the afternoon.

"Who can explain it?" Maguire asked.

It was two hours to showtime. August wasn't hungry. He had no more auditions. He eyed his pocket watch, considered the stern weather, and decided to risk it. He bundled up, hailed a hack, asked the driver if he could reach Mountain View and return by seven, and hopped in. The horse, whipped by wind, hastened south, the enclosed coach rocking gently. Night was crawling down, and he'd return in full dark.

The cabby knew exactly where to go. Death and Butte were familiar with each other. He pulled up at the naked grave, raw earth shoveled over Mary Mabel Markey's tomb. The bleak twilight revealed a hastily filled grave, the clay not yet smoothed, and patches of snow dotting the yard.

"Give me five minutes," August said.

"I'll bring a lantern, sir."

"Thank you; I'll be all right, and won't be long."

A rim of last-light lay on the western horizon.

The cold air off the mountains took the breath out of him. There on the grave was a wreath of pine boughs. Someone had remembered.

"Well, Mary Mabel," he said. "Here's where it ended. In a town that loved you. Buried by your friends. You came out of nowhere, and touched the sky. I just wanted to say good-bye, and tell you that you've got a corner of my heart."

He had nothing to give her, and then remembered the new Indian head penny in his pocket, and this he placed at the top of her grave. Even in the near dark, it shown oddly bright, a bronze coin in a copper town.

"Good-bye, sweetheart," he said. "We've played a lot of towns together, you and I."

The ride back deepened his melancholia, and he knew that he must banish all that before the show. He was no good at concealing his feelings, even in tux and topper, ready to open the show. He paid the cabby extra, thanking him for braving the wind, and walked through the stage door, feeling better for having the communion he needed with his old friend and occasional nemesis.

Butte was the coldest place he had ever been, and the opera house was slow to warm. He wondered whether people would show up this evening, braving the relentless wind and the smoke from the boiler stacks that was whipping along the streets.

The stage felt like an icebox. He spotted The Profile hurrying his way, a grimy rag in hand.

"The catarrh and a bad throat," Wayne Windsor said, his voice a growl. "I should shorten the act—if you're willing."

"Fever?"

"Feels like one."

"Go to bed," August said. "Whenever I push too hard, we pay for it."

Windsor looked shocked. "I'll do the act. I can't let you down."

"Rather have you away from the rest."

"Two of the Wildroot girls have it, and Harry the Juggler, he's wiping his nose. Got a faucet running from both nostrils. Hope he doesn't sneeze when those scimitars are flying."

The juggler was a silent act. August could use the silent acts to fill in. The tap dancers, too. They didn't sing. The Marbury Trio had several routines. LaVerne Wildroot could sing, if she was up to it.

"Which of the Wildroot Sisters? Is LaVerne sick?"

"No, she's good. Cookie and Marge caught it, Marge with a cough."

"What about Mrs. McGivers?"

"Who knows? Maybe it'll be a monkey night," Wayne said. "They're our ancestors."

"They can catch what we catch," August said.

He headed for the Green Room, hoping to find ways to put a show together. He wouldn't cancel. Never cancel. Work it all out. He found Harry the Juggler there, and asked him to do a third, maybe a fourth act if he could. Harry listened closely; August never knew if Harry was grasping words, or just nodding. But yes, Harry would add the cup-and-saucer act. Drop one and it'd break; drop several, and there'd be a lot of ruined pottery onstage. The deal was, break the whole lot. It was an amateur juggler act, and usually got some laughs. But pottery was costly, and that act didn't come cheap.

"Break it all, Harry," August said. "We'll buy more in the morning."

He corralled Ethel Wildroot next. "What's the score?" he asked.

"The girls are ready. LaVerne'll sing. Cookie and Marge'll squawk a little, but they'll do it. They'll do the job, and no one will guess."

"Twice? Second act? And LaVerne can solo?"

"They grew up in the business. Speaking of that, dear boy, I could do the Dumb Dora act if I had to. That's what the act was, before the girls took over. I'd put on a blond wig and he'd deliver the questions and I'd deliver, and the crowd got a chuckle out of it."

"Well, not tonight, Ethel."

"You could do it. Just slide me questions, like where are we, and who's on first, and what day of the week is it?"

"We'll work on it. Not tonight. We'll go with whoever's here."

"Break a leg," she said. There was something tender in her response.

He found Mrs. McGivers in the wing, fussing with the capuchin monkeys.

"Run long if you can. About half the acts are sick."

"Sweetie pie, I was just thinking Cain's not looking so hot, but Abel's fine. Don't worry. We can add the organ grinder routine; the little buggers squeeze some coin out of the crowd while Joseph cranks the accordion. That can get juicy."

Somehow they'd put on a show. It had been the longest day in memory.

17

Somehow or other, the company delivered that evening. That was the thing about veteran troupers: they could fill in, make do, improvise, put on a show, get out there in the limelight and keep the songs and laughs coming.

Ethel Wildroot watched the girls perform, not once but thrice that evening, and they managed somehow. But just barely. Truth was, she was disappointed in them. They'd grown up in the business, knew the ropes, and still didn't quite deliver whenever something was amiss.

It annoyed her. She'd spent years teaching, cajoling, demanding, encouraging, and the best they could do was get some pleasant applause. She wished that her late husband, rat that he was, could hammer something of the business into their heads. She would even prefer their old stand-up comedy, rat that he was, to this. At least they were an act, and it got laughs, rat that he was. It was called a Dumb Dora act, because she made sure to be the dumbest dame up there that anyone had ever seen. She was good at it. She picked up his cues, his questions, and her responses guaranteed that every male in the audience felt superior to every female ever born on this earth. Rat that he was.

But that was long ago. If she could put a comedy routine together, it would be the reverse of the Dumb Dora act. She'd feed questions to some old goat and let him dither. She'd looked around the company some, but no one qualified. Even the accordionists were smart.

The company headed for the hotel, and sleep, and maybe better health in the morning, but Ethel was ready to roam. She often stayed up late, never got sick, and sometimes had fun. Especially in Butte, with a saloon for every nationality and taste. What's more, most of the places didn't mind a lone woman, even if the precincts were entirely male. And it helped when she said she was from the Follies. Where else could one get a drink from barkeeps like Butt Bean or Dago Jim or Stuttering Alex or Big Jerry or Whistling Sammy?

Butte was the best town she had ever played. It was lit up all day and all night, and there was nothing like it outside of New York. That night, half frozen, she burst into a saloon with the mysterious name of Piccadilly, which offered few clues about its clientele. It turned out to be a haven for Englishmen, especially those who wouldn't rub shoulders with the Irish, and would cross the street before tipping a hat to the Italians.

Decorum ruled. She feared she wouldn't be served, but this was Butte, after all, and pretty soon a barkeep with a soiled apron supplied her with a rye and water. Well, fine. She would listen to the galoots. Maybe she would get into an argument. Maybe she would huff out, into the cold night.

There was one particular gent who interested her. He had a kingly way about him, and for some reason people kept buying him drinks. He was carefully groomed, but shabby, the sort who had seen better days but still got into his boiled shirt and cravat, even if his attire was worn at the sleeves, even soiled. But there he was, often with a crowd about him, listening intently.

She caught the attention of the barkeep. "Buy the gentleman a drink," she said.

"He's got four ahead of you, madam."

"He's good for a quart," she said.

The keep poured some amber fluid and set it before the gentleman, nodding in her direction.

"This is a portentous event, and history will remember you kindly," the man said.

"What have I done?"

"You have wet the whistle of a man destined to be remembered throughout the ages," the man said. "It's my fate to be the Shakespeare, the Newton, the da Vinci, of the ages."

Several of his auditors were listening now, following every word, plainly enjoying the exchange. She had walked into something, maybe a running joke at this saloon.

"What have you done?" she asked.

"Done? Done? I am recorded on the pages of

history. I am the Napoleon of empire, the Hannibal of ancient times, the Julius Caesar of modern times. I will be remembered as the conqueror of Asia, the Lord High Chamberlain of India, the Christopher Columbus of all the oceans, the conquistador of Argentina, the man who raced his sled dogs to the South Pole and lived to tell about it. The British Isles are in my rear pocket."

"What haven't you done?" she asked.

"I have not yet set a record for wives," he said. "I've had a few, disposed of many, but so far, I'm no match for a typical Italian."

"I'll marry you if you want."

"Madam, you are already touched by history. My numerous biographers will remember this fateful day when you bought me a drink, thereby entering that select world of those who will be read about a thousand years from now."

"I gather you're important," she said.

"Important! I disdain the word. That suggests merely a berth in the first rank. I leave that to the multitudes who toil and sweat. In truth, madam, I am unique. Throughout the history of the world, of all the civilizations, in the jungles and deserts, on the steppes of Asia, and in the frigates of navies, there has been none like me."

She took the plunge. "Would you like to tell it to the world, sir?"

"There's nothing to tell. I'm already known from pole to pole, and clear around the equator."

"But not everyone's seen you, sir. I think you should be granting audiences to those who have admired you from afar."

His gaze bored into her. "What's the proposition, eh?"

"First tell me your name, sir."

"If you don't know it, you are grossly deficient."

"Here's the proposition, sir. I will display you. I'm with the company at the opera house in town, and I will put you in front of large crowds, who then may catch a glimpse of your genius, and remember it the rest of their natural lives."

He mulled it.

"You will be fed, clad, sheltered, and will have your choice of beverages at any time."

He turned to the rest. "There, you see? It took a woman to recognize the unique person before you. She wasn't content to offer me a drink or two; she has offered me sustenance worthy of my unique calling."

"I'm Ethel. We'll call the act, The Genius and Ethel. All right?"

"Madam, I'm your liege lord," he said.

"Come along now. I'll get rid of some girls and put you in the Butte Hotel, where it's warm."

"Madam, genius has met its match," he said.

"And we'll tour Philipburg and Missoula next."

"Abominable towns, but I will suffer cruelties until the whole world has gathered at my feet."

The observing crowd was smiling. That was the

deal. He was half the act. She would need to be the debunker and skeptic, and puncture the gasbag now and then, and if it all worked, she'd have a comedy routine.

She got him out of there, fed him some soup at an all-night café, and stowed him in her room. He was not fragrant but that could be dealt with. She moved in with the girls, who didn't want another in their two beds, but so what?

"I've got an act, The Genius and Ethel," she said. "And don't ask me his name."

Her tone was belligerent enough to quell questioning, so they grumbled instead.

The next morning she pushed some porridge into him, found August Beausoleil, and arranged for an audition at the opera house.

"Who's the genius?" he asked.

"I haven't beaten that out of him yet."

Beausoleil's smile spoke loudly.

She insisted on some spotlights, and the olio drop, since this would make a good olio act. And she wanted the focus on The Genius.

Beausoleil sat about four rows back, looking impatient. But Ethel was an old hand, and he'd give her careful consideration. She wished there could be a small audience, able to pick up on details, but August was as much a veteran of auditions in empty theaters as she. She settled The Genius in a wicker chair with a high back that looked vaguely like a throne.

"All right, Genius, away we go," she said. "Who are you?"

"I'm the greatest man who ever lived, from the beginning of time," he said.

"What have you got against Napoleon?"

"Utterly incompetent. Now, if I had been in charge, Waterloo never would have happened."

"Have you ever served in an army?"

"That would be an utter waste of my talents," the Genius said.

"What about Shakespeare, Genius?"

"Pedestrian, madam. I could write circles around him. Hamlet's the worst bit of stagecraft ever written."

"So are your plays better?"

"Good Lord, woman, why bother? Plays are an inferior form of storytelling."

It went along for a while like that, and she didn't see Beausoleil crack a smile. That wasn't good. She put more heat on the Genius, making fun of his windy assertions, but it wasn't softening up Beausoleil any.

"Ethel, that's enough," Beausoleil said. "I'm going to say no to this, for several reasons. Thank you, sir."

"You mind telling me what?"

"You have the germ of an idea, but it's not going anywhere. It's not building. It's not an act, with a finish. But there's more, I'm afraid." He eyed The Genius. "The audience may be discomfited by you picking on this fellow. If he were an entertainer, that would be one thing, but he's not."

"Well, sir, I am an entertainer, and I'm glad you've put your finger on it," The Genius said. "First, let me introduce myself. I'm Cromwell Perkins. I don't use my name much, so as not to embarrass my family. Let me explain. I grew up in comfortable circumstances in the East, and got a good education, but I was born with a fatal flaw, at least a troublesome one. I have a great aversion to honest labor, and I'll find any wretched means to avoid toiling as a grocery clerk or a surveyor or a shoe salesman. The thought of practicing law, like my father, makes me faint. I sank deeper and deeper into want, and then figured out my salvation. I became a barstool entertainer. I am a frequent visitor to saloons of all sorts, and the places eventually gave me my living. I learned how to collect a crowd.

"It was there, sitting on more stools, or putting a foot on more brass rails, than I can remember, that I evolved into The Genius. I learned how to startle and amuse. I learned how to shock and dismay. People bought me drinks. They fed me lunch. They gathered around. They brought others in to hear The Genius. It didn't matter which saloon; I could wander into any, and pretty soon I collected a crowd, and sooner or later, they'd be buying me drinks, or offering me a tip. Not much of a living, I declare, but one that allows me a bunk in a basement, and a little heat in winter, and the chance to make a fool of myself day by day, to avoid honest toil."

He stared at Beausoleil, who stared back, and chuckled.

"So you're in the business after all," he said.

"It beats working for a living, sir."

"You know, this could turn into something. Not today or tomorrow, but soon, if you and Ethel turn this material into an act, something that doesn't sputter and die every other minute. I can do this much: I'll give you a free ride for a while, bed and board, but no pay until you've got an act that we can put on the boards with some confidence. And then we'll talk pay. Does that make sense to you, Cromwell?"

"It sounds suspiciously like toil," The Genius said.

"Take it. I'll work with you daily. We'll work up some material. We'll make this into the best comedy on the circuits," Ethel said.

It was strange how it worked out. August was dead right. The act needed some refining. And in two minutes he had gotten the man's name and history out of him, and put a halt to the idea that Cromwell Perkins was half mad, or delusional, or that he was being paraded in front of audiences just to make fun of him.

"Come along, Cromwell. We'll have a bite,

and then we're going to work, and I mean work, whether you like that idea or not."

"The thought makes me dizzy," The Genius said.

18

Mrs. McGivers had two sick babies. Cain and Abel lay on her hotel bed, listless, their nostrils lined with phlegm, their long prehensile tails limp. They wore diapers. Their red-and-gold band uniforms had been brushed and set aside for the next performance. But now it seemed unlikely there would be another performance anytime soon.

She scarcely knew what to do. She wondered who might help, or whether it was useless to consult with anyone. She already knew what the trouble was: both capuchin monkeys had pneumonia. They were tropical animals, living in lowlands mostly, moist and warm, with good air. Not like Butte, over a mile high and numbingly cold, no matter how much heat warmed the room.

She had asked the Butte Hotel to summon a doctor, and wondered if the man would flatly refuse to treat a pair of sick monkeys. She could only wait and see. She rarely had trouble keeping the monkeys in her hotel room. In fact, the hotels usually enjoyed the prospect of a pair of primates in diapers in a room.

They were the only babies she had. She fed them, nurtured them, played games with them, and occasionally practiced the act with them. She had fitted them out with custom-made cymbals and a small bass drum, and had shaped them into an anarchistic band, with each song spinning off into chaos until the audience howled.

But she had nurtured them, too, brought them fruits and various vegetables, beverages, sweets. Monkeys had a sweet tooth. And sometimes, when they were unsettled, she took one in her arms and held it close, felt its little monkey arms wrap around her neck. She was mother and counselor and teacher to Cain and Abel.

Joseph, the accordionist who actually put the melody before audiences, had a room of his own, and lived oddly separated from the rest. And yet he was as sensitive to the monkeys, and the act, as she was. Indeed, he had been a street-corner organ grinder, and both of the monkeys had once been his wards until Mrs. McGivers bought in and reshaped the material into an act for the vaudeville stage.

Now she sat and fretted. She was more than worried; she felt panic, which she ruthlessly suppressed.

At the knock she leapt up, opened, and found a bearded man carrying a black Gladstone.

"Dr. Mortimer, madam. You are ill, I take it?"

"Ah, not me exactly, sir. There." She pointed at the small primates on her bed.

He stared, registering that, and smiled. "I'm afraid that's outside of my competence, madam."

"I thought you'd say that. They have colds, coughs, rattling in their throats, and maybe worse. Pneumonia, I'm thinking. Any help—well, they're my babies."

He peered at her, at them, at the small bed filled with two beasts with long tails.

"All right, let's see what I didn't learn in medical college," he said.

He settled on the edge of the bed, while Cain and Abel eyed him listlessly. From his Gladstone he extracted a listening horn, and placed it on Cain's chest, and paid close attention to what he heard. Then he placed the horn on Abel's chest, listening closely. He dug out a tongue depressor.

"Will he bite?"

"He won't like it."

"I'd like a look."

"I'll hold him, and hold his tongue down, and you have your look."

It worked pretty well. Dr. Mortimer lit an electrical torch and got a good look inside the mouth of each.

"It's a pulmonary disease, certainly. As for a name, that is beyond my competence. Pneumonia, bronchitis, catarrh, common cold, sore throat, cough. Not that naming it would do much good. This is not the healthiest climate for a pair of tropical animals. Your best chance is to get them lower and warmer and dryer as fast as you can."

"And where might that be, sir?"

He stared into space. "Salt Lake City. I'd not trust them to survive the trip if you took them any farther than that."

"Any idea when they'll get better?"

"You're with the vaudeville show, I believe. I can hardly hazard a guess. But diseases come and go faster in smaller animals."

"Are there any remedies, sir?"

"I would hesitate to dose an animal with anything. The best I can suggest is a trip to a climate more suited for these little fellows."

"Are they dying?"

"They have a lot of fluid in their lungs. Especially that one there. I can hear it."

"I have some cough syrup with opium. . . ."

He shook his head. "I wouldn't."

"These monkeys, I love them. They're my act. My life depends on them."

The monkeys watched intently from their sickbed, somehow knowing this was all about them.

"See if you can get some honey in them," he said. "A little warm whiskey and honey, or tea and honey. It has mysterious powers."

"The whiskey or the honey?"

"Tell me about it," he said.

He charged her two dollars, two for the price of one, he said, and wished her success.

She closed the hotel door, and eyed her sick babies, and felt a wave of desolation crawl through her. There wasn't much hope. She couldn't get them to Salt Lake City; she lacked the means to rent a Pullman compartment, and they'd die before she got there. She couldn't leave the show. She couldn't stay in the show. She hardly dared leave the little capuchins alone, but she had to deal with this.

She found August Beausoleil in his room.

"Cain and Abel are sick; maybe pneumonia. I got a doctor, and all he could say was that it was in the lungs, and the monkeys were far from home. He thought the nearest dry and warm place was Salt Lake."

"No act, then?"

"No act."

He seemed to sag, and then straightened. "What may we do for you?"

"Keep us in the company for a while."

"Of course."

"The doctor said diseases come and go fast in smaller animals."

"Did he say whether the monkeys would recover soon?"

"No, he said that was beyond his competence.

He said I should try to get some whiskey and honey into them; it has properties."

"Drunken monkeys," he said. "I'll send someone for some honey. There's no shortage of whiskey in Butte. Madam, I'm so sorry."

He hugged her. It felt comfortable, his gentlemanly hug, and reassuring. She was almost beside herself. The monkeys were all the children she would ever have, and they loomed so large in her life that she couldn't imagine a future without them.

In due course she mixed some steaming water, some honey, and some whiskey together, and coaxed first Abel and then Cain to swallow some, which they did listlessly, accusation in their dull eyes. She gave them as much as they would swallow, and kept trying every few moments, until they rebelled and spit out anything she coaxed into their mouths. Then she sat, the bedside vigil, even as the next performance, another matinee, cranked up.

She couldn't imagine how August could fill the bill with so many acts disabled—or dead. But that was the business. Limp along, improvise, and hire claques to laugh and clap.

She clung to the room, even as the capuchins slept peacefully. Maybe it was the whiskey, she thought. Once she placed her hand on their fevered brows, but they barely stirred. She made room between them, and settled herself on the bed, her babies on either side, her rough browned hands clasping her little ones, until she dozed the afternoon away.

She was awakened by a knock, and opened to Ethel Wildroot, and welcomed Ethel even though they'd not gotten along, and Ethel was brimming with schemes and plots.

"Those poor little things," Ethel said.

"I've got them whiskeyed up," Mrs. McGivers said.

"That's as good as any," Ethel said. "We got through the show. LaVerne did it. Three solos. There's hope for the girl in spite of bad blood on her father's side."

"Someone comes through, and the show limps along," Mrs. McGivers said.

"You want some monkeys? We can come up with monkeys."

"In Butte, Montana?"

"Don't I look like a monkey? And I've a friend I can turn into one."

The thought of it alarmed Mrs. McGivers at first.

"I can follow a beat; I can whale away at the cymbals when the moment comes. I can do monkey business. I can turn into an anarchist. I'm half monkey myself."

Mrs. McGivers stared, speechless.

"I have a new friend, a natural-born monkey we can put on the drum. Cromwell Perkins. He'll get the idea in no time. We can climb into some costumes, something evil, something that speaks of jungles, and we can do your monkey act without Cain and Abel."

"I could never leave Cain and Abel alone in the room."

"We could get a nanny. Cookie, my daughter, she likes monkeys. She's a little slow. I'll send Cookie over after the matinee, and we'll practice for tonight between shows. Get Joseph, and I'll get Cromwell, and we'll see what happens."

And that was how it played out. About five that afternoon, Mrs. McGivers and her new monkey band assembled at the opera house, under the skeptical eye of August Beausoleil, and soon were hammering out the revised act, this time gradually sliding from disciplined calypso music into utter anarchy. And then Mrs. McGivers shouted imprecations, and the culprits returned to rhythmic calypso, only to have that born rebel, Cromwell, begin to foul up the music.

And August Beausoleil was laughing.

"I don't know why I'm saying this, but I'll put you on. Be ready fourth slot in the first act, and we'll see."

Cromwell was a natural subversive. He caught the idea instantly—start with disciplined music, veer into anarchy, give it a tropical twist. Mrs. McGivers wondered about him. He almost looked like husband material to her jaded eye.

That evening, with Cookie Wildroot nursing the sick monkeys, Mrs. McGivers got her act costumed, absurd hats and gaudy pants, and then they were on.

"Gents and ladies, the one, the only, the sensational Mrs. McGivers and her Monkey Band," August intoned to a good crowd that had braved the dark cold evening.

It was a funny thing; she had a way of seeing success or failure in advance, and now the eve was bright with promise. The costumes were outlandish enough so the audience chuckled at the very sight of them. Joseph wheezed away on the accordion. Mrs. McGivers plunged into exotic calypso, strange rhythms from distant places. Ethel Wildroot whanged a cymbal at just the right moments, an odd sound against the tropical beat. And the insidious Cromwell was poking along on the bass drum, perfectly attuned to the music, until they had finished the first stanza. Then everything began to fall apart. Ethel whacked the cymbals. Joseph wheezed the accordion. Cromwell loosed a thunderous volley that rumbled out upon the crowd.

The crowd was discomfited. Something was wrong. And then Ethel loosed a clatter of cymbals that shook the rafters, and that monkey Cromwell battered the bass drums mercilessly, and now the crowd was chuckling, then laughing, then howling. The whole act tumbled into chaos, with

Mrs. McGivers screeching, in turns, at Joseph, at Ethel, and at Cromwell. She grabbed a drumstick and beat Cromwell on the noggin with it.

The crowd howled. Mrs. McGivers' band had deserted her, poor old dear.

And August Beausoleil stood in the wing, delighted.

"How was that, ladies and gents?" he asked, when the crowd had quieted a bit. "Mrs. McGivers and her Monkey Band. Come out and take another bow, Mrs. McGivers! And the rest of you, come out and face the music! You're all fired!"

They did. People laughed and clapped. It was a different act, not a monkey act, but it worked. And August was smiling.

19

Wayne Windsor hated to get out of bed before ten, but there were tasks to perform. Butte had ignored him. In fact, the papers had been silent, the coverage abysmal. He made a point of getting into every paper in every town the company played. On this cold morning he pulled the blankets away, fled their comforting warmth, and prepared himself for an excursion.

He scraped away the day's whiskers with his well-stropped straightedge. He took special care not to nick his cheeks, because the profile would be under close observation within the hour. He was an immaculate man, taught the virtue of cleanliness and grooming by his immaculate family. Unlike most people in vaudeville, who rose from the depths, or arrived on an immigrant boat, Windsor had grown up in privilege. He had achieved a bachelor degree, and he ascribed his success as a monologuist to the fund of wisdom and knowledge that he had acquired in New Haven. And, of course, his career had started in those hallowed precincts, the debating society.

After tea and a poached egg and muffins dripping with jam, he ventured out upon Butte's cruel slopes, after ascertaining the locations of several newspapers. He found *The Inter-Mountain* first, which was fine. By all accounts, a good, sober paper, not given to conniption fits.

He discovered a squinty gent in a sleeve garter at an oaken desk; behind him was the inky plant, where skinny compositors toiled at their type-sticks, and half-formed pages were spread on iron tables known as stones. He had been in many a plant, and knew the language.

Sleeve-garter took notice, and approached the counter.

"Yes, I have a story for you, sir," Wayne said. "I'm Wayne Windsor, top-billed at the Beausoleil Brothers Follies, at the opera house. I've stopped by to give you an interview."

"An interview, ah, yes, some publicity."

"Well, look what I have here, sir. Here's an attractive portrait of me, from the side of course, which is the most flattering vantage point when it comes to depicting any vaudeville performer. Precast, ready to drop into your forms. And here, sir, is a complete interview, precast in type metal, so all you need do is drop it in your forms, and you've a story without further labor. Very handy when you're rushed. We'll be playing two more days, extended engagement because of the fine reception we've received, and I thought you'd like to run it in the afternoon edition. A good way to sell copies."

Sleeve-garter eyed Windsor, eyed the portrait etched in metal, and the two-column interview.

"Sir, if you want to run an ad, you have to pay for the space," he said.

"It's a balanced interview, finest journalistic tradition. All you need do is write a headline mentioning that I'm at the opera house these two days."

Sleeve-garter sighed. "We could use some news today. I tell you what. I'll run that image of you, and interview you myself. We'll have to hurry, though."

Windsor was delighted. He followed the reporter to his grimy desk, and settled in for a good talk.

"I'm Bruce Key," he said, grabbing a pencil and

a pad. "Now then, you're with the Follies, and you do what?"

"I'm a monologuist. I spin stories. You might say I'm a Mark Twain drifting through Butte."

"Who's that?" Key said.

"Tom Sawyer? Huck Finn? Never mind. I like to tickle funny bones, and I do this by poking a little fun at people."

"Ridicule, then?"

"Oh, nothing so blatant. There's plenty of people who beg to be examined. You might say I like to throw some light on their foibles."

"You amuse people on a stage. How'd you get there?"

"Debating societies, college, you know. I am among the fortunate, having a well-rounded schooling. I'm from an old Massachusetts family, textiles, shipping, slavery, rum, and various learned professions. A good name is worth a lot, of course. Here from the early seventeen-hundreds, prominent in Boston. Not quite up to the Cabots and Lowells, but certainly a peer, as families go. You know, that gives me a vantage point to view this country. I must say, sir, the tide of immigrants coming in now is very inferior. Not up to snuff. Half can't even speak English. The other half do nothing but breed. I'd support laws restricting immigration to the English, and no one else."

Key was busy scribbling all that, to Windsor's great satisfaction.

"You'd exclude the Irish?" Key asked.

"They don't really speak English, do they?"

"Dutch, Germans, Norwegians?"

"Yes, the stock would improve if they were kept out."

"What about those in your vaudeville company? Are they all English?"

"Well, you have to understand there's exceptions to any generalization, sir. Some people succeed, in spite of their genetic and social deficiencies. That's show business. Home of the mentally defective."

Windsor was enjoying it all. And Key had opened him up and was mining Windsor's richest veins. It turned out to be a fine interview. Even brilliant. Windsor explained that the country's strength was based on good English genetic stock, and the more it was diluted and debased by the hordes of people flooding through Ellis Island and spreading out across the continent, the weaker the republic became. These new people didn't understand the common law and tradition that had gone into founding the republic, he said. And they were lazy by nature.

Key cheerfully recorded all that, and then explained he would have to rush to get the story into the afternoon paper, but it should be on the streets around four. Windsor debated whether to take his interview material to other papers, but decided he had done a good day's work, and he would enjoy a leisurely tour of the town, if it wasn't too cold, and then prepare for the evening show.

He never knew which of several monologues he would employ, and he often sounded out his audience a little before plunging in. Maybe he would talk about future janitors and farmers pouring through the golden gates, and see where that would lead him. The ethnic roots of pig farmers fascinated him.

At four, he bought the paper, hot off the press, and was delighted to see his interview prominently displayed on page one. Good. That would help to fill the opera house that evening. The troupe would be pleased with the publicity he'd managed to get on his own.

But in fact no one said anything. Beausoleil was more concerned about having enough acts to run a normal show. The monkeys were sick, and that was a blessing as far as Windsor was concerned, but so were half the acts. And there were some strange faces around; some dubious sorts filling in, which made Windsor irritable. Beausoleil must be desperate.

The Profile saw it all as golden opportunity. During his first stint, in Act One, he had some fun with the copper kings of Butte, getting rich off the sweat of thousands of miners toiling deep in the pits. That got him a lot of nervous laughter. In fact, he was the real star of the Follies, since none of the other acts were drawing the sort of applause and delight that he was enjoying.

Mrs. McGivers was working with two human monkeys, and they weren't half bad, but it wasn't as bizarre as when the capuchin monkeys were whaling away. And the Wildroot Sisters were all sniffling and sick, and their stuff wasn't up to par. And Harry the Juggler wasn't up to snuff, either, especially when a scimitar fell to his feet. But the tap dancers, the Marbury Trio, were in good form.

All of which made Wayne Windsor glow. He was the top act, and the audience knew it. He did even better in the second act, with an improvised monologue about trying to converse with people who didn't speak English. He had a knack, and soon was imitating Norwegians, Italians, French, Bohemians, and Eskimos, much to everyone's delight. The new stuff was so good that he resolved to polish it up and make it part of his standard repertoire.

The show ended with the usual patriotic finale, and The Profile was looking forward to a drink or two, and bed. But John Maguire approached. "Windsor, you've got four admirers at the stage door, wanting to take you out for a beverage or two."

"Women?"

"No, miners, unless I miss the mark. They said they wanted to treat you to a few, and hope you'd accept. They said you're the man they'd like to visit with."

"Tell them I'll be there in a bit, soon as I get into street clothes."

Sure enough, there were four gents waiting for him, two of them burly, one tall, one short, and all grinning.

"Windsor, is it? We're looking forward to a visit, sir. We'll take you to a miners' pub, and buy whatever it is that wets your whistle."

"I'd be pleased to bask in your admiration," Windsor said, wondering if these louts heard him praise himself. But they didn't.

"This is Martin Murphy, and that's Will McNamara, and this is Robby Toole, and I'm Mike Hoolihan," said one of the burly ones. "We all work the Neversweat. We'll share a toddy with you, if you're inclined."

"Of course. I relish time with my admirers," The Profile said.

They headed northeasterly, toward the great complex of mines that seemed to be the heart of the city, and in that zone where the downtown fell away and dreary streets with mining shanties and flats spread darkly into the night, they paused at an obscure saloon, ill-lit and strangely lonesome looking.

"Pile on in, Mr. Windsor," said Hoolihan.

Windsor found himself in a long ill-lit saloon with lithographs of horses tacked to the walls and only two lamps illumining the place, front and rear. Pipe smoke hung thickly in the air; most of these cobs had a pipe stem clamped between their teeth. Twenty or thirty silent men nursed ale or a shot of something.

"What'll it be?" Hoolihan asked.

"Some Jameson's, if it's to be had," The Profile said. That was good Irish whiskey, and this saloon might not stock it. But a bottle promptly appeared, and was set before the guest, along with a tumbler. He could pour his own. That was all fine with The Profile, who awarded his hosts with a long look at each side of his visage.

"We all work for Marcus Daly, and his Anaconda," Hoolihan said. "He brought us across the sea, by the thousands, and put us to work here. There's more of the Irish here than anywhere else away from the old country."

Windsor was beginning to see what this was about. He'd finish the good whiskey, and duck away.

"You know, my friend, it's mean work, and it wears a man down, and it's work few Yanks want to do, because it'll kill a man quick. Now, we thought you might like to see how it's done. You know, we're only a little hike from the Neversweat, and we'd like to take you down and show you men knocking rock. I'm a shift foreman, and I have the right to go where I want. You'll see men working in their underdrawers, it's that hot. They're all sheened up with sweat, and have to sip on the cool water they send down the shaft. But we keep on. The muckers break up rock and load it into the one-ton cars, a little noisy for your tastes, and those get pushed or pulled to the shaft and taken up. Others, they're using pneumatic drills on the face, to pound holes and set the charges. There's a lot of dust, and nowhere for it to go, and a lot of men get silicosis, miner's lung, or maybe consumption, because over the years they breathe a lot of that busted-up rock into their lungs, and they die young. So maybe all these immigrants are being led to their doom, wouldn't you say?"

"I'm sure you're very strong, sir."

"But maybe dumb, too, wasting our only life down there, far from the sun, breathing killer dust, and getting laid away at age forty-two. All so you can have copper to make wire to light your cities. Take that opera house. It's wired, and you get to do your show with incandescent lights, courtesy of mostly immigrant miners like these boys here.

"We were thinking, boyo, that there aren't many as strong as us or brave as us. Mr. Daly, he couldn't hire enough Yanks to fill his mines, and so he went and fetched us, and brought us here. What does that say about all the ones living here, boyo?"

The Profile smiled. "Thanks for the drink, fellows. I'm worn-out from the show, and looking forward to bed. You've been most entertaining."

He rose to leave, but a strong hand clasped his shoulder and pressed him into the bar again.

"Not so fast, boyo. We've decided to take you down the shaft. You ready to go?"

Windsor laughed. "I must say, sirs, it's not my line of work, and it's time for me to head for the hotel, with thanks, of course, for your hospitality."

"You're staying a while, boyo. We're not done with you—unless, of course, you wish to show us that you don't enjoy our company."

They were itching for a fight. Well, Windsor hadn't been on his college sculling team for nothing, or the baseball team, or the tennis team, either.

He grinned, tucked a leg behind Hoolihan, shoved and twisted at the same time, and unbalanced the miner, who toppled with a mighty thud. The Profile headed for the door, but only to run into several fists. The others closed in. One caught his left profile with a jab; the other caught his right profile with an uppercut. Hoolihan bounced up and landed a hairy fist square in Windsor's mouth. He tasted blood. He felt his lips swell. He knew he had bitten his tongue. His mouth was a ruin. He could hardly form words. He fled into the night as they smiled.

20

August Beausoleil clutched the yellow flimsy with the bad news: GEO PARSONS BARITONE AVAIL BUTTE THREE DAYS YOU PAY FREIGHT.

That was from a Chicago booking agent, Abe Stoop. Even if August added the Parsons act, it would be too little and too late. And he didn't have the cash to buy a two-thousand-mile ticket to Butte, Montana, from St. Louis, where Parsons was doing a club.

No, not Parsons.

That morning Wayne Windsor had shown up with a battered face, swollen lips, purple bruises, saying he couldn't work. His speech was slurred. All he would mumble was that he had been beaten by hooligans, and Butte was a dangerous place. He'd be out of the lineup until he could speak, and that would be a few days. The Profile had gotten himself into a jam somewhere. Beausoleil had a good idea how it had come about, but he didn't push the issue. That Butte newspaper with the interview sat on his hotel room table. It was a reckless interview in a mining town teeming with people straight off the boats.

That left a major hole. Windsor was good for

two monologues a show, always richly humorous, and always an audience pleaser. But that wasn't all. Mrs. McGivers had come to August that morning with more bad news. Cain had perished from pneumonia but Abel lived on. Cain had died in the night, his prehensile tail wrapped around Mrs. McGivers' ample arm. He'd coughed and stopped breathing. Butte's brutal altitude and cold had overwhelmed the tropical monkey. Mrs. McGivers, in her night robes, had carried the dead monkey around and about the hotel, haunting corridors, until someone in uniform had finally steered her to her room and took the dead creature away.

Maybe that act was done, too, but for the moment, if Mrs. McGivers was up to it, the act could continue with a pair of humans playing monkeys. It didn't look good. He worried less about the substitute monkeys than about Mrs. McGivers, who was suffering a mother's loss of a child, and might not be able to open.

Suddenly the follies was falling apart. He could manage a short performance, with extra work by the Marbury Trio, and possibly get by. Or he could cancel, lose the box office, but still owe the theater. It was morning; he had a few hours to decide.

He would need to wire Pomerantz. If they were too crippled to play Butte that night and the following, they were likely to be too crippled to play Philipsburg. He wondered if he could even reach Pomerantz, who was off honeymooning after a reckless marriage. Dream girl. Ginger was her name, girl in white, singer of opera and ballads. Funeral singer. Did a good job at the service for Mary Mabel Markey.

He hiked to the telegraph office in the next block, and hastily fashioned a message: NEED GINGER TONIGHT TOMORROW.

Maybe if there was passenger service, he'd have a singer.

But not an act. The girl would just sing some songs. But she was good at it, and that counted.

The odds weren't good, but he sent the wire anyway, and hoped for a quick reply. It wasn't anything he could count on.

Catching all the acts in their rooms would be tough, but he could spread the word. He found a Marbury in the hall.

"Delilah, wait."

"More trouble, I suppose. I hear The Profile got beat up."

"You know more than I do," August said. "But yes, he's out for a spell."

"The word is, some miners didn't like his piece about immigrants, and let him know it."

"He hasn't revealed the source of his affliction, only that he's lacking the means to talk."

"I heard it at breakfast. They wanted to take him into the mine, and show him where copper comes from. It doesn't come from people with social connections and college degrees."

"I think he learned that last night."

"In spades," she said, grinning.

"Delilah, we're short of acts. Mrs. McGivers' little monkey died of pneumonia, and she's not fit."

"Oh no, oh no."

"We'll see. She's a phenomenon."

"Tough old performer."

"The thing is, Delilah, can you and your gents do three different deals tonight?"

"We've been working on one. This house has hardwood on the aisles. We're thinking of a deal tapping our way through the audience, and up and down some stairs. But we've barely tried it."

"You're on, and you've rescued me."

"We'll work on it this morning. Which monkey, Cain?"

"You know, I don't remember."

"Poor Mrs. McGivers. She might kill husbands, but she loves monkeys."

"Delilah, get the word out."

He headed to the opera house, braving a smoke-choked morning. The north wind drove the acrid mine and mill smoke straight down the slope of the city, burning up lungs and tempers. He marveled that anyone lived to be forty in this miserable city. He wondered whether this mean city would be the ruin of his company, whose ranks were thinning by the hour.

He found John Maguire in his office, staring at the horizon.

"I've heard," Maguire said. "Word gets around fast. You have some acts?"

"Maybe cancel; have to make up my mind."

"Tonight and tomorrow?"

Beausoleil just shook his head. Butte had defeated him.

"The Profile sure chose the wrong place to tout his ancestry. Frankly, August, I'm surprised he got away with it as long as he did. This town's famous for saloon fights; I mean, the Cornishmen invade an Irish saloon, and bust it up, or the Irish and Italians tangle over some alleged insult. So Windsor simply walked right into the middle of it. I know who did it, and they were kind to him. He could have been busted wide open."

"You have any ideas, John?"

"Headline: Wayne Windsor not in show tonight. Turn it to good use. In this game, turn everything to good use. Fill the seats, one way or another."

That was it. One way or another. "Thanks, John. I'll see," August said.

That was a novelty. But so was Butte. And by now, Windsor's fate was the gossip of the whole mining town. It was a town that enjoyed rough humor. August weighed what to say, and finally decided that the gaudier the story, the better. He bundled into a thin coat—he hadn't fathomed how early cold weather would descend here—and headed for *The Inter-Mountain*. He'd get it into all the afternoon rags if he could, but he might as well start with the paper The Profile visited.

A stern gent in a sleeve garter greeted him at a counter.

"Beausoleil here; I own the show. Have an announcement," August said.

"I imagine you do," the gent said.

"One of our acts, Wayne Windsor, won't appear this evening or tomorrow. But the show will be better than ever."

"That's what I figured," the gent said. "Incapacitated? On both sides of the profile?"

This gent knew a lot more than August had imagined.

"Yes, he's a bit out of sorts."

"And how did all this happen, sir?"

"He didn't tell me. Maybe he ran into a doorknob."

"I'll quote you."

"That's what I want. Tell your Butte readers that the star of the Follies ran into a doorknob and won't appear."

"Beausoleil, you're a genius," the gent said. "Is this a scoop?"

"No, I'm going from paper to paper, varying the story considerably. Whoever gets it out first will have all the advantage."

"I might improve upon the story, sir."

"Good. You'll sell more papers and I'll sell more tickets."

Impulsively, Beausoleil shook hands with the dour reporter. He counted it one of his best interviews ever.

He braved the dank cold and arrived at the *Miner*, owned by one of the copper barons who rode herd on the town. This time, the reporter who met him was stern, gray, with wire-rimmed spectacles. He oozed skepticism.

"So, what's the story?" he asked.

"Why, sir, our lead performer may not appear this eve."

"So why are you telling me this?"

"So our customers will know in advance; it's the thing to do."

"Why won't he appear?"

"He's been injured, sir. He hasn't told me how. But it impairs his performance. Now, of course, he may change his mind and appear; one never knows. In that case, he would bravely do his monologues even while words don't form easily on the tongue. The audience might be treated to a performer's courage."

"Word is, he got whaled in an Irish pub. Yes or no?"

"He hasn't told me, sir."

"Are you weaseling?"

"I have heard the rumor. But he hasn't told me.

I also heard that the assault was a response to Wayne Windsor's comments about immigrants of all descriptions."

"Maybe you're square after all," the man said. "I might run something. Maybe not. It's not the hottest story in town."

"Read all about it," yelled a newsboy on the next corner. "Actor loses his teeth."

That was *The Anaconda Standard*, published in the next town by copper king Marcus Daly, but a lively presence in Butte. It was Daly who had imported Irish by the thousands to work in his pits.

Beausoleil laid out his two cents, and examined the sheet. Sure enough, on the front page, was the Wayne Windsor story.

Some gentlemen who worked at the Anaconda Company's Neversweat Mine invited the performer at the opera house, Wayne Windsor, to tour the pits with them, which the performer declined, and in the process of escaping the hospitality of these gentlemen, ran into a few knuckles.

It was an elegant story. The Beausoleil Brothers Follies were mentioned more than once, along with the opera house. But the story's real focus was Wayne Windsor's observations about new immigrants, their deficiencies, and the virtues of solid, old American English-speaking stock.

So it was all over town, both the rumors and now a story on page one. But it went on to discuss the performer himself.

"Mr. Windsor is enamored of his countenance, according to our sources, and is known in the company as The Profile, because he turns one way and another as he addresses his audiences, so each half of the crowd may admire his noble brow and aquiline nose and jut jaw.

"By all reports, he has a good line of repartee, mostly poking gentle fun at assorted groups. He does a whole routine based on trying to talk to various Norwegians, Swedes, Irish, Bohemians, or Italians, and this is said to amuse not only the English-speakers in the audience, but the more recent arrivals on our shores.

"We await word as to when The Profile will be back in commission. There's been no one quite like him in Butte."

August had the odd sensation that this evening's performance would be well attended. That was the odd thing about publicity. Even the most negative would draw a crowd.

When he reached the Butte Hotel a flimsy was awaiting him: NO TRAIN UNTIL TOMORROW GINGER READY FOR LAST BUTTE SHOW.

Tonight, then, his beleaguered company would sing and dance themselves into exhaustion. He headed for Mrs. McGivers' room, wondering if madam would perform this cold evening.

She opened to him, with an apparently restored Abel on her shoulder. The little criminal looked lonesome for his lost pal.

"You have an act?"

"You damn betcha," she said. "We're going to put on an act, one way or another. Work or starve, that's my motto. We'll crank something out. Abel, he'll pick pockets, the organ grinder act. AndI've got that fake monkey Ethel pulled out of a saloon. Hey, it don't take much to keep Butte happy."

She was smiling broadly, but there was a sadness around her eyes.

21

Charles was waving a yellow paper. "Hey, sweetheart, you wanted to sing? You get to sing."

"What, Charles?" Ginger asked.

"August needs you, right now. He's got sick acts."

"But he said I'm not, what was it? Not a draw."

"You put on a show or you cancel. And if you cancel, you return the ticket sales, and you still pay the house, and you still have expenses, and people waiting for their money. So you do the show, baby."

This was dizzying. These days had been dizzying. She had recklessly plunged into a universe she knew nothing about, and that included much more than a sudden marriage.

"What do I do?"

"You take the train back to Butte. I'll go with you partway, but then I've got to go to Missoula. We're nearly done here anyway. You go back, try out your tonsils, and knock 'em dead, twice, first and second acts."

"I haven't practiced."

"Neither have half the acts. You put a smile on your mug, you go on out there, and you do what you can do, and maybe you'll score, maybe not."

"What do you think I should sing? You know better than I ever could."

He eyed her cheerfully. "Here's where you're the boss, baby. I don't know what's stuffed in your head; I've barely heard you. We've got an amateur marriage. Singing, you're the pro. So you pick the numbers, and you dish the numbers, about three each act, if August wants to stretch it out a bit. And have an encore ready."

"Who'll accompany me? I often sing at a piano."

"Improvise, baby. If it bombs in the first act, do something else in the second."

"But what should I wear?"

"Nothing."

She reddened. She'd been wearing a lot of nothing in the hotel room in Philipsburg. She'd gotten the whirlwind tour of marriage. She'd expected a lot of sweet nothings, a lot of whispered kisses, a lot of hand holding, and instead, she'd been carried to a mountain top and hurled into space. She hadn't had time to figure it out. She was plunged into a river of impressions, feelings, odd loneliness, yearnings for the home she had fled, aching for whatever might come next. And her first real awareness of her lithe body.

He'd been furiously busy. Apart from making arrangements to house and feed the company, an advance man was involved in publicity, first and foremost. Tell the world about the show. Get three-sheet playbills up on barns, ads in papers, notices in cafés; start barkeeps gossiping, start editors muttering. Hire someone to hand out flyers.

He was off and gone all day and half the nights, so she barely knew her husband, and knew even less about the marriage she had contracted, and had spent a lot of time cloistered in the room, waiting for him. She had felt like some useless baggage, and maybe that's all she was. But then he'd burst into their room, beaming, and the world was aglow again.

One thing she knew: this world was nothing like the bourgeois one she had escaped. And she wasn't sure she liked this one at all. What was the axiom? Act in haste, repent at leisure. But there was this about it: She had made good her escape. She had fled the world that was crushing her and arrived in a world rife with possibility. And somehow, she had left no trail. They wouldn't be coming after her. She was free!

He was eyeing her. He had been curious about her, curious about how she was taking all this. He had learned to read her, and she marveled at it. She'd barely known boys; now she had a man. A stranger. More of a stranger than the day they had met. The odd thing was, she liked this jittery life. Even when she was scared, she liked this business. She was ready to hug the world.

"The shuttle leaves at seven; we reach the mainline at eight; Helena by nine; Butte by ten thirty. You'll have the afternoon to work up an act. It's the last show there. That makes it easy on you. If you flop, you won't let anyone down. But you won't flop. You've got the goods, babe."

Philipsburg lay at the end of a long spur off the Northern Pacific. A short smoky train carried freight, ore, passengers, and hoboes each way, each day.

She couldn't remember where she had put her sheet music. Or what dress to wear. Or what she should do out in front of people. She had given recitals, but this wasn't a recital. And after the company was together and well, she'd be back with Charles, Mrs. Pomerantz, out in front of the troupe, living in hotel rooms. Well, she had bought the ticket, and now she would see where it would take her.

She had barely gotten some sleep that wild evening when he was awakening her.

"Up, baby. This is your big day."

Big day? For what? As she went through her ablutions, she understood. They all thought she had wanted to be a vaudeville star, that she was some stagestruck girl with ambitions. Well, there was that, but the thing that had driven her to this point was simply a passion to escape.

She hurried into gray woolen travel clothes, and they hastened to the small barn-red station where several other people huddled in the morning cold. The ancient coach wasn't much warmer, but steam from the engine gradually wrought a measure of comfort.

For a change, every train was on time. They boarded the lacquered eastbound NP express, and were soon in Helena. Charles left her there with a kiss and a squeeze, and caught a train to Missoula. She boarded another local and rattled through a mountain valley to Butte. A hack sent by Beausoleil was there to meet her and carry her and her several bags to the hotel. She had been billeted with the Wildroot girls, for lack of any other room. And no sooner had she dropped off her bags than August was at the door.

"We'll go to the opera house. You'll want to work out an act," he said.

She realized he hadn't welcomed her, hadn't made small talk, hadn't engaged in pleasantries.

He had brusquely commanded her presence. Keeping a touring company afloat was serious business.

"I don't have my music," she said as they walked along Broadway.

"Sing from memory or tell me you're not in," he said. "And right now."

"Is there a pianist?"

"We've got a fiddler, an accordionist or two, but not a pianist. We can't be hauling a Steinway from stage to stage."

"But doesn't the house have one?"

"They sometimes do. John Maguire probably does."

"Can someone accompany me?"

"What are you, some opera diva?"

This was not going the way she had hoped. Charles had vanished; he always seemed to have more business than he had time. There were shadowy things in this new life she was leading.

He pulled open the side door to the opera house, and steered her toward the stage, pulling a switch that lit a single spotlight that flooded a down-stage area with white light. Then he clattered down some steps and into the cavernous darkness, filled with row upon row of empty seats, and settled in one, about five rows back. He made no effort to find a piano for her, or an accompanist, or Mr. Maguire, the boldly dressed gentleman whose place this was.

Then Beausoleil's voice softened. "Warm up a little, Ginger, and when you're ready, give me music."

She ran a few scales, a few high C's, and nodded.

"Introduce yourself and your song," he said.

It frightened her. "I'm Ginger," she said, tentatively.

"No, no, tell the audience how fine they are."

"I'm so pleased to see you good people this cold evening," she said. "I'll do a few ballads, songs that tell stories."

"Okay, okay, not exactly riveting," he said. "But you'll figure it out. If they yawn, try something else."

"Here's a favorite of mine, from Old Mexico," she said.

Dead silence out there. At least Beausoleil wasn't barking at her. "It's called 'Cielito Lindo.' "

That was greeted with a long silence.

She sang, her voice sailing into oblivion, swallowed up by the cavernous space in front of her. She was tense, and then relaxed a little, and caught the complex rhythm, and made it Mexican bright.

"Give me another," he said, afterwards.

She did.

"This isn't a recital," he said. "Sing to someone. Sing to me. Make contact with your audience."

"I don't understand."

"Tonight, pick out some gent in the fifth row,

and sing to him. Make him think you're up there for his sake. Get him in your vision, and keep him there. Like he's a lover."

She hadn't the faintest idea why she should do that, but she nodded.

"If that bothers you, pick someone else. Sing to the old gal in the third row with the hearing horn. And that brings up another thing. Your voice is weak. Make it strong. Make it bounce off the rear wall, behind me."

"You don't like my voice?"

"Sure I do. Nice for operas and recitals. This is vaudeville, show business. It's not a voice for that. Not like Mary Mabel Markey. She could deliver, know what I mean?"

She did, actually.

He softened again. "Glad to have you here, Ginger. You'll do. You'll be fine tonight, and maybe we'll use you some more, if the acts stay sick. I'll borrow you from Charles for a while. Once you get the hang of it, you'll pick up some steam. Mostly, you need to connect with people. At recitals, you just sing. Onstage here, you have a different task. You'll seduce every male and enchant every female."

"But that's—not . . ."

"It's show business, sweetheart. See you a half hour before showtime. Might have other things to tell you. Get gussied up so you look like everyone's favorite girl."

That was it. He wandered off to talk to Maguire. She stood there, in the spotlight, feeling two things at once. She seemed to be soaring, and she felt crushed, and she couldn't reconcile the two.

Charles wouldn't be in the audience that evening. She wouldn't be singing for him. She wouldn't have his assurance. If she failed, there'd be no hug, no arm around the shoulder. Now she was in the troupe. She was a performer. She had crossed some sort of bridge. She realized, suddenly, that show business could be the loneliest profession, and sometimes the loneliest moment of all would arrive when she was surrounded by well-wishing people, and a warm audience, and a happy manager.

The Wildroot girls were annoyed by an addition in their crowded room. It meant they would all be sleeping two to a bed, and any disturbance in the night would keep them all awake. But they were veteran troupers, and would joke it away.

"How'd it go?" asked LaVerne, the one who seemed most caring, even if she was a rival with a singing act of her own.

"I don't think Mr. Beausoleil was very happy," she said.

"They're all like that, sweetheart. It's not the managers and coaches and any of us you should worry about. It's the crowd. It's those folding-money folks who lay out the moolah, come in out of the cold, and sit down and want you to give them something good, something that they enjoy, in the bright lights. You pay no attention to us, to me, to the owners. Just ignore us. Go ring their bells. You listen to the crowd. You listen to their clapping. You listen to their smile. Yeah, sweetheart, listen to that. When they're smiling, the sound is different. When they ain't smiling, you'll hear something else. And sweetheart, don't give up after one bad show. It's a big ladder, and not very many climb to the top. Keep trying. Keep working new stuff. But if you get a few rungs up, that's fine. We're out here on a rinky-dink tour, not big time. No big-timers do Montana. This is the end of the earth. Beausoleil couldn't afford them. He can barely afford our two-bit sisters act. But now you're in the business, and you'll have a good time—mostly."

22

Wayne Windsor watched dourly from the wing. Harry the Juggler was tossing teacups and saucers in perfect form, a blizzard of pottery flying in perfect arches. The audience was rapt. Harry was doing things people had never seen and could hardly imagine.

The opera house was full. That spate of publicity had filled it. Windsor had read the articles grimly, aware that Butte was rubbing it in. He was in a foul mood, and August Beausoleil, dressed in his majordomo tuxedo, was eyeing him carefully. Windsor was not beyond causing trouble, and took some pride in it.

His lips and cheeks were swollen, his tongue bore some lacerations, and his noble visage was in ruins. The latter, more than his inability to enunciate clearly, was what kept him in the gloom offstage.

He envied Harry the Juggler, who needed only to smile, gesture, and plunge in. The man was actually billed this time as Harry Wojtucek, The Exhibitionist Extravaganza. He spoke enough English, after Polish, or whatever, to get along, but he remained a mystery to the company, and chose his own lonely ways. Harry didn't need to say a word. Harry could mesmerize audiences with the dash and daring of his skills. Wayne was always a little contemptuous of all that. Wayne Windsor had to go out twice an evening, fathom his audience, tickle their humor, and adapt his monologues to all sorts of conditions. Now that took mental skill. That took finesse far beyond what Harry the Juggler possessed. It was another case of the gifted American standing above the crowd.

Wayne wearied of it. Wearied of being in shadows, ignored, distrusted, and even laughed at by the company. He knew they were laughing. He truly did have a noble visage, a stunning profile, but no one much cared, and a few rubes were ready to make fun of him. The Wildroot Sisters were ready; silent acts were followed by noisy ones. And after that, who knows? This was an odd show, patched together. Maybe that girl in white, the one Charles Pomerantz wanted to bed badly enough to turn himself into a sucker. The girl who was standing rigidly in the shadows, far from anyone.

Beausoleil turned to the girl in white next. He was dealing with a cheerful crowd, but a quiet one. Nothing had ignited them this eve. Windsor watched the majordomo stride out to the spotlit center, peer out to the crowd, and lift his top hat.

"Ladies and gents, a new voice, the sweetest voice I've ever heard, a young lady I'm proud to present to you, as a farewell gift, the one, the only Ginger!"

He paused there, awaiting her, and she finally strode out, smoothing her dress as she went.

He nodded and left. She bowed, deep and long, and smiled. She had borrowed Joseph, on his accordion, and he struck a tentative note. And then the lively "Cielito Lindo," a bright tune up from the lands below the border. She sang well. Windsor watched, fascinated. She received polite applause, and he knew why. She wasn't connecting. In vaudeville, you play your audience, you nearly reach out and touch those people. Her voice sailed straight over their heads, and died at the farthest walls.

Two more ballads, same response. Not bad. She really did have a sweet voice, and a discipline rarely seen on the variety stage. Not bad at all, just not a success, and not really vaudeville. For her, it had been another recital.

But Beausoleil had filled some time, kept his patched-up show out there, in the limelight, everyone digging deep to entertain this Butte crowd. Windsor watched the girl, wondering if she could read the performance, and decided she could. She left the stage quietly, even as Beausoleil led the crowd through a final round of applause. And then she was alone again, hugging the dark, while the rest of the crowd steered away from her because that was plainly what she wanted.

"The one, the only Wildroot Sisters," the majordomo was saying.

Windsor headed her way. "Good start, sweetheart. You'll get the hang of it soon."

"I forgot to sing to the gent in the fifth row," she said, smiling suddenly. "The bald gent with the big wife wearing fake pearls."

"Yeah, I try to talk to the wiseacre in the seventh row, the guy who's going to head for the saloon and tell the town my act was lousy." He had trouble saying that, but it didn't matter. This was whisper time, with the three girls out there, getting primed to wail away.

214

"It's not like I thought it would be."

"It's better, sweetheart. Wait until you connect. Wait until that guy in the fifth starts nodding or grinning or mouthing words, until his wife elbows him and the couple behind him catch the fever."

"I hadn't thought of that. I'd thought of a perfect high C, or a slight pause, or a gentle fade, or making sure I didn't betray the composer."

"You've been trained, right?"

She seemed to freeze up a moment, and then nodded.

"Throw it out. Make use of it, but throw it out. Next time you sing a song, put a stamp on it. It'll be yours more than whoever wrote it."

"That would be—a sacrilege," she said.

"Then commit sacrilege."

He swore she turned pale, there in the shadows, as she absorbed that, while the sisters out front were doing a high step. She smiled, excused herself, and headed toward the safety of the Green Room.

She'd never make it. She should go back to giving recitals at tea parties. They came, they went, they had a round or two onstage, and they disappeared. He'd seen a thousand, each hopeful, each with stars in her eyes or a smile on his lips, and they didn't pass muster, and after a few tries, they knew it. And left the stage.

Windsor listened a while. The audience wasn't exactly giving the Wildroot girls the big huzzah, either, but they were professionals, and they could even turn an act around in the middle, picking up a better beat.

Beausoleil didn't look happy. But this was the last shot in Butte. What did it matter. Openings, those counted.

Windsor found himself itching to escape. They wouldn't use him this eve. He thought of Butte, raw, cruel, teeming with ruffians who had muscle and no brains, and not enough schooling to fill a third-grade classroom. He pulled a coat over himself, slid out the stage door, and into a black night while arctic winds caught his sore cheeks and tugged at his bowler.

Any saloon would do. No one knew him. A drink or two or three would comfort him. He needed several to quiet the pain. And he could watch the animals, watch them sip ale and tell stories. He drifted upslope and east, and found himself at the edge of the commercial district, staring into a well-lit eatery. It looked to be crowded, the patrons all male. He suddenly realized he was starved. He had eaten little; his lacerated tongue and lips and mouth simply hurt too much. But now a ravenous need propelled him into the warmth and cheer.

These were rough men, ruddy, and cheerful. And he didn't understand a word they were saying. It seemed to be English, but he swore it was some dialect beyond his fathoming, with broad yeowls and mews and barks. But the fragrance of food caught him squarely. These men were mostly buying a single product, a warm pastry served in a paper wrapper. The customers collected one, sat down at trestle tables, and devoured the fragrant thing, eating it straight out of the paper.

"What'll she be, boyo?"

"That," he said, lacking a name.

The server wrapped one up, handed it to him, and muttered a price, some amount he couldn't understand.

"Two bits," said the customer behind him. "Beef pasty, a quarter."

Windsor paid.

"New here, eh? These are Cornishmen, and their English is so thick you need to slice it with a knife."

"I hope I can eat this. I need something soft," Windsor said.

"Half the miners in Butte lack most of their teeth," the man said, as he picked up his own pasty. "Have a seat, and I'll tell you a little about this town."

They found room at the trestle table, and settled on its bench. Windsor bit gingerly into the hot pastry, and was rewarded with some tasty, soft mixture within, mostly beef that had been reduced to small pieces.

"Your first one? It's cubed beef, onions, and

potatoes, baked in a pastry shell. Miners love them, take them into the pits, call them 'letters from home.' They're a filling meal, no fork needed, usually still warm in their lunch buckets. And a Cornish delicacy."

Windsor swallowed gingerly, having no trouble working the tasty food past all his wounds.

"Good," Windsor said.

"Lots of Cornish here, sir. They were miners in Cornwall, had the knowledge to help over here. They're often shift bosses, or people with special skills, putting all they know to work."

The pasty filling was warm and fragrant, and slid down easily. Windsor thought he might like a little more spice, but this was a good hearty meal, and he was filling his empty stomach with little bits of pasty.

"We've got all sorts flooding in. Norwegians, Finns, they're the ones to work with wood, and they do the timbering of the mines, employing skills they seem to have been born with. Seems like just about every corner of Europe is sending people here, each with a specialty."

"And you, sir?"

"Shift foreman, actually German."

"You'd come here into a workingman's restaurant?"

The German stared at him. "In Butte, sir, every-one's a workingman. Including the owners."

"But there's no plates and napkins and silverware and all. Why come here when you can enjoy better?"

The foreman eyed Windsor, somehow assessing him, and smiled, a recognition.

Windsor was suddenly aware of his battered face, the notoriety, the papers, and knew he'd been found out.

"And all you get along?" he asked.

"No. The Irish jump the Cousin Jacks; the Cornish wreck dago restaurants; the wops bust every mug in an Irish saloon; the bohunks heckle the norskies, and once in a while someone gets hurt. Like you. It's a matter of national pride."

"What are Cousin Jacks?"

"Cornishmen. Half of them are Jack, so that's the name for them all."

Windsor watched the foreman polish off his pasty and wipe his hands on the paper.

"I saw your act," the man said. "The best was when you were mimicking the immigrants, when you had Norwegians trying to talk to Hungarians in rough English, and everyone got a little crazy."

"That didn't bother you?"

"Windsor, that's Butte humor."

"I thought you kill each other when you can."

"That's in between laughing at each other."

"Then why did the Irish do this to me?" Windsor pointed at his bruises.

"You've got to understand the rough humor

here. If you'd just laughed, they'd have bought you a mug of ale."

"But they were going to take me into the pits."

"Just to see you soak your pants, my boy. All you had to do was grin back. Now, it's getting on to shift time, and I'm heading toward the Anaconda to put in my hours. Want to come along? See how it is, a thousand feet down, and hot as the tropics?"

"Sir, I'd be scared."

"Well, fella, I'd be scared standing up in front of an audience and spinning out jokes and stories. I think I'd be the one staining my britches, my friend. Whenever I tell a joke I forget the finish, and feel like an idiot. It's what you're used to, and what you can bear. I couldn't stand it, myself."

The gent clamped a shapeless fedora over his head, headed into the night, and left Wayne Windsor sitting alone at the bench, contemplating a world he little understood, but had suddenly started to appreciate.

Maybe he'd be healed up by the time they opened in Philipsburg, a booming mining town a little ways away. Another pasty, and some more good company, and Windsor would be ready to go once again.

23

The Butte box office wasn't bad. August Beausoleil sat with the opera house owner in John Maguire's dim-lit office, counting out the singles and two-spots and change. There was hardly a fiver or a ten in the lot.

This final night they had filled most of the seats; another seventy would have packed the house.

"Pretty good," said Maguire.

"Nothing to complain about. Are we even?"

"Far as I know. You want to stow it in the safe?"

The troupe wouldn't be leaving Butte until mid-morning. "Best place," August said.

"You'll be the first road company to play Philipsburg," Maguire said. "Let me know how it went."

"Three-hundred-fifty seats; matinee and evening."

He and Maguire knew the Follies would need to fill the house both performances to come out ahead. And there would have to be no surprises. That was the thing with a touring company: no matter how carefully you worked out the arrangements, the acts, the accommodations, the travel, there always were surprises. And the only thing between you and disaster sometimes was the cash box.

"Enjoy Butte?" Maguire asked.

"Not enough people speak English."

Maguire smiled. "They know how to count. And miners make a good day wage, usually three and a half. And they spend it."

They did spend it. Unlike people in a farming town. There was a lot of cash circulating in Butte. And miners were not the sort to save and scrimp.

"August, I'm pleased you booked the house." The natty Maguire, in his dove-gray waistcoat and tailored coat, offered a hand, and Beausoleil took it.

"You helped us through some troubles, John."

"That's the biz," Maguire said. He slid the cash box into a small safe and spun the dial.

The house was dark, save for a single lamp high up. Beausoleil was feeling that odd loneliness he always experienced upon finishing an engagement. No sooner did he have a relationship with a town than he was torn from it. He couldn't explain it, and it made no sense. The next town would probably be better. The future was always better than the past.

Out on the cold reaches of Broadway, he discovered Mrs. McGivers waiting patiently for him. "Caught you. You're not going to bed yet. The night's halfway along."

"Mrs. McGivers—I'm worn."

"We have business. And I'm buying you a drink and a supper."

She stood there, formidable, the wind whipping her thin coat, the monkey nowhere in sight. He knew what the business was. Her act had been a disaster this eve; it never caught the crowd, people yawned. Ethel Wildroot and what's-his-name were no substitute for the monkeys, and messed it up. Calypso had an odd beat, an odd secondary syncopation, and this evening nothing worked. It hurt just to watch the disaster unfold on his stage. She was going to apologize, or maybe propose changes, or who knows?

"Okay. We don't have to get up early," he said. "Ten o'clock at the station."

She steered him south, the wind at their backs, while the commercial district faded into nondescript two-story shops, and then into something else entirely. She was taking him straight into the district. Butte's bordellos were famous and sprawled over several square blocks, and did a booming trade with a few thousand miners on the loose, shift after shift. He eyed the area curiously. Lamplight from windows spilled on the cobbled street. Which street, he wasn't sure. It didn't matter. She steered him past hurdy-gurdies, noisy saloons, dark and quiet buildings with a single lamp at the door. There were few pedestrians, all male, braving the night air eddying off the peaks above Butte.

"Here," she said. "Number fifty-two."

She opened upon a well-lit saloon, with a small

stage, and an adjoining eatery to the left. And a stairway along one wall, leading upward to whatever was going on up there in Butte, Montana, in November, 1896.

The bar was doing a trade; keeps in soiled aprons were serving up what probably was rotgut. But these precincts were not all male. Here and there were gaudy serving girls, in wrappers, who seemed available for anything a customer desired.

"We'll eat," Mrs. McGivers said.

"I could use a bite."

"They serve stew out of a pot, two bits, and drinks are one bit."

He knew the stew would be bland, and without flavor, but it would do on a cold night. Butte's food matched its weather, he had discovered. A lady with peroxide hair, in a blue kimono that hung loose, took their order, and brought him a bourbon.

"You like it?" Mrs. McGivers asked.

"It's as good as any, I guess."

"I bought it this afternoon."

That stopped a lot of conversation. She smiled, lifted her glass, and touched it to his.

"I've got seven girls upstairs, a suite to live in, me and Joseph and Abel, a stage to play on if I feel like it, a bar, and this eatery. How's that, do you think?"

"Well, your monkeys knew how to rattle the tin cups, didn't they?"

"Hell yes," she said. "Some shows, twenty, thirty dollars. Who could resist giving a dime to two monkeys, more on matinee days?"

He sipped the bourbon. Or whatever it was. It tasted like varnish. He remembered sipping stuff like that on State Street in Chicago.

"Okay, what?" he asked. This all had sudden implications.

"Crappy act today."

He nodded.

"Ethel Wildroot, God love her, she's no damned monkey. And neither is whatever his name is, Cromwell. And Joseph, he wasn't caring, and Abel, he's in mourning. So you got the worst performance on the tour, from an act that flew apart and can't be put together again."

He grinned. It was all shaping up.

"You saying adios, are you?"

"If you need me, August, I'll play a few shows until you can get another act."

"I'll miss you, Mrs. McGivers."

"I'll miss you, too, August. It was a great tour. You're a great manager. We had some good shows."

"Long way from home, I guess."

"Not so long. I was born in Scotland. Cold weather, it's not something I've never seen."

"I know nothing about you."

She smiled. "I guess you never will. But now I'm a madam, with a dive in Butte, and some commercial ladies upstairs, and a monkey who's ready to retire and entertain the customers. Joseph gets in free. So do you."

"I'd sure like to know more about you."

"If I started confessing, they'd lock me up."

"Do they know you here? These people?"

"Not yet. They will tomorrow. . . ." She let it remain a question.

"Tonight, if you wish," he said.

She laughed suddenly. A big, hearty, meaty yowl. "Maybe I'll move in. Joseph's got the itch. And Abel's telling me he's half froze. That hotel is not tropical."

"Mrs. McGivers, I'll be leaving a piece of myself here. The show, it'll be leaving a lot of itself in Butte. I suppose we should celebrate, but the truth of it is that I'm feeling blue."

"August, you need to get laid."

The kimono-clad bleached blonde showed up with gray stew, which August ate delicately, fearful of an upset stomach. But the stuff settled amiably in his belly, and he supposed he would survive Mrs. McGivers' famous and maybe dubious hospitality. He wondered if the blonde was a working girl. They probably were all working girls.

"I'll have Joseph bring the stuff, and the monkey," she said. "We've got a big square room at the back, upstairs where I can keep an eye on the ladies."

"You stay; I'll tell Joseph," he said. "He can bring the monkey and your stuff."

"I got a woolen scarf," she said. "The little guy wraps it round and round, and pretty soon there's nothing but wool and a tail."

She laughed, big and booming again, and reached across the table to kiss him.

He sat there, amazed. He had just lost an act. A woman he loved, and her entourage. Life flowed on around them: men at the bar, ladies serving stew, stairs leading to quieter precincts. The loss of a monkey had killed her act, but maybe Butte had killed it, too. Butte was where everything happened. A troupe might arrive in Butte for a run at Maguire's Opera House, and it wouldn't remain the same company for long.

She knew what he was thinking, and patted his hand.

"Whenever you come here, everything's free," she said. "On the house."

They laughed.

"You won't get rich," he said.

"There's always a way, a door, a future, if you're willing," she said. "Lots, they aren't.

"Well, if I'm free . . . ," she added, pausing, waiting for a nod, "I'd better move in. And tell the bunch here. They don't know."

He nodded, stood, and welcomed her hug.

"Thank you, August. Not everyone would do that."

That was true. But he had learned a few things about acts, and one of them was that unhappy acts made bad vaudeville. He smiled, clapped his hat on, and sailed into the night, not looking back.

The air was still and crisp, and it was an easy hike up to the hotel. He liked Butte. But he kept a wary eye for footpads. One could never know, around Butte.

He found Joseph, the accordion, some packed bags, and the monkey in the hotel room.

"It's fine," August said.

"Yah, good," Joseph said. "Hey, it's auf Wiedersehen, eh?"

"I'll fetch a cab if I can. The city never sleeps."

Abel perched on the rumpled bed, subdued. The star of the Beausoleil Brothers Follies seemed mournful since his pal had vanished. August realized he had never touched the little fellow, and was more inclined to cuss him. But suddenly everything had changed.

"You mind?" he asked Joseph, reaching for the monkey.

Joseph grinned. He was watching closely.

August picked up the little fellow, feeling the surprising weight in his arms. The monkey snugged right in, his little paws clasping Beausoleil's arm. It was an odd feeling, holding this creature so like a child. He held the monkey for a bit, found the long gray scarf, and wrapped it around the monkey, who helped him with it. There was a blue child's receiving blanket, too, and August caught it up and wrapped that around the monkey, who rewarded August by pulling the blanket up over his monkish head and burrowing into it.

Beausoleil had never had children. He had lived a while with a Latvian woman, Katrina, who had drifted away, or maybe he had drifted away, and he knew he was a stranger to hearth or home. He had grown up on the streets and scarcely knew what a quiet, serene home might be. There had been two or three other women, mostly very young and worldly, but never a home. Never a quiet refuge from the world. Never a Christmas tree, with strings of popcorn on it. Now, with Abel snugged deep into wool and bundled in his arms, he suddenly longed for the thing he had never had: a warm hearth, a home, a welcoming wife.

Joseph wrestled bags and accordion down the narrow hall, down a flight, to the lobby, while August followed with the bundled-up monkey, who curled trusting in his arms.

The deskman summoned a cross-eyed boy, who braved the night to find a hack, and after a few minutes one rolled up, the back of the dray horse frosted, the driver's breath a haze in the deeps.

The monkey shivered. The hack driver loaded bags and the accordion, and then Joseph climbed into the cold interior. August handed the bundled monkey to Joseph, feeling as if something had been torn away from him. Joseph gathered the bundle, and pulled the monkey tight against his massive chest, his big hands cupping the blanket.

The cab door snapped shut. The driver clambered up, slapped the lines, and the cab, carrying the best act, carrying a creature August hadn't realized he loved until that very moment, slipped into the hushed Butte night.

24

August Beausoleil woke up to a grim day. He had to move his troupe to Philipsburg, a miserable U-shaped route involving two transfers, and at the same time revamp his broken company. There would be a matinee and evening performance the next day at the new opera house there. He collected his company at the Butte station, told them that Mrs. McGivers had departed, and that he would be revamping the show en route.

"Not her," said Delilah Marbury. "She held it together."

"Her act died when Cain died," August said. "She was brave enough to keep on trying."

"What is she doing now?"

"Running a joint."

He spotted some smiles. Wayne Windsor announced he'd be fit to perform the next day, and that helped. But the company was still strained to the breaking point. They boarded a short train, a baggage car and two cigar-stink coaches, that would take them back to Helena, where they would transfer to a westbound Northern Pacific train. The stubby engine soon wrestled them out of the toxic smoke of Butte, and into a serene valley.

The coach had banging wheels, which added to the travel headache, but August didn't have time or energy to lament. He found Ethel Wildroot, sitting with the new man, Cromwell Perkins. The sisters were huddled together in the seats ahead.

"You have an act yet?" he asked.

Perkins started to reply, but Ethel cut him off. "We've tried to come up with something."

"In other words, no." He stared at Perkins. "This one won't get you any drinks. But sometimes things work. Could you insult everyone in Philipsburg—the town, the miners, their kin, and anyone else around there?"

"Mr. Beausoleil, sir, I am in a class by myself when it comes to insult." He turned to Ethel. "Just ask me what I think of the locals."

"You sure you want to do this?" she asked August.

He smiled. "It's practice. We're out of there after one day. What I want is to get him cranked up for Missoula. It's a college town. Be merciless."

"I loathe college students, miserable parasites bleeding their fathers of fortunes, learning how to ruin their own lives."

August thought he could like the man.

"We'll try an olio act, three or four minutes, for the matinee. Expand it to seven or eight in the evening. If they don't threaten to put you in the hospital, I'll call it failure."

"At last, a chance to enjoy life," The Genius said.

"It's a small house. People halfway back can toss the tomatoes. It's also new. We're the first big show." He smiled. "Maybe the last. If you don't rile them up, I'll hook you."

Perkins was mystified, so Ethel explained. "It's a big hook on a stick, to drag off people who are boring the house half to death."

"As long as I can use it on you, I'm fine with it," The Genius said.

That was a novelty. August wondered whether there were moments when he should be hooked. He headed down the aisle to Ginger, who sat alone, staring out the window. She wore a gray teacherish suit, almost as if it were armor. The coach was chilly. She had been almost aloof since joining the troupe, and August could only guess at the reasons. Maybe show business wasn't the lark she had imagined when she fled from somewhere or other.

"May I?" he asked, sliding in beside her before she responded.

"I'm revamping the show," he said. "You know. What act follows what act. How do you think you did last night?"

She looked uncomfortable. "I tried to do what you asked," she said.

"And?"

"There was, I don't know how to describe it. An invisible wall. A glass wall between me and the audience. It's as if my voice stopped traveling."

"Your voice reaches the rear. I checked."

"Then I don't know. They applauded."

"Yes, they did," he said. They applauded politely, waiting for the next act. There were all types of applause, and they all sent messages, and the message they sent Ginger was indifference.

"No one wanted an encore," she said.

"Maybe you could experiment some. Different songs. You must have lots."

"But I haven't practiced them."

"It's not a recital, Ginger."

She brightened suddenly. "It's not at all like I thought. I mean, I'm trained. My voice is good. I was considered a prodigy. They all said so. I always thought that was it. I was at the top, the whole world would see it." She smiled. "Some joke."

"I wish you could be a saloon singer. Up close, getting something back from the people watching you, people with drinks in hand, and you a few feet away, trying to entertain them."

"Entertain them?"

"Of course. Entertain them."

She seemed puzzled. "But I perform."

He grinned. "Ginger, try something different. A nice, sentimental ballad or two. Don't worry about getting high C or B flat right. Just wink at some gent, and see if he winks back."

"I don't know how you put up with me," she said.

"I know some reporters," he said. "They tell me about their training. How to write a lead that's interesting. How to make sure the story has a who, when, why, where. The four Ws, they call it. How to catch a reader's attention. How to be spare, not waste words. Good reporters, with years of training, years of mastering the art, the lore. And you know what? One or two of them switched to writing novels, and they crashed. They said it's different; they had to unlearn everything they had mastered as newsmen. The lore didn't help them write a novel. They lacked voice, the personal thing a novelist puts into his work. Maybe it's that way for you."

She stared out the window at the passing slopes. "Maybe I was naïve," she said.

"I'm not giving up on you, Ginger. Let's just see what you do. Let's see what part of yourself you put out there."

"Oh, well," she said, not believing.

"Philipsburg is a good place to try something new. Brief engagement. Then on to Missoula, and big crowds."

"Maybe this is a train to nowhere," she said.

The engine lurched around a bend, the bad roadbed bucking the coach, and August patted her hand and left her there. Show business wasn't whatever she had dreamed long before. But she was flexible.

They were passing through anonymous forest that largely blotted out the scenery, so the train seemed to crawl through a place of no beginnings and no endings.

Wayne Windsor was sitting on an aisle seat, but there was space across the aisle, so August settled there. Windsor was no longer masking his damaged face with high collars and scarves.

"You'll play tomorrow?"

"One act, maybe two for the matinee. I'm talking, anyway."

"Small house," August said. "But we don't know much about it. No big show's played there."

"I didn't think I'd ever love a monkey," Windsor said. "But I do. She had a great act, Monkey Band. It loosened people up. I always wanted to follow her, because everyone would be in a cheerful mood."

"Butte air's hard on monkeys."

"She bought a joint?"

"Whatever it is. With a little stage. She's still got some box office. Along with a bar and some working girls."

"I never thought she'd end up in Butte. Cuba, maybe, but not Butte."

"Where will you end up, Wayne?"

"In a big city, full of people. Not Montana. This is the hardest tour I've been on."

"Yeah, and a lot still left. Thanks for sticking with me, Wayne. You're the draw now, always were."

Windsor sighed, rubbed his wounded profile, and stared at the anonymous forest. Montana was a lot of nothing.

August managed to visit with each of the people in the company, as the train huffed north. The Marbury trio were doing fine; Harry the Juggler was as surly as usual. LaVerne Wildroot was cheerful. The other girls were a little blue. It would be their last tour, and they knew that, though nothing had been said about it.

"Your music's holding it together," August said. "You're out there when I need you."

They probably didn't believe it.

Butte sliding away, minute by minute. Mary Mabel Markey dead and buried there, lying beside a thousand miners who died young. Mrs. McGivers and the remains of her Monkey Band running a joint there. One monkey left. He felt an odd pang. Ever since he had carried Abel down to the waiting hack, swathed in wool, he had known that Cain and Abel were the true stars of the Follies. It took death to give him some insight.

They waited in a sturdy frame station off Last Chance Gulch for the Seattle Express, which

236

would whistle its way to Garrison Junction, and another square-wheeled local that would shuttle them down to the sprawling silver camp that would soon see the first touring variety show ever to show up there. He hoped Pomerantz would meet them and settle them there. He knew the turf.

By the time the troupe finally boarded the train to Philipsburg, which consisted of three box cars, a gondola, an ancient coach, and a caboose, everyone was ready to crawl under two blankets and into bed. August could not remember a more grueling and bone-cold trip in all the years he had been on the road with a touring company. He had an odd thought: it was no place for monkeys. Mrs. McGivers had saved the little guy's life, staying back there in that bustling city. Abel and Butte were made for each other.

They chuffed in at dusk, noting a snowy landscape. They had come to the end of the world. If Butte was isolated, Philipsburg was on another planet. The train halted shy of the gravel platform, leaving passengers to wrestle their way along the roadbed after a long step off the coach stair. Whatever was in those boxcars was more important than mere mortals.

But there was Charles Pomerantz, collecting his crowd, opening his arms to his bride, who fell into his embrace as if were the only comfort left to her. The engine hissed steam, which enveloped them and smeared grit on them.

"There's no hacks here, but the hotel's over there. And I've got some boys to help you," Charles said. "The opera house is around the corner, a block beyond that."

Indeed, there were four boys in knickers and leather caps, ready to help. Pomerantz steered the boys to the larger trunks and satchels, and studied the troupe.

"Am I missing something?" he asked.

"We've got a lot to talk about. Including changes in the playbills," August said.

"Where's the show? I mean, the acts?"

"We've got a show. Just not the show we had when you left Butte."

"Mrs. McGivers?"

"Dead monkey. She pulled out, opened shop in Butte. Don't ask what she's selling."

Something heavy settled on Pomerantz. "Okay, we'll work it out. The paper wanted to interview her." He stood on the platform—the town had an unheated station—counting his company, act by act. He seemed almost to forget his bride, who clung to his arm, her face strained in the dusk.

They walked slowly toward the clapboard-sided hotel, two stories with barracks windows in a military row. Pomerantz finally turned to Ginger.

"How did it go, sweetheart?"

She didn't answer at first, choosing her words. "All right. I guess."

"She's off to a good start," August said.

He and Pomerantz exchanged a glance. "And how's the advance?" August asked.

"We've got a good house. We'll sell out the matinee. Maybe the evening."

They passed a building with a playbill plastered to it. Mary Mabel Markey, it said. Wayne Windsor. Mrs. McGivers and Her Monkey Band. The juggler. The trio, the Wildroot Sisters.

"Who's that?" Pomerantz asked, pointing at Cromwell Perkins.

"New act, The Genius and Ethel," August said.

For once, Charles smiled. "Where did he come from?"

"Ethel collected him from a saloon. He's a bar rail comic."

"What'll he do?"

"Insult the crowd, I hope."

Charles Pomerantz wheezed, laughed, and steered his weary bunch into the small hotel, which at last offered a modicum of comfort. "We'll put on a hell of a show," he said.

25

Mrs. Charles Pomerantz lay abed homesick. The hotel room was small, mean, and cold. Barely enough morning light filtered through a listless curtain for her to see her quarters. Her husband had hastily abandoned the room, en route to Missoula again, to publicize changes in the show.

Her brief moment with him had been melancholic. From the moment he met the troupe, stepping off the bone-jarring coach, he and August Beausoleil had been consulting, and he had barely given her a kiss on the cheek, much less the warm embrace a newlywed woman might expect.

He had, finally, unlocked the door and entered, long after she had pulled the covers over her and tried to banish the chill. He lit a lamp, eyed her, kept his long johns on, and slipped into the narrow bed beside her.

"Glad you're here, sweetheart," he said. "Sorry to be so busy. But we'll have some time in Missoula."

"Oh, Charles . . ."

"I hear good things about your act," he said.

"That's more than I hear."

"We've had to change the billing. You'll be on the playbill. How's that?"

Oddly, she didn't care. "That's more than I expected," she said.

"I'm worn-out. Nothing but troubles these days, losing our biggest draws. I'll be out of here before you're up; see you down the road."

He squeezed her cold hand, turned his back to her, and swiftly fell into a soft snore.

She didn't sleep. The cold made the wooden

hotel snap and creak and pop, startling her. The stranger she called husband lay inert, not caring, not holding her tight, not kissing, not even wondering how she fared, or how she had spent the long, hard day. Everything for him was the show.

She turned away, on the cold pillow in the cold room under the cold blankets, next to a cold husband, and wished she were somewhere else.

Like home.

A handsome, spacious, secure home. Her family. Comfort. They cared about her, showed her off. Pocatello was clean and gracious, with grand vistas in most directions. She had never shivered in bed in her life. Even the thought of her intense mother, who treated her like a windup doll, didn't seem so awful, the way it had a few weeks earlier.

She wondered if she should go back. She could disappear back to her home, just as she had disappeared from her home, took a new name, and left no trail. She could abandon Charles Pomerantz, abandon the show, abandon Ginger, and walk through the door as Penelope, virginal, unmarried, a prodigy who was the wonder of southern Idaho. Not say a word; just return to her own home, her own spacious bedroom, resume the name she had abandoned, and let them wonder where she had been.

If she was not pregnant. She wished she knew.

She didn't know much about anything, and there was no one she could ask. Maybe she couldn't go home again; maybe she couldn't be a vaudeville player, either. Maybe she would be a mother whether she wanted to or not, at age eighteen. She corrected herself. Nineteen, if it happened. That made her all the more homesick. Maybe she couldn't go back home. Maybe she was doomed, a castaway of some worldly impresario, who probably had more women than he could remember.

She watched him awaken, get up, vanish down the hall to the water closet at the end. She had barely seen a man do his morning rituals, scrape away beard, comb his hair. Men were mysteries. One moment he was fawning over her, kissing and seducing, and the next he was doing business. He would soon return, dress, abandon her without a word unless she lit the lamp and waited for his morning greeting.

She did that. She lifted the glass chimney, struck a match, and lit the bedside kerosene lamp. It slowly bloomed to life.

When he returned, he was shaven and combed.

"Well, well," he said, discovering her staring, the lamp spilling yellow light over her and piercing into the dark corners of the room.

"Are we married?" she asked.

"I'd have to check," he said.

"I don't think I like this business, and I might go away somewhere."

He paused. He was buttoning a clean shirt, but he stopped.

"Ginger, this is rough on you. Some people aren't cut out for it. Some people try hard, and it defeats them. I hope you'll give it a chance. As for marriage, it's for you, not for me. You're a girl from a proper home, and marriage is the way you feel comfortable in a hotel room with a man. It's what you need." He smiled. "But I'm glad we did it. I'm glad you're my wife."

"I guess that's your declaration of eternal love," she said, and from somewhere a big laugh boiled up in her.

He didn't say a word, but leaned over and kissed her. She tasted mint on his lips.

"I'll stick," she said.

"After Missoula, it's Spokane, and then a few days of downtime. Just right for us to figure out who we got married to," he said. "Damned if I know."

"If I don't find another gentleman first," she said.

That startled him more than it startled her. "I think you're gonna fit right into the business," he said, but she thought there was an edge in his voice.

She watched him tie his blue polka-dot cravat and straighten it, shrug into his fawn waistcoat and button it, climb into his gray woolen suit coat, and eye himself. These theater men were natty dressers; they were careful with appearances. He looked to be a man of substance, no matter what condition the show was in.

"We've got a big rendezvous in Missoula," he said. "It'll knock your socks off."

"We'll see whose socks come off," she said.

His eyes lit up.

He lifted his black bowler, saluted her with it, collected his bag, and vanished. She stared at the door. That had been her husband and now her husband was going away to a town she knew nothing about, but was probably evil since it harbored the state college.

She wasn't homesick anymore. In fact, she wanted only to find a place to practice, to try some other songs she knew, to see about hugging her entire audience. The hour was early, the sun not yet sailing, but she could not bear her hotel room another minute. It took only a little while to don her gray travel suit and slip outside, discovering an oddly mild day and an orderly city in a broad valley, built around a smelter. Philipsburg lay in the heart of a silver mining district, but the mines were well away from the town.

She saw hardly a soul on the streets, and certainly did not expect to discover any of her troupe. Show people rose late and retired late. But she had always flown into each day from its very start, because that's how she was. She would soon sing to those who lived in this place. Who were they? What would they enjoy? Could she please them? The one thing she had garnered from her brief visit was that this town was orderly and its cottages well kept. But what did that imply for her performance? She felt a little foolish for even wondering about it. What was she? An eighteen-year-old prodigy? A genius, able to fathom an audience and respond to it? A canary in a cage.

She was amused by her own presumptuousness. She felt the weight of her parents' expectations, and knew it was a millstone on her back, and she should escape that burden once and for all. That was one thing about vaudeville: she wasn't in a concert hall singing grand opera.

She spotted a well-lit café, and decided it was time for breakfast. Uneasily—she had yet to live life on her own terms, her own volition—she entered, discovered an all-male patronage, with one exception. Ethel Wildroot sat at a table, a coffee cup before her. Ethel saw her at once, and hailed her. Hesitantly, Ginger joined the mother of rival singers, wondering where all this might lead. Discomfort, probably.

"You're up early. A rara avis in show biz," Ethel said. "Park your little rear in the chair, and tell me about it."

There was always something a little edgy in Ethel, and it made Ginger smile. She settled in the chair, and soon was ordering a bowl of oatmeal and tea. Ethel was demolishing a breakfast steak that a smelterman would have considered large.

"So, how do you like the Beausoleil show?" she asked, sawing a piece of pink meat loose.

Ginger was discreet. "I don't think I'll be in it long," she said. "All I really want is to be a good mate to Charles."

"Oh, horse apples. Your act isn't catching on, and I can tell you why."

"August wants me to sing to my audience, and I'm doing that."

"Well, that's half of it," Ethel said, sawing another slab of meat off the steak. "You've got everything you need. Great voice, fine training, poise, all that." She waved a knife. "But you can't just be the goddess, singing songs."

Ginger braced herself. Something was about to knock over the tenpins.

"Girl like you, you should talk to them. You go out there, smile, start a song, and you never talk to them. That's a killer. You come from a concert background. I can tell. Concerts, you just stand there and sing. Or start playing the piano, or whatever. Well, that's what the fuddy-duddies want. Hold your hands together, stare at the far wall, and sing. But this is vaudeville, sweetheart. Quit being the Virgin Queen."

The waiter arrived with a bowl of cereal, and Ginger made a great show of spooning it.

"Talk to them, dammit. Don't just clasp your hands together and start warbling away. Hey, they're people, just like you. And don't be so polite, either. Don't thank them. August, that's his job. He thanks them for coming. You, though, that's not your job. You need to connect with them. Just get it through your head. Be their best friend."

"What would I say?"

Ethel masticated the beef a little, and then smiled. "Hey, that Mexican drill. Don't just sing it. Say it's cold around here, and maybe the way to warm up is to sing something south of the border, and maybe something about a señorita. And tell all those miners, they'd like to hear something about a señorita."

"I'd need a script, Ethel."

Ethel waved her spoon. "If you need a script, you shouldn't be in vaudeville. All you do is introduce the song, tell them about it, about yourself a little."

"Myself?"

"Tell 'em you've been singing all your life, and it's much more fun singing for a lot of grown-up men. You've been waiting for the chance!"

"That's too forward, don't you think?"

Ethel sighed. "You probably shouldn't be in the business, sweetheart."

The curtain rolled down, or so Ginger thought. But Ethel wasn't done. "You've got the best voice in the company. Sure beats my girls and LaVerne. That kind of voice, you can wind a man around your little finger. It's sweet and sultry."

"Sultry?"

"You haven't been married long enough to figure that out, Ginger."

"I haven't figured anything out yet," Ginger said.

"Charles, he'll be a good husband if you keep a leash on him."

"So far, it's been a few hotel rooms. Neither of us know why we did it. It sort of bubbled up. But he just smiles and says it'll be fine."

Ethel eyed her assessingly. "Beautiful, naïve, innocent maiden."

Ginger pulled into herself. Somehow, marriage, show business, this new world, were full of shoals that could sink her. These were worldly people, and she knew she was nothing but a small-town girl adventuring into a hard world.

"Hey, Mrs. Pomerantz, if you need any crystal ball reading, call on me. I know a few things about men," Ethel said.

Ginger was itching just to spill out everything she didn't know, every mystery of marriage, every odd thing about males, why they shaved, what they expected, who they thought they were, and how a wife fit in.

Ethel sensed it, and patted Ginger's hand. "You're the star of the show, sweetheart. You just don't know it yet."

26

Show day. August Beausoleil hurried through a late November chill to the glistening opera house operated by Marshal McFarland. It stood a block from the hotel, seven or eight from the smelter grounds. The hotel had been cold, and his body felt numb. He found the place, noted that it was devoid of ornament, a utilitarian frame and fieldstone structure washed white. A playbill in a case at the front touted the Follies. He found a side door and entered, only to meet with a blast of icy air. A side corridor opened on the auditorium, also bone cold and dark, and led to a small cubicle where, August hoped, he would find the proprietor.

That office was as cold as the rest, but at least McFarland was present, wrapped in a woolen waistcoat, gray woolen pants, and a woolen coat. A loose scarf lay about his neck and fell down his chest.

"Beausoleil, is it? You're late," the manager said. His mantel clock announced the time as 9:15.

"Sorry, the hotel was slow to serve."

"There's some messages for you, sir," McFarland said, all business. "The Methodist women wish to conduct a bake sale in the lobby before each performance. I said I would let them know as soon as you appeared."

"Bake sale? Breads, muffins, tarts?"

McFarland glared at him. "They raise money for injured miners."

"What are the buyers supposed to do? Sit with an apple pie in their lap during the show?"

"Usually, they throw whatever's in hand at the performers, sir."

"No. No bake sale."

"Then there's Mrs. Wall. Josephine. Wife of the general manager of the Granite Mine. That, sir, is one of the finest silver mines in the country. You would do well to accommodate her."

"Which is what?"

"She wishes to play her harp during the intermission."

"Harp? It takes a couple of strong men to haul a harp around."

"She has footmen in abundance, sir."

"What will she play?"

"She tends toward light airs, sir."

"Is she good?"

"I reserve judgment."

He didn't want her, but knew that rebuffing powerful people might have consequences. "Are you going to start heating up the building?"

"Firewood's dear in Philipsburg, Mr. Beausoleil, and it's a habit in town to get along without it."

"I will want the building fully heated as soon as possible."

"Your footlamps will do it, sir. Light the lamps, and your limelight, and you'll have plenty of warmth. That and a full house, warm bodies."

There was some reality in it, but not much. "Mr. McFarland, our contract provides that you'll supply a house suitably prepared in all respects. And that includes heat."

McFarland looked annoyed, but finally rang a bell, and soon a lackey appeared. "Start the stoves," he told the man.

He turned to Beausoleil. "There are two potbellies flanking the stage."

"I have new acts, and people wish to rehearse, and disease has already damaged my show, sir. We had a death, and the loss of an animal, and that meant two acts down."

"So I heard. We're hardy people here, sir. We don't need all that coddling. Miners are used to having bad lungs, so cold air makes no difference to them. That's reasonable. I'll add a firewood surcharge."

"Surcharge! The contract calls for suitable conditions."

"You're in Montana, Beausoleil. What's suitable here is not suitable for hothouse flowers."

A great clatter interrupted them. McFarland leapt up, opened the door upon two footmen hauling a great, gilded harp on a dolly. And they were followed by a formidable woman, swathed in layers of gabardine formed into a high-button suit.

"That stair there leads up," she said, steering the liveried footmen toward the stage. She spotted McFarland and Beausoleil. "I shall be with you directly, once we station this up on the platform," she said.

Beausoleil wondered how much choice he had in any of this. He watched silently as the experienced men slid the great gilded harp up and onto the dark stage.

"There, that's done," she said. "Marshal, put the heat down. It will affect my arms when I play. I don't want droopy arms."

"This is Mr. Beausoleil, whose company will perform today," McFarland said. "And this, sir, is Madam Wall."

"Mrs. Wall, I'm pleased to meet you. I only now heard of your proposal to play during the intermission, but I'll have to decline your generous offer. All the acts are paid, of course, and the budget doesn't permit the slightest change. But it's most generous of you."

Her face pinched up. "Then put me on. I will play for you, sir."

"I'm afraid that's impossible. We have a regular troupe, you see . . ."

She reached out and patted him on the arm. "My dear sir, you'll accommodate an old lady.

Your audience will forgive you, knowing that my husband can fire the whole lot of them."

She lifted a thick handful of skirt, and climbed to the stage, and settled beside the harp, which she began tuning, sometimes letting her fingers trill out a chord. The notes were throaty and lingering. She was a gray presence on a dark stage.

"It will only be during the intermission, in front of the olio," she said. "The rest of the evening is yours to ruin."

August sighed. Philipsburg had a few surprises, but so did most of the towns he booked. He said nothing. Perhaps the dowager queen of the mining town could stumble through some music. Most of the audience would be out in the lobby, or visiting the water closets, or next door downing a fast one at the Quail saloon. On the other hand, she could chase the crowd away, and the second act would play to a few survivors.

But then, after she had fiddled a little, and ran nimble fingers—probably numb with cold—across the strings, she slipped softly into melody, the name of which he didn't know, but it was sweet and lyrical, and not at all painfully wrought. She was playing on a dark stage, barely lit by light spilling back from the lobby.

It depressed him. Keeping some sort of lid on his show was the hardest of all his tasks.

She was accomplished. He confessed to that.

And she was playing sentimental ballads, the sort of thing a miner might appreciate.

He resolved to say nothing at all. He wouldn't approve; he wouldn't get into a predicament about pay. This was between the formidable lady and McFarland.

"Count me out of it," he told the proprietor. "It's not my show. She's not an act. I don't know what she is."

Marshal McFarland grinned. "She owns the town."

"And I'm not paying for firewood. I'll have my people in here shortly to set up footlights, the limelight, and stow the props. There may be some people practicing. Especially Charles Pomerantz's wife."

He had barely spoken the name when he heard her singing, picking up on a ballad the harpist was playing. Her voice, the harp, the sound was gold. The harp was made for Ginger, and Ginger was made for the harp.

And that meant trouble.

"Now sing one I don't know," Mrs. Wall commanded.

Ginger launched into "Cielito Lindo," singing it in Spanish. Flawlessly, Mrs. Wall added chords and flourishes, creating an eerie beauty even though the song was intended for brass, for a mariachi band. It was a tender thing, this accord between Ginger and the dowager empress of Philipsburg.

August knew when to bend. "All right, Mrs. Wall, you're hired for two performances," he said. "I'll have cash for you after the second show."

"Oh fiddle, I don't want money. I want this child to savage the hearts of those knuckleheads, the smeltermen in the audience. And with a few flourishes from me, she'll do it."

"How shall I introduce you, madam?"

"You won't. Every man and woman in that audience will know who I am. If you introduce me they will applaud, for fear of not applauding. I could wear a mask and they still would know who I am. I could play badly and they would still applaud. They believe my husband knows all, and punishes his critics. They believe he has snitches in the mine, who report to him. Maybe Marshal McFarland is a snitch. Let them think it. In fact, I play quite well. So let them gossip and worry. That's how it all works, you know. Some gossip rescues all enterprises."

Beausoleil gently entertained the notion that Mrs. Wall was a godsend. But swiftly dismissed it. He tended to be superstitious.

A thin warmth began to welcome mortals to the opera house. Ritually, August began a tour of the place. It always helped to know everything. He eyed the olio drop, and lowered it himself, making sure it fell behind the harpist and singer. He walked out to the rear of the auditorium and listened. Ginger's voice carried well. This was a small house. It would likely carry well even when packed, but there were always surprises.

The seats were hard and uncomfortable, rising in slightly canted rows. McFarland had not concerned himself much with comfort, but perhaps he was right. He had the monopoly on entertainment in this place, and his customers could take it or leave it.

They would need footlamps here. He surveyed the front of the stage and found a shallow metal trough intended for the lights. Each light burned inside a hood that threw the light onto the performers and hid the flame from the audience. A mirrored interior assured that the light would be reflected forward, upon the artists. The company carried eight of them, and a limelight, which was also a hooded device, larger, that directed a hot gas flame upon a cylindrical column of quicklime until it threw brilliant white light. He would use that, also. Most of the acts would be as far downstage as he could manage them. Upstage was poorly lit. He could burn a lot of fuels in a single performance. Running a show in an opera house that had not been electrified was far tougher than one that relied on incandescent lights.

Even as the morning quickened, his two hands placed the footlights, made sure their reservoirs were filled, and set up the limelight. He watched Mrs. Wall and Ginger shape an act, and hoped it would work. Instinct told him it might. But who could say what a notional, powerful woman might do?

Around one, his troupe drifted in. The house was almost warm; the footlights and crowd would do the rest. Some had eaten lunch. Others would wait. A few wouldn't touch food until both shows were done. He eyed The Genius, Cromwell Perkins, and hoped for the best. He hoped Ethel, a veteran of the stage, could steer the man away from shoals. An old professional like Ethel was a comfort and consolation to him. She was capable of marching The Genius off the stage if things erupted badly.

A boy showed up with a wire for Ginger. She read it and beamed. Break a leg, it said, and it was from Charles, who was working the advance in Missoula. She was puzzled, momentarily, and then smiled. Well, this would be one hell of a show. New acts, untried talent, new town, cold weather. But that was the business. You bent, you ducked, you stood tall, you improvised, you wrestled the dragons, especially illness, the thing that caused more cancellations than anything else. Especially in cold weather like this.

Outside, a thin layer of cloud softened the sun, but the Saturday was bright and the air was quiet. The smeltermen and their mates and families drifted in. He stood quietly near the box office, watching the crowd, largely male, almost all young, dressed in work clothes for the want of anything finer in their wardrobes. Mostly men, lonely men, bored men who had only a few saloons in this isolated town between themselves and dreariness. Their wives, if they had any, were far away, in the East, in Europe, across the seas. Not here, not in the wilds of a new state. This opera house, where no large company had yet appeared, was the magnet. But they laid down their greenbacks and settled in the hard seats. He did spot a few women, mostly the wives of managers, he guessed. They would be looking for anything that would color their isolated and slow lives.

He saw a reporter, brandishing a pass, come in. There'd be a review, but it wouldn't appear until after the second show, the morning they pulled out. Even so, August itched to read it, and thought to hunt down the twice-weekly paper to see the verdict.

He hoped to give them a memorable time. And if Mrs. Wall said to clap, they would, and if she didn't raise her hands in applause, neither would they. August thought it was the damndest bind he'd been in.

27

August eyed the crowd. The house was full. McFarland had sold some standing-room tickets, and now twenty more stood at the rear. Philipsburg was flocking to the new show in the new theater.

He nodded. A stagehand stepped out, lit the footlights, struck a match to the jets that fired up the limelight, and retreated. It was six minutes past two. The acts waited quietly in the wings. He signaled a stagehand and the curtain parted. This house had draw curtains, and no flies. The limelight caught him in his top hat, tuxedo, white bib, a gold-knobbed cane in hand. Before him, a dim-lit gulf of pale faces peered upward.

"Ladies and gents, welcome to the Beausoleil Brothers Follies," he said. "It's our pleasure to play here in Peoria—or is it Altoona?" He glanced toward the wings, awaiting an instruction, an old joke. "Ah, forgive me, it's the noble city of Philipsburg, Montana. The finest town on the continent!"

They laughed.

"Thank you for coming this cold afternoon. And now, ladies and gents, those gorgeous and talented ladies, the one, the only Wildroot Sisters!"

The girls trotted out along with the accompanist, and away they went. They put their hearts in it; Ethel had drilled that into them. And they always had a good opener to warm up the crowd. They hugged the limelight, a trio of bright-lit song-stresses, a stage full of butterflies.

"What a trio! Give them a hand, ladies and gents. You'll be seeing more of the beautiful Wildroot girls. And now, as a special treat, the country's finest monologuist, the gent who'll tickle your funnybones, the gent who taught Mark Twain how to do it, the one, the only Wayne Windsor!"

He led the applause as Windsor, still a little rocky from his laryngitis, stepped out and was met with polite acceptance. This crowd was male, and it was looking for female entertainment. Windsor had a little spring to his step, no matter how he felt. And a wry smile that anticipated some delicious bon mot. He faced right, then left, letting the crowd admire him.

"I'm pleased to be here, in this great, rich, jewel of the Rockies—at least that's what the mayor says," he began. "I think I'll talk about robber barons today. I'm all for robber barons. Are there any out there? If so, stand up, sir, and take a bow."

He peered out upon a quiet crowd.

"I don't see any. A pity. I was going to heap praise upon him. The world needs robber barons. They clean out pockets of ore; they clean out workingmen's pockets. They clean out the till of every merchant in town."

August watched from the wing. The gifted Windsor had his audience, and that act would be fine. There was always an edge to his humor. He did best picking on someone or something. He rarely reduced an audience to fits of laughter, but his sly humor worked its way through the crowd, gaining chuckles and smiles. And today he was in good form, his voice holding up, bouncing off the rear wall, where those standing customers lounged.

August rolled out the Marbury Trio next. "Ladies and gents, this afternoon you'll see something brand new. Some incredible footwork, called tap dancing, that will make you snap your fingers. It's all the rage in Memphis, and now it's flaming in all directions, conquering audiences everywhere. This is talent, my friends. This is music as you've never felt it. I'm proud to offer you the one, the only, the sensational Marbury Trio."

The trio tapped their way out from the wing, their rhythm perfect, the gents in black dinner jackets, Delilah in a daringly short red skirt. These miners had never seen the like, or heard a dance done with tapping of shoes, and they sat silently, blotting it up, and finally smiling, and even laughing at one of Delilah's extravagant solos. Her partners peeled back, turned her loose in the limelight, where the dress shimmered in the brightness, and her feet lifted into a staccato that was broken now and then by a whirl of the skirts, and a new rhythm. August was suddenly aware he was watching a virtuoso. That was the thing about the business. Something grand always cropped up.

When they took their bows, he applauded along with the happy crowd.

"Weren't they a sight? That was just magnificent. The Marbury Trio. Take that home and tell the world about it." He paused a moment, letting the crowd settle down. "Next, ladies and gents, is Harry the Juggler. He's got three names I can't pronounce, and all I know is that he is not from the South Pole. And he's the best juggler on the planet. It's a miracle he doesn't break all the china in Montana. The one, the only . . . Harry."

That went fine, too. And then it was time to try Ginger. She was waiting quietly in the wings, wearing that white dress of hers that made her all the more girlish.

He signaled, and Josephine Wall's men rolled the golden harp out, but kept it away from the limelight. Mrs. Wall wore a glittering brooch on her bosom.

"And now, friends, a special treat for you all. The loveliest singer you've ever heard, with the voice of an angel. Miss Ginger, my friends, Miss Ginger."

Ginger floated out gently, and settled herself in the limelight, which caressed her white gown. She smiled, took her time.

"I see many faces before me," she said. "I know you come from many countries, far across the sea. And many of you remember the lady you left behind, the one you dream about, the one you hope to bring to the New World . . . someday soon. I will sing 'Far Across the Sea' for you, and for your sweethearts."

She started gently, alone, her voice indescribably rich, rising from some heartland within her, and then Josephine Wall picked up the chords on her harp, instantly catching the melody and mood, not so much playing as adding resonance. Ginger sang to those men, her gaze slipping from one to another, and sometimes to those who stood at the back.

A different sort of applause greeted her. It was respectful and firm, polite and glad. Beausoleil listened knowingly. This was exactly what he had seen in her. A tremor coursed through him. She had added an introduction, and now she had an act.

She sang two more. First, "Frost Upon My Garden," a gentle song about love lost before it could ripen. And once again, Mrs. Wall added the melodic company of her harp, this time with more flourishes than before. It was as though they had practiced this over and over, getting it right. But they hadn't. Mrs. Wall was gifted in her own right, and the honeyed voice and gentle harp seemed made for each other.

There was, oddly, no applause. No one wanted to break the spell Ginger had cast over the darkened theater.

"It's cold outside," she said. "And I think you just might enjoy something spicy and warm, from Old Mexico. Of course it's a love story, too. It's called 'Cielito Lindo,' and it won't be in English, but I think you'll know just what it means."

And that was fun. This one was lively, the middle song had been sad. And after the first chorus, she invited her rapt listeners to join in.

> "Ay, ay, ay, ay,
> sing and don't cry, heavenly one,
> for singing gladdens hearts . . .
> Ay, ay, ay, ay,
> canta y no llores,
> porque cantando se alegran,
> cielito lindo, los corazones."

Now they loved her. With each wave of applause, Mrs. Wall added a resonant flourish of her harp, somehow deepening the acclaim. August watched, feeling the glow work through him. He chose a moment to return to the stage, swept a hand toward Mrs. Wall, who rose and bowed, and then Ginger, who lowered her head a moment, as if saying grace, and then slowly exited the limelight.

That closed the act. The curtains rolled. The cheerful audience drifted out. A hand extinguished the limelight. The footlights soon revealed Mrs. Wall, before an olio, playing intermission music, pale hands plucking harp strings, and plainly enjoying her moment. August looked on, entertained. In the business, who could ever predict a thing?

August led off the next act with the Marbury trio again, this time all three clad in tux and tails, each with an ebony walking stick that doubled as a baton. He had never put them in that spot before and he wanted to see if they launched the second act with gusto. They did, and he moved easily into the rest of the afternoon's entertainment.

"And now, ladies and gents, a brand-new act, The Genius and Ethel. I'm not sure which of them is The Genius, and which of them is Ethel, but you'll figure it out. We found The Genius in a saloon in Butte, and life hasn't been the same since he joined the troupe. I give you the one, the only Genius on the planet, and the one and only Ethel."

The Genius showed up in a brown tweed jacket and a deerstalker hat, and Ethel followed in a dowdy dress that turned her into a sort of pyramid, even as the olio drop closed behind them.

"Well, sir, how did you get to be a genius?" she asked.

"It's my vocation, madam. Some people choose

to be carpenters. Or miners. I chose to be a genius."

"What makes you a genius, sir?"

"My natural superiority, madam. I am the world's greatest expert. I know more about everything than anyone here."

"Well, you don't know much about women," she replied.

The audience enjoyed that.

"Ask me anything, madam, and I'll prove it."

"Okay, genius, tell me how many people are out there watching you."

Perkins swelled up and gave her a withering glare. "More than you or anyone out there can count, so there's no reason to be specific."

"How do you know you're smarter than anyone out there?"

"Madam, that's simple. They live here."

"You don't think much of Philipsburg, do you?"

"Madam, being a genius is lonesome. If there was even one genius out there, one genius equal to me, I'd be happy to live in Philipsburg. Until then, though, I'd have to consider the place poor and deprived."

"I like Philipsburg," she said. "They came to our show."

"That's why they're not geniuses," he said.

The banter went along like that, pretty entertaining, Beausoleil thought. It would be fine if they didn't run too long, or let the joke get pretty thin. It made a light act, a diversion. And they'd probably improve it as they worked the audiences. Maybe Cromwell Perkins could be a little more outrageous.

They quit after a few minutes, and got a good hand. That sort of braggadocio was a novelty, and the miners out there were entertained.

"The Genius and Ethel," Beausoleil said. "Let's hear some applause for Ethel."

That won more cheer.

He ran the acts in order. Harry did his juggling act with knives and scimitars. Wayne Windsor did a brief monologue on misbegotten English, which the miners appreciated, since they were misbegetting English constantly.

And then it was Ginger's turn, and once again Mrs. Wall's men rolled out her golden harp, and Ginger appeared, this time in a powder-blue dress that glowed in the limelight.

"I love ballads because they tell a story," she said. "So I'll sing three ballads now, ballads that seem to rise right out of the longings of people who are far from home. The first is 'Shenandoah.' Across the wide Missouri. I guess a lot of you have left your own Shenandoah behind."

That surely was true. The old American ballad evoked tender thoughts. Beausoleil could see it in their faces. These were men who had come some vast distance across a virgin continent to find a new life here, in an obscure corner of the Rockies.

She sang that and "Swanee River," and "Down in the Valley," and then "My Old Kentucky Home" for an encore, and the hush that followed was more eloquent than applause. She had won hearts here.

It had been a good afternoon, and bore the promise of a fine evening, and in spite of a small opera house, they would do better than break even.

"My dear sir," said Mrs. Wall. "After the evening's show, I would like to invite your entire company to my home for a late supper, and a farewell from the grateful people of Philipsburg," she said. "It would be our farewell."

"I'm sure our people will be delighted," he said. "I'll tell the company."

"It's the house on the hill," she said. "You can't miss it."

She was right. No one in Philipsburg could possibly miss that house.

28

The Steinway grand piano in Mrs. Wall's music room caught Ginger's eye. Near it stood the golden harp. Both instruments seemed out of place in Philipsburg, a raw and hastily built mining town. But there they were, in one of the few brick buildings, a fine Georgian home over-looking much of the town. She had seen only one other Steinway grand piano in the region, and that one was in her parents' house, and she had spent hours at its keyboard. The nearest piano tuner was in Salt Lake; it was journey enough to Pocatello. Bringing a tuner here would require an arduous journey.

The piano evoked memories, and she fled into the spacious parlor and dining area, where the entire cast and crew of the Beausoleil Brothers Follies congregated around a buffet supper, with Mrs. Wall presiding as a vivacious hostess. It was a grand farewell party, even though the company had played Philipsburg only one day. Few in the company had ever been in a home like this.

Ginger saw no sign of Mr. Wall, and presumed he was away somewhere. The Granite Mine lay several miles distant, and by all accounts was a superb producer of silver ore. Mines rarely lasted long, and most mining towns were built with that in mind. But some sort of optimism had embraced this district, and now the Walls were living in a solid home built to last for generations.

Mrs. Wall spotted her and bloomed before her.

"Ah, there you are, Penelope. Come with me to the music room for a little visit."

Ginger's world stopped cold.

"Mrs. Wall, my name is Ginger. Ginger

Pomerantz," she said, the words hollow in her dry throat.

But Mrs. Wall steered her into the quiet music room. "I think not," she said.

"I'm married," Ginger said, feeling her life fall into pieces.

"Of course you are, my dear."

"But I want to thank you for your interest," Ginger said. "Your backing with the harp worked well, I think."

"Would you like to play the piano?" Mrs. Wall asked. "I remember when you were the child prodigy, playing in Pocatello, your hands so small they didn't stretch across an octave. But you played marvelously. Of course you had tutors, brought from distant cities by your parents, to impart the best that the world could offer you."

"I am Ginger, madam, and I'm sure you are thinking of someone else."

"No, my dear. Your father and my husband were classmates and close friends. They still are in touch." She walked to a bric-a-brac and plucked up a portrait in oval gray pasteboard, the gilded name ADAMS BROTHERS, POCATELLO, embossed in its base. The portrait had been taken when the young pianist was sixteen, a time when she was past girlhood and taking lessons from another set of tutors to develop her glorious voice.

"I think it's grand that you are engaging in

show business, even if it's not what your parents expected."

"I think I'm ready to go back to my hotel," Ginger said. "I do want to thank you for the evening."

"Yes, of course. But first you must play me Chopin's Polonaise," Mrs. Wall said. "Here, I'll collect some of your colleagues."

The Polonaise had been Penelope's triumph. Mastered at age fourteen, her body still growing, her hands still maturing. A prodigy. To play it would amount to an admission, but she could think of no way to escape.

Even as Ginger was braving herself to bolt, Mrs. Wall returned with several of the troupe, and then more, and finally August Beausoleil, who eyed her contemplatively, obviously not sure what to make of this.

Very well, then. Ginger seated herself. She would make no apologies. She hadn't played it or practiced on a piano for as long as these people had known her. They would understand. Still, this was something strange, some facet of Ginger they knew nothing about, and now they settled quietly, some of them with hors d'oeuvres in hand.

She glanced at August, wishing he would intervene, send his singer home to rest, but he didn't.

She played, the soft introductory measures, and then the great theme, so familiar to all, played as

271

if she had never stopped playing, her fingers dancing, the Steinway leaping to respond. She played out of desperation, not looking at anything, played in a crowded room lit by a dozen kerosene lamps that lifted heat and light and a faint odor. She played grandly, even as the troupe absorbed this surprising skill in the young wife of Charles Pomerantz.

They didn't applaud, but smiled when her fingers caught the last notes, and the sound lingered.

"Thank you, Mrs. Pomerantz," Mrs. Wall said.

Ginger felt her body sag. The worst had passed. But who could say what might come next?

"That was spendid, Ginger," August said, an odd smile upon him. "I had no idea."

"It isn't often that this piano is put to such good use," their hostess said. "Mining towns— well, they come and go." She smiled. "I'm sure you could offer us a concert, my dear."

"Thank you," was all Ginger could manage.

Was Mrs. Wall implying that all of Ginger's training, and tutors, and practice, was being wasted? Yes, probably.

But maybe this would be the end of it; in the morning they would all be on the shuttle to the Northern Pacific mainline, and then to Missoula. She would leave Mrs. Wall behind. But maybe not.

Nothing more came of it. Mrs. Wall did not corral her. And her name continued to be Ginger Pomerantz. And yet the evening was wreathed with worry, and she knew it would not easily slip away; a night in her hotel bed would accomplish nothing to allay her fears.

Later, carriages and footmen conveyed the troupe to the wooden hotel, and only then did her friends in the company pour out their admiration.

"I had no idea," Ethel Wildroot said. "You have kept it all a secret."

Ginger bobbed her head uncertainly. There were hidden shoals here. She had risked everything to escape the gilded prison her parents had built around her.

"Thank you," she said, and turned away. She did not welcome questions.

August collected them all in the lobby. "Train leaves at seven forty-five. Be here at seven fifteen. Sorry to cut into your beauty sleep."

"Where in Missoula?" asked Windsor.

"Bennett Opera House, second floor of the European Hotel, downtown. It seats five hundred. We're there four nights, Saturday matinee, but tomorrow's free."

"Lumberjack town, bad for business," Ethel Wildroot said.

"We have a good advance sale," August said. "Prosperous town. It supplies timbers to the mines. Also a school. Helena got the capital, Missoula the state college."

"We'd better play it while we can," Ethel

said. "Students want comedy; faculty wants symphonies."

"You'll be awakened at six," he said. "Eat before you leave or wait to get to Missoula."

Ginger had discovered that managing a troupe took a lot of work, including herding the company to train stations on time. None of it was effortless, and often it involved smoothing ruffled feathers.

He turned to Ginger and handed her a yellow flimsy. "From Charles," he said.

HEARD YOU WERE SPLENDID SEE YOU SOON, it read.

She longed to be with him, and now there was something new about it. He was her husband, and protector if trouble followed her from Pocatello. Her mother would stop at nothing.

August grinned. "I second that."

That night she lay abed in the room she shared with two of the Wildroot Sisters, but sleep eluded her. She dreaded what might happen soon. So willful was her mother that anything could happen, even a kidnaping. The morning arrived with a knock, and soon the troupe was settled in the sole passenger coach of the mixed freight train that would carry them to the mainline. She was soon watching the forested slopes drift by. She had never been east, to settled country, where farms surrounded towns, and forests mingled with pastures and plowed fields. This was different. She had a sudden impulse to catch the next train to New York, and try a new life once again. But the moment died. She sat passively, with the company, and transferred passively to a west-bound express with plush maroon seats and a tobacco odor. She stared anxiously from the window as the train screeched to a halt at the Missoula station. She ached to see Charles.

The line crawled slowly to the end of the car, and then the conductor was helping her down the steps, onto the stool, and then the gravel platform. And there he was, a bouquet of yellow roses in hand, his derby cocked on his head, his gaze feasting upon her. She swept toward him, and he gathered her in, and pressed her tight, and she felt the brusque warmth through his gray topcoat, and then he was placing those roses, wrapped in green tissue, in her hands, and smiling, an odd sadness in his eyes.

"Oh, Charles . . ."

"It's himself," he said. "I've been hearing about you. And now you're going to sing for me."

"Private concert?" she asked.

He liked that. He squeezed her, pulled her back, looked her over, and helped her collect her stuff. A trainman had deposited her travel bag on the platform. A small trunk would follow, delivered by expressmen.

A hack stood ready to carry them to the Florence, near the opera house, where they had rooms on the ground floor. He waved at August.

"I'll see you at the hotel," he said. "There's things."

August nodded. The cryptic message eluded Ginger, but managers were like that. They always had things to resolve. The hack driver, dapper in his ankle-length black coat, steered the dray horse over to Higgins, and set a fast pace. Inside, the Wildroot girls were jammed in beside Charles and Ginger, and also Harry the Juggler, who sat impassively, studying the city.

It seemed a harsh place. Wood smoke layered the city and there were no breezes to carry it away. But that didn't matter. Charles, her husband of a few days, sat comfortably beside her, his quietness suggesting that there would be intimate conversation only when they were free from company. Maybe at dinner that evening. Yes, surely then. An odd anxiety wormed through her. For some couples, this would still be a honey-moon.

The hack driver unloaded them quickly, intent on collecting more customers, and Charles escorted her inside and straight to a room she realized was his. The bags would catch up, somehow. He let her in, flipped a light switch—Missoula was electrified—and a table lamp burned inside a Tiffany shade.

He caught her close and kissed her.

"Long time; too long," he said. "I tell you what. Rest a little, and I'll be back in time for dinner. We'll have a grand evening."

"You'll be back?"

He looked apologetic. "There's some things to talk about with August. You know, business interferes with everything, and it's interfering with us, with our rendezvous." He smiled woefully. "It can't be helped. The company, you know, is on the road, and things shift and change, and we need to adjust, or work out details."

He sure wasn't telling her much. "What is it, Charles?" she asked.

"Nothing for you to worry your pretty head about."

She didn't like that much. She'd had some notion that marriage would bring them a complete sharing. But now . . . she didn't know.

"Make yourself beautiful," he said. "And we'll go out and have a fling."

"When will I see you?"

He sighed. "Hard to say. But don't worry; I'll be back soon."

He pulled free, kissed her on the cheek, smiled, and pointed at the roses. "Put them in water," he said. "Keep them fresh."

And with that, he opened the door, stepped into the hall, and closed the door behind him. She peered around the comfortable room, peered at his things hanging in an armoire, peered at the bed, and then sat down on it, hardly knowing what to do, or why she was there, or who her husband was.

29

Charles Pomerantz knocked and was let in instantly.

"We've got this," he said, placing a yellow flimsy in August's hand. It was from the manager of the Spokane Auditorium, and it canceled the booking.

August stared. "Why?" he asked.

"I don't know much. It's been sold. New owners aren't honoring bookings. They own the Orpheum, San Francisco."

"You argue with them?"

Pomerantz shook his head. They both knew what good that would do. And a lawsuit would only throw money away and take a year to settle. "It gets worse. I picked up a little from the bill-poster there. When I tried to start him pasting up the playbills, he wired back that a combine in San Francisco was buying up houses up and down the West, a chain. It'll be a new circuit called Orpheum."

"What else do you know?"

"There's no other houses anywhere near Spokane. None in northern Idaho. In other words, we don't have options near there. Can't book another house. Spokane was our bridge to the coast."

"We saw this back east. Combines, buying up theaters, controlling the acts, moving acts from stage to stage, new show every week, shows twice a day, nonstop. I hoped we might escape that here."

"There's another option, August. We can duck south, try to book the houses at Pocatello, Boise, and maybe more towns around there. Good houses, and a good chance they're dark. Pocatello, the Grand Opera house, town of five thousand. Boise, eight thousand, Columbia Theater. But we'd have to get down there. That means back-tracking to Butte, and taking the Utah and Northern south. And booking rooms. But we could do it, and fill the two weeks before we do Seattle, Tacoma, and Puyallup. And start down the coast."

"Charles, are we still booked solid out there?"

"No word otherwise."

"And Oregon?"

"We're still booked."

"And California?"

"We're in."

"So we have only this one hole in the schedule?"

Charles wished he could say so, with some finality. "I don't like this. I'd better wire. Get some confirmations."

"Find out fast. We may have a lot of dodging ahead."

Charles' thoughts raced ahead, to ticket refunds,

new tickets, reserving rooms, booking alternative houses. But they'd done all that before. And they had a five-day run in Missoula, time to squeeze it out.

Money. They needed to fill the house every performance. They had payroll. Those brown envelopes they doled out each Saturday had to hold greenbacks. Most players got fifty a week. A three-person act like the Marburys, a hundred fifty a week. Some favorites, like Wayne Windsor, collected more. Seventy-five a week for him. Mary Mabel Markey had gotten eighty. The billing order, who got top billing, and who was stuck at the bottom, usually set the pay. Larger companies did it differently. Their home office paid the agents, who paid the players. But August had no home office.

The troupe was working toward San Francisco, where the show would disband. Some would be hired on the eastern swing a few weeks later, across the middle of the continent, to Chicago, the terminus as well as the starting point. The Chicago agents were booking the return east, burning up the telegraph lines. Now he would have to let the agents know about this. They got a cut of every booking. Everyone wanted a cut and usually got it.

"All right, Charles. Wire Pocatello and Boise tonight. Book what you can. Tomorrow, tickets and rooms, if we're going there. And wire Seattle,

Tacoma, and Puyallup—confirm our bookings. And we'd better look at Portland, Salem, Eugene, and keep on going. Yuba City. Sacramento. Stockton. Oakland. Berkeley. Confirm bookings all the way. But tonight, deal with the dark two weeks."

It was a tall order. Shifting a schedule en route, with no time to settle the details, was rough.

"How are we fixed?" Charles asked.

"If we have a good draw here, we should be able to weather it."

"I put out extra playbills."

"I've never played a lumberjack town before. Have you?"

"They eat a lot of pancakes; that's all I know."

August smiled. "We'll do what we always do."

But Charles didn't like the weariness he saw in the manager's eyes.

He hiked up Higgins in a mean wind, and found the Northern Pacific station empty, save for the telegrapher in his cage behind a grille. A clear-glass lightbulb lit his wicket and the empty ticket counter. Missoula had juice. The man bolted upright with a start. He wore a white shirt with a sleeve garter, and had removed his celluloid collar.

Pomerantz found a pencil and filled out forms. One to GrndOpHs Pocatello. Booking Dec 2–10, ASAP Beausoleil Follies Pomerantz, Florence Hotel Missoula. The next would go to Columb Theat Boise, booking December 12–16.

The telegrapher eyed them and counted, and yawned. "Four fifty," he said.

Charles winced. He had it. He had to have it. An advance man operated on cash. The show did, too. Payroll was greenbacks, and part of Charles' job was to deal with banks along the way. Suppliers wanted cash from road shows; most wouldn't take a check or send an invoice east.

"These'll take a few moments," the mustachioed operator said. "You gonna stick around for replies?"

"No, they won't reach their destinations until morning when things open up. But we'll be here four days."

The man nodded. He took his time, reading each one, and then hunched over his brass key, the device with which he tapped out coded messages, usually in a flawless and fast staccato, the device clicking and chattering as it hastened its message out upon miles of copper wire.

Charles did stick, making sure the wires went out, watching the skinny, bored telegrapher depress the key in some sort of rhythm, letter upon letter, word upon word, space upon space, his concentration total.

That was it. An SOS shot into a void. He would be sending more wires in the morning. More and more, a pile of yellow paper the next few hours and days. The show was dark, and putting it into houses was up to him now.

He nodded to the telegrapher, who had returned

to a Horatio Alger novel, and headed into the eve. His thoughts were on Ginger. She would be pleased. She had been his wife a few days, and he had barely given her a kiss. Tonight would be fragrant in their memories.

She was waiting for him, sitting primly in the room's only chair. She had waited a long time.

"Put your coat on, sweetheart, and we'll eat."

She looked a little pouty.

"Hey, in this business, you'll spend your life waiting for someone. Namely me. Managers have to put out fires."

He steered her into the breeze, which had a hint of snow in it.

"There's not a decent eatery in town. Believe me, I know. Advance men know everything. But there's a hotel, down the street here, that's got something edible."

Missoula wasn't his favorite place. He had his doubts whether all those sawmill men and timber cutters cared to be entertained, but he'd soon know. The state college would only make it worse. Academics never cared about a feed, and sat long-faced through a show, right to curtain.

He steered her into a folksy place named Mrs. Williams' Appetite Chastener.

It chastened appetites, all right.

Its walls were jammed with embroidered samplers, most of which flaunted biblical verses, or mottoes encouraging rectitude of one sort or another. Charles had been there a few times during his advance forays, and had offered to buy the samplers to hang temporarily in the Green Rooms of the houses they played. But Mrs. Williams had declined. He had thought to instill virtue in his troupe, wherever they played. His favorite sampler, and one he really itched to own, was "Let us eat and drink, for tomorrow we die." But Mrs. Williams would not even take a five-dollar greenback for it.

He had the sense that Ginger had been in better restaurants, but she kept her silence. That was one of her becoming traits. He talked and she listened. The perfect wife. That separated her from almost all other females.

"Want me to order for you, sweetheart? I can separate the good, the bad, and the ugly."

She smiled at last.

He ordered something or other she had never heard of that sounded southern. Like grits.

"All right, tell me. What took you away from me this afternoon?"

"I need a double rye to unload all that on you. But the chances of getting one from Mrs. Williams are slim."

"I will ask her," Ginger said.

When Mrs. Williams returned with some bread and butter, Ginger caught her.

"My husband would like a double rye, on ice if you have it," she said.

Mrs. Williams stared. "In a Limoges teacup, and it'll cost a dollar. And don't let on."

Charles stared, amazed.

"Maybe I know some things," Ginger said. "Now tell me what happened."

He waited until the rye materialized, sampled it, and found it was the real stuff.

"We're not going to Spokane. New owner canceled us."

That troubled her. "Can they do that?"

"Easily. They didn't buy the old contracts. They bought the house. We could maybe sue the previous owner and get two cents next year if we're lucky."

"But why?"

"Vaudeville's changing fast, sweetheart. Shows like ours, a complete company on tour, we're being beaten out by the new chains and associations. Circuits. The owners of theaters think they can make more money with continuous shows, or at least two shows a day. And the shows are all acts, booked from one town to the next. It's acts, like yourself, or Windsor, or a magician, or a trio like the Wildroots. The contracts don't include us; the Beausoleil Brothers are being squeezed. But it's not all bad. It takes big towns with big houses to keep a circuit going. This is how it is back east, where there's people. And now, maybe the West Coast."

"But wouldn't the acts prefer a company like ours?"

"Money talks, sweetheart. Those acts are getting a hundred a week, some of them."

"Dollars?"

"It's a tough life: shows all day, moves each week. The circuit's a treadmill."

"What's going to happen to us, Charles?"

"Not over, sweet. Not by a long shot. We've got a few aces. We can make money in smaller houses. We can get talent for less."

She smiled wryly. "Which reminds me . . ."

He reached across to her. "I'll talk to August. You were, well, tentative. Now you're not. I'll get you something. Maybe not a lot; you need to be a draw before you can start dickering with August. But you've got a foot on the rung, and you can climb the ladder."

He sipped his rye from the teacup, and smiled, even as Mrs. Williams brought two plates of sliced beef and mashed potatoes mixed with chives, called Le Grande Eau de Cologne.

She ate tentatively, but dug in after a bite or two. The dish had seemed off-putting to her. He sipped from the teacup, thinking the Limoges improved the rye.

"We're going to try another route," he said. "We've a two-week gap to fill, and I'm heating up the wires looking for bookings. We've got an option worked out. Pocatello, Boise. I sent queries this eve. That was what delayed me. If the houses are dark, we can detour. It's a pain. We'll need to print a lot of playbills and slap them up. . . ." He stared. "Something wrong?"

She was staring into space, her knife and fork down.

"I'll be all right," she said. "It's just a spell."

"Anyway, it's a tough haul. Backtrack from here almost to Butte, go south on that UP branch, Utah and Northern, and then move through southern Idaho. Pocatello's got the Grand Opera House, town of fifty-five hundred, good enough for a stay. Boise's got the Columbia Theater, eight thousand there, good potential. And I'm looking at Moscow, even though there's no direct route. It's got five thousand, and the G.A.R. Opera House. Grand Army of the Republic. I guess we know what side the owners were on. But that's way out of the way."

She had quit eating, and sat rigidly in her seat, staring.

"Vapors or something?"

She smiled, woodenly. "I'll get over it," she said. But she didn't eat. And said not a word.

After that strange meal, he took her back to their room, anticipating a delightful renewal of their honeymoon. But she lay rigid and pale, her mind drifting somewhere, and he wondered what the hell sort of marriage he had gotten into.

30

Ethel Wildroot, Wayne Windsor, and The Genius were exploring Missoula, having first settled in their rooms. Their first stop was The Woodcutter's Bowl, which had but a single dish, beef stew, all drawn from a pot. A large bowl cost two bits. It wasn't bad if one didn't examine the meat closely. That done, they ventured out once again, this time southerly, and found themselves at the Bennett Opera House, which occupied the second floor of the Hotel Europa.

Some event was unfolding there that eve. The lamps were lit.

"Want a look?" Windsor asked.

Of course they all did, so they entered, climbed a gallant set of stairs, and found a placard on an easel announcing the evening's fare: a lecture by Mrs. Amelia Woodcock of the Women's Christian Temperance Union. It had started at seven, and was no doubt mostly over, unless Mrs. Woodcock was particularly windy.

They entered, found the place lit by electric lights. Mrs. Woodcock, a handsome woman in a gray suit with a jabot at the neck, stood at a walnut lectern. She was flanked by two other ladies and some gents in full white beards, suit coats, waistcoats, with gold watch fobs dangling across their middles. They were all paying rapt attention to the speaker. The three vaudevillians settled quietly at the rear. When Ethel's eyes had adjusted to the light, she discovered several of the acts had slipped in. Show people liked to do that: see the house, see what was playing ahead of them.

Her daughters and LaVerne were sitting nearby. The Marbury Trio, too. Harry the Juggler.

The opera house was a third full, the listeners gathered forward. An olio drop behind Amelia Woodcock barred a view of the large stage behind.

"The rising tide of drunkenness comes from lax immigration laws," Mrs. Woodcock was saying. "There are, of course, certain nations and cultures that actually welcome intoxicating beverages and even use them in religious rites. Even small children are permitted to sip wine, a sure way to begin them upon the road to ruin. It doesn't matter whether it's wine or ardent spirits; they are all evil, and destroy the character and decency of those who take the fateful step of drinking them. The Woman's Christian Temperance Union is staunchly opposed to imbibing alcohol of any sort, in any circumstance.

"We are, of course, opposed to lax immigration laws, which have opened the gates of this great nation to morally loose people, especially those gathered around the Mediterranean Sea. They tend to be people of darker hue, a sure sign that they are vulnerable not only to drunkenness but also to social disorders, crime, cruelty, and wantonness of all sorts. But wine drinkers aren't the only problem. Head north and we find the Germans, celebrating life in beer halls, drinking all sorts of ardent spirits, and delighting in it. Such people can never make good citizens of our republic; neither can the Irish, another race imbibing ardent spirits. Look at Butte, a city lost to inebriation, a city in perpetual turmoil because moral bonds are loosened, and widows and orphans suffer.

"This organization is devoted to curbing promiscuous immigration, and maintaining a civil order intended from the beginning to reflect the ideals and cultural traditions of its founders. That means, largely, those who cannot speak English ought not to be welcomed here."

Ethel listened closely, peering at her vaudeville colleagues, wondering if they felt what she felt. Her alienated husband's name was not Wildroot but Wildenstein; he was German. Ethel herself was Irish. Her daughters were a mix of both peoples and would not meet this speaker's approval for citizenship in the United States.

Harry the Juggler was Polish, or at least from some country around there. Who knew which? The Marbury Trio, golden-fleshed, were mostly Italian, from the boot of Italy. Charles Pomerantz was a Polish Jew. August Beausoleil was French, and who knew what else? Mary Mabel Markey had been Irish. Heaven only knew what Mrs. McGivers was, all told, but only part of her could have been Scots.

And that was true of the whole business. Vaudeville was a creation of recent arrivals, people distinctively different and not on this lady's approved list. Not native, but arriving in immigrant boats from Italy, Ireland, Germany, the Continent. And they were giving these native people like Mrs. Woodcock the best entertainment and humor they had ever seen.

"Now, then," said Mrs. Woodcock, "to sum up, the community can cleanse itself of tragedy and grief and loss and financial ruin, all of it wrought by spirits, if it quietly removes and destroys all the drinking parlors, making it impossible for the weak to appease their ravenous appetites, or bring further sorrow to their families and friends and colleagues. How great is the ruin they visit upon their loved ones, friends, associates, and neighbors.

"We calculate costs, which go far beyond the financial sort, and include children denied food and shelter and the loving paternal hand; we calculate that the presence of spirits ruins an entire city and county. The solution does not lie in Washington, or in the Montana capitol, but right here. In your village ordinances. In your county laws. Make this beautiful county dry. Make it a crime to operate a saloon, or a store where spirits are vended. Drive out the demonic presence of spirits, which corrupt a whole community until it bleeds with tragedy, and no household is spared.

"Yes, begin here, and then take the issue to the state, and then to the nation, so that at some future date the United States Constitution will forbid the sale or possession of intoxicating spirits. And then, dear people, we will see safe and secure communities, sober and industrious fathers, each neighborhood dotted with white churches watching over the flock. Then we will see the orphanages empty out, the work of constables diminish, the available jobs increase because a sober workforce is far more productive than a dissolute one. Yes, we will swiftly see all these things come to pass. Not all at once, but as a tidal wave rolling toward shore, carrying a clean and bright new world on its crest.

"Start here, dear people. Start right here in this opera house. Make it the home of lectures, enlightened musicales, uplifting sermons, exhortations to achieve a good life lived in quietness and service. Ah, dear friends, begin right here in this theater, and choose carefully what might be played here. Let it inspire and reward."

She paused, collecting the polite applause, and sat down.

A gent with a massive white beard stepped up to the lectern.

"We do thank you, Mrs. Woodcock. We all have profited from your inspiring talk, and your vision of the future, and the remaking of America. And now, as always, I invite inspirational comment from our audience."

A matronly lady in blue arose at once. "Mrs. Woodcock," she began. "We're all inspired by your lecture, and also by your guidance. We know now what to do, and how to do it. The WCTU has a great history of picketing saloons, but also picketing undesirable places that endanger public morals. I do believe I know of some places right here, in Missoula. In fact, this opera house tomorrow will be turned over to a troupe called the Beausoleil Brothers Follies. That's the word, *Follies*. That says it all. It's time for us to drive pernicious influences out of Missoula, wouldn't you say?"

"Madam, you have caught the letter and spirit of my lecture, and if that's what's coming here, then let the world know. A firm line of picketers has been known to drive such company out of a town."

"Count on us!" said the lady in blue.

"We'll organize the event right now," said someone else. "Those of you wishing to join us, have a sign ready. I believe the Follies starts at seven."

Ethel watched, fascinated. And so did the rest of the troupe.

The crowd around the stage stirred, and the lecturer and her contingent abandoned the stage. Few people were leaving; most of the Missoulians were collecting around the woman in blue, who was plainly organizing the surprise party for the vaudeville company.

"I guess we'd better talk to Charles, or maybe August," Ethel said.

"I've been in a couple of these," Wayne Windsor said. "And I'm English."

"I bet," said Ethel. Windsor laughed.

"This place sure isn't Butte," The Genius said.

Some of the company, notably the Marbury Trio, were drifting forward, boldly intent on listening in, while others, such as the juggler, were quietly donning coats and pulling out.

LaVerne Wildroot eyed her aunt. "What are you going to do?"

"Talk to August if I can find him."

"He'll know what to do?"

"I think so. He can turn something like this into box office."

"I'd never thought of that," LaVerne said.

"Any publicity works," Ethel said. "If it's put to use. All right, Genius, let's hunt down the boss. You coming, Wayne?"

"No, I'm going over there and listen in. I might have a new monologue ready when we open."

"You coming, LaVerne?"

"No, I'm going to volunteer to picket us."

"I always knew you had talent," Ethel said. She eyed the rest of the company, including a couple of musicians and stagehands who obviously didn't know what to do.

"Go listen," she said. "Make a picket sign."

They smiled.

Ethel headed into the evening, Genius at her side, passing a knot of dignified men in topcoats, waiting for their wives within.

"Scandalous," Ethel said to one, who sputtered something that vanished in the wind.

She tried Beausoleil's room at the hotel, but no one responded, so she headed for the nearest saloon, and entered, with The Genius, against a wall of frowns. Sure enough, there was August, nursing a drink, maybe his third or fourth, in one of his melancholic moments. She knew about those. Sometimes the remembrance of an abandoned youth, desperately surviving on tips around theaters, caught at him, even now, and sent him reeling into a bleak private world.

Beausoleil smiled slightly as Ethel plowed down a long bar. An oil portrait of Cleopatra, thinly veiled about the loins, was prominently displayed above the handsome, mahogany Brunswick back bar.

Beausoleil nodded, even as a serving man showed up.

"I can only serve the gentlemen," he said.

"Then your life is half as valuable," The Genius said, ordering a rye.

"We're going to be picketed tomorrow," Ethel said.

August stared, sipped, and waited.

She spilled the story swiftly, and he absorbed every word.

"What set them off?" he asked.

"Follies."

"That's why I use the name," Beausoleil said. "I almost used *Scandals*, but the times aren't ripe for it."

"Those ladies were all Presbyterians or Baptists or something like that," she said. "There wouldn't be a Catholic in the lot. Probably not an Anglican, either."

"WCTU—ban the spirits, along with Italians, French, Germans, Irish, and the rest," he said. "Missoula isn't Butte. All right, we'll give them something to picket about." He nodded to Ethel. "Have the girls show an ankle. I'll want the Marbury Trio in blackface."

"Blackface?"

"Biggest acts back east are blackface. Burnt cork's selling tickets. And tap dancing's straight out of minstrel shows. I'll go talk to the newspaper. The minstrel show's arrived in Missoula."

"LaVerne's been itching to show a lot more than some ankle, August."

"Let her rip," he said. "A girl needs to make good use of her assets."

The waiter delivered the drinks, and The Genius shoved his glass at Ethel, who downed it neat, in three coughs and two sputters.

"I'm a case history for the WCTU," The Genius said. "Maybe I can turn it into something."

"Give it a shot, and if it bombs, I'll give you the hook. You play something like this for all it's worth."

August finished up the dregs in his glass, reached for his black topcoat and black derby, and swept into the night, with Ethel and The Genius in tow. The newspaper, the *Missoulian*, was just a block or two away.

31

Charles Pomerantz opened his room door to August, who bore news.

"We're in luck. The WCTU's fixing to picket us tomorrow."

"What's their beef?"

"Follies. They don't like follies, so they'll get more than they bargained for. I've asked the Marbury Trio to go blackface, and they'll be the Marbury Minstrel Dancers. And LaVerne's going to show a little limb and chest. And The Genius says he'll try to work the theme. I headed over to the paper and bought a small ad, program change, minstrels, etc. With some luck, we'll get a lot of picketers."

"How'd you get wind of it?"

"They were at the opera house. Lecture by some temperance lady or other. She doesn't like spirits or Italians. She doesn't like Catholics or Episcopalians or Latvians or Norwegians. Half our company was there, enjoying the show. It could give us a few sellouts. Speaking of which, what's the word?"

"Won't know until morning. Wired Pocatello and Boise. We're covering two weeks, and need two theaters or a long run in Boise, which is big enough."

"Let me know fast."

"I'll wire the houses in Washington and Oregon tomorrow to confirm our dates," Charles said. "And California. If a circuit's buying houses out there, we need to know, fast. While we can still maneuver."

"I sure get tired of the scramble," August said. "What a business. Nothing's firm. We need houses that won't cancel us. We need acts. I'd pay good money for an animal act, but where do you find one in Montana?"

"So we stir the pot," Charles said. "Got any more scandals?"

"I'll invent some."

Charles thought that August looked drawn. Road managers careened from crisis to crisis, and this tour had been full of them. It had always been hard to read August. He was the loneliest man Charles had ever met, keeping everything to himself. He was always affable, always affectionate—and distant. There was an interior life in August that no one knew, or would ever know. A man without intimates carried a terrible burden, especially in critical moments.

"I will do something," Ginger said, suddenly. "I have assets."

"That's sweet of you, but you just keep on the way you are," August said.

She smiled suddenly. "The way I was. I'll never be that again."

Charles sensed something that he couldn't quite fathom. She had been almost rigid, silent, withdrawn all evening. Something was burdening her. And then suddenly, this. Her assets. He wished he could fathom what was inside of her. And what she meant. Whatever it was, she wasn't spilling any beans, not now.

"You'll be the draw," he said.

"Not if I stay the way I was."

This was beyond him. August stared flatly, nodded, and a moment later the door clicked shut.

She sprang from the chair where she had sat in locked silence, raced to him, and crushed him in her arms with an eagerness that astonished him.

She clung fiercely, and only after a long moment did he respond to her, drawn ever closer to her pliant body, which for the first time seemed to shape itself to his.

He felt the rush of need, and returned her kiss. But still this sudden change in her very nature bewildered him.

"There, now," he said, softly. "What is this?"

She didn't respond except with her eager hands. And he was discovering a Ginger he hadn't known, a woman of such intensity and passion and willfulness that he simply surrendered to her, a circumstance as strange to him as marriage itself. He was married, and he hadn't ever grasped how it happened, or why. A crazy impulse.

Their brief honeymoon was fraught with tension, and she had surrendered piecemeal, unloosing bit by bit those parts of her that no man had ever known, and always a little removed from him, even analytical as if she were an observer. And when they had at last achieved union, he had no sense of whether she enjoyed it, or whether it repelled, or perhaps made no inroads upon her heart at all. Maybe it didn't matter. And in the end, before he was compelled to leave Butte, he had concluded that he knew little of her, and might never know much about her, and least of all about their union. He had married a woman far removed from anyone—

from him, but also from the world, a woman with a chest of secrets she shared with no one.

Still, as he thought back, there had been tenderness, and tentativeness, and experiment, and she had not resisted as she experienced his caresses, and weighed his advances. But she had been a mystery, and now in her passion she was even more so, the heat in her shredding the moment, hurrying their bodies along.

It took little time, actually, a great tugging of clothes, rending of buttons, yanking of stockings, and he discovered a different bride this time, one he had never fathomed. And was it tears he was finding on her cheeks in the midst of passion? When, finally, they lay spent in that narrow hotel room, it seemed that this really was the first of their matings, that all that had gone before was little more than removing locks from doors.

Then she was there, her tangled hair nestled into his shoulder, an utter stranger in bed with him. And along with his peacefulness was curiosity; who was she, and why?

"Who are you?" he asked.

"A bird out of her cage."

"And what cage?"

"My mother's cage. What she expected of me."

"Which was?"

"Charles, you can't possibly know. It's beyond, I mean, there's no words. A clockwork doll. A windup toy. A prodigy to be displayed and put back on her shelf. A prisoner. A girl whose will was trampled, stolen, who could never be herself. My mother has no self, so she invaded me, possessed me, stole me. She doesn't even see me as a person."

"Your father?"

"He went along, bought the tutors, paid for it all, and never questioned it, or objected, or asked me. But he always, oh, it was like he was the law."

An old story, he thought. And no doubt all out of proportion, an eighteen-year-old woman who had yet to see the world. In a year or two, she'd see it differently. Mothers against daughters. Daughters against parents. Escape, somewhere, anywhere, even into vaudeville, so impossibly distant from her quiet, bourgeois life.

"Ginger, where was this?"

She didn't speak for a long time, and he felt her stir in the comfortable dark. "I'm afraid to tell you," she whispered, and then pronounced it: "Pocatello."

No wonder, he thought.

"My father's superintendent of a Union Pacific division."

"And has railroad muscle behind him," he added, finishing her thought. "So, you don't want to perform there."

"You don't know my mother," she said.

"You're married. So what's going to happen?"

"If you knew my mother, you wouldn't ask."

"Ginger's not your name, right?"

"It's Penelope."

"And lots of people there would spot you the moment you walked into the limelight. And you're hoping we don't book Pocatello."

She clutched him and buried her face in his shoulder. Her fear was palpable.

"Penelope, there's no reason to worry about anything. We're married. You're old enough."

"Please, please, don't ever call me that. Please."

He pulled her tight. "You're Ginger to me; that's who I married."

He felt her quake, and felt the heat of her tears in the hollow of his shoulder.

"Hey, it'll be all right, Ginger. For one thing, we haven't gotten a booking there. Maybe they're running something. For another, we need two. If I can book Boise, we've got most of what we need."

"My mother would pull the ring off my finger. My father would send railroad workers to take me away."

That seemed wildly unlikely to Charles. The woman he'd taken to wife was brimming with feverish fantasies. "Ginger, brace up. You go out there, on that stage, on any stage, and you bowl them over. You've got it; you'll strut it."

"They'll take me and lock me in my room. They'll charge you with things. They'll say I was stolen."

"Ginger, you're of age. You have a right to your own life."

She burrowed closer, and clutched him desperately. It amazed him. Rampant fear had caught her even though the company was not yet booked in her hometown. He didn't know what to do. Terrified people made bad performers. He'd seen performers quit the stage in the middle of an act. He doubted she would even walk out there, smile at the crowd, and offer up something they might like.

But there was this: A long run in Missoula, time to get used to the idea of playing Pocatello. Time for her to grow a little, pitch out the demons, collect herself. And time for him to work out a schedule.

"Hey, sweetheart, you're a long way from home," he said.

"You don't know," she replied.

The dread was there, alive, lashing back and forth like a lion's tail.

He hadn't known the woman he married. Marry in haste, repent forever. But the thing was, he had no regrets. This half-girl, half-woman enchanted him. There was a dimple in her cheek that he loved. It somehow doubled her smile.

Her quietness signaled sleep, or at least those peaceful moments of surrender to sleep. But he was starkly awake. The troupe was suffering for the lack of acts. Markey and McGivers gone. You couldn't just add a new one, not in Montana. He and August were pinning their hopes on this girl in his arms, hoping she would soon be a draw, have the magic, the power, the reach, that would bring crowds to their show. All the signs were there, but she hadn't quite connected yet; still too much recital, and not enough performer, or whatever it was called. Magic, that's how he described it. She needed magic, and they needed her magic, and so far there was no magic.

He'd know more in the morning when he heard from the opera houses in Idaho. What houses were dark, what houses weren't. A two-week break in the tour could be fatal. He had to book something fast, in the sparsely populated Northwest. He'd avoid Pocatello if he could, but even as he considered that prospect, he knew he couldn't avoid any house that was dark. Any house where the Follies could light up the stage, perform, and bring in the crowds. And cash.

The next morning, long before she stirred under the thin gray hotel blanket, he dressed quietly, braved sharp cold, and hiked to the railroad station. He didn't expect responses until the managers began their own quotidian routines and saw what Western Union brought to them. But it turned out he didn't need to wait; the managers had received the wires in the evening and had responded.

"I was just going to send a boy out to find you," the telegrapher said.

The news was good. Pocatello was dark the first four days, booked two days, and dark the next days. Boise was booked the first four days, dark the rest.

Pomerantz knew what he had to do. He booked the Grand Opera House at Pocatello for four days, with two travel days following the Missoula run. He booked the Columbia Theater in Boise for the next leg, one travel day after Pocatello. After that the Follies would head west, Washington and Oregon, solid cities, big houses, some safety. And then California.

From the *Julius Cahn Official Theatrical Guide* he carried, he wired Pocatello for hotel rooms, Boise for hotel rooms. Then he wired the bill-poster at both sites, saying three-sheet bills would be expressed. The bill-posters would need to add a paste-on with the date of the appearance. They were skilled at that. They would get the sheets, post them on barn sides, walls, structures beside the roads, add the dates. There was more to do: wire the papers with small ads, wire or mail publicity material, find out from the house managers what worked best in their towns.

That's what an advance man was for. He would have to leave Ginger behind, set up the shows in Idaho, and hope for the best.

32

Two redoubtable ladies, armored against the evening cold with thick woolen coats and over-sized hats, hoisted picket signs that evening. One sign said AMERICA FOR AMERICANS, and the other said KEEP US FROM FOLLIES.

They stood placidly in front of the Bennett Opera House, drawing only idle glances from those planning to see the show. August Beausoleil was, in a way, disappointed. A rowdier, snaking picket line would have been more to his liking. But these respectable matrons, armored in the attire of their bourgeois lives, generated only mild curiosity. And they were polite enough to stand to one side, not interfering with theater patrons.

He knew what the signs were about. The Woman's Christian Temperance Union was not just about removing every last ounce of alcohol in the states; it was also about immigration, and about a variety of other sorts of conduct it deemed immoral. It did not open its membership to Catholics and Jews, and was actively opposed to immigration of these groups, as well as Germans, French, Italians, Irish, and most everyone from Eastern Europe. Show business was the peculiar realm of these people, such as himself. So show business itself was the target this cold eve.

In 1882, a New Yorker named Tony Pastor had turned variety theater into vaudeville. The old variety shows had been racy, and Pastor had reasoned that their bawdiness was keeping women and children away. He could lure them into theaters with the promise of clean, cheerful shows. He called his new variety shows vaude-ville, a little French, and swiftly turned them into a bright success. August Beausoleil, along with countless others in the business, had learned the lesson. Especially Oscar Hammerstein, whose shows soon outdid anything that Pastor put onstage.

August Beausoleil adhered to the new variety forms, but with a small caveat: he believed a little bit of spice could draw people into the theaters. He would even generate a little bad publicity if it improved his sales. But these polite ladies would only disappoint.

He headed toward the ladies, confronted them with a slight bow, and waved four tickets at them.

"My show," he said. "Please be my guests. You and your husbands."

"Over my dead body," said one. But she pocketed the tickets.

Beausoleil smiled, bowed once again, and headed inside. The ladies probably wouldn't attend, but they would find friends to "report" what they saw inside.

He found Pomerantz backstage, looking worn. The other half of the Follies had spent the day in the railroad station, keeping the telegrapher busy.

"Where are we?" August asked.

"Looking good. Booked Pocatello December one to four; Boise seven to eleven with two holdover days reserved. I've got hotels in Boise and Pocatello. I've got the paper hangers alerted; they'll get playbills tomorrow, and they'll print paste-overs locally. I've got rail schedules and worked out the backtrack from here to Butte to Pocatello. I'll be leaving here tomorrow; got to be on hand forward. But it should get us through the gap, in time for the year-end stuff around Seattle."

"Any trouble I should know about?"

Pomerantz sighed. "My wife."

August said not a word. He studied the dark wing, offstage, empty of performers. Stages are sad, bleak places except for the few explosive moments they come alive with light and song and magic.

"Pocatello is where she's running away from," Charles said.

"And she doesn't want to return."

"Mother-and-daughter deal; sounds bad but I've seen a few daughters swear their mothers were straight out of hell."

"What's the deal?"

"I don't know. She's silent. She's a lot of things,

but you know what? I'm tied to someone I'm just starting to know. So, all I can say is, coax her along."

"We're short of acts. She's getting better. We need two more acts, and can't get them fast around here."

"I'm away from here after the show; milk run to Butte. I've got more to worry about than mothers and daughters. If I don't get publicity out, it won't matter that we're booked across Idaho. So," he said, sounding amused, "she's your cookie."

"All right, what's your guess? At Pocatello?"

"She's got a stage mother, nah, call this one a recital mother, and Mama's spent a few thousand tutoring her little prodigy, and Mama's gonna drag her out the door."

"You married her, right?"

"Yeah, to a girl named Ginger. Her name's Penelope. So it's your guess."

"Showtime," said the stage manager.

Swiftly, August donned his tux with the snap-on bib, and stole a look out there. The house wasn't full, but there were people drifting in. And there were four empty seats where the temperance ladies would never sit. Seating in the gallery was spotty. But there were a pair of reporters out there.

What was it about showtime? Everyone who'd been in the business felt a galvanic current run through him when the moment arrived when the curtain would roll away and the performers and audience would greet each other. At each curtain time, not a few performers were sucking spirits from flasks. Beausoleil checked his acts; the Marbury Trio had applied the burnt cork this time, and looked lean and lanky. That would be one to watch. You never knew how a minstrel act would work. The Genius looked ready to go. He'd improved his line, making himself more and more outrageous, and at the same time more vulnerable to Ethel's little asides. He would probably pick on the WCTU. Harry stood quietly, waiting for his turn, and the Wildroot Sisters were ready, this time in the shortest skirts in their wardrobe, which showed plenty of white stocking at the calves. Strangely, Ginger had a new dress this time, one borrowed from somewhere, with a bit of ankle showing, and a scooped neckline. That should please the gents, if not their ladies. And there was Wayne Windsor, the old professional, a slight mocking in his face, as if to say he'd reduce this audience to fits, the way he often did.

Let it roll, then, August thought.

Then he was out there, introducing the Follies, waving the curtain up, thanking the crowd, and introducing the Wildroot Sisters.

Another show, another town, another audience to please, one of a thousand or two he had stood before, welcoming them, and welcoming his show.

The girls knocked them dead. What was it, the

air? The perpetual smoke? The frowning ladies with their posters? He didn't know. He only knew that Cookie and Margie and LaVerne were singing, shimmying, and showing a little ankle out there, and Ethel was looking smug. The crowd warmed up. You could feel a crowd warming. It wasn't applause, it wasn't laughter, it was some-thing else. Everyone in vaudeville knew what it was, but no one could put a word to it, or explain it to someone not in the trade.

Had Ethel reworked the act?

That proved to be a great opener, and the audience was ripe and warm.

He introduced the Marbury Minstrel Dancers next, and Delilah and her gents clattered out in blackface, their faces pitch black and shiny, the hands encased in white gloves, the men in tuxedos, Delilah in a loose glittery gown that bared some calf. That drew a ripple from the crowd as the trio clattered into the limelight. Minstrel was new to most of them. It had been a part of variety theater for many years, but this was frontier Montana. No one knew just where tap dancing came from. It seemed to combine English clog dancing with the movements and rhythms of southern blacks, and it had swiftly become a staple of vaudeville, with many blacks in blackface as well as whites.

The trio clattered and dodged and set the audience to swaying. They leapt and split and tiptoed and whirled. This was a controlled dance, small gestures, intense and disciplined, and Delilah and her gents were masters of it. The clickety-clack, the explosions of Gatling-gun chatter, the slow and syncopated taps of six shoes with metal cleats toe and heel; it caught an audience that had barely experienced any of it. They used the limelight, working into it, retreating from it, and then, finally, rattling down to a finale, three statues, halting, finally, in the white light center stage, hiding the pumping of their lungs.

That won a surprised gasp, and applause.

They danced two more, the second loose and louche, the accompanist on the accordion discovering ways to coax New Orleans out of his squeezebox. The third round was quite the opposite, the dancers barely moving about the stage, but their legs and feet working in syncopation, bright and chattery.

That won a great and steady round of applause, as August finally strode out and introduced The Genius and Ethel. A quiet act following an expansive one.

The pair bowed.

"Well, Genius," said Ethel, "is it true that you're the brightest man in Montana?"

"I wouldn't want to exaggerate," he replied. "No doubt the brightest in North America."

"What makes you so bright, Genius?"

"I didn't buy a ticket to tonight's show," he said.

That got them laughing. It was a good act, getting better as the pair worked out their patter, August thought. The Genius would make outlandish claims, and Ethel would puncture them. And the fun was, the audience usually ended up on the side of The Genius. They didn't stay long in front of the olio. The joke wore out fast.

They got a cheerful round of applause, and August strode out once again.

"Ladies, and usually gents but not always, I'm pleased to introduce Harry the Juggler. He's got a last name, but I can't pronounce it. He comes from one of those little nations near New Jersey. Here's the Juggler!"

Harry came out, followed by a stagehand pushing a cart loaded with stuff, and after some bowing and scraping, Harry pitched a couple of saucers up, and soon added enough tableware to seat four at dinner, and somehow managed not to break so much as a teacup. The crowd enjoyed that. He bowed long and low, and trotted off.

Then it was time for Ginger. He introduced her softly, conversationally. Some acts he introduced with fanfare, but not this young woman. She floated out on polite applause, wearing a borrowed dress this evening, with some of her golden shoulder and neck glowing in the light.

She seemed different somehow, though August could not say how. Only that she had never seemed more tender.

She sang alone, without accompaniment, her voice floating out upon a quiet crowd. She always chose familiar ballads at first, Stephen Foster or "Shenandoah," and let the familiar strains find their home in a hundred hearts. The crowd listened quietly, blotting her up. She was reaching them this evening. She seemed a little older, perhaps. August couldn't tell exactly, but he knew that she was connecting, and that she had the whole crowd in her grasp, and that it was a sweet and memorable moment. She finished her first one to polite applause, slipped solo into another, and finally a third, and after the last note died, she bowed.

Her auditors clapped politely, and kept on clapping, and she bowed again, and they clapped on and on, not letting her leave the stage. August finally rescued her, striding forth and lifting a hand.

"Miss Ginger, that was the most beautiful singing I've ever heard," he said.

The crowd enjoyed it, but finally let her go.

August caught her eye, and winked. She smiled and retreated, the respectful clapping still echoing in that house. It had never happened like that. August made note of it. That performance, Ginger had transformed herself into the biggest draw in the show. There would be some out there who would return for the next performance and the next, just to listen to her.

Wayne Windsor wound up the first half, turning right, turning left, treating the crowd to his profile. His monologues always had a good-humored edge to them, and August knew the crowd would enjoy some good times.

"I understand that Missoula captured the state college," he began, and paused a moment. "What a pity. You should have applied for the state prison."

They liked that. He managed to do ten or twelve minutes on the shortcomings of students and professors, with a few asides about how colleges subtracted more from the local economy than added to it, and then he was done, and the audience headed for a halftime break in a very good mood.

The second half went just as well, and the crowd seemed especially eager to hear Ginger sing. But the moment she was done, she vanished into the Green Room, and August knew that the booking at Pocatello was tormenting her. The small bare room was empty, save for her. The show wasn't over, and he had more introductions, but maybe he could listen and learn in one quick interlude.

"You were great this evening, Ginger. You'll have top billing."

She looked haunted, and stared away from him.

"We've had to make a few quick changes," he said. "But once we get to the coast, we have the best houses lined up. Big ones. I just want you to know that, and know how much Charles and I like your act."

She pushed her golden shoulders back and met his gaze. "Mr. Beausoleil, after Missoula, I'm leaving the show," she said.

33

The opener in Missoula was a success. A good box office. A dandy show. A profit. August could meet payroll.

He lingered in the opera house office long after the building had emptied, doing payroll under a naked bulb. He carried with him a stack of small brown envelopes, which he filled weekly with greenbacks and hand-delivered on Saturdays, the last day of the week, when pay was due. All his transactions were cash. His players didn't want checks they couldn't redeem. They wanted spending money, and that's what he gave them. Each show night brought in a load of small bills from ticket sales.

He kept his accounts in a small vest-pocket notebook, often using cryptic initials rather than writing entire entries. Now, in the creaking quiet of the Missoula house, he doled out bills and stuffed them into the envelopes. A hundred fifty for the Wildroot Sisters, who would pay their mother and manager. Eighty for LaVerne, who had a separate act, and would give thirty to her accordionist. A hundred for Wayne Windsor. Seventy for Harry the Juggler. Greenbacks, carefully counted out, stuffed in the envelopes, and an initial or name on each envelope. Fifty for Ginger. He hesitated a moment, and then pushed the folded fives into the envelope. She had earned it.

There were four musicians in the company, paid by the various acts. A guitarist, a banjo player, an accordionist, and an all-around percussion man. He did not pay them. He did pay his sole stagehand, Vince Leo, thirty a week.

He finished the payroll, stuffed everything into the opera house Mosler safe, and swung the door shut. Those safes, used by each company, were common accouterments in opera houses, and resolved a dilemma for touring companies: where to store their cash. The other options were the hotel safe, if one was available, or keeping the cash in his hotel room, under the mattress as a bonus for the chambermaids.

It added up. This payday would eat up the evening's take, and then some. The take of other matinees and evenings had to pay for train, hotel, theater rental, playbills, advertising, Charles' expenses, and sometimes payoffs for officials who threatened trouble of one sort or another. All cash. All grubby greenbacks, in heaps, collected at the box office or the drugstores that did advance sales. Arrangements varied from theater to theater. Some simply rented, but others wanted a percentage, and their owners usually hung around through the counting. Keeping it all straight was a headache.

On the road, with its ups and downs, he careened from confidence to panic. There was never enough cash. Sometimes he had to struggle to buy fuel for the lamps, where there was no electricity. Light your own spots, and buy the kerosene. Once in a while, at the end of a tour, there was actually some cash, and this he split with Pomerantz. It was the only salary they ever got.

He sometimes wondered why he did it. It wasn't because he loved show business or was infatuated with the players and the acts and the excitement. It was because this was the only thing he knew how to do. He had been a part of it, squeezing dimes out of it, since he was a boy, cadging tips and trying to fill the hole in his stomach and quell his loneliness, when he had no home to go to and spent a night in a trolley barn or railroad station. But it had taught him the business from the ground up.

He was slipping deep into the blues. He had lost Ginger. And much more, there were things that filled him with foreboding. The cancelation in Spokane heralded more cancelations. Someone on the West Coast was putting together a circuit. That was the new thing: own a string of houses, put acts out on the circuit in rotation, keep the lights lit with two shows a day. And drive out competition. In New York, that meant building a rival house across the street from whatever house was holding out. The whole vaudeville business was coalescing into a few owners and a few circuits. And the casualties were the touring companies like his own.

There wasn't much he could do about it unless he had an act so top-dog that he had some power to book his show wherever he wanted. But Ginger had folded her hand for some reason known best to a young woman barely out of school. Show business was a tough game and what she was doing would get her booted clear back to her hometown, but she was his partner's new wife, and in any case she was wrestling with something no one else could fathom. So he'd just let it go. And his show would be stuck with one less act.

He didn't feel like going to bed. The opera house was dark, hollow, and as bleak as his own feelings. He was lonely but didn't want company. He could never make sense of it. The very times when he starved for friends and lovers, that was when he turned solitary. Like now.

He wore a gray cape, a utilitarian garment that could double as a blanket on the road. And now he wrapped the cape about him, pushed his plug hat down low, and departed, switching off the light, locking the opera house doors. Any saloon would do, and he found one a few yards from the hotel. He smacked into a wall of heat, picked up the scent of hot wool and rank armpits, and settled in a dark booth.

"You serving food?' he asked the pimpled man who loomed over him.

"Chili, that's all."

"A bowl, and a glass of red wine."

"This is a timber town," the youth said, which translated to the absence of wine.

August would have liked a glass of Beaujolais, but settled for Old Orchard, one of Kentucky's more lethal products. He had inherited a French palate, and that didn't include whiskey of any sort.

Too late he spotted Wayne Windsor at the far end of the bar, entertaining some rummies there. Even as Windsor spotted him and waved slightly. The monologuist would stay on his stool, indulging himself with his favorite narcotic, conducting a discourse to an attentive crowd, winning their chuckles, their smiles, their nods. Windsor was doing exactly what he enjoyed most, both onstage or off. With some spirits in him, his monologues edged toward the bawdy, especially late in the evening.

August nodded, slipped chili into himself slowly, savoring the spice, washing it all with sips of bad bourbon.

But then Harry the Juggler materialized, looking as alone as usual. He was by far the most isolated and distant of his acts.

"Have a seat, Harry," August said.

The juggler did, at once, in a way that suggested that Harry had something in mind.

"I yam working on a new act," Harry said, his peculiar accent barely discernible. "Maybe not for this tour. The next."

August smiled. He welcomed new acts, especially by someone with the skills of Harry.

"There's an illusionist, magician, escape artist back east. Just a boy, not yet twenty, but already causing a lot of talk. His name is Weisz, but he's calling himself Harry Houdini, same first name, like me, and he's on the vaudeville circuits in the East."

"I've barely heard of him."

"His big act is to invite the local police in, tell them to cuff him, manacle him, put on leg irons, and give him a little time behind a curtain, and soon he's free and walks out. They can't lock him up."

"But the audience doesn't believe it, I hear."

"Now they do. He's thrown away the curtain, and they see him wrestling with it. He's strong. He's double-jointed. He can move his bones in and out of their sockets. He can somehow compress his muscles, shrink his wrists, like he was India rubber."

"That's a good act."

"Yes, and now he's adding to it. He's putting himself in jeopardy. They're putting him manacled in a tank of water, and he's got to get free before he dies."

August pondered that. "Not sure I'd like that on my stage."

"Houdini never fails," Harry said.

"Well, that's the sort of big-time act I can't afford, Harry."

Harry stared, checkmated by August's dismissal. "I am working on such an act," he said. "I will keep the audience transfixed."

"You already have one. The scimitars. Drop one, catch one wrong, and you're likely to lose a finger. And they know it. You can tell. There's not even a sneeze. It's so quiet out there, you know they're waiting, waiting, waiting for blood."

"Yah, it is good. They're waiting for me to behead myself. That's going to be the new act. You think this one is waiting for mistake, wait until you see my guillotine act."

"Your what?"

"I will juggle lying in a guillotine, my head on the block, facing upward. The blade above, held in place by a small cord. If a scimitar drops and cuts the cord, the guillotine falls and my head rolls. That will keep the audience on the edge of their seats, eh?"

August stared at Harry, stared at the soaks along

the bar, stared at Wayne Windsor, whose jaw was rising and falling, and stared at his empty chili bowl.

"Harry," he began delicately, "this is a road show. We can't be hauling a guillotine around from house to house. Not even if you pay the freight."

"Houdini has big tanks of water, and derricks, and hoists to lower him in."

'Yeah, and a thousand-seat house in New York."

"I will perfect the act. And join you on the next tour. I could do something like it even now. A small guillotine and a rabbit in it. I make a mistake, and it's rabbit for dinner."

"Ah, Harry . . ."

"That's the trouble with acrobat acts. Sing and they love you. Talk and they laugh. But acrobats, jugglers, the silent acts, all we can do is worry them. Scare them. And when the bad doesn't happen, everyone applauds. It's a small pleasure. That boy, Houdini, he doesn't talk. It's all silent. But he does great things. I hear even coppers are amazed. They think they've got him locked up solid, but they don't. Audience likes that. Nothing like a red-faced copper."

Harry smiled. A rare moment.

August didn't want blood on his stage. Drama, fine. Getting out of manacles, that was Houdini's game. But no guillotines. "Harry, there's something you might do. Magic. Combine juggling

324

with some magic. I've always wanted a magician, but they're hard to find, and don't like road shows so much. But if you can do some magic, pull rabbits out of an empty top hat, put your assistant in a long box on sawhorses and saw her in two, until she steps out of the box, that stuff would work fine, and I'd put you on."

"So it is fine for me to saw a woman in two, in a box, but not to put myself under a guillotine blade, eh?"

"The one's an illusion, Harry. Every person watching the magic act knows the young lady will be just fine, and what interests them is how it's done, the illusion. But you're talking about something else, the possible horror if something happens."

"So? What does Houdini do, eh?"

Harry won that one. But August was damned if he'd put a potential bloodbath before people, and ruin his company and maybe vaudeville in the process.

"That's my decision, Harry."

"Magic, that's not the real thing, eh? I do the real thing."

"I'm in the entertainment business, Harry. I want people to go home happy and come again the next night."

"Well, I'm thinking about another act. The Firing Squad. Latin America, sombreros, bandannas. The soldiers drag a prisoner in, white shirt, tie him

325

to a post, lift their rifles, all aimed at his heart. The *capitán*, he lifts his hand holding his sword . . ."

"Then what?"

"A beautiful girl rushes in, waving paper, a pardon."

"Then what?"

"*El capitán*, he lowers his hand, the sword drops, the line of soldiers fires."

"And?"

"The victim, he smiles, takes the big sheet from the girl and holds it up. It says, *Intermission,* and he kisses the girl."

August laughed. And in the wash, his melancholia vanished. He loved the business. It owned him.

34

J. J. Sharpey, manager of the Pocatello Grand Opera House, proved to be a fountain of useful information. Charles Pomerantz had contacted him immediately upon arriving in the southern Idaho town, and was welcomed at once.

It had been an exhausting trip, clear back to Butte, and then down to Pocatello on the Utah and Northern, and he was ready to call it a day. But on the road, anything can be urgent. He needed to know whether the bill-poster, J. W.

Kelly, was putting up the posters, and pasting the new billing in. With his wife, Ginger, getting top billing.

"You have a concert grand piano here. Is it available?" Charles asked.

"Unusual, right? A gift, sir, of the Joneses. He's the superintendent of the Idaho division of the Union Pacific, and a prominent man here. They have a daughter, Penelope, you see, and employ the house for regular recitals. But of course they had to give that up. She was a prodigy, you know, trained by masters, but no master can make a hand grow large enough. Hers didn't span an octave, the minimum for concert pianists, which disappointed the family. I once heard the mother, Mazeppa, inform the young lady that she had to grow her hands, fingers half an inch longer, an inch for the thumb, and no ifs, ands, or buts. But the dear young lady, Penelope, wasn't able to accommodate her mother, though no doubt she tried. Growing one's hands is a tricky business. So the piano goes unused. A Steinway, too. We charge two dollars a night, simply to pay for the piano tuner. He comes clear from Salt Lake to keep it right. We can also put on an orchestra if you need one. Six people."

"So the young lady gave up her career?"

"Oh, no, not at all. Thwarted by small hands, the mother, lovely but firm lady named Mazeppa, put the girl into voice. A sweet voice, that girl. A parade of voice teachers reached town, one after another, and before long the young lady could not only play the piano, but could sing. A nightingale, they call her. Two great skills in a girl not yet an adult. Oh, she slaved, she sang, she comes here for recitals, with her proud parents front center, sir, front center, best seats in the house for the man who more or less runs Pocatello. Front center, to see their precocious daughter sing."

"Her parents sound a bit ambitious for her, sir."

"Oh, they are capital people. I would never say a word otherwise. But they do have a program for that girl, an only child, the vessel of their dreams, it seems."

"What does she think of it, Mr. Sharpey?"

The manager sighed. "She is a dutiful girl, but sometimes I see something, almost haunted, yes, haunted. That's the mark of genius, you know."

"How old, sir?"

"Late teens, out of school now. A whole life on the concert stage ahead. I'm sure the parents are arranging it, but I haven't heard recently."

"I've met a few stage mothers in my day," Charles said. "We even have one in our show, managing her daughters. They are, well, impressive, most of them. But sometimes I feel sorry for the child, the one who's a vessel of someone else's dreams."

"Actually, that girl, she's fortunate. Her folks laid out a fortune, brought in the best teachers.

Did it all here in a growing town, too. I've heard tell they've spent seven thousand on her. They could have sent her off to New York, some academy, but now Pocatello, Idaho, has a top-notch talent to boast about."

"And it is all fine with this girl, Penelope?"

"She puts her heart into every performance."

"Does she have any other life? A young gentleman?"

"Nope. None that I ever heard about. I think her parents discourage it. The music is the beginning and end of everything, that's how I figure it. Must be a quiet life, everything depending on a B minor or a C flat."

"Why here in an opera house? Why not a small hall, or someone's parlor?"

"Fame. We seat six hundred. That's a corker of a number for a town this size. Penelope's fame. It rubs off on the parents, I think. And this is the best place in town for all that. She sings and it rubs off. You should see her mother, just waiting for the compliments. Like the compliments were meant for her, and not the daughter. They always have a reception afterwards. Poor girl has to shake a thousand hands."

"These people, they seem to own the town."

"Well, sir, let me put it this way. He runs the railroad. He can hire or fire most of the people here. And a suggestion to the city fathers, well, you get the idea. Their house is on a little rise, and it gives them a view of Pocatello. You'll see it when you step out."

The manager suddenly reined in his comments, caution restoring his decorum. "You saw the playbill coming in?"

"I did. It's just what we want."

The playbill filled a varnished frame at the front of the opera house. The Beausoleil Brothers show was well displayed. Not like a big-city marquee, but that playbill would be noticed by anyone passing by.

"You going to Boise after us? And what's after that?"

"Reconnect with our West Coast bookings. Three around Seattle, then Portland, Eugene, Corvallis, Klamath Falls, on down, Sacramento, Stockton, Oakland, Berkeley, finish this tour in San Francisco."

"Yeah, if it happens, sir."

"You know something I don't?"

"The new circuit. Everything's changing. The Orpheum man out there, Leavitt's buying every West Coast theater he can put his hands on."

"With what?"

"He's not asked me so I don't know. But he's offering stock in his company, all of that. He's got a couple dozen, and he's locking up the talent now. He'll move the talent city to city, once a week, or hold it over, it doesn't matter. The talent's mostly back east, so Leavitt's got a hold on what's here. He can give an act a forty-two-week contract, good billing, and good pay, and mostly playing big towns. Most show people would snap that up."

"Is that what happened in Spokane?"

"I heard so. And every day now, I hear something new. It's like falling dominoes. Get a few and the rest fall. They threaten, you know. If you don't sell out to them, they'll build a house across the street and steal your patrons. It's not what you'd call a genteel game."

"We're booked solid," Pomerantz said, suddenly wondering whether that was still true.

Sharpey just grunted.

"And there's a hundred smaller houses. And we're a name show."

"The new vaudeville, there's no show at all, just acts, catching trains from town to town, connected by telegraph. Even phone sometimes. Lots of trains, take you anywhere, fast service, some with sleepers."

Pomerantz had a bad moment, and pushed it aside. "We're booked. We've got good acts. We're paying our freight."

Sharpey didn't argue. Instead, he went upbeat. "Lots of smaller towns, like this one, each with a house that's dark too much, and the ones putting the circuits together, they don't pay attention to us. What do they care about Pocatello or Boise, when they can have Portland?"

"It doesn't make sense to run circuits in places where they can fill a house just once a day," Charles said. "That's for us. A few matinees, but the cash comes in after dark."

"If you can get talent," Sharpey said. "They're locking that up, too."

"We've got a young sweetheart, Ginger, she's going to the top," Charles said. "And she's not going to jump ship." He smiled. "She's my wife."

"Ah, a syndicate," Sharpey said.

Charles smiled. He wondered what Sharpey would be saying in a few days.

There was business to be done. Sharpey had ordered the tickets, a set for each night, with the bulk of them on sale at Ransome's Drugstore. The store got a nickel an orchestra ticket, two and a half cents for a gallery seat. The newspapers had been contacted. Ads purchased. Tickets sent to the reviewers. Some handout releases had been given to the papers. Sharpey was as good as his name. There was a good handout of Wayne Windsor, and a fine one on Harry the Juggler. The stuff that Ethel had printed up about LaVerne Wildroot was embarrassing, but it didn't matter.

Pomerantz yawned. "What hotel?"

"Pacific Hotel. Just a hop away. Dollar seventy-five single, two dollars double."

"I'd better book us in," Pomernantz said.

He stepped into a velvet evening. The town's commercial district was solid, permanent, and bustling. He could begin to like a place like this, if it weren't so far from everything. Sure enough, on a rise to the north was a house that lorded over the town, a light shining from most of the mullioned windows. It was not a mansion, just a spacious house with a regal view over the town and the valley.

His parents-in-law. He wasn't sure he wanted to meet them. But then he decided they would soon relax, maybe take some pride in their daughter's new career. Maybe welcome him. He could hope for the best. Ginger was a miracle he couldn't explain. She had slipped into his every thought, and the sheer joy of her colored his days.

He got a room, payable in advance, and then sought to book the company into twelve rooms, doubles, four nights.

"This a theater outfit?" the clerk asked.

"Yes, the Beausoleil Brothers Follies. We'll be playing at the opera house, then off to Boise."

"Theater company, is it? That'll be in advance, of course. Twenty-four times four, that's ninety-six."

"I don't have that much. But the company will, when it arrives, sir. How about a deposit, to be applied to the tariff?"

The clerk, a thin fellow in wire spectacles, slowly shook his head. "My instructions are, sir, enterprises of your sort, they all pay cash on the barrelhead."

"Is there a reason?"

"Certainly. Skipping town with bills unpaid. That's one. But this town, we have certain standards. I'm sure you'll understand."

"No, I don't. Tell me."

"I will leave it to your imagination, sir." He pushed his spectacles upward. "Cash up front, that's it."

"Is there another hotel?"

"I'm sure you'll find that out."

He kept his room for the night, but bowed out. The European was down the street, and he soon had rooms for his company, four nights, doubles at one-fifty, five percent discount. Payable on arrival. But the place smelled odd. And it had no plumbing in any room. That was all down the hall.

The clerk there was just the opposite of the one at the Pacific: short, garrulous, and bursting with cheer. For some reason, he wore a battered bowler, even behind the check-in counter.

"People go to the opera house much?" Pomerantz asked.

"Depends on whether you empty a pay envelope or fill one," the clerk said. "Them that fill the envelopes, the proper ones, they don't much care for entertainments."

"Is there a reason?"

The clerk eyed Pomerantz. "There's an idea around here that this nice place, it should keep out a lot of people and just welcome some. And the easiest way to do that is to run a watch and ward, looking after morals and such. There's some, want to take the town dry. There's others, want to make tobacco costly, put a big tax on. There's others, they want some people to live in certain wards, and other people to live in other wards, all sorted out. There's some, they want to have the public schools, they won't take anyone that don't speak English. We got some railroad workers around here, they're from all over everywhere."

Pomerantz was filling in the blanks fast. "Suppose we do a minstrel act. How'll that go?"

"Blackface?" The clerk grinned, baring a snaggle tooth. "You sure don't know Pocatello."

"We've got some gals singing. They show a little ankle."

"Yeah? They'll get hauled away, likely. Two-dollar fines."

"We've got a monologuist. You know, like Mark Twain. He pokes a little fun."

"Who's this Twain?"

"Man with a sharp tongue, wrote some stories."

"He'd best keep his trap shut," the clerk said. "Take my advice."

That was good to know. That's what advance men did, and why advance men worked ahead of a show. Pomerantz felt the burden. It was his task to keep the show out of trouble, and trouble often came from the least-expected corner. But this time, he thought, Pocatello would run him through the wringer.

35

Ginger read the telegram she had just received. It was printed in capital letters on porous yellow paper, the blue ink blurred.

SING AND THE WORLD SINGS WITH YOU STOP MISS AND LOVE YOU CHARLES

She clutched it. A boy had knocked at her door and handed it to her. It seemed a marvel, something bright and new in her life. Charles was such a worldly man, and each hour with him had brought riches to her.

A wire, just for her! The yellow sheet diverted her, if only for the moment, from the looming menace that was threatening her life. Pocatello. Her parents. Or rather, her mother, ready to impose her will at whatever cost. She hoped that she could simply hide in her hotel room there, not appear, not let anyone in her town see her or know she was there.

She hoped she might return to the stage in Boise, having escaped the confrontation she dreaded. She hoped she might just continue,

Charles' wife, then the cities around Seattle, then Oregon, each show, each day one step farther away from Pocatello. She had told August she would leave the show, but she hoped she wouldn't. She hoped she could just slide through. Or maybe go with Charles on his advance tours, putting things together in Boise, far, far from her home.

That afternoon she had ventured into the bright November sun, strolling Higgins, looking for some small token to give to Charles. And in front of a chocolate shop a well-dressed couple had waylaid her.

"Miss Ginger, is it?" the gentleman said. "Ah, we saw you, and simply want you to know what a delight. A treat. I wish we could see more beautiful girls singing."

"Me?" she asked.

"Yes, young lady. You are the beau ideal."

She wasn't sure about that beau ideal business, but she nodded.

"I teach rhetoric at the college, and if you should ever like to address my class, I'd be pleased to have you. Just six students, just getting the college under way, of course. Beaumont, my name. Sterling Beaumont, and my wife, Clarice."

"A lovely performance, Miss Ginger," the lady said. "Our students will be so pleased to learn we encountered you."

Ginger nodded. Her first admirers! So many people had come to her recitals, and they were quick to say how well she had mastered Chopin or whatever. But she had never considered them admirers, as this couple were.

"Well, goodness, thank you," she said.

Beaumont tipped his felt hat, and the couple proceeded on its way.

She bought a small paper bag of chocolates laced with almonds for Charles, and retreated buoyantly to the hotel.

If this was show business, she was all for it.

She was noticed. They liked her singing. The whole world lay just ahead. All she had to do was sing, sing, sing, and everything life had to offer would be hers. She hastened back to the hotel, looking for August Beausoleil. She needed to talk. He was not about. She hastened to his room, knocked boldly, and after a moment the door swung open. He was half-dressed. He stared, no warmth at all in his face.

"I want to talk to you, sir."

"I will not have my partner's wife seen entering or leaving my room. I will be in the lobby in five minutes."

With that, he pressed the door shut. She found herself staring at the blank door instead of his flinty face. Well, then, the lobby.

It wasn't much of a lobby, and this wasn't much of a hotel. It was an enlarged corridor, the registration desk on one side, and a bench on the other. It seemed all too public, with all the hotel's

338

traffic walking straight past her. But she had to explain. She had to try it again.

He appeared in less than five minutes, nodded to her to step outside, and she followed, having to exert herself to keep up with him.

"What is it?" he asked.

"I was hasty," she said. "I want to sing. Just not in Pocatello, that's all. I'm sorry I was hasty."

"No," he said.

"No what, sir?"

"You're done. You'll not come to me one day, wanting out, and another day, wanting in. Every such choice turns my show upside down. I don't care who you are, or how you're married, you're through."

There was wrath in him. She'd never seen it, never imagined it, because Beausoleil was a man firmly in command of himself.

"Go to Pocatello or not, but not on my stage," he added. "Travel with Charles if you want, but not in my show. Sing on the streets if you want, but not in my show."

"Could I rejoin in Boise?"

"Never. The best thing for Charles to do is ship you back east. Are we done?"

She felt a wave of sorrow steal through her. Everything had gone wrong. She had fled her parents to find a new life, and now she had thrown away that new life, and there was nothing ahead. Not even if Charles loved her, not even if her sudden marriage bloomed, would it make up for what she had just done.

"I deserve it," she said. "But you deserve something, too. A warning. My father is a powerful man, and he and my mother can make trouble for you, and will. I was seen by a friend of theirs. They may know I'm in the company."

"I'll deal with whatever comes."

But then he relented a little. "What should I expect?"

"I don't know. But it could be courts and lawyers."

"They're like that?"

"My mother . . . she's poured all her ambitions into me, and the least of her ambitions is to join a vaudeville company. For her, that would be like—getting a bad reputation."

"I'll deal with it. I've dealt with worse. I've opened in towns with officials who wanted to bust the company."

"What for?"

"They see a company come in, make some good money, and leave town with a bag full of greenbacks. To them, it's almost like we stole it. So they think of ways to break the company. Get the money before it skips town. Fines, jail, lawsuits. I've dealt with them all. And I'll deal with your family, if it comes to that. Are we done?"

This was a different man than the quiet one she had met only a few weeks ago.

"I will sing tonight and each show in Missoula."

"I will expect no less of you."

"I will sing better than I ever have."

"I expect that from every person in the company. Those who don't, they don't last. I've hardly ever ended a tour with the same company I started with. And this is no exception."

He was softening a bit. But she knew better than to think that would affect her fate.

"I've said what I wanted. Now I'll go warm up," she said.

He grunted and left her there, and she made her way into the darkened theater. Not even a bare bulb lit the stage, but there were two small windows on the left-side corridor casting gray light into gloom. The place echoed and its hollowness caught her. Why were theaters so sad, so much of their lives?

Backstage she found a simple light switch on the wall, and pressed the button. A lamp glowed up at the top of the flies. A deep chill weighed upon the dark interior.

What would this be, a recital or a vaudeville act? Recitals barely needed an audience. The performer was looking for perfection, and if the audience assented or approved, that all was fine but not critical. There wasn't a soul in the cold theater. She peered into the gloom, somehow comforted that no one was sitting there, not a single soul. That gave her liberty. She could experiment. She could perfect a note, a breath. Until recently, she had begun recitals with barely a nod to the auditors before her. Her task, her mother's wish, was to prove to the world that her daughter was a prodigy.

She would sing to the audience that wasn't there. Not long. Even at her tender age, she could wear out her voice. She would have to pretend. She imagined that the opera house brimmed with gentlemen in tuxedos with slicked-back hair, the women in gowns and tiaras, all aglitter. She imagined that these people out there were urbane; they had seen a thousand performances and were hard to please. And her task would be to pleasure them, an eighteen-year-old girl wishing to triumph over all the jaded minds waiting for something to happen worth applauding.

She pulled off her coat, letting the chill reach her. In a moment it wouldn't matter. She ran a few scales, knowing that her vocal cords were muscles that needed warming, just as an athlete's body needed warming.

Then she sang this or that; pieces of song. She would try one, try another, discovering only the emptiness of the cavern that swallowed her voice. She sang her folk songs, not forgetting Stephen Foster. She was in good voice, the notes liquid and sweet, but they sailed into a great hollow, where each word was instantly doomed. It would live in no one's memory. She sang an aria. It didn't matter. The place was empty. She felt dissatisfied, and knew at once that she needed the audience. She could never return to recitals. Not until this quiet, hollow place was filled would she find what she was looking for.

She left the building, having gotten more from her singing than the exercise. She had gotten a need and vocation. She had walked into the cold edifice a girl still fleeing her family; she had walked out changed. She was a vaudeville trouper. Nay, a vaudeville star. She might be married to Charles, but in fact her spouse was her audience.

She didn't know how it would work out, but she knew she had a destiny. And she was no longer afraid of going to Pocatello. Or having it out with her mother. If trouble came in Pocatello, her mother would find not a servile daughter, but a firebrand.

That evening in Missoula, once the opera house had warmed, and the crowd had packed in, and the bright lights of the show were burning, she rocked the house. Whatever it was—and who could say?—she owned the stage from the moment she set foot before that crowd. She walked straight to the light, an arc light serving as the limelight, and there she poured out her ballads, some old and familiar to the heart, and then a little of *Carmen*, and finally a couple of love songs, the verses settling like velvet upon all those good people there.

It was a dandy show. Ethel and The Genius finally found their stride, with The Genius insulting everyone in Missoula, and Ethel deflating The Genius at every opportunity. Just as surprising, LaVerne Wildroot was working a new repertoire, a little swing to it, and she was sporting a new smile, too. She was so good that Ginger felt a moment of envy—and fear.

Wayne Windsor went hunting for robber barons in Missoula, and when he couldn't unearth any in the audience, he settled for city council members who were saying smoke was good for the city, proof of its vitality, so what did it matter if it irritated the lungs? He punctuated all that with lingering left and right profiles. And the Marbury Trio, in blackface, tapped minstrel music into the receptive ears of an eager audience that eve.

When Ginger had completed her second-half gig, to rolling applause and an encore, she discovered August Beausoleil staring from the wing, his gaze dark and maybe even bitter.

She smiled but he stood rigid, in his master of ceremonies rig, scowling.

"Well, August," she said, "if you'll let me sing in Pocatello, I'll knock 'em flat."

He glared angrily, and walked away.

36

Cromwell Perkins waylaid August Beausoleil after the curtain call.

"Want to talk to you, old sport. Did you notice? The wind has shifted. Ethel and I got thirty-seven good laughs. Thirty-seven belly-whoppers, in a few minutes. Quite a bit better than Wayne Windsor, I'd say. He got twenty-something."

"Yes, you're coming along. I like it."

"I'm the top dog now, better than Windsor, but it's not reflected in my pay."

Beausoleil caught the drift of this, and said nothing. Around him, people were packing up, heading into the night.

"The Genius is your top draw now," Perkins said louder, as if August were deaf. "And I'm not getting top pay. Windsor gets his hundred, plus top billing. The Genius gets fifty, split with Ethel, and fifth billing." The last was almost a shout.

Beausoleil chose his words carefully. "You're coming along well. But Windsor is known, and draws crowds, and a veteran, able to change his act for any audience. That comes only from experience. This is your first tour. We're proud to have you, and it's my good fortune to feature you and Ethel."

"I'm requiring a pay of a hundred a week henceforth, sir. Ethel will get twenty-five."

He had used that unusual word, *requiring,* deliberately. It was a demand.

"I see," said the manager. "I'm afraid I can't afford that even if there's merit."

"Then you can't afford the best talk act in the business. You can lock me in for the tour, or not. There's never been a contract. You're so short of acts that I'd think you would go out of your way to keep each act satisfied."

"Then the answer's no."

Beausoleil was being a lot tougher than Perkins had expected. It obviously galled him. For weeks, he and Ethel had worked on their drill, spiffing it up, jumping on each other's lines. It was not only rich comedy, it was also becoming a hit. Actually, Beausoleil had been delighted with the improvement.

"You would also need to give me top billing, starting right now, sir."

"Then we are at a parting of the ways. I trust you will finish our Missoula appearance?"

"I shouldn't. I'm just giving away talent. The Genius part of it is real. Can you name any other act that comes close? Of course not. We can pick up any theatrical agent and soon have work at four or five times what you're paying. Fifty dollars in a brown envelope for two. That's called cheap."

"And Ethel would go with you?"

"Ask her. She's tired of her daughters. And LaVerne doesn't need her. And she likes my, shall we say, bed and board. I'd rather be a bar-stool entertainer again than earn ten percent of what I'm worth."

"I can add ten dollars, make it sixty, and move you up to third billing, but only if you and Ethel commit to the entire tour, ending in Frisco in March."

"Not nearly enough. We'll pull out when we close here."

Beausoleil smiled. "Your choice," he said. "Your act means a lot to me, and I'm hoping you'll stay."

"Your loss," said The Genius.

August thought that Perkins' head had expanded several hat sizes.

"I'll wire New York for an act starting Pocatello," Beausoleil said.

If The Genius was disappointed, he hid it well. "And we'll wire an agent ourselves," he said.

"You're done with me? Definitely?"

The Genius hesitated. "I have to talk it over with Ethel. She doesn't always appreciate my contributions. Let you know."

"I'll bring in an act," Beausoleil said. He needed one in any case, with Ginger out. He was stretched way too thin.

It was a costly option; he'd have to pay the freight. But when the opera house had emptied, he braved a cold night, hiked straight north to the rail station, found a sleepy telegrapher with muttonchops, composed his message to theatrical agents in Chicago, Weill and Branch, who used the wire address BWELL: NEED COMEDY OR ANIMAL ACT OPEN POCATELLO DEC 4 TOP SIXTY BEAUSOLEIL.

"Thirteen words, twenty a word," said the agent. "Two dollars and sixty cents, please."

"I should buy some Western Union stock," Beausoleil said. And coughed up.

He probably would be covered. Train to Pocatello took three days. He'd probably greet some eccentric with two talking dogs. Or a raucous parrot. Or a cat with two heads. Or two midgets with top hats taller than themselves. Who could say?

He stepped into a harsh night, feeling the old melancholia again. He was alone; he had been on his own for as long as he could remember. Sometimes he caught glimpses of families, children at the table, the girls in pigtails, the boys happy and well fed. He had no family at all, but he had a good substitute for one, the talents who came and went. Just like The Genius and Ethel, and just like Ginger. All of them quitting at the end of the booking. Well, Ginger was a puzzle. Now she was saying she'd play Pocatello. Suddenly she was ready to take on her family and quit running. He'd think about it. He disliked talent that signed on, signed off, couldn't be steady and reliable. But in spite of himself, Ginger's new feistiness brought a little cheer to him.

He headed back to the dark opera house, let himself in, headed for the safe with the evening's take in the cashbox, lit the overhead bulb, and did his usual count, sorting the grimy bills and adding them. Five hundred and forty-seven this evening, very good. He made a small notation in his vest-pocket ledger, slipped the cashbox back in the Mosler safe, and locked it tight, giving the dial an extra spin. Hartley, the manager, would change the combination after Beausoleil Brothers pulled out. Each visiting troupe got its own strongbox.

Payday was coming, and August would spend the next eve filling brown envelopes. One with fifty for The Genius. Same pay as most of the acts. The Genius was unique. There wasn't another act like it in the business, some knucklehead turning himself into a genius, scorning everything, everyone, every hero or saint in history, all for a surprise and chuckle out there among those folks who often sat on their hands. August was tempted to add ten more to his offer, seventy, try to keep the act around, but he knew what the result would be . . . unless Ethel laid down the law. It really was Ethel who turned Perkins into an act. She figured it out, became his foil, sometimes puncturing him with a wild riposte. And that inspired an interesting idea. He would offer Ethel a fifteen-dollar raise, but nothing for The Genius. She might take it. And then The Genius would discover whose act it really was. The Genius was her prisoner, a thought that entertained August.

It was late. Gust's Saloon stood kitty-corner across from the opera house, and August headed in that direction. After each show, the place was packed. And before the show, too. It was a long, narrow place with a few tables and a dartboard at the rear, and a homespun bar and back bar forward. All pine cabinetry, made from local wood. No Brunswick mahogany bar furnishings here. The rear overhead light had been turned off.

Almost empty. One old soak in a white shirt and corduroy coat occupied a seat. The saloon man was polishing glasses. He looked annoyed, probably because he wanted to close.

"Make it fast," the barkeep said.

Moments later August was nursing a bourbon several stools away from the old soak.

"You're with the show," the soak said. "I can tell."

"Manage it."

"We're in the same business," the soak said.

"You? Variety shows?"

"No, I teach rhetoric at the college. My task is to entertain about twenty bored students and stuff them with what they don't want to know."

"How does that make us alike?"

"I am a showman." The soak sipped amber

juice from his glass. "The enemy is boredom. They are eager to be entertained, but not educated. But if I fail to educate them, then it reflects on me just as bad box office reflects on you. No paying customers, and you're done for."

"I can fire an act," August said. "But you're stuck. At least until grading time."

"No, no, I'm talking about my failings, sir. Some academics inspire students, draw them to their courses, turn them into good scholars who get good grades. But, sir, you are not talking to one of those. I'm the sort who drones through the hour, and the students avoid rhetoric the rest of their unnatural lives. I envy you. Entertaining well is a rare gift. Not one person in a thousand can entertain others."

He downed a mighty slug of amber.

August scarcely knew what to say.

"This is our fourth academic year, sir. A new college in the sticks. We're missing an ear, have six fingers on one hand, and webbed toes. But we're open. No scholar in his right mind would voluntarily come to Missoula. That says something about me, correct?"

"Yes. It says you had the courage to come and build a university, sir."

The old soak laughed. "And everyone has a fairy godmother."

The barkeep set down his towel. "Drink up, gents; I'm closing in five."

"Professor, I'd like to give you two tickets to our show," August said, digging into his vest pocket for the front-center seats he always carried.

"Have I earned them?" the man asked.

"Anyone who survives classes of daydreaming students year after year has earned them."

The old gent stared, plucked them up, and smiled. "This is the best thing that's happened to me in Montana," he said.

The professor tucked the tickets away, swallowed the dregs, nodded, and left.

August was about to follow, but the keep suddenly poured another shot into his glass.

"That's for making the old sob-sister happy," he said. "He's got a cloud over him and leaks rain every time he comes in."

"We've all got troubles."

"Sure we do. And professors got more troubles than anyone else. If I had to deal with a lot of wet-behind-the-ear squirts I'd be a souse. You know what? You've got the best business on the planet. You open the curtains, and you make people happy. They forget their cares for a bit; you run your acts out, and they take us away from ourselves, and for just a little bit, the world is good."

"Well, you do that here, just listening to your customers."

"Nah, I just get them soaked enough so they quit complaining. No big deal."

"Life's mostly drudgery. You open up your pub, and they come in and tell stories or make friends, and they go away content."

The keep didn't argue. "That's what pubs are for. And you're what opera houses are for. I keep an ear out, you know. My regulars, they see whatever comes into town, and they're talking about just one thing. The girl. The one in white. She comes out, into the limelight, and she's just right. I mean, not brassy, not glittery, but like the girl most lads dream of, and she starts to sing, and she's smiling at them, and she sees them, and she sings to them, and that's how she's got about half the men in Missoula in love with her."

"Ginger."

"That's the one. She's giving every lad in town a dream, including the married ones. You know what? They talk about her. They say they'd trade any two women for one Ginger. They say they'd never have a chance with her, because some millionaire's gonna snap her up."

"Yes, she's a great one. And she came to us just a few weeks ago. Out of the blue. Wanted to audition. I wasn't even going to do that. She sang at a funeral; we lost one of our acts, and this girl sang. And my partner got interested in her, and here's the thing. They got married. I thought it was just because she wanted a ticket into the business, but the thing is, she loves him. She's got that, you see. That innocent beauty."

"And now she's your draw."

"For the moment," August said.

He found two more tickets and proffered them, but the barkeep shook his head.

"Gotta work," he said. "We all gotta work."

37

August read the terse wire from Weill and Branch, theatrical agents. An act, The Grab Bag, would be in Pocatello December third. Good. August had not seen it but knew about it. The act was the work of Harry and Art Grabowski, acrobats, and it featured a stooge. Art would sit in the audience and insult Harry, who would begin with some indifferent acrobatic stunts, and sometimes fail to execute them properly, landing in a heap.

That's when Art would start yelling insults, and Harry would take offense, and Art would boil up to the stage and there would be a comic brawl. Harry would throw a haymaker, and Art would do a cartwheel or a flip-flop. The mock fight was a work of acrobatic genius, each blow resulting in a comic response. That was all good. Sixty a week, two hundred twelve to get them to Pocatello. That was painful. He was lucky to collect six hundred a night to support his entire company.

But it was necessary to put them in the lineup.

Who knew what The Genius and Ethel would do next, or whether the girl would sing, or who'd get sick. The whole tour had been like that. The Grabowskis were insurance, and could vary their routine. They could do a variety of straight acrobatic acts, some combined with music.

This was closing night in Missoula and he was eager to put the show on the road. They'd had enough of smoky air, and were hoarse. The night was going to be hell. An eastbound express rolled through at ten thirty, and he was tempted to cut the show short and board it; but he refused. It had been his cardinal rule to give every audience its money's worth. The next train was a milk run, stopping at every crossroads, and leaving Missoula at two in the morning. And when it got to Butte there would be another wait for a southbound Utah and Northern local to Pocatello, and the company would not get a wink of sleep.

They would spend night hours in the Missoula station, sitting on its varnished pews, waiting. They would spend hours more in Butte, waiting in the dimly lit waiting room, waiting, waiting, wanting only the comfort of a warm bed.

It was all because of an improvised schedule through Idaho, upsetting the careful planning that smoothed a tour. Still, these were troupers, used to it, and he was satisfied that the company would hold together and that they'd soon be in the footlights.

But it was an oddly listless show that eve, before a house only two-thirds filled. There were two bright spots. Ginger sang eloquently, and caught the crowd once again, and The Genius and Ethel topped everything else. His two departing acts had saved the night. Then it was over. The troupers climbed into winter coats and left the darkened theater. Their bags had already been carted to the station; they had only to walk the seven blocks through the gloomy city and begin the long wait.

By eleven they had all settled on the hard pews in a semiheated building, and began a three-hour wait, always assuming the local was on time. Wayne Windsor seemed resigned; he had done this a hundred times on the road. The Marbury Trio were restless, pacing the room, sliding outside, letting in gales of cold air, wishing the train along, peering down the empty rails, and seeing nothing. A freight at midnight stirred them all. No one was saying much. No one was reading. They had all sunk into their private worlds. Or wishing hellfire upon the new operators of the Spokane opera house. Or trying to sleep sitting up. Or wishing for a stiff drink.

Why were they there? What bleak turn of life had brought them to this stern waiting room on a wintry night? Why were they patient? He stared about, seeing not performers but wounded people driven to the performer's life, just as he had been from childhood onward. Most were first or second generation. Harry the Juggler was a new arrival, and wrestled with English; what had driven him to abandon a quiet life in Europe, cross the sea, and find a living in vaudeville?

Most had arrived in the business because it was the only door open to them. They certainly hadn't come from bourgeois families; they were outcasts, prevented from walking through polished doors that might lead to law or medicine or political office or academic life. Some had changed their names, shedding the one that imprisoned them in favor of something bland and English. August could guess the origins of most of his troupe. He knew of only one who had arrived in his company from the upper crust, and that was Ginger.

She sat alone, encased in a shroud that seemed to isolate her. He watched her, knowing that the trip back to Pocatello would be a trial, but also her passage to independence. He didn't know just what awaited her there, but she had chosen to confront it, and if she won the forthcoming battle with her family, she would bloom.

She was not inviting company, and there was something in her face that suggested a private ordeal. The rest of the troupe, sensing something, had left her to her imaginings.

August approached gently. "Want to walk?"

She nodded. He led her into the quiet dark. The air was harsh but not moving, and they could ease their way along the streets, which were largely devoid of paved sidewalks in the area.

She seemed almost companionable, though she was utterly silent.

"Going home's going to be hard, I imagine," he said.

"I knew you wanted to talk about that. If I don't find the courage, then I'll be afraid the rest of my life."

"You left your family?"

"My jailers."

"I have good friends in the business who escaped, like that."

"You do?"

"Sure, in the East. One's the son of a cantor in Brooklyn. His father wanted him to sing and taught him all the sacred music; he was going to have his son become a cantor, too. Except the son couldn't stand it, and bolted. Flat ran out. He's singing in vaudeville now. All that training, it's making him a living."

"My mother wants me to be a singer, like in concert halls. First she wanted me to be a pianist, and when my hands didn't grow enough, she wanted to stretch them every night."

"She has ambitions for you, Ginger."

"Ambitions, yes. But for her, not for me. She sees me as a vessel for her dreams."

"And that's why you need to confront her now."

"At first I fled; I'd never look back, but when I

learned we'd play in Pocatello, I suddenly had to face the music."

"Do you think you can? May we help?"

"It's something I've got to do, Mr. Beausoleil."

"Ginger, I like it. Most of us in the business are running from something. We ended up in the business because it's the only open door. Our families fled the old country, where we were shunned or outcasts or desperately poor, or trapped in a life without hope. You fled, too, and now you're willing to finish up, return, and face them, if that's the word for it. You've got some things on your side: eighteen, employed, married."

"I'm christened Penelope, and you'll hear that name if they come, and I know they will. But I'm Ginger, and I won't let them take Ginger from me."

"Everyone in the company will help, if you need help."

She stopped walking. "I need to do it myself," she said. "But thank you."

He admired that. "Ginger, there's not a man in the company who isn't in love with you," he said.

She didn't know how to manage that, and slid into quietness.

"Call on us if you need us," he said. "The whole company."

"You don't know my mother," she said.

That was all. They strolled back to the station through lonely darkness.

They welcomed the local when it finally chuffed in, two boxcars and an ancient coach, just in case someone wanted to travel somewhere through a long night. They boarded, put all their show baggage in the coach, and soon the engine was wailing through the blackness, with pea snow clattering against the grimy windows. The train was literally on a milk run. At Deer Lodge it stopped to load casks of raw milk, destined for a Butte creamery, along with a ton of potatoes destined for the mining town.

Then the local cranked its way east, its weary passengers swaying through the wee hours and the very late hours of night. Butte, perpetually alive, seemed quiet at four when they wearily debarked, heaving all their show stuff to the platform because there were no teamsters or cabbies to help them.

August eyed his company; they were shell-shocked with weariness and lost in silence. The only one who seemed impervious was The Genius, who had been working the contents of a flask through his innards. The Utah and Northern, a branch of the Union Pacific, loaded them at dawn, this time into a clean coach that was warm, and soon they were en route to Pocatello.

Ginger was staring at nothing, lost in her own world, but the rest brightened at the thought of a hotel room and sleep. The Grand Opera House in Pocatello would be dark that eve; the next day, the Follies would be up in lights.

Beausoleil lost track of time, but in the middle of the next morning the train chugged into Pocatello Junction, a mountain-girt town of about fifty-five hundred. The troupe wearily collected bags, and discovered Charles Pomerantz waiting for them with two hacks and a dray to carry luggage and equipment.

August peered about, looking for signs of trouble, and found none. The whitewashed station rested peacefully in the bright sun, indifferent to those who flowed through it day and night. He watched Ginger step onto the conductor's stool, and then the gravel platform, peer about cautiously, discover Charles, and race to him. He greeted her with a sweeping hug that lasted a long moment, and then led her to a hack. He had business to attend to: getting the weary troupe to its hotel, along with all their baggage.

The hack carrying Ginger was soon loaded, and Charles sent it on its way, and then the rest, until the company had been cared for.

That left just August and Charles, partners in a precarious enterprise, standing there.

"So far, no trouble," Charles said. "I've learned a thing or two about the Joneses, her parents. They are well liked and greatly respected here. But I haven't met them, haven't heard a word about trouble. They may not even know their daughter's here. But we'll see."

"Ginger's holding up. She's not running;

361

she wants to get it over, so she can quit running."

"That's my girl."

"New act in?"

"Yes, at the hotel. The Grabowski boys. They seem fine, ready to go."

"Tickets moving?"

"Yeah, good news, sold out tomorrow. Filling up the next nights. You want to walk? It's a few blocks."

"Do me good," August said.

They walked through a bright and comfortable town, well set in its valleys, which branched outward into arid slopes. Maybe a good place to visit, but not a place to live if you enjoyed variety.

"How are we in Boise?"

"They're pasting the bills up, they say. I think we're set. But I'm not hearing from our bookings on the coast. And it's been three days since I wired Seattle. The manager in Boise says he's heard a rumor or two about buyers offering good money for houses up and down the coast, but he said it's just talk. Things are going along."

Charles had booked them into the Bannock Hotel, white clapboard place next to a Mrs. Wilson's Pancake Parlor. It would do, even if they charged two dollars, a steep price for a small room. The opera house was half a block away.

The Grab Bag boys were waiting in the small lobby. Art looked like a muscular boxer; Harry was a slim gymnast.

"We're ready to roll," Harry said. "Art's the stooge. He's twice my size, which works real good. Sets up the crowd. He's gonna get up on the stage and flatten me. We're ready for a few laughs."

"Can't wait to see it," August said. "We'll run you twice, before and after the break. I hope you've got several routines."

"Oh, we got a bunch," Art said. "We can knock 'em senseless. You mind paying us in advance? We're flat."

"I'll lend you two bucks," August said.

"We eat that in a day," Harry said. "Acrobats chow down."

August sighed, and forked over two singles. "Earn it, then," he said.

38

Ginger had been in this building before. Twice she had played her parents' Steinway grand piano on this stage. The piano had been carried down to the opera house from her parents' home on the heights. Three times more she had sung at this hall after her mother had switched her from piano to voice. There had been other recitals in more intimate venues, but this was the stage where her mother had presented her to the world.

After a few desperate hours of rest at the

Bannock Hotel, the weary troupe was gathering at the opera house ahead of its opening in Pocatello. They had rattled along silver rails, finally settling in their rooms around eleven for whatever rest they could extract from an early December afternoon with the low sun brightening the streets.

It soon would be dark. The Grand Opera House loomed solidly in the dusk. In Pocatello they built things to last, in part because her father insisted on it. Pocatello Junction, as some still called it, was no fly-by-night railroad construction town, but a durable city of brick and stone with spacious houses of well-cured pine. The Union Pacific was going to put this town on the map to stay.

Ginger was oddly passive. She had come to accept that she could not thwart a confrontation if her parents chose to have one. She had her majority, a wedding ring, Charles and August to shield her, not to mention a performance contract with Beausoleil Brothers Follies. Still, her parents were a looming presence, and she could hardly take a step onstage without imagining that they were watching and waiting.

Charles had mercifully let her rest. Marriage was still a puzzle to her; she hadn't been at it long enough to learn how to live with a man she barely knew. He, the urbane showman, seemed a lot more comfortable with it than she was.

"This is where you'll be the star of the show, baby," he had said.

The troupe soon collected there in the cold building. Theaters were never warm except when they brimmed with people. The stage was lit by one bare bulb, casting sickly light upon the gathering company. She met The Grab Bag act, thick Harry, slim Art, gymnasts with a streak of comedy.

"Miss Ginger, all I've heard about you is true," Art said, which made her curious. "Here's my greeting card."

He leapt upward, did a complete back flip, landed on his feet, and bowed.

"Do I shake your hand or your big toe?" she asked.

"I'm your slave for life," Art said.

"Have you met everyone?" she asked.

"Not if I can help it," Harry said.

"He's the stooge," Art said.

The term was beyond her, but she would soon figure it all out. She watched the Marbury Trio, looking just as tired as they did in the morning, loosen up. And Wayne Windsor was loosening his tonsils, sipping something she decided was a private brand of tonsil tonic. But what startled her the most was The Genius, who was singing scales, *do re mi fa sol la ti do . . .*

"Genius, why are you singing the scales?"

"The train ride wrecked my voice."

"But you could just talk to Ethel."

"Ethel is in no mood for talk. All she wanted was her matrimonial rights. No sooner did we get off the train than she attacked me."

"I think I will go say hello to Harry the Juggler," she said, escaping the hand that shot out to stay her.

"Once a genius, always a genius, at all things large and small," he said.

Harry was unpacking his trunk, filled with lethal knives, scimitars, and cups and saucers.

"Did you sleep, Harry?"

"I am working on a guillotine act," Harry said, his voice thick. "Soon I will have it. A guillotine, the blade above me, suspended by a cord. If I drop a knife on the cord, I drop my head in a basket."

"That would make the front pages," she said.

"It would be an India rubber head. I will work it like the magician who puts a girl into a box and saws the box in half."

"Where would your real head be?"

"I haven't figured that out yet, but I will. Then I will show the act to Monsieur August."

"I think at the end, you should stand and hold your head at arm's length," she said.

"I'm perfecting it," he said.

She greeted the Wildroot girls, who seemed none the worse for wear. They were from an old theater family, and somehow knew how to get through exhausting times. She discovered August eyeing her, and knew he was keeping close tabs on her.

"I will be all right," she said. "There's nothing they can do."

"But will it upset you?"

"Maybe. But Mr. Beausoleil, I left home. I did it on my own. I made my plans, got some cash together, figured out an escape, and did it, and they never found me. That was harder than this. Now I have friends."

"My empty stomach is what started me," he said. "Get into the business or steal."

Then she was alone. She had to see what was least wrinkled in her trunk, and put it on. She slipped down the steps into the orchestra, three hundred and fifty seats stretching back to a perimeter that defined the lobby. A balcony curved overhead, with another two hundred fifty seats. This was a fine, solid house for a small town. It had 110-volt alternating current, the latest type, and the company would not need to light foot lamps or fire up the limelight. It had a skilled bill-poster, who had pasted up the notices all over town, notices that placed Ginger in second billing, behind Wayne Windsor. One of the bills graced a cabinet at the front of the opera house, between two sets of double doors. And Charles had not neglected the press. There in *The Tribune*, that day, was a story, and a paragraph about her, Ginger, wife of the co-owner, Charles Pomerantz. Maybe that was a form of insurance, she thought.

Charles would do what he could to keep her from being molested.

She selected a bottle-green velveteen for the first act, a tailored dress that flattered her and also seemed suited for the American ballads she planned to sing her first round. She had exploited familiar songs, old songs children had learned from their parents. Her second act was often classical, sometimes operatic. And she welcomed encores.

Showtime.

August had donned his tuxedo and top hat, the white bib a little worse for wear, but no one would notice. She caught him gazing at her. He waved gently; everything would be fine.

Backstage, the acts readied themselves. The new one would be different. One of them was seating himself on an aisle seat. The other, Art, was wearing blue tights, a gymnast outfit, and looked pretty snappy, she thought. The Wildroot girls were looking glorious, as always; they were the real troupers in the show.

Ginger slid the curtain aside a bit so she could peer out from the edge of the proscenium at the gathering crowd. She couldn't make out faces, nor did she see her parents. If they came, they would be front center, but they weren't. Still, there were people she knew, people who knew her, who would puzzle at the transformation of Penelope Jones. They would know her voice, her style, her face, her walk, and her parents. She could not hide that, nor would she try. If there was trouble with her parents, she would cope—somehow. She wasn't sure of it. The thought made her jittery. But she had songs to sing, and a voice to warm up, and she concentrated on readying herself. A few quiet scales, anything to loosen the tightness in her throat and body.

Then the moment came. An opening was always electric. It was just as electric to veterans of the stage as it was to new arrivals. An opening, new town, new audience, caught in the throat and held, as the curtain parted or rolled upward.

And there was August, his stride confident, pushing out to center stage as the crowd quieted.

"Ladies and gents, good evening. The Beausoleil Brothers Follies is proud to play in, what is it? Peoria? Billings? Ah, Pocatello, in the great state of Idaho, home of the potato," he said. "And now, to warm your evening, the one, the only Wildroot Sisters, sweethearts of song."

And away they went.

August returned to the shadowed wing, smiled at Ginger, and the show rolled ahead, one act upon another, a clockwork procession of song and athletics and talk. Wayne Windsor warmed up the crowd. The Marbury Trio did a jaunty tap dance. Harry the Juggler tossed his scimitars. And then August announced a new act, the one, the only Grab Bag. Art Grabowski sailed on, found the brightest spot, did a few flips, walked on his hands, did several cartwheels, and whirled around the stage on a monocycle. But there was a fellow out in the crowd who didn't like it.

"What's this, a joke?" he yelled.

Art stopped. "My good man, if you don't like my act, you can always leave."

"Leave? Then all these suckers would have to sit here for another ten minutes."

"You're interrupting the show, sir."

"I'll show you what it means to interrupt a show, pal."

Harry, in street clothes, bulled up the aisle, found the stairs, pushed out onto the stage, while the audience waited breathless at what looked to be a fight.

Harry was about twice as big as Art. Harry pushed on, while Art backpedaled on his monocycle, a precarious retreat. And then Harry charged, but Art cycled out of the way, abandoned his one-wheel bike, and stood his ground. Next time big Harry swarmed in, Art unloosed a haymaker, and Harry did three backflips and a cartwheel.

Suddenly, the audience chuckled.

The act turned into a choreographed brawl, the little guy against the big tormentor, with the pair tumbling and rolling. Every time the big guy swarmed in, he overshot, or the little guy tripped him and he ended up doing cartwheels.

The audience soon was laughing, then hooting, then applauding each time the little guy foiled another assault and sent the big guy to the floor. But the moment came when the little guy won the fight, and stood with a foot on the big guy's chest, and then the Grabowskis were up and bowing and looking a little sweaty.

This was a world that Ginger knew nothing about. She had never seen anything like it in her gently raised life, and at first she recoiled, but then the audience's enjoyment tugged at her, and from her perch backstage she began laughing, too. The Grabowskis were not only acrobats but gifted comics, and their act was winning a lot of laughter from the crowd.

She knew something then: Vaudeville was for all people. It wasn't a bit like her high-toned recitals for cultivated people whose tastes had been schooled and refined. Vaudeville was broad, earthy, universal, and fun. Which is perhaps why her parents were not out there; vaudeville was beneath them.

It had almost been beneath her, too. But in the few weeks of her touring, she had come face-to-face with thousands of working people, miners and shop girls and clerks, all of them laying out their dollars for an evening of fun.

She watched the two grinning acrobats slip off the stage, even as August, looking chipper in his top hat, trotted out as the applause faded.

"The Grab Bag, come out for a bow, boys," he said.

And Art and Harry hurried out for one last bow, and then cartwheeled away.

"And now, the lady you've been waiting for, the singer with the voice of a silver bell, the one, the only Ginger! Please welcome our new nightingale, Miss Ginger."

And then she was on. Her heart pattered. She heard an immediate buzz, the whispers, the questions as she made her way to the bright-lit center stage. Some of them knew her. Another name, an earlier time. She paused, knowing she looked good in that green velveteen.

She smiled. She bowed gently. There were three of the company's musicians in the orchestra pit. An accordionist, a guitarist, and a banjo player. They would simply pick up whatever she started.

She filled her lungs. She chose some ballads first. Stephen Foster. "Jeanie with the Light Brown Hair." And the more she sang, the more she knew that all those people were dreaming of Miss Ginger, and wildly curious about the girl they knew as Penelope.

39

Standing in the wings, Charles Pomerantz thought that maybe this show, this evening, was the finest the Follies had ever wrought. The performers, exhausted from the hard trip, had somehow drawn from their last reserves to delight the audience.

His surprising bride had done even better after the intermission, turning to ballads that evoked generous applause. And it was her audience. These were people who knew her, who were speculating about her new life and name.

She knew it. She sang with a warmth he had never heard in her. It was almost as if she had minted a new voice for this event; as if the new Ginger-voice would separate her from her Penelope self. Was she seeking their approval? It occurred to him that, yes, she wanted it badly. She was offering herself to them.

And still no sign of her parents. But the run in Pocatello had just begun, and if word had not yet reached them, it soon would. He thought she just might cope with it. But it worried him. He hoped to be on hand, to help, to defend, to encourage, and if there were tears, to wipe them away.

But it wasn't just Ginger who was transfixing

the crowd that night. The Genius and Ethel had them chuckling. The Marbury Trio was introducing tap dance to a lot of people who had never seen it, and they were swaying in their theater seats, and enjoying the svelte athletics. Even LaVerne Wildroot, doing a solo or two in front of the olio, was catching waves of applause.

August seemed to know the evening was rare, and fairly strutted out to introduce the acts, choosing to be conversational and quiet. And so it went on opening night in Pocatello Junction, Idaho. When at last the curtain rang down on a generous evening, the performers stood quietly, aglow. How long had it been since any of them had enjoyed an audience like this? A perfect show, like this? Even the newcomers, Art and Harry Grabowski, who had contributed much, listened to the happy crowd in wonder.

It was only after a peculiar pause that the performers began to drift to the dressing rooms. Ginger looked oddly restless; whatever she had been expecting hadn't happened. Not yet, anyway.

Charles watched a bespectacled man work through the performers and close in on Ginger. He was a skinny drink of water with a polka-dot bow tie and gummy lips.

"Parkinson with *The Tribune*," he said. "Like a word."

Charles caught the flash of uncertainty in Ginger's face, and watched her stiffen and nod.

"Okay, miss, you're Penelope Jones, right?"

"Sir, I'm not *miss*. I'm Mrs. Pomerantz, and this is my husband, who's an owner of the show."

"How do you spell it?" the reporter asked.

Charles obliged him.

"Okay, the word is, you're the same as left here a while ago, dodging the old lady, and now you're an actress. Right?"

"I am Ginger now. I am not an actress."

"You saying you aren't the Jones babe?"

"I'm saying that I left her behind me."

"So, your parents, they approve of it?"

"I haven't talked with them."

"So, you mind telling me how this happened?"

"I am of age; I chose to leave. I chose to make my way in the world, and I did."

"You defying them, are you?"

"Thank you for your interest, Mr. Parkinson. Are you done?"

"Hey, relax, sweetheart. I'm just getting at the nitty-gritty. Word is, you flew the coop, and the old lady's having a conniption fit."

"I wouldn't know, not having talked to them."

"The buzz is, they put a fortune into your training, and now you're wasting it all on, what is this? Sideshow. Carnival stuff."

Charles was ready to barge in, but Ginger smiled at the reporter and touched his arm. "Thousands of people have enjoyed my singing since I joined the show. I'm proud and pleased that

I've had the chance to sing for the whole world."

He liked that, and scribbled it into his spiral-bound notepad.

"I'm grateful for the training. It gave me my chance to fulfill my dreams. Mr. Beausoleil, and my husband, here, have opened doors for me, given me a chance, brought me along when I was learning the ropes, and here I am."

"Yeah, but sweetheart, your old man and old lady, they had different plans for you."

"Yes, my mother did. And I'm sorry to disappoint her, but it's my life, and my choice to enter vaudeville. I love vaudeville. I love the company. These are the sweetest people I've ever known. They have great gifts. They entertain. They have, well, a knowledge of how the world works, and what pleases an audience, and I've learned more from them than I ever learned from voice coaches and tutors. Singing is more than hitting the notes."

"Holy cats, lady, that's a mouthful," the reporter said, scribbling away.

"Get it right. Write what I said. I've learned more about singing, and voice, since joining this company, than I ever did through my girlhood. These are my teachers."

"Man, you're gonna tick off a lot of people."

Charles started laughing. Ginger was a champ.

"Get it right, Mr. Parkinson," she said.

"Or what?"

"I like your bow tie," she said. "I'm all for polka dots, but I prefer blue. Really good reporters get the facts."

The skinny bird laughed. "Hey, you're a story and a half," he said.

He hurried off. Charles caught her elbow, and winked.

The company was too exhausted to head for the usual watering holes, and Charles quietly walked Ginger back to their hotel in a darkness that seemed almost ominous. She wrapped her cape tightly about her, and then they were safe in the thin warmth, and soon entered the quiet privacy of their room.

He helped her out of her cape and then hugged her.

"You're my star," he said.

"You're my heaven," she whispered.

"I'm still trying to figure out how we ended up hitched," he said.

"Destiny," she said, and kissed him.

He hugged her, and she melted into him.

"I need to lie down a little," she said.

He helped her to the double bed and eased her down. She smiled up at him, her eyes full of promise, and she clasped his hand and held it.

And fell asleep.

It took him a moment even to realize it. One moment, full of promise, the next, surrendering to exhaustion, the conclusion of one of her hardest days. Her body seemed to sink into the mattress, and she was gone, her breath gentle, the rise of her chest steady and quiet.

He undid some of her buttons, giving her room and air, and stared down upon her, his miraculous bride of just a few weeks. There were dark circles under her eyes.

"My shooting star," he said. "A comet across the dark."

He was disappointed. He had been looking forward to this night, for many nights. But there would be more nights, each more delightful, and for now, sleep was best. The kindness of the quiet night was the best tonic for the long trip and the brave front before the people of her hometown.

She wasn't dozing; she had slipped over the cliff, her weariness at last compelling her young heart to rest. He felt closer to her than he had ever felt, and marveled at it. There she was, exhausted and asleep, and he was watching over her, keeping her safe from harm. He had never been in the guardian angel business, and was liking it.

A sharp rap on the door halted his reveries. The rap soon became a clatter.

"Tomorrow," Charles said at the door. "Whoever you are."

"Police. Open up."

Charles stood, knowing what this was about. He eyed Ginger, who had barely stirred, and opened the door. There indeed was a large, blue-uniformed policeman. And a hawkish, small woman with blazing eyes. And a tall, lantern-jawed man with a stern look to him.

"You have my daughter," the woman said, pushing in.

"My wife," Charles replied.

She ignored him, pushed to the bed, where Ginger was stirring.

"Penelope, you're coming with me," the woman said.

"Madam, who are you? You are talking to my wife."

"If you interfere we'll throw you in jail and toss away the key," the woman said.

"Jones here, and that's my daughter and we're taking her."

"Taking her? She's my wife."

"She's not anymore, if she was at all," the woman said.

She reached over, grabbed Ginger's left hand, and swiftly stripped it of her wedding ring, and tucked the ring into a pocket. "Get up," she said.

"Now just a minute. This is my wife. She's of age. She's committed no crime. And she's staying right here. You're in my room. Get out. Right now."

"Get up," the woman said.

Ginger, groggy still, finally realized what this was about. "No," she said. "You can't do this. You don't own me."

"We're taking you away from this filthy carnival. They abducted you and we're taking you away. We've sunk a fortune into your career, and they're stealing you from us."

"I'll stay right here," Ginger said, sudden ferocity in her. "It's my life. My choice."

The woman turned to the cop. "Carry her out."

"Get out! You're kidnapping her," Charles said.

"I'm me!" Ginger cried.

That was the most poignant cry that Charles had ever heard.

A crowd had collected at the door, among them the reporter, Parkinson.

"Hey, what's the deal?' he asked.

"None of your business," Jones said, "and if you print a word, we'll sue."

"You kidnapping her? How come you got the right to do that?"

"Get away from here, Parkinson."

Outside the door, the Grabowskis were watching, and so were Harry the Juggler and The Genius.

"Go on, get away from here," Jones said.

"You gonna kidnap her in front of all these witnesses?" the reporter asked. "That's front page. We'll use the war type."

"She's coming home, and that's that. Pick her up and get her to the carriage," Jones said.

The cop slid his arms under Ginger, who refused to cooperate, and lifted her from the bed. She lay inert, resisting.

Charles saw how it was. The prominent Joneses had the cop on their side. Nothing else mattered, including wrong or right.

Ginger suddenly struggled. "What are you going to do with me?" she asked her mother.

"You're going to return to the concert hall."

"No. I'll never sing again. Not as long as I'm your slave."

"A few days of bread and water will cure that," the mother said. "We've spent a ransom on you. We'll get it back."

"I'll never sing again," Ginger said, and there was something so strong in her voice, in the forceful way she said it, that it sent a shiver through Charles.

"Don't think this is over," he said, directly to Jones. "You'll be dealing with me every day of your life."

"Hey, copper, put her down," The Genius said. "Or you'll spend a few years behind bars."

"And who are you?"

"I'm the voice of conscience, the whisper in the night, the wrath of the gods."

The cop ignored him, and pushed through the crowd carrying Ginger, wrapped in a sheet that pinned her like a straitjacket.

"Holy cats," Parkinson said. "Stop the presses. This'll sell a lot of papers."

The big cop bowled through the door, into the hall, scattering spectators like tenpins, and carried Ginger away. She was squirming now, struggling, no longer sleepy, fighting to break free. The parents followed behind, the hawkish woman glaring at everyone, her gaze withering, while the Union Pacific superintendent Jones, with balled fists the size of hams, walked behind, daring anyone to resist.

Outside an enclosed carriage waited, and the copper stuffed Ginger into it, the parents climbed in, the father slammed the lacquered door, and a hack driver pulled away with its human contraband.

Charles followed the carriage, step by step by step, before it vanished in the darkness.

40

The big copper carried Ginger, under the watchful eye of her mother, to her room in the spacious house. The copper left. The maid, Maude, stripped away Ginger's clothes, without Ginger's cooperation, and finally got Ginger into a nightdress.

There was nothing to say, so Ginger kept her silence.

The maid removed every bit of clothing from the armoire while Ginger's mother watched.

"There," she said. "There's not a slipper or shoe or coat or dress anywhere about. Just in case you try to leave. There's snow on the ground, and it's cold."

"You have taken my life from me."

"Exactly."

"Where's Father?"

"He's off at the paper, putting out fires. The paper will understand that you were abducted by the vaudeville company, and we have rescued you and restored you to your rightful life. That will quiet that reporter."

"It's not true."

"Now it is."

"I will tell everyone it's not true."

"You won't be here. Tomorrow you will be on a private car, carrying you to the American Academy of Symphonic Arts in New York, where you will study voice. It will take some arranging, getting a car here isn't easy, and a chaperone and a guard. But he has ways."

"I will never sing a note as long as I am not free."

Her mother smiled, her lips curling upward. "Time will tell," she said. "And by the way, never use the name Ginger again. That's gone and buried. It'll take some effort to escape the blot on your reputation—vaudeville! Vaudeville! Cheap shows, cheap people, mostly off the immigrant boats."

"They're the best people I've ever met."

"Who assaulted you, demeaned you, and exploited you. Like that fake husband."

"Charles . . . ," Ginger started to defend him, and gave up. Whatever she said would be ignored.

Her mother suddenly turned cheerful. "Good night, Penelope. You're back."

She clicked off the electrical light. Penelope lay in fragrant darkness. Her mother was a great one for sachets, and the house always had a pleasant scent of exotic spices.

So there it was. In the space of an hour or so, she had been abducted, imprisoned, returned to the life she had fled, and reduced to nothingness. No amount of fragrant spice in the air could conceal the odor rising from this house overlooking Pocatello. The blankets covering her felt like shrouds.

She was weary beyond words. The night of travel, the new town, the show, the longing for sleep, deep sleep, sleep until she might wake rested, all of it weighed her down. The temptation was to crawl under those clean, fresh covers, and fall instantly into oblivion, and accept whatever fate awaited her.

But she couldn't. And there was no time. A private car, actually a prison, carrying her away, carrying her to a distant place across a continent, silencing her, forcing her into the life her mother planned for her. Even now, her father was out in the night, summoning a railcar, wiring people in New York, putting it all together.

She crawled wearily from bed, drew aside the curtain, and stared into the wintry night, the snow cover giving ghostly light to the scene. It would be a long way to the hotel. In a nightdress. Without a scarf or coat or anything for her bare feet. And she might be picked up and returned by that big copper. And when she got to the hotel, she would be wearing her nightdress, and they would stop her.

She could freeze to death. That was one way to die. But she would die a worse death in a rail-car under the eyes of an armed guard.

The house was not yet quiet. She heard her mother, and the servants. They were making sure she had nothing to cover her feet or body, making very sure, making the wayward daughter a slave once again. Even as her father was busy at *The Tribune* giving them a monstrous lie, quieting the sensation.

She would wait an hour. And she would freeze her feet, if that's what it took. And she would wrap herself in her Hudson's Bay blanket, which covered her bed. And she would find a way to wrap bathroom towels about her feet.

So she waited. She heard her father return, and the houseman take away his hack, and the doors click shut. She heard muffled voices. She watched the moon rise, turning the snow silver. She waited in the silence. She discovered she had no good way to wrap towels about her feet, so she would go barefoot, and if her feet were frostbitten, she would pay the price.

She wrapped the blanket about her, headed downstairs, and gently tried the door. It was bolted, and she could not grasp how to release the lock. She tried the rear door, and found it was locked also. She gently pushed the sash on a downstairs window, and it wouldn't move. The generous house was more a fortress than she had known or imagined.

She returned to her room, opened the sash, which slid upward easily, and crawled out on the roof of the generous verandah, wondering if she could find the courage to jump. She could hurt herself badly. But her liberty was worth the risk. She edged through patched snow, down the slippery shingles, and reached the edge. The frozen ground was a long way down. It was bitter cold. Her feet were already numb. Doubts flooded her. And a renewed weariness. A bed would be so welcome.

"Ginger."

The voice floated upward.

"Ginger. Harry Grabowski. Me and Art, we came to help out."

"Oh!"

"You sit down on the edge, feet over the edge, and I'll be ready to catch you. Then just push off."

She needed no invitation. She slipped to the edge, sat slowly, slid her bare legs over, discovered massive Harry, dressed darkly, waiting, a welcome shadow.

"All right," she said, and pushed off.

He caught her easily, so easily she marveled. One moment she was falling, the next, his strong hands caught her at the waist, and gently settled her.

"Barefoot, are you? It figures," he said. "In the old country, keep 'em barefoot. That's how they ruled."

"All clear," said Art, who was keeping watch.

Harry lifted her up, tightened the blanket about her, picked his way carefully to the drive where broad carriage tracks would obscure footprints, even as Art whisked away the footprints in the snow around the veranda, obscuring everything.

"Hey, Ginger, you mind walking in the snow a while?" Art asked.

"I would be proud to."

Harry eased her to the ground, and she felt the snow bite her bare feet, and she walked artfully, now and then in the carriage tracks, but now and then leaving small, feminine prints which Art did not touch. She wanted each print in the snow to be an indelible record, a signature, of her will. For all the world to see, including the reporter at the paper. So she walked, and walked, and oddly her feet did not go numb because it was a record of her flight, a record of her determination.

And then, when they reached the end of the drive, Harry swept her up and carried her along moonlit lanes, and into the slumbering town.

Near the hotel, Art eased ahead, checking things out. He entered the hotel, looked around, stepped out, and nodded. A few moments later, Harry tapped on a familiar hotel door, and Ginger found herself peering into the face of her distraught husband. His gaze ran deep and gentle.

Charles reached out, touched Ginger's cheek, and nodded.

Harry gently lowered her to the bed, and drew the red blanket tight about her.

"We were right," Art said. "Nothing holds this lady in a cage."

Charles shook hands heartily with The Grab Bag, and the brothers slipped into the peaceful corridor, clicking the door behind them.

Then he held her, warmed her, pressed her to his solid body, and finally eased her to the bed and settled her in it.

She told him about the escape. And about her parents' plans for her. And about the barefoot prints she left in the snow, a mark of everything she was and intended to be.

"Those prints may tell the world the truth," Charles said.

He found her feet and began massaging them, warming them, awakening the circulation in them, and she enjoyed the sensation.

"Your father went to the paper? With a story that we abducted you?"

"Yes."

"I don't like it," he said. "I'll talk to August."

"I'm so tired."

"We have one matter to decide," he said. "Shall we slip you out? To Boise?"

"I've already decided it. I'll sing tonight. I will sing right here, before this city. I want the world to know it's my choice."

He smiled. "I knew it. I knew it when I proposed," he said. "Who you are. I saw it."

Sleep crept up once again. And this time, she slept the night through. And there was no one hammering on the hotel door. She didn't hear Charles, who was up and down, and she didn't hear when he got dressed and left the room in the night, or hear him return at dawn, or feel him slide into the double bed beside her.

And yet when sunlight at last teased her awake, she sensed at once that her new husband was taut with worry.

Yet he smiled. "How's my girl?" he asked.

"I could sleep for days." She watched him pull out fresh clothing from his satchel.

"You're worried about something."

"Worried about your parents, yes."

"What is it?"

"He's been telling the paper that we abducted you, and they rescued you."

She was puzzled.

He didn't elaborate. "There's trouble in it," he said.

Indeed, when they saw *The Tribune* that morning, the headline read, "Singer Rescued," and the story was about the Joneses and their success in rescuing their daughter, Penelope, from a notorious vaudeville company that had captured and exploited her. A vivid description of the rescue, penned by their ace reporter, Studs Parkinson, put Miss Penelope Jones back in her ancestral home, with help from the city police. She was reported to be at rest in the bosom of her home, grateful to be freed from vile servitude. And Jones was reported as saying he intended to take legal action against the vaudeville company.

No wonder Charles was restless.

He sipped coffee and sighed. "It's the lawsuit part that's worrying August and me," he said.

She felt blue. Her flight had triggered all this. And yet, maybe some good would come of it. "I'll sing tonight, Charles. Just put me on, and let me sing. Let them see me, singing. Let them see me smile. That'll say what needs saying."

"Lay low today?"

"No. I'll be here. I'll be with the troupe. And if anyone asks, I'll tell them I left, of my own free will."

He smiled suddenly. "What else did I marry?"

"Most of an iceberg's below water," she said.

"You're more of a volcano," he said.

It proved to be a quiet day. She moved freely about, window-shopped, looked at ready-made dresses, lunched with some of the troupe, and showed up early at the Grand Opera House. But it wasn't quite normal; a line of people stood at the box office, thirty, forty, plunking down cash to see the show. And not a one recognized her. She wondered how that could be, and remembered that any publicity, good or bad, would sell seats.

Backstage, August eyed her sharply, noting her new blue dress, purchased that afternoon.

"We've got a full house," he said. "Thanks to you."

"Are my parents out there?"

"No one's seen them, and the word is, they wouldn't set foot in the opera house as long as we're billed."

She thought that was true. Maybe it was all over. But when she thought of her mother, she thought it wasn't over.

41

August Beausoleil couldn't remember when he had felt so melancholic before. He was often a little blue; that was his nature. The melancholia was a sort of thermometer that registered how well his life was going. He had learned that when he was particularly blue, something bad was looming. He had an intuitive understanding: the blues heralded trouble.

As they did now. He shouldn't be melancholic at all. The young star of his show, Ginger, had weathered a brutal confrontation with her family. All her fears had been justified; they were quite ready to imprison her and deny her the life she had chosen. And somehow, at a tender age, she had weathered it. She was singing with a richness that he ascribed to adulthood; the girl had vanished in a leap from a roof; the woman was now walking out on the stage.

All the uproar had been duly chronicled in the Pocatello paper, *The Tribune*. At first readers were treated to a colorful story about a girl from a prominent family who had been abducted and used by Beausoleil's Follies. And how her enterprising parents had freed her from her degraded estate and returned her to the bosom of her family. But the story hadn't ended there. Next, readers learned that she had been kept a prisoner in her family's home, deprived of clothing and foot-wear, but had escaped barefoot, with only a blanket against the wintry night, to return to the life she had chosen on the variety theater stage. "Jones Girl Returns to Stage," was the first headline. "Married to Owner," was the subhead.

All of which generated intense interest. The Joneses were Pocatello's first family; he ran the railroad. Their daughter was a prodigy, destined for great things. And then, it seemed, she wished to live a life of her own. And she was packing the house. There was not a ticket to be had to any performance. Lucky people got to see her twice, thrice, if they could find the tickets. With each performance, August looked out upon a jammed house, with standing room only. It was all a miracle.

Charles had left for Boise after making sure his bride was well and weathering the worst ordeal of her tender years. He had the usual advance work to complete, and could delay no further.

Then, one bright December morning, a man with a sheriff's badge pinned to him thrust some papers into August's hand. It was a summons issued by Bannock County District Court. *Notice! You Are Being Sued,* it said. It was accompanied by a complaint. The Follies, Charles Pomerantz, and August Beausoleil were being sued by the Joneses. The complaint was a lengthy one, and August skimmed quickly over it. It had to do with damaged reputation, theft of property, alienation of a family member, and a lot more. It was a legal mishmash, likely to be dismissed, but that was not the real purpose.

The defendants would need to appear the next day. The court would place a heavy cash bail on the vaudeville company to prevent flight.

The real purpose was to wreck the company, prevent it from playing its next engagements, and require surety so drastic that it would drain the company of its last cent. It was a very old game. Want to destroy a traveling show? Lower an enormous performance bond on the entire show and its performers. Lawsuits like this were the Achilles' heel of any touring company. It didn't matter if the complaint had merit; the idea was to disrupt the show's schedule, destroy its income. In most cases, the odds were stacked against a touring company being sued by a local citizen, with the case heard by a local judge.

Suddenly August Beausoleil needed a lawyer, and a lot more money than he had in his cashbox. More than those things, he needed liberty; the freedom to move his company to its next billets, keep the income rolling in, day after day, town after town.

The sadness that engulfed him was old and familiar. It harkened back to the days when he was a boy so alone he scarcely knew his mother and had never known his father. He could go find a lawyer, or he could go to the Joneses' lawyer. He had, actually, a stronger suit than the Joneses did. They had kidnapped his star, the wife of his business partner, who was of age, and they had done great damage.

But he knew better. Lawsuits would mire the company. The Beausoleil Brothers Follies would be stalled in Pocatello, and swiftly starve to death, its players unpaid, its bills unmet, its credit run into the ground. A company on the road had to fix its troubles in other ways.

Charles had gone ahead to Boise. August would wire him; they had a code word, *RED,* which meant emergency, return at once. But that would be tomorrow. And the Follies was due to open in Boise in three days. Tickets were on sale there. August was on his own, alone, as he had been from his earliest memories. The stage-door errand boy would depend on his own resources once again.

Jones himself operated from his superintendent's office in the railroad station. Their lawyer, whose name was Brophy, was also a Union Pacific lawyer in the same offices. August could go there, three blocks distant, and endure the test of manhood.

Instead, he collected his worn topcoat, hoping it would do against the sharp cold, and headed toward the generous house on the heights, the house that overlooked much of Pocatello, and was meant to be seen from below, by lesser people.

The long driveway up the grade was caked with ice, and treacherous, so August walked carefully, as much in snow beside the road as on it. But he did not fall, and eventually found himself stepping to the front door, located at the center of a broad verandah.

The door opened even before he knocked. A manservant, tall, with slicked-back hair, confronted him.

"Mrs. Jones said to talk to their lawyer, if you must," the manservant said.

"Please tell Mrs. Jones I'm not here to argue, but to listen. I wish to know what her grievances might be, and how I might be of assistance."

The manservant debated that, and finally vanished into the gloomy interior.

When he returned, he had a simple message: "Madam says you cannot be of assistance, and good day."

"Very well, tell her I'm on my way, but I'd hoped to hear all about her daughter. A remarkable young woman, sir."

The door closed in August's face, and he turned to leave, his next stop being Superintendent Jones himself. But then, suddenly, the door opened. It was Mazeppa Jones, looking thin and waspish.

"I will give you ten minutes," she said.

"I will listen," he replied, as she waved him in and escorted him to an ornate parlor done in reds: red plush horsehair, red velvet drapes, oriental rugs. She took a seat but let him stand.

"You are French," she said.

"Mostly orphan, madam."

"Penelope was destined to be the finest concert pianist in the world, but her hands never grew. You need an octave, you know. So I switched her to voice, a good soprano that altered downward as she matured, but not perfect. It was such a blow to me. But training can perfect a flawed voice, and I was about it when all this girlishness happened."

"What did happen?"

"You destroyed her reputation. She's ruined."

"Ah, I am not following, madam."

"Of course you wouldn't. And I'm not going to explain it."

"What of the future, madam?"

"Penelope is dead. Let her lie in an unmarked grave."

"And you, madam?"

"My daughter took my life. I will spend the rest of my days scrubbing her from the world. Until nothing's left of her. Not a memory."

Beausoleil became aware of a ticking clock, a mantel clock over the fireplace.

"Is there anything you want from me, madam?"

"Put her on the streets. Here. She must never sing again. Do that, and I will drop the lawsuit."

"Is the suit yours, rather than your husband's?"

"My intentions entirely. Now I have given you your salvation. You are going to snatch at it. One could not expect more from your sort. You may leave."

"She is married to my colleague, madam."

"You heard me. On the streets. After that, your company will be free to go."

He bowed slightly; the manservant materialized at once from behind velvet, escorted him to the door, and moments later he was in fresh air, under a cloudless sky. He edged carefully down the icy drive, and into town. He stepped around ice, avoiding black patches, checking each step before putting weight on that foot. And so arrived back at the hotel, unscathed by broken bones.

The price was a glowing young woman, whose talent was larger than any he had ever known. The day was still young. He headed for the chambers of the Union Pacific lawyer who was also handling this matter for the superintendent. Pierce Brophy, according to the signature.

August was ushered in the moment he gave his name to the clerk. The office was far from opulent, but the railroad preferred oaken muscle to show when it came to legal affairs.

"Mr. Brophy, what sort of surety will you seek in court?"

"Five thousand."

"And is the judge likely to set bail at that?"

"Always."

"Thank you, sir," August said.

"Just a minute, Mr. Beausoleil. Mrs. Jones required me to supply you with another option."

"I was just there, and heard it."

"Well?"

"Mrs. Jones will not succeed."

"I think I like you," Brophy said.

"Then ask the court for a more appropriate surety."

Brophy stuck a finger in his left ear and twisted,

apparently gouging out wax. August thought Brophy hadn't heard the expected.

"Ten thousand?" Brophy asked.

"I will be there at eleven tomorrow," August said.

He left, somehow knowing he had gained ground. There were lawyers who did not like to do what they were commissioned to do, and he sensed that about Pierce Brophy.

He was done. Fate would play out in the morning. A weariness settled through him. He might not be the proprietor of the Follies for much longer. But he had weathered worse, and the Follies was actually the second of his variety companies. The first had collapsed under his own mismanagement, which had been instructive.

The show went splendidly that eve, with every seat filled and thirty people standing along the rear wall. Again, Ginger was the attraction. The battle with her parents, flamboyantly described in the paper, had ignited the curiosity of people for miles around, and all eyes were on Ginger, who did not fail to sing her golden songs, in her golden way.

In the morning, Charles showed up on the first train in from Boise, and August filled him in. Charles looked stricken. At eleven, the pair showed up in the chambers of Henry Rausch, district judge, and waited for events to unfold. The courtroom was empty, save for a clerk and a bailiff. And *The Tribune* reporter, Parkinson.

The bored jurist eyed the defendants cursorily, and Pierce Brophy petitioned the court to set bail at one thousand dollars, that being a reasonable estimate of the presumed damages suffered by the complaining party.

Judge Rausch, from the bench, set the trial date as January third, and set bail at the thousand dollars, August agreed to provide it forthwith, and that was the end of the proceeding.

"Can we do it?" Charles asked.

"Yes, and with a little to spare."

"I don't know how you managed that," Charles said.

"I don't know, either," August said. "But it had to do with honor."

42

Parkinson trailed them out of the Bannock County courthouse, annoying Charles Pomerantz. Ginger had suffered enough from *The Tribune*'s sensationalism.

"What was all that about?" the reporter asked.

"Ask the Joneses," Pomerantz said.

"It's a public document, a complaint. You may as well tell me."

"Read it, then. We have nothing to say."

"You posted bail. That cuts you loose, right?"

"We will lose a large sum unless we appear in this court in January."

"What have the Joneses against you?"

Parkinson was amused by his own question.

"Look, sir, talk to them. We have a show to put on tonight."

August was listening as the reporter dogged them, walking back to the hotel. But suddenly he intervened. "Here's your story, sir. You tell the Joneses there will be two seats, front center, for them this evening, and the company would be pleased to host them, and let them see their magnificent daughter perform."

"Holy cats, that's a story, all right. Who do I talk to?"

"I gather that Mrs. Jones makes all the decisions, sir. At least she says she does."

"I can work this into a great story either way. An invitation and two empty seats tonight. Or the Joneses, bitterly opposed to their daughter's entry into vaudeville, show up for a gander."

Charles smiled in spite of himself. It reminded him that reporters often manufactured news, especially when there were no good headlines at the moment.

"Go ahead, Parkinson, fill our house for us," Beausoleil said. "Here's a pair of tickets. Give them to the Joneses."

"Hey, this is a story and a half. And if I can't unload them?"

"Bring your lady and enjoy the show. But let me know if the Joneses accept the tickets, all right?"

"Yeah, sure, I'll give you the word."

Actually, the last performance was nearly sold out. The hurly-burly reportage of Ginger's tussle with her parents was filling the opera house. So far as Charles or August were concerned, any publicity was good publicity. But Charles worried about Ginger, whose courage was being tested each hour in Pocatello. How would she feel, singing in front of her mother?

He found Ginger lying on the bed, looking worn.

"Bail was a grand. We can manage, sweetheart. We'll be opening in Boise."

"I've cost you a fortune."

"Hey, sweetheart, you're our new star."

"You'd be better off . . ."

"If we hadn't found you? Nah, you're our fortune cookie. But there may be something going on tonight you should be ready for. Like maybe your parents in the audience."

"They are?"

"We don't know. August sent some prime tickets to them."

She stared up at him, looking forlorn.

He sat down next to her. "Maybe some good will come of it," he said.

She just stared, and he could only guess what torments were flowing through her now. August had been impulsive, the fixer making things good, but maybe this time he had overstepped. The gulf between Ginger and her mother could not be bridged, much less fathomed.

"I've come this far. I'll go the rest of the way," she said, and squeezed his hand.

She was tough.

That afternoon, Parkinson reported that the Joneses' attorney, Brophy, had accepted the tickets. Parkinson had gotten nowhere with Mrs. Jones. He didn't know who, if anyone, would claim the seats.

And that's how they went into the final performance. Pomerantz hoped it would be a door-buster. That surety for the court appearance came to the entire income for two shows. And that meant they'd barely make payroll and expenses, going into Boise. But that was nothing new for the Follies.

By seven, the troupe had assembled at the opera house. Ginger was costumed early, and spent her time peeking out at the empty house, looking for her parents. And then, at the first signs of people arriving, the Joneses appeared, he in ordinary business clothes, but she in black taffeta, with a black hat and black veil, looking funereal from head to toe. Mazeppa Jones made a spectacle, which was plainly what she intended. They took their seats as the opera house began to fill. There was whispering out there, but nothing untoward, as show-goers slipped in, found their seats, and settled down for the evening. Mrs. Jones sat immobile, wrought from stone, not so much as a finger moving inside its black glove.

Oddly, Ginger smiled.

"It figures," she said.

But by then the whole troupe was curious about her, about her parents, about the quiet hubbub out there as this final audience in Pocatello realized the sort of drama playing out right there between the wayward daughter and the rejected parents. As far as Charles could tell, the town was divided, many siding with the parents but some standing up for Ginger. It had all played out in the paper, and people had rushed to their own conclusions no matter whether they knew the Jones family or not.

She stood quietly, a wall of privacy around her, waiting in the wings. Charles couldn't say what was passing through her then, only that she was composed. She had stopped peeking from the edge of the proscenium. Her parents were there, a pool of darkness in a festive crowd, and then it was showtime.

The curtain rolled up; August Beausoleil, jaunty and eager, a spring in his step, sailed into the center of the stage, the bright place, and began all his familiar routines, welcoming the ladies and gents to this, the final performance of the Follies.

And then, to everyone's astonishment, he changed the order. It would not be the Wildroot Sisters opening this time.

"Ladies and gents, I bring you the star of our show, the one you've been waiting for, the beautiful, the sublime, the engaging Miss Ginger!"

Ginger was caught utterly unprepared, and in the ticking seconds, she processed this shocking thing, collected herself, and plunged out to a warm applause, once again in her bottle-green gown, looking as heavenly as Charles had ever seen her. She paused, center stage.

There was a great hush.

She bowed, she smiled at the balcony, she smiled at the orchestra, and she smiled at her parents.

"I wish to dedicate this performance to my mother and father," she said, into the deepening silence.

Charles, from the wings, ached for her and rejoiced in her, all at once.

She began with "Jeanie with the Light Brown Hair," which she sang sweetly, and with the warmth that Stephen Foster had intended.

Mrs. Jones sat motionless.

Soon, Ginger was singing her repertoire of American ballads, one after another, while her mother sat like a gravestone, and the crowd was craning to see how the Joneses were responding to their daughter. Something was happening. Ginger was pouring beauty and joy into these familiar songs, transforming each of them into something magical. She was singing as she had never sung before.

But they saw nothing. The pair sat silently, a black pool in front-center seats.

She bowed and abandoned the stage, and August swiftly continued the show, bringing on the Wildroot Sisters, and Harry the Juggler, and then Wayne Windsor, who had worked up a new routine.

"I'm going to tell you about a railroad man who figured out how to get rich," he began. "This fellow knew where the traffic was, and found a way to make his fortune. His secret was simple. He built a railroad to Hades. A high-speed state-of-the-art railroad, that hauled multitudes down the slope. At first he thought coaches would be all he needed, but he soon discovered that parlor cars were in great demand. The more luxurious the better. He was catering to clientele of the better class. So he began adding luxurious and roomy cars, one after the others, and his business improved. . . ."

The audience was plainly enjoying this, enjoying Windsor's attempt to entertain the railroad man in their midst. There were chuckles and cheer, but not from that bleak little pool of darkness front center.

The performers were watching from the wings, watching to see if the couple would ever smile, ever settle in and enjoy the show. And gradually, it all became a contest, with each act striving to entertain the Joneses.

Harry and Art Grabowski put on a fine show, choreographing a brawl that set the crowd to howling. Every time Art threw a haymaker, Harry did cartwheels, until laughter rippled through the opera house and continued almost nonstop. Then the Marbury Trio tapped out to center stage, tapped intricate steps, did a buck and wing, delighted the crowd—except for the two who could not be entertained, and who didn't move a muscle.

And August had never been better at introducing his acts, one after another, each given a special send-off that wrought eagerness in all those people out there in the dusky seats.

The Genius and Ethel wrought good cheer that eve. The Genius was especially outrageous and superior, comparing Pocatello to Butte, scorning everything and everyone, while Ethel bled the hot air out of the blowhard. The crowd chuckled. Many of them had run into self-serving people bent on letting the world know how superior they were. And still the Joneses sat, immobile.

Ginger watched them anxiously, and was so restless backstage that Charles finally caught her hand and held it quietly. She looked stricken at first, but his smile wrought one in her, and she was all right.

When intermission came, the performers watched anxiously to see whether the Joneses would rise, retreat to the lobby, and vanish.

Instead, they sat silently, unmoved, unmovable, while the patrons refreshed themselves and drifted back to their seats.

The second act was much like the first, with the crowd enjoying the performers while Ginger's parents sat sternly, revealing not so much as a smile or raised eyebrow. They did not clap. They did not nod, or share their delight with those in neighboring seats.

When Ginger returned, she told her eager listeners that she would sing more ballads, and invited the crowd to sing along. She offered them "Careless Love," "Swing Low Sweet Chariot," "Clementine," "Down in the Valley," and concluded with "Buffalo Gals."

Nothing could be further from what her mother intended than these old songs, and Charles knew that Ginger was carefully, deliberately, staking out her independence. He watched them closely, but saw not the slightest shift of a muscle. They had been cast in bronze.

Ginger was watching them, too, as she sang, and registering her mother's every movement. And then it was over, and the crowd clapped politely, almost as if these people were afraid to appreciate the wayward daughter.

The show ended that way, the crowd subdued, as if the stern disapproval of the Joneses had triumphed over their own appreciation of a happy evening. They had seen good vaudeville, and had enjoyed top talent, and yet when the curtain rang down, they left quietly, soberly, defeated by Ginger's parents.

Charles watched them rise, stretch a little, and make their way to the aisle, and up the lobby, and vanish into the night, where their enameled cabriolet was waiting. He could not fathom what they were thinking, and no one else could, either. The performers felt blue; they had turned the whole show into an effort to break the ice, win the good cheer of those two people. And had failed.

Ginger was inscrutable, too. Whatever she felt, she was not sharing.

This was the end for Pocatello. He watched the performers pack up. There were accordions and guitars to put into cases, a few props to bundle, Harry the Juggler's array of cups and saucers and knives to box up, costumes to return to trunks, and they did these things in deep silence, unsure of themselves. It was as if Ginger's mother had not only thwarted the entire audience, but thwarted each performer who had sought her approval. She had approved of none, and now it lay like a blanket over the company.

But there was always tomorrow. They would catch a train for Boise early in the morning, and would be setting up shop in the opera house in the state capital late that afternoon. Another opening. Another crowd, this time more likely to enjoy the talent.

Charles walked back to the hotel with Ginger, both of them lost in silence.

He was worn, and crawled into bed ahead of her. She took her time washing up, and when she did emerge she was in a bright crimson wrapper.

"Let's leave Pocatello behind, forever," she said, and reached for him.

43

Boise was surely the place where good things would happen. It was a bustling state capital, with plenty of cash. It had a fine, large theater, the Columbia, with a thousand seats. Fill those seats for several performances and the troupe would bridge the gap in late December, and start along the West Coast with the new year.

Charles Pomerantz brimmed with hope. He had done everything it was possible to do. In a short time, when Spokane canceled, he had put together two Idaho dates, looked to all the details, and somehow managed to move the company, which was now quartered at the comfortable Overland Hotel, close to the theater. The Union Pacific had delivered them on time. The trip was restful. The performers were lodged, and spreading out to look at the handsome town. And they had a day of rest. The first show would be tomorrow eve.

There was one worrisome puzzle. Only three hundred seats had sold for opening night, and a handful for other nights, and none for the matinees. He contacted the owner and operator of the Columbia to find out a few things. The man's name was Pincart, James Almond Pincart. Maybe Pincart could point to something that needed doing.

The man had not been helpful. He charged a flat rent, not a percentage, which gave him little incentive to fill the seats. He was of the crafty, calculating sort, always with an eye to protecting himself and his property. In the early negotiations, Charles had learned to expect nothing, and to follow through on everything, from printing of tickets to making sure the bills were posted and the ads scheduled in the daily *Statesman*.

He found Pincart peering at his ledgers in the small office at the back of the Columbia Theater.

"Well, you're not selling seats," Pincart said. "I knew it. You'll have empty houses."

"What's not working, sir?"

"The ads in the paper. They buried them, back of the classified. They like to do that."

Charles pushed an issue of the daily across the prim desk, and thumbed it open to the inside of the rear page, where the announcement of the Beausoleil Brothers Follies was buried.

"The publisher, Wool, he doesn't like money leaving town. He says every cent taken out by a touring company's a cent that Boise merchants don't get, so he buries ads like yours."

"But not locals?"

"Nope. When the Boise Marching Band advertises a concert here, Wool runs the ad on page two, prime spot, where it gets seen. A Boise band, the ticket money stays in town, you see."

Charles stared. "I wish you had told me. We could have insisted it get better play in that paper."

Pincart shrugged. "No skin off my teeth," he said. "Wool's right. Keep the money in town, not let it ride the next train out."

"I was called away, couldn't be here, and now these ads are buried. And you let it ride?"

"Small crowds, it's easier to clean the house," Pincart said.

"What else isn't right?"

"Bill-poster, name's Thompson, he never got them up. You got cheated."

"What?"

"Cold spell, he didn't feel like going out, got only two, three pasted up. Don't know what he did with the rest. Hid them, I guess. Here's his invoice, sixty playbills up, eighty-seven dollars."

"Say that again?"

"He didn't paste up the playbills, worthless sort, and here's his charges."

A desolation stole through Charles. "And you didn't wire me, or inform me?"

"No skin off my teeth," Pincart said.

"Where are the sheets? Who can I get to paste them up? Can you show me the walls where they go up?"

"Thompson's probably used them to start fires in his stove by now. They're evidence against him, you know, so he no doubt burned the whole lot."

Charles stared. "I've got no ads anyone's seen, and no playbills around town, and no seats sold. And you let it pass?"

"Saves me work, cleaning up. I hate to fill the theater. Janitors complain and want overtime. People are all swine, leaving stuff on the floor. I ought to charge a clean-up fee on top of the tickets."

"Are the tickets all printed?"

"Here's the invoice."

"May I see them?"

"Printer's holding on to last three nights until you pay him."

"Steer me to Thompson. I want to get the bills and find someone to paste them up. He must have a sub."

"Now, you don't want to disturb a sick man, and I'll say absolutely not. He'll catch the pneumonia."

"Where can I get flyers printed fast? And boys to pass them out?"

"I despise flyers. People bring them in, drop them on my floors, and I have to cart all that rubbish out."

"What is the other paper?"

"*The Evening Mail*, just out today."

Pincart looked almost triumphant.

Charles snapped up the Thompson invoice. It had a street address. He stuffed it in his pocket.

"I'll expect rental from you for the next five days, before showtime tonight," Pincart said. "Or the curtain doesn't go up."

Charles wrapped his coat and scarf around him, bolted through the cold theater and out into bright light, and waylaid the first man he came across. The capital was serene.

"Pardon, sir, looking for an address. Can you direct me to Myrtle Sreet?"

The man could and did, and Charles raced in that direction. There was no time. No time at all. But maybe he could prevent disaster. Four blocks later he found Myrtle, and a shabby bungalow at 400 south so poorly marked it was all guesswork. But he bolted up two stairs, rapped on the white door with peeling paint, and soon confronted a whiskery man in his grimy union suit and britches.

"Ah, you've come to pay up," Thompson said, looking Pomerantz over.

"Maybe, maybe not. It depends on whether you do your job, now, this afternoon, every bill up."

"Too cold," Thompson said.

"How many were you to put up?"

"I dunno. The usual."

"How many did you post?"

"Two, three."

"I want the playbills and you can give me the name and address of a sub."

Thompson yawned. "You sure are making a fuss."

The man was soaked in rotgut, and exuded it.

"You mind if I come in and look around?"

"Well, truth to tell, the bills are at the theater. Pincart's sitting on them."

"You mind if I look?"

"There's two, three here."

"Why is Pincart not putting them out?"

"He doesn't like vaudeville, but doesn't mind renting the stage."

"You mind putting up the bills you've got, and any you can find?"

"It sure is cold, old boy."

He saw three or four large playbills lying in a corner. "I'll take those," he said, and tried to edge past the owner of the manse, but a hard arm shot out and blocked him. "They'll cost you a dollar apiece," Thompson said, a smirk building. "Lay out five."

"I'll find the ones in the theater," Charles said. "If Pincart's got them."

The door turned him back to Myrtle Street. It was too late to paste up three-sheet playbills around Boise. He needed a printer. In the space of an hour he had gone from optimism to utter desperation. It was time to get August and the performers in on it. They could hand out flyers as well as anyone, and it might generate some interest in the show.

The job printer on Fourth Street turned out to be a gruff old pulp-nosed codger in an ink-stained smock. Charles sketched out his needs: Beausoleil Brothers Follies, Vaudeville, Columbia Theater, December seven to thirteen, featuring Ginger, Wayne Windsor, Harry the Juggler, The Wildroot Sisters, The Marbury Trio, The Genius and Ethel, The Grab Bag. Each evening at seven, two o'clock matinees on the eighth and twelfth. Advance sales at Rubachek's Pharmacy. Fifty cents to a dollar fifty. The biggest show ever.

"Small flyers, you choose the size, a thousand, as soon as possible, an hour or two if you can manage it."

The printer eyed Charles as if he were daft. "An hour or two! Have you the slightest knowledge of my art? An hour or two. Judas priest, where have you been all your life?"

"Sir, you can set that type in twenty minutes, I can proof it in one, you can make corrections in five, and crank out a thousand in an hour on that flatbed right there."

The printer's eyes gleamed with malice. "Supposing I can. What makes you think I will?"

"I'll pay extra. Half again your charge."

"Oho, bribing me, are you? You can pick up the

first hundred at noon, day after tomorrow, and wait for more stock to come in before I print the rest."

"Sir, I see all sorts of sheets on your shelves, different sizes, but they'll do, if you don't mind. We can hand out all sorts of flyers. Whatever's in stock. Colored paper, too."

"You think that, do you? And has it never occurred to you that those sheets are reserved for printing jobs ordered locally, in time for Christmas?"

"There's a paper cutter, sir. Sitting right there. I'll cut large sheets myself, and ready them for you."

"Just so you can walk the cash out of town. That's the trouble with you travelers. You think you can come in and skim the cash from good folks here and catch the next train out with a pocketful."

Charles had heard that before. "You own this job shop, sir?"

"Nope. I run it, but the *Statesman* owns it."

"Is there another job shop here?"

"I leave that to you to discover, my good man. Now, if we're done?"

Charles plunged outside, into an icy wind, the sort of wind that withered and killed anything fragile. Boise, a bustling, prosperous town, didn't know the troupe was about to open, stay a week, and generate marvels, laughs, musical delights, and amazing feats of dexterity. If there were any playbills up, Charles had not seen them, but some tickets had sold even so.

He hurried back to the Overland, against the arctic wind, and hunted down August, who was in his room with the cashbox, filling brown pay envelopes.

Tersely, Charles outlined the events of the past hour, sparing his colleague nothing. August stared at his pay envelopes, at the declining stack of greenbacks in the cashbox, and nodded. The show was in peril again.

"And Pincart wants the balance in advance," Charles added.

"Anything left?"

"*The Evening Mail*, we might persuade to print flyers. Or some sort of extra edition. If it's not too late."

August seemed almost to fold up. "I suppose we could just tell them what we're up against and see what happens," he said. "We could bring some acts with us. They've got stories. A good reporter could make something of them. Maybe we could give the weekly a scoop—if they'd go for it. But we're down to the wire, Charles."

There weren't many of the troupe in the Overland Hotel that hour, but they found Wayne Windsor, Ethel Wildroot, and Art and Harry Grabowski. That would do.

The weekly, it turned out, was near the capitol, and survived largely by publishing legals, the endless public notices that emanated from a seat of government. Its editorial content was sober, with business stories dominating. It seemed the last place for a special edition about a vaudeville troupe. But who could say?

Its owner, Harvey Pelican, greeted the visitors cordially. Considering that he published a weekly loaded with legal notices, he seemed almost jovial. Nothing so exotic as a vaudeville troupe had ever penetrated his sanctum sanctorum.

"If you've time, sir, I'd simply like to tell you our story, and our dilemma," Charles said.

"Have a cup of cold mean java, there, and spill the beans, Mr. Pomerantz," the owner said. He plainly wished to be diverted. And that's how it went, the next hour. They diverted him. They told him their tale of woe. And asked for help.

"You tickle my funny bone," Pelican said. "Let's whip up a few and see how it goes."

44

The Western Union boy found Ginger in the lobby of the Overland Hotel, and handed her a yellow envelope. A telegram? Who could be sending it? She pulled it open and found the message printed in block capitals: MAZEPPA JONES DEAD OVERDOSE TODAY PARKINSON.

She could not fathom it. Her mother? Dead? Overdose? Suicide? The reporter had swiftly sent word. And probably had another sensational story. She read and reread it, trying to unlock its terse message, more and more shaken. Her mother did have laudanum and used it frequently for whatever ailed her. And it was dangerous. But overdose?

Her mother? Had Ginger's flight from her family anything to do with it? Of course, of course. Disobedient daughter, mother gives up living. Her mother's revenge. *You failed me, so I will give up my one, my only life. You are what I lived for, and now I have nothing, except the blue laudanum bottle and a teaspoon.* A flood of something unfathomable flowed through Ginger. She could not say what. Her mother was hanging a crown of thorns upon her, and she felt the thorns cut into her heart.

She felt no rush of sorrow or loss; that was impossible. Maybe sometime, a few years away, she might. She didn't feel weighted; quite the opposite. Her spirit seemed to float free. No longer was her mother trying to work her will upon her daughter without the slightest thought of what Penelope might want from life.

And yet, somehow, Ginger felt sadness steal through her. There was love, too. She suddenly understood how starved Mazeppa was for atten-tion, how hollow was her mother's passage through the days and years, and how desperate her mother had been to find a reason to live, finally settling on shaping her daughter.

Then Ginger couldn't think at all, and sat numbly, the yellow telegram in hand, her mind a jumble of conflicting feelings. She did not know the passage of time, only that she was paralyzed, in the hotel, and that was how Charles found her some while later.

"Where've you been, Ginger?" he asked.

She handed him the yellow sheet. He glanced at it.

"Oh, Ginger," he said. "Oh my God."

She nodded.

"Let me take you back to the room," he said.

She let him lift her out of her chair, and let him guide her down the dark hallway, let him unlock the door, let him guide her in, let him guide her to the bed and ease her down upon it, she looking upward at her husband.

He shut the door, and sat beside her.

"You don't have to make any decisions," he said, which puzzled her.

But then it grew upon her that there were decisions that needed to be made. Whether to sing that opening eve. Whether to go back to Pocatello, the funeral, her father. But she could not make them. She felt small and helpless, and just wanted to lie quietly, without decisions.

But he made one for her, then and there.

"You won't want to sing at this time," he said.

She wasn't so sure of that. She thought she might, she might sing a canary song, a bright song, a song of her own. But his decision had foreclosed that.

"I'll talk to August," he said. "Change the show around. This would be a good night to do it. Small crowd."

"Small crowd?"

"Yeah, a lot of trouble. The bills didn't go up; no one knows we're here. But tomorrow we'll have flyers to hand out, and maybe make some money."

She understood none of it.

He vanished. She stared at the ceiling. Oddly, she could barely remember her mother, or anything about her. She could draw her father's image into her thoughts, but not her mother's. She liked her father; she was not afraid of him. But mostly, she just lay quietly, uncertain, uncomfortable with any thought or plan.

When Charles did return some while later, he handed her a train ticket. "There's an eastbound express at seven, gets you to Pocatello before dawn. Lousy schedule, but that's all I could do. You'll have a room at the Bannock Hotel there for as many nights as you need. I can't go with you. There's trouble here, so you'll be alone. But I know you'll be all right, and secure, and doing what needs doing."

"I don't know what needs doing."

"You'll want to be at your father's side, for your sake, for his. And to quiet the newspaper, which is likely to make much of this. Be thinking of what you'll say to that reporter, Parkinson."

"What to say?"

"He will want to know if your mother, ah, abandoned life because of you. Your departure."

"I think I should stay here. I have nothing left in Pocatello."

"You have ghosts, and they need to be laid to rest, Ginger. Memories . . ."

"But I'll miss the show. Several shows."

"Yes, and the shows will miss you."

"But Charles . . . ," she said, knowing she would go. Knowing it was something she had to do.

"You'll regret not going, and always be grateful you put your mother to rest," he said.

She wasn't so sure of it. He could not know what her mother was like.

The talk ended that way, she uneasy, he firm. But she welcomed his firmness. It was as if he was, momentarily, more father than lover.

She whiled away the afternoon, packed a small valise, grew fretful when the performers headed for the Columbia Theater and she was not among them. But then Charles escorted her to the Union Pacific station, and waited with her until the east-bound local huffed in, sending up clouds of steam in the chill air.

"You have everything? Money?"

She nodded, and he escorted her to the coach, gave her a squeeze, and helped her up the stool, and onto the steel step of the coach. And then he was gone. He didn't linger. He didn't wait on the platform while she settled in a seat, but was gone, and it reminded her that something was amiss, and he was trying to deal with it.

The train lurched eastward, its whistle mournful in the inky dark. Beyond the lights of the city lay nothing at all, and nothing but night lay beyond the windows. The coach was mostly empty, the passengers mostly male, and all were keeping to themselves. The coach exuded an odor, and she wondered what it might be, whether a leaking water closet, or ancient sweat, or scratchy wet wool, but most of all the odor was despair. It was the train to nowhere.

She sat quietly through the night, occasionally passing a flash of light that signaled something, perhaps a town. But mostly she was tunneling toward the unknown. When at last the weary conductor announced Pocatello, she collected her wits, pulled her satchel off the rack, and waited for the train to squeal to a halt. Then she stepped into a cold night. There were no hacks. She waited for someone, anyone, and found no one. The two others who left the train vanished.

Well, this was her hometown. The bag was heavy, so she left it on a luggage shelf. She would send someone from the hotel for it. And then she walked toward the Bannock Hotel, through the wee hours, a time so devoid of life that not even footpads would be about. When at last she turned into the hotel, its entry barely lit, she found no clerk, nor did ringing a counter bell bring one.

But a while later, she didn't know how long, a skinny man appeared, apologized, put her in her room, and volunteered to go for the bag himself after she had signed in as Mrs. Charles Pomerantz.

"Never see anyone at this hour," he said.

"Here's a dollar," she said.

"Holy cats," he said, fingering the bill as if it were a thousand-dollar note.

Fifteen minutes later, he was knocking on her door with the bag, looking like he wanted to come in and see where the waning night might lead.

"My mother died," she said, and closed the door.

She lay inert, dressed, on the bed until mid-morning, when a thunderous thumping on the door galvanized her. She rose, slowly, feeling unwashed, knowing who it would be. Parkinson, the reporter, who regularly read hotel registers.

"Please wait," she said, and without listening for a reply from the other side of the flimsy door, she found a washbasin and pitcher, poured water into the basin, and wiped away the travel from her face with the cool water.

"Hey, it's me," Parkinson said.

She took her time, all the while wondering what he might ask, and how it might hurt her, or how it might inflame Pocatello. When she felt more presentable, she opened, but did not invite him in.

"Saw you were here," he said, doffing a fedora. "Ask some questions?"

"Thank you for wiring me," she said.

"Yeah, and that's the story. You came back to bury her. How come, given the little spat or two? And escaping from her upstairs window?"

"I came to bury my mother."

"Yeah, but why?"

"I think that is my business. Now, if you don't mind, I'll try to nap."

She started to close the door, but found his foot blocking her. "Not so fast, sweetheart. Now, here you are, even before your old man's set the funeral day. You regret ditching your old lady?"

"They sent me," she said, and regretted it.

"Who's they? The Follies? They want to keep their nose clean, right?"

"I came because it was the thing to do, and now please remove your foot. I need rest."

"Naw, my foot in the door's gotten me more stories than my pencil in hand."

"Then your foot will feel what comes next," she said, and swung the door hard. He yanked his fancy shoe away in the nick, and the door clattered shut.

"That's how you treat the man who wired you?" he asked in the hallway.

"I will talk to you after the funeral," she said.

426

He tried a few more gambits, and finally left, and she was back on her bed, engulfed in the silence of the morning, and an odd sense of loss for her mother. She understood her mother at last, and the understanding freed her. For Mazeppa Jones, marriage had been a prison.

But she was allowed no rest. When she opened to the next knock, an hour later, she discovered her father, in black, solemn, his gaze gentle. She hesitated.

"May I?" he asked.

She nodded. He stepped in, eyeing her quietly. "The reporter, causing trouble," he said, trumping her question. "I'm grateful you came."

He saw her weariness. "If you'd like, I'd like to take you out. I have a club, and we can dine quietly, away from prying eyes."

She nodded. "Let me freshen," she said.

He met her in the lobby, and he walked briskly toward the river, and a brick building there he said was the Bannock Club. In short order, he was seating her in an obscure corner. They were left to themselves, the dinner courses arriving.

"I'll tell you about it, if you want. If not, I'll just have a quiet meal, and be on my way."

She nodded.

"Mazeppa always had dreams for you," he said. "I never paid heed until you left us, and never really understood. I think I do now. I didn't understand, and went along with it, paid the bills, thought we were simply giving you the best that we could give a gifted daughter. I missed the other. Until your barefoot escape . . ."

"Thank you," she said.

"I make no apologies," he said. "Not for me, not for her. No matter how you add it up, you had a privileged upbringing."

"But it wasn't me," she said. "I didn't count."

He quieted, dabbled with his potatoes, and stared.

"Let bygones be bygones," he said. "I need you. The house is empty. I'd like you to stay on, live as you choose. I will make sure you have everything. I'd be pleased if you resumed your life as a concert performer, but wouldn't insist on it."

Oddly, the arrangement tempted her. The person who had tormented her, driven her to flight, was gone. Her father, well, she could manage life in the same house with him.

But the yearning for that vanished.

"I . . . I'm afraid not," she said. "I love my husband, I love the stage. I'll catch the next train to Boise. But thanks."

He grinned unexpectedly. "Now I'll have to deal with that rascal reporter," he said.

45

The Boise opening went badly. The cavernous Columbia Theater was mostly empty, as bad an omen as there was. August peered out upon row after row of blank seats, each a rebuke to his company. Out there in the darkness a couple hundred people were scattered about, many of them in cheaper balcony seats. The hollow theater subdued them as much as it subdued the performers.

August was used to bad shows, but somehow this one abraded him. His ceremonial posture was too jaunty. His apology for not offering the star of the show, Ginger, was too forced. His easy humor, intended to put the people out there in a good mood, fled him.

"And now, ladies and gents, the one, the only Laverne Wildroot," he said, and she bounced out to the limelight in the middle of silence. And trilled her songs in a vacuum.

"And now, ladies and gents, the masters of acrobatics, The Grab Bag," he said, but the act fell flat. Harry, out of what should have been the audience, was off. Had he bulled his way onstage from a packed house, it would have been comic. Instead, it seemed like a ritualized rehearsal. But they tried. August gave them credit for that. They careened about like demented gladiators.

Wayne Windsor's monologue fell flat. He tried several tacks, trying to pick up a thread that would delight those scattered people, and he couldn't. They didn't chuckle. They didn't appreciate. And they didn't clap.

Harry the Juggler performed flawlessly, and no one noticed. The Marbury Trio tapped and two-stepped as elegantly as ever, and the tapping sounded like hail on the window, and the audience stared. The Genius gave it a try, insulting Boise, insulting the audience, insulting Idaho, insulting men, women, and children and dogs, and no one howled.

At the intermission some of the audience vanished, leaving even fewer to enjoy the second set. From the wings, the company watched inertly, knowing they were witnessing something as bleak as they had ever seen onstage. Ethel Wildroot stood there, shaking her head. LaVerne Wildroot looked to be ready to weep.

August himself was about ready to weep, too, with cash receipts for the show running about two hundred dollars, and bills piling up by the hour. He watched the critic from the *Statesman* clamp his felt hat over his slicked hair, and slouch his way toward the exit. No telling what would be in the paper, if anything. The ultimate thumbs-down was to say nothing at all.

The show seemed to end with a whimper, and after a scattered clap or two, the remaining patrons wound their scarves around their necks and vanished. The theater was large, quiet, and empty.

August noted a fair-haired man in a topcoat working his way through the performers, who were standing mute in the wings, reluctant to call it quits.

"Where may I find LaVerne Wildroot?" he asked, politely.

The Genius jerked a thumb in her direction, and the local gent headed her way, hat in hand, and introduced himself as Stanford Sebring. It was easy to see he wasn't poor.

"Miss Wildroot, I just had to come back here to tell you how enchanted I was, and how much I liked the opening song," he said.

A stage-door Johnny. That was the last thing August anticipated on a night like this, when there were no stars in the sky.

"Why, I'm so glad," she said. "You came all the way back here to say that? My goodness. You've surprised me."

"It took some doing," Sebring said. "I thought, if I don't try, she'll never know. So I found an unlocked door. In fact, I think you are the finest songstress I've ever heard."

August had never seen a stage-door Johnny flatter the cast after a debacle like tonight's. But that was fine. If there were stage-door Johnnies around, all wasn't lost. LaVerne was swiftly turning into a coquette, and August heard her say she'd like to get into street clothes, and yes, she'd love to do a turn with him, and yes, wait in the Green Room.

It gave August odd solace. It was still show business, even in Boise, in the worst opening in recent memory. He glanced bleakly at Charles, who was holding a strongbox with the night's take, which was going to be pathetic.

"Bad, right?"

"Worst ever," Charles said.

"Well, maybe we can make it up when we get out to Seattle."

"August, I wired them days ago, and haven't heard a word."

"Carelessness. It's December, and people have other things in mind."

"I'm glad you think so," Charles said.

August didn't like the sound of that. But there were pressing things, such as paying bills, keeping the theater open, and in a couple of days, another round of payroll for the acts.

They repaired to an alcove off the Green Room and counted the take, which came to a hundred ninety dollars and change. Pincart wanted two hundred just to keep the doors open for the remaining performances.

"Guess we'd better shovel it all his way. We can add the rest. If you have it," Charles said.

"I was keeping it for the flyers."

"Better tell the acts they'll be out pushing flyers all day tomorrow."

Harvey Pelican over at the weekly would do a thousand flyers, gussied up with a few stories about the acts. He thought it would be fun, and a way to needle the daily. But the flyers wouldn't be ready until morning. And then August intended to push them into every store and restaurant and bar, hand them to people on the street, drop them into government offices, leave them on counters in stores, tacked to electrical poles, stuffed into mailboxes, and pushed under doors. He would have his entire ensemble at it, including the hands, the musicians, the acts, and Charles and himself. One way or another, Boise would be given the message: The Beausoleil Brothers Follies was in town, at the Columbia, and tickets were going fast. See Ginger! See Wayne Windsor! See the Marbury Trio! Laugh with The Grab Bag. Enjoy The Genius and Ethel. Get your seats fast at Rubachek's Pharmacy, open all day, every day.

"What was the takeout?" Windsor asked.

"Under two hundred."

"And how long can this keep up?"

"About another hour," Charles said. "Or maybe a half hour."

"Never fear. LaVerne's new Johnny will fork over. He's not wearing cheap rags."

August had entertained fantasies like that in

years gone by, and had never seen one materialize. Maybe someone would like to own a piece of a vaudeville company.

"I should have been a barber," Windsor said. "You get to talk to the guy while you're shaving him and he can't talk back, and if he does, you nick him. He's in the chair and he's gotta listen. I'd like that. Captive audience every time, and if he whines he bleeds. And barbers have a regular income."

August didn't contradict him.

"I live high, never worry about the future. There's no point in show business if you don't live life to the hilt," Windsor said.

"Then you'll do better on the big-time stages."

"Hey, August, here I'm top banana."

August made some notations in a pocket ledger, and closed his cashbox.

"Hey, what are you going to do with that?" Windsor said.

"Add eight dollars of my own, making it two hundred, and then I'll give it all to Pincart. He wants cash in advance to keep the doors open the next four performances. Fifty a day."

"Out of our paychecks, right?"

"We have to fill a lot of seats starting tomorrow."

"This company is sitting here without a dime?"

"And a stack of bills. Like the hotel. Maybe that'll inspire you to get the flyers out tomorrow."

"Nah, it'll inspire me to wire my agent about work."

"I've had the same idea," August said. "If we make it to the coast, we'll be okay. But that's a ways off. I don't know who'd employ me."

"Is this secret?"

"Anyone who has eyes can see it. No, it's not."

August left the rent money in the manager's strongbox, and headed into a bitter night. The acts had been alerted. Show up at ten for duty on the streets. The show needed a jolt, and fast, and flyers were the only route open. There had been very little grumbling. Anyone who had looked out upon all those vacant seats, each with its bleak message, knew something needed to be done. He'd send men into women's stores, and the show girls into men's stores, and see what that did for sales.

He debated whether to spend something on a nightcap, and decided against it. His early life had taught him a few things. Just now he was wondering whether that would be his fate once again. But not if he could help it, and he thought he could.

In the hotel lobby he ran into Charles, who was bundled up for a cold walk.

"I got a wire from Ginger's old man. She's on the westbound ninety-seven, due here in a few minutes. Want to come?"

"He wired you? Did he wire you about canceling that suit?"

435

Charles stuffed the yellow sheet into August's hands. It was terse.

"I'll come along," August said. "Maybe she'll have full pockets."

They braved the whipping air that scoured warmth from Boise along with smoke from a lot of chimneys. They walked grimly, straight into the wind, and that's how life was in Boise, so far. The station was cold, but a relief from the wind. The ticket window was shut. Anyone boarding here would need to buy passage from the conductor.

But the express train did roll in on time, and first off was Ginger, carrying her satchel, and glad to be welcomed. Charles pecked her cheek and grabbed her bag. There was no hack in sight, and August was glad of it. A dime saved was a dime to eat with.

"So, what happened? Did you bury your mother?"

"No, but I did go to a private visitation with my father. I said good-bye, and he put me on the train again."

"You contacted your father?"

"That reporter was busy. He's still looking for stories, like a runaway singer who scorns her mother's funeral. He told my father I'd arrived, and my father came to me, and we met privately."

"What happened, if I may ask?"

"He asked me to stay on, take my mother's

place in the house, and resume a concert career."

"And?"

"I told him I loved my husband and I loved show business. He accepted it, and that was all. He upgraded my ticket; I came back in a palace car."

"Did he talk about the lawsuit? Like dropping it?"

"We talked about honoring my mother."

The wind blew them back to the hotel, a gale gently pushing at their backs.

"Tomorrow, Ginger, we have work for everyone in the show, handing out flyers. But Charles will tell you about it."

She nodded. August left them there, in the lobby, and headed into the night once again. He had one more mission, which was to drop in at the *Statesman* and see what sort of review the critic had penned. You never knew. Dour critics, sitting three rows back, sometimes wrote fine reviews. Other times, the affable critic, looking plumb happy, would butcher the show. Most reviews were mixed. That was all right. It was vaudeville, variety, and no one had to like every act.

The paper was easy to get to, in the shadow of the capitol. He entered a well-lit pressroom, found a live body, reading proof, introduced himself, and asked to see the review, if any.

The gent, in a stained vest, wire-rimmed spectacles, and a green-billed visor, nodded, pulled off galley proofs from the spike until he found what he was looking for.

"Dull," was the tagline.

"The Beausoleil Follies opened last eve to a sparse, cold, and bored crowd, a condition that didn't change an iota the entire evening, except the audience diminished as the evening crept onward."

There was more of that, and a concluding line. "Keep the cash in Boise, and spend it locally," it said.

Beausoleil read it carefully and handed it back.

"Thanks," he said.

"Glad to be of service," the proofreader replied.

46

The telegram, this time from Chicago, made Charles Pomerantz's knees go rubbery. It was from an acquaintance named Martin Beck, who was now employed by the Orpheum circuit on the West Coast. It announced that Orpheum had bought the Olympia Theater, the Puyallup Opera House, the Seattle Theater, the Tacoma Theater, and was negotiating the purchase of Reed's Opera House in Salem, Parker Opera House in Eugene, the Marquam Grand Opera House in Portland, Cordray's New Theater in Portland, and Park

Theater in Portland. And bookings made by the previous owners would be canceled immediately. Circuit vaudeville on the coast would start in January.

There went the tour.

He should have guessed. Circuits were fast replacing individual vaudeville companies. Circuits put individual acts on tour forty weeks a year, moving from city to city, providing constant fresh entertainment along the circuits. The arrival of a rail network offering swift transport from town to town had made circuits possible. New shows, on the move.

Charles stared at the offending yellow paper, feeling the clutch of despair grab his chest. Of those on Beck's list, five had been booked by the Beausoleil Brothers Follies. Nothing in the telegram said anything about Northern California, but the Orpheum was already strong in San Francisco, and the outlook there was just as bleak.

Charles paced his room, knew he must find August, and fight—if there was any way to fight anything.

He found August in the lobby, handing out stacks of gaudy flyers to the show people. The whole troupe was there, save for The Genius, who refused to demean himself with anything resembling work, and had wandered off looking for a saloon that served pretzels for breakfast. Oddly, The Genius' loutishness didn't affect the rest. They had seen the empty house, and knew what needed to be done.

"On the streets, to anyone who'll take one," August said. "Don't neglect children. In stores, to any that will post them in the windows. In restaurants and saloons, any livery barn, on any counter, in any office, in any station of public place, state office, on any tram, in any seat of any hack—it all depends on you," August said, quietly. "Hire a newsboy to hawk them."

"What if we run out?" Ethel said.

"There'll be more here. We ordered a thousand. Eight thousand people live here."

"Why didn't the bills go up in time?" LaVerne Wildroot asked.

"That's complicated. The bill-poster claimed it was too cold. The house manager seems to enjoy embarrassing touring companies. The newspaper's gospel is to keep all cash in Boise."

Several laughed. Boise was cleaning them out of their last nickel.

"What happens if no one buys tickets?"

August smiled. "I hope you don't mind selling apples on street corners."

The whole crowd was pretty serious. They each collected an armload, arranged among themselves what areas they would cover, and hastened into the biting wind. There wouldn't be many people lounging along the streets this December day.

August watched them go, and grinned at Charles. "There's always a way," he said.

Charles did what he hated to do, and placed the telegram in August's hands. August read it slowly, reread it, and seemed to turn into marble. He said nothing for a while, stared into the distance, even though they were in a warm hotel.

"We were running from this," August said.

"It came faster than we thought."

"Do you have a *Julius Cahn Guide*?"

"In my bags."

The *Official Theatrical Guide* listed every opera house in every state and in Indian Territory, with all relevant contacts.

"Maybe we can reroute the tour," August said. "Wherever the rails go. Nevada, who knows?"

"Not much in Nevada," Charles said. "But there's houses on the coast not bought up. We'd have competition from the circuit."

August laughed shortly. Operators of the new circuits knew how to deal with competition, including buying up opera houses, cut-rate ticket pricing, bringing in big-name talent, bribing suppliers such as printers, paying off bill-posters to do bad work, stealing acts. Their inventiveness knew no boundaries.

"Wire Graeb. We need cash. Two thousand. Book us straight down the Rockies, Wyoming, Colorado, starting now. If we can."

Bland Graeb was the company agent in

Chicago, the man who usually cut deals, booked theaters, auditioned acts when needed. It would have to be Graeb's money, and he would be the naysayer.

"There's no north-south rail in the Rockies. We're heading for the coast. Like Portland, there's the Park Theater, and the Baker. Smaller places. Not bought up—yet."

"Right into the circuit. But that's the game."

"What have we got?"

"Bills. Printer, hotel, payroll coming up."

Charles grinned. August grinned back. It helped to grin when your neck was in the guillotine.

"How are we gonna get out of here?"

"Sell The Genius to the nearest medical school for a cadaver."

It would be up to Charles. He was the wizard with the telegraph, and could say more in fewer words. He wondered how he'd pay Western Union for the amount of wire traffic he would launch.

"I'll go push some flyers," August said. "We've got to fill the house tonight."

With that, Charles headed for his room to get his *Theatrical Guide*, and then to the Western Union office, at the station. He had the sinking feeling that it was all for show, all to be able to say that they tried every avenue, every angle.

But August had a firsthand acquaintance with miracles, and scrambling on the streets of Gotham had taught him a thing or two. They had booked this area because the circuits hadn't started up here, and a touring company could still schedule its route. Back east, there were cut-throat syndi-cates, swiftly turning the enter-tainment business into a few fierce rivals. Some of them would even throw up a new opera house across the street from the competition, and then get into price wars to cop the trade.

He collected his treasured copy of the *Julius Cahn* directory, with all its resources, along with ads on most every page pushing theater products, makeup, costumes, lighting, baggage. Charles would need to consult every Oregon and California page to put a schedule together.

There were plenty of houses in Oregon and Northern California. But he had no way of knowing which ones the Orpheum circuit was buying. Graeb would know, and would know how to set up a tour down the coast. Compete with the circuit.

He composed the most important telegram of his life: ORPHEUM CANCELING FOLLIES COAST TOUR REBOOK FOLLIES COMPETING HOUSES JANUARY FEBRUARY ENDING FRISCO WIRE TWO THOUSAND REPAY WITH BOOKINGS URGENT POMERANTZ

Twenty-one words. Reroute the tour, send money. Twenty-one words that could start the wires humming with bookings and confirms and credit. Graeb would know what to do—if he chose to do it.

He took it to the Western Union office, paid the per-word tally, and watched the grouchy telegrapher start tapping on the brass key. Everything rested on it. If Graeb could set up a tour, and send money, Pomerantz could book hotels and passage. It had to be. He didn't like to think of the alternatives.

He watched the man finish up, knowing the SOS would reach Graeb swiftly, and a reply would come swiftly from across the continent. He had an odd, hollow feeling as he braved the cold.

It was odd how Ginger intruded on his thoughts just then. Ginger's father had made an offer. Return to Pocatello. Prepare for the concert stage. And, unspoken, get rid of her husband. But she had rejected all that. And if Graeb didn't produce, she might find herself broke and stranded. But she had plowed ahead with all the optimism of an eighteen-year-old, a trait that Charles Pomerantz no longer possessed. The thought opened something tender in him.

Graeb replied with breathtaking speed. Sorry. He was now contracted to book acts for the Orpheum Circuit and could no longer operate as booking agent for the Follies. He would be glad to book acts into the Orpheum circuit.

Graeb was throwing the dog a bone. He'd rescue the acts but not the show.

Somehow Charles had sensed it. He hadn't heard from Graeb for a while.

So this is where it all ends, he thought. The flyers wouldn't do much, maybe fill a few seats, and then there would be bills unpaid, the acts unpaid, the Follies falling apart. Maybe even before they had finished their run in Boise. You had to deal squarely with the acts. Not ask them to work if you had no way to pay them. Maybe there would be no shows, not the one tonight, not tomorrow, not the next day.

He guessed that this evening's performance would be the last one. And then what?

Maybe the end of his marriage to Ginger, too.

He hurried back to the telegrapher, this time with a reply to Martin Beck. Book Follies in Orpheum Circuit? Buy Follies? Need answer fast.

He sat down on a hard bench in the rail station, hoping for a fast reply, and one clattered in twenty minutes later: NO.

The *Idaho Statesman* was next. He corralled the manager, who stared flinty-eyed at the offending visitor from the dubious world of theater.

"We'd like to do a free Christmas show at the Columbia, a matinee the day after tomorrow. Absolutely free, to celebrate the holidays. Would you give it push?"

"An ad costs the same for out-of-towners as for locals," the manager said. "Three columns, ten inches, twenty-seven fifty."

"Ah, I'm talking about a free show, a Christmas

show, for all the good people of Boise, and we need a good story in your paper tomorrow."

"You could have a column-inch in the classified section for eighty cents. A bargain, given what it's worth."

"Ah, we're not talking business, Mr. Hardesty, we're talking a free show. Good, lively variety, free to men, women, children of Boise."

"We don't give anything away, especially at Christmas, Mr. Pomerantz," Hardesty said.

"That I believe," Charles said.

"You sell theater seats; we sell advertising space," Hardesty said.

"Merry Christmas," Charles replied.

Charles clamped his hat down, and ventured into the cold. At the hotel he discovered some of the troupe, cold, rosy-cheeked, and cheerful. They had unloaded every flyer, and maybe it would fill those seats. But in his pocket were wires that would wipe away that cheer in an instant. He spotted August, who was looking cold and gaunt, and with a nod, summoned August to an alcove.

August read the wires, and seemed to sink into himself.

"I just offered a free matinee, Christmas matinee, and asked the paper to push it, and guess what?"

"Eighty cents an inch in classified."

"You were there?"

"Same idea. Ahead of you. Fine fellow, Hardesty."

"You want to tell the acts?"

"We're a square outfit. The worker deserves his pay. My earliest lesson in life."

"Now or before or after?"

"Not before. It colors the show. Not now; they've headed for their rooms. After the show. I'll keep the acts around for a few minutes."

That's how it would be. Charles found himself peering straight into August Beausoleil's soul just then. He knew August's story, at least in general terms, and what he saw then, he swore, was the abandoned boy, get tips or starve, cadge a nickel here, a nickel there, buy candy, live on, find a basement warm enough to keep from frostbite, watch the people, the ones who never noticed a starving kid watching them. August was still young, or would have been if fate hadn't broken his body. But now his face was the color of whey.

There it all was, radiating from August's worn face. But there was more. August Beausoleil had survived from his eighth or ninth year by his wits.

"Come on up, Charles," he said. "We have things to talk over."

Charles was glad to. It was fine to be in a warm hotel room, proof against the cold streets of Boise, drawing up a last will and testament for the Beausoleil Brothers Follies.

47

No line formed at the Columbia Theater box office. August watched a few people, hurried by a bitter wind, buy tickets and scurry inside. The flyers had little effect. The weather wasn't helping. The sarcastic review in the *Statesman* didn't improve matters.

Beside him stood the manager of the Overland, a Mr. Poole, who wanted cash immediately or the troupe would be evicted forthwith. August had persuaded him to wait for the box office receipts. There were twelve rooms to pay for, at two dollars each.

Minutes before showtime, August slipped into the box office, extracted the cash, and handed it to Poole, who smiled maliciously and hurried back to his hotel. The troupe would sleep warm one last night.

August hurried into his tails and top hat, and peered out upon a sea of darkness. There were so few people they seemed to vanish. And more were in the balcony than in the orchestra. He focused hard, and counted fifty-something. They sat in deep silence, and one could swear that there was no audience at all. Not even a sniffle or cough to signal human presence.

The performers were oddly quiet. They knew. And just because they were performers, and proud, they'd do their best this night. They had already figured out the rest: There was no brown pay envelope awaiting them. And no more Beausoleil Brothers Follies. And no tickets back to Chicago or New York, where they might scrape by until they could find a job. They knew that at the end of this show, he would gather them on the bare-lit stage and apologize, and tell them it was over, and he had no remedy. He hadn't said it, not yet, but they already understood it. Some would be angry, some bitter, some blue, and most would put up a false front, joke, and wonder what the next day would bring.

He eyed his pocket watch.

"Throw on the footlights, and lower the olio," he said.

A moment later, he stepped onto the narrow downstage strip, peered out into the silence, and tipped his hat.

"Ladies and gents, I'm August Beausoleil. This is my show. I want you to enjoy it. You all gather right here, in front. You up in the balcony, come down and have a seat right here. We're about to give you the best show we know how to do, and we're all hoping you'll have a fine time this eve. We'll start in a few minutes."

With that, the curtain rang down, and he watched the handful gradually filter in, and settle in the rows just a little back. Those were the best seats. No one sat in the first row. Just a few people settled there, many solitary, leaving empty spaces between them and the next person.

At a nod, the curtain rose, and he welcomed them, and introduced the Wildroot Sisters, who did just fine, lots of sparkle and smiles. August relaxed. Every performer would do whatever it took this evening. Do it from the heart. Do it without pay. Do it without knowing what would happen on the morrow.

The crowd clapped tentatively, a small, hollow chattering of hands, and then August headed into the next act, and next, and next, and the show glowed, and the audience had a good time, and no one left at the intermission. And when the show ended, the audience clapped, stood, and left, braving the Idaho winter.

Everyone in the show, including the musicians, simply waited on the stage, in the dim light of a naked bulb above. August wouldn't be surprising them. "I'm sorry," he said. "It's over. We had enough to pay your rooms tonight. We don't have pay for you. Tonight's take came to fifteen, after the hotel took its cut. Each act and hand gets a dollar. It buys a telegram or a meal."

"What happened?" Wayne asked.

"Orpheum Circuit bought several houses where we were booked, and shoved us out. Our agents won't lend us cash. One went to work for Orpheum."

"You owe us," The Genius said.

"Yes, I do."

"Then shake what you've got in a sock and pay us."

"You gave people a lot of fun, sir. You added to the show. That's all I have in my sock."

"What are we supposed to do?" asked Art Grabowski.

"Wire your agent," Wayne Windsor said.

"Orpheum is hiring," August said. "Wire Bland Graeb in Chicago. Our agent. Or Martin Beck, who's running the circuit from Chicago."

"Oh, God," said Ethel Wildroot.

"I'll help," Wayne Windsor said. "This is show business. I've been there. Most of us have. Anyone wants to send a wire, tonight, tomorrow, I'll pay. Anyone needs a meal, I'll arrange with the eatery next to the hotel for tomorrow."

No one thanked him.

"If acts want to send a joint wire to Graeb, I'll word it," Windsor added. "One wire, several signing it."

The odd thing was that no one agreed. The theater was growing cold. The manager didn't burn an extra nickel's worth of coal.

"This is a badly run deal," The Genius said.

August didn't argue. If there was justice, The Genius would soon be back in Butte as a bar-stool entertainer, cadging drinks and sleeping in cellars.

The whole company stood paralyzed. For a loquacious band of performers, they were oddly mute, struggling with fear, maybe anger, maybe helplessness. And there was the cold, the piercing, bitter cold worming straight into them.

That's when LaVerne's stage-door Johnny, Stanford Sebring, showed up, warmed by a black alpaca topcoat.

"Hey, baby, I'm taking you for a nightcap," he said.

"I don't think so, Johnny."

"Hey, what's this? What's the trouble?"

"We're closing, Stanford."

"Well, we'll have a party. I'll spring."

It seemed surreal. At the last, most of the company repaired to Darby's Saloon, down the street, to make merry, and lift a glass to the Beausoleil Brothers Follies, though a few including Harry the Juggler and some accordionists headed back to the refuge where they would welcome one last warm night. A familiar thought passed through August's mind: eat and drink, for tomorrow we die.

Charles helped Ginger into her coat, and donned his own. They would go, of course. August could almost name the ones who'd go for the last hurrah; the ones who were less anxious, who'd weathered storms, who'd fallen from peaks, climbed out of troughs, figured out ways, made compromises, bandaged hurts, smiled at life. He would go, too. No matter what he felt.

He wanted to soak in guilt, but wouldn't let it happen. He had not let anyone down. But some stern executioner in him was surveying his neck. He had wrestled his demons since boyhood, wrestled the Accuser who blamed him for his misfortunes. It was the Accuser lurking in him, condemning him, even now, with a new tragedy unfolding by the hour.

"I will join you," he said.

Darby's proved to be a politico's saloon, redolent of cigars and sharp with whiskey. The place was almost empty. Boise was not known for its nightlife. The keep eyed the women unhappily; this was the home of sovereign males. But when the performers were at last seated at what was probably a poker table, the keep eyed the clock, which said ten thirty, sighed, and approached.

"Closing in half an hour, but I'll serve up a quick one," he said.

Bourbon neat all around, except for their host, Stanford Sebring, who settled for a sarsaparilla. August thought the Wildroot girls were exploring new ground; LaVerne, though, seemed at home with the amber fluid before her.

Most of the troupe looked ready for a drink. The Marbury Trio, Delilah and her brothers, sticking close as usual; Ethel Wildroot; the girls, Cookie and Marge; Cromwell Perkins, The Genius; the Grabowskis; Wayne Windsor; Ginger along with

Charles; and even Harry the Juggler, who had changed his mind and joined the company. August wished the rest could be present at this farewell: Mary Mabel Markey, Mrs. McGivers. The musicians and hands, too. Sebring was putting a fitting ending on it, lubricating a sad moment, giving them all a memory. A small company, doubling their acts to fill the bill.

The keep eyed them all sourly; he preferred politicians.

Sebring rose, suddenly. "I must say, ladies and gents, I'm honored to be included here. All this talent. All this grief. If I'd known, earlier, what awaited you here, I could have done something. I have a few resources. At any rate, you fine people, I wish to raise a toast to the Follies, and may you all prosper."

He lifted his sarsaparilla.

"You won't raise a glass of spirits with us, sir?" Windsor asked.

"No, not for me, friend. I'm L.D.S."

August didn't have the faintest idea.

"Latter-day Saint?" asked Windsor, turning to expose his better profile.

"Why, yes, so of course I must abstain. At any rate, here's to you all, to the Follies, to your success."

They sipped gingerly. August was some while sorting it out. A Mormon, toasting them. Boise was an odd place.

"And here's to our benefactor," Charles said, raising a glass to Sebring.

"It's not over, not by a long shot. Here's Act Two," Sebring said. "It's my one and only chance. You shall all be witnesses."

He stood, turned to LaVerne, and took her hand. "LaVerne Wildroot, my nightingale, will you marry me?"

LaVerne startled, spilled some of her bourbon, and stared.

Stanford Sebring was smiling.

The clock ticked. She eyed her mother, her sisters, the troupe at the table, the company she had kept all her life. She gazed at Sebring, in his costly suit and cravat, his alpaca coat nearby.

"Yes," she said.

"Ah, ah, a great moment for us all," Sebring said. He gently collected her, drew her close, and raised his glass.

There should have been congratulations, but no one in the company could manage them.

"I should add, friends, that if any single lady here wishes the security and happiness of a good marriage, I know of many fine and virtuous men who seek to start a family."

No one spoke.

"And of course, if any gentleman wishes, we have jobs and opportunities open. Here and in Utah. Say the word, and your future will be secured. Our people know what it's like to struggle, to be outcasts, to build our own Zion. And now we offer a helping hand."

No one spoke for a few moments.

"Thanks, Mr. Sebring, but I'm addicted to coffee," Windsor said. "My left side favors java; my right favors bourbon."

With that, everything eased. They ordered another round, courtesy of Sebring, stayed way past the keep's closing hour, and finally drifted into the streets, to the hotel. Sebring accompanied LaVerne to the hotel, where he kissed her cheek and promised to collect her in the morning.

The next hours proved to be the strangest in August's life. He stood in the Overland lobby, watching his troupe head for their rooms that last night, wondering if he'd see them again. He didn't. After a restless night, mostly awake, he headed for the lobby and found no one he knew. He knocked on the doors of his troupe, but no one answered. Strangers wandered through the lobby, checking in, checking out.

He looked for his company in the adjacent restaurants, and saw no one. He was alone. He didn't know where Charles was, or Ginger. He couldn't fathom how his colleagues could simply vanish, leaving no word, no trace of their existence in Boise, Idaho. There were no messages left at the hotel desk. He had several trunks of gear stored at the express office of the depot, and after an arduous search, he found a secondhand dealer who would buy the stuff for a few dollars. That was all he had; he had shared the last receipts with the troupe. He wandered through the stuffy Overland one last time, his raging curiosity pushing him into every corner, wanting to reconnect with his company. But the Follies were dead; his acts had vanished.

He had enough cash from the sale of trunks and costumes to take him to Butte, where he hoped Mrs. McGivers would shelter him a brief time, or where he could wait tables or serve drinks or run errands. The lamps were always lit in Butte. He carried his sole remaining satchel with him to the Union Pacific station, purchased coach fare to Butte, and boarded an eastbound back to Pocatello, and a change of trains to Butte. If Mrs. McGivers could not help him, he would have to think of something else.

Epilogue

Only the Wildroot girls remained in Boise. LaVerne married Stanford Sebring that very day, and never returned to show business. Sebring graciously provided shelter and sustenance for Cookie and Marge, and introduced them to eager young men in woman-starved Idaho. Years later, long after they had started families, they enjoyed roles in Christmas pageants and reenactments of pioneer life. LaVerne named her second son August, even though Stanford was not enchanted with the name, preferring Brigham. Her cousins, Cookie and Marge, raised happy families and gradually concealed their vaudeville past and their father's profession, but once in a while, at a graduation or school play, they would lead an audience in song.

Delilah Marbury, her husband Sam, and brother-in-law Bingo immediately wired their agent, Morrie Gill, and he booked them in the expanding Orpheum circuit and advanced them ticket money to Seattle. They caught the next train west. They had mixed success on the West Coast. Some inland towns didn't like to see her dressed in tux and tails. Other towns thought that tap dancing was corrupt and degrading. But mostly, audiences delighted in the rat-a-tat and clatter, and enjoyed the trio. They toured the vaudeville circuits for many years, and opened the way for other tap-dancing acts, including blackface ones. For a while, blackface tap dancing was all the rage in vaudeville.

Harry the Juggler was booked instantly by the Orpheum circuit, but they changed his name to King of the Jugglers, and had him dress in a glittery gold costume festooned with fake rubies. He succeeded brilliantly for the next two years, but one day a train whistle caught him just as he was juggling his scimitars; he slipped—one scimitar cut his wrist to the bone, severing nerves and ending his career. He did attempt a one-handed juggling act, but it never caught on as well as the original. He ended up a celebrity bartender in San Francisco, able to do amazing things with glasses of booze.

Cromwell Perkins, The Genius, made his way back to Butte, and reverted to his former life as a barstool entertainer cadging drinks from amused customers in several saloons. The harsh winters took their toll, and he eventually vanished. Rumors abounded. Some said he was shot by an irate drinker. Others argued, in Butte parlance, that "he woke up dead" one day. He was not missed, but was the source of good Butte stories, some even true.

Ginger never looked back. She never regretted her flight from Pocatello, her escape from the clutches of her mother. She and Charles caught the next Union Pacific train eastward, riding in a Pullman Palace Car in comfort. Charles, veteran of the rails, not only had letters of credit on his personal account in New York, but also a few double eagles salted away in his effects. He found employment with the Keith empire, and later Keith-Albee, applying his endless knowledge of travel and hotels and arrangements to get acts from town to town, on time, and in comfort.

Ginger's career took an odd twist. Ginger found

regular employment at Oscar Hammerstein's new Manhattan Opera House, at Thirty-fourth and Broadway. Her success in the Northwest was unknown to New Yorkers, and it took a year before she recouped the billing status she had known far away. She was celebrated in New York for the aura of innocence that somehow clung to her. She was well ensconced in the business, happy with her life, and close to the heart of the world of vaudeville, where Charles governed over hundreds of acts on the road.

August scraped together enough to get to Butte, where Mrs. McGivers immediately gave him shelter. He discovered Ethel Wildroot also there, waiting tables in exchange for shelter. August didn't have a nickel. But in time, he scraped together enough to ride coach to New York, where he soon found work doing what he did best, introducing acts at Tony Pastor's Rialto Opera House, which was doing vaudeville nonstop all day, every day. It wasn't much, but it afforded him a room, and he gradually paid off his debts to Boise printers and restaurants, sending a few dollars from each paycheck.

But the failure, the collapse of his Follies, and the new, ruthless world of competing vaudeville circuits, had taken their toll on him. He was frequently ill, and developed a tumor on the stomach, and less than three years after he returned to his hometown, he lay dying in Bellevue

Hospital, his life dwindling as he lay on a narrow cot in a charity ward under an army surplus blanket.

Charles and Ginger found him there, staring upward into emptiness.

"August, we just found out you're here," Charles said, reaching for a cold hand.

"Good of you," August said.

"Are they treating you well?" Ginger asked.

"The one, the only Bellevue," August whispered.

"August, thanks to you, my dreams came true. I just want you to know."

"Same here, August. I took what you taught me and made a life," Charles said.

For a long moment, August didn't respond. Then, quietly, "The business. The business gives us life. It's a refuge."

"I hadn't thought of it that way," Ginger said. "But yes, it puts its arm around us; it put its arm around me, and after that . . ."

August smiled thinly. "Vaudeville's like this hospital. It's for the ones coming in or going out."

He closed his eyes, and his visitors wondered if he had slipped away, but they stayed, and clung to his hand. The person who had transformed their lives was adrift.

Ethel Wildroot found him then, noted his closed eyes, and her face formed a question.

"Ethel, I'm glad," August said, mysteriously fathoming her presence.

"Oh, August," she said.

"You were my reliable," he said. "Always ready with an act. I'm glad you came for the curtain."

"Oh, August, oh, baby."

The Profile showed up, too, his visage ravaged by age and spirits, but still somehow noble.

"I'm going to talk about showmen tonight," he said. "Is there any showman in the audience I can honor this evening? Raise your hand."

"Never made the grade, and flunked at Boise," August mumbled.

"Never made the grade? You're one of the great ones. You cleaned cash out of a thousand towns. You bankrupted whole cities."

August laughed gently, and then faded into blessed memory.